She'd taken her phone out of the silly clutch purse and returned it to her proper handbag when they got back, pleased with herself for remembering to do so, but had *not* remembered to get it out again and put it within easy reach for alarm clock purposes.

When it rang a little past two in the morning, it woke her out of a sound sleep—but for a moment she couldn't work out why it was ringing on the *floor*, disoriented in the dark.

You left it in your bag, idiot, she thought, and sighed, rolling over to reach out an arm. Her fingers had just brushed the worn leather when *something warm and solid covered in hair* nudged itself firmly under her hand: something very like a head.

Greta's scream hit, and sustained, high C.

Praise for
Strange Practice

"An exceptional and delightful debut, in the tradition of *Good Omens* and *A Night in the Lonesome October*."
—Elizabeth Bear

"An excellent adventure."
—Fran Wilde

"*Strange Practice* is written with elegance, wit, and compassion. The prose is gorgeous, the wit is mordant, and the ideas are provocative. Also, there are ghouls."
—Laura Amy Schlitz

"Shaw balances an agile mystery with a pitch-perfect, droll narrative and cast of lovable misfit characters. These are not your mother's Dracula or demons....*Strange Practice* is a super(natural) read."
—*Shelf Awareness*

"An appropriately dark breath of fresh air."
—*Booklist*

"Readers will look forward to more of Greta's adventures. An imaginative, delightfully droll debut."
—*Kirkus*

"A book to settle into. A warm quilt of a thing that's made for curling up with....I miss this newest Helsing already."
—*NPR*

"This book is a joy to read, unlocking every bit of delicious promise in the premise."
—*B&N Sci-Fi & Fantasy Blog*

DREADFUL COMPANY

A

DR. GRETA
HELSING

NOVEL

VIVIAN SHAW

www.orbitbooks.net

Copyright © 2018 by Vivian Shaw
Excerpt from *Grave Importance* copyright © 2018 by Vivian Shaw
Excerpt from *Prudence* copyright © 2015 by Tofa Borregaard

Cover design by Will Staehle and Lisa Marie Pompilio
Cover illustration by Will Staehle
Cover copyright © 2018 by Hachette Book Group, Inc.

Orbit
Hachette Book Group
1290 Avenue of the Americas
New York, NY 10104
orbitbooks.net

Simultaneously published in Great Britain and in the U.S. by Orbit in 2018
First Edition: July 2018

Orbit is an imprint of Hachette Book Group.
The Orbit name and logo are trademarks of Little, Brown Book Group Limited.

The publisher is not responsible for websites (or their content) that are not owned by the publisher.

The Hachette Speakers Bureau provides a wide range of authors for speaking events. To find out more, go to www.hachettespeakersbureau.com or call (866) 376-6591.

Library of Congress Cataloging-in-Publication Data
Names: Shaw, Vivian, author.
Title: Dreadful company / Vivian Shaw.
Description: First Edition. | New York, NY : Orbit, 2018. | Series: A Dr. Greta Helsing novel ; 2
Identifiers: LCCN 2018010014| ISBN 9780316434638 (paperback) | ISBN 9781478945161 (audiobook) | ISBN 9780316434645 (ebook)
Subjects: | BISAC: FICTION / Fantasy / Contemporary. | FICTION / Fantasy / Paranormal. | FICTION / Fantasy / Urban Life. | FICTION / Action & Adventure. | GSAFD: Paranormal fiction | Fantasy fiction.
Classification: LCC PS3619.H39467 D74 2018 | DDC 813/.6—dc23
LC record available at https://lccn.loc.gov/2018010014

ISBNs: 978-0-316-43463-8 (paperback), 978-0-316-43464-5 (ebook)

Printed in the United States of America

LSC-C

10 9 8 7 6 5 4 3 2 1

For Jane Mitchell, with love and profound appreciation.

CHAPTER I

There was a monster in Greta Helsing's hotel bathroom sink.

She stared at it, hands on hips, and it stared back at her. After a few moments it apparently decided she wasn't an immediate threat, gave a froggy *glup* sound, and settled down in the marble basin for what looked like an extended lurk.

"What on earth are *you* doing out of a well?" she inquired of it. "You ought to be guarding treasure, not preventing me from brushing my teeth."

It blinked at her—its eyes were large, also froglike, with a coppery iridescence to the irises—and then shifted a little to reveal that it was in fact guarding something: Greta's amethyst earrings, which had been sitting beside the sink and were now clutched tightly in a clammy grey-green hand.

She sighed. "I need those, they were a present. If I get you something else pretty to hang on to, can I have them back?"

Another slow coppery blink. She went back out to the

bedroom and returned in a few minutes with the watch she had been meaning to have repaired for several months now and which had not benefited from rattling around in the bottom of her handbag for the duration. It was at least still fairly shiny, even if it didn't work, and when she held it out to the wellmonster, it reached for the watch right away, grabbing at it with both little hands, her earrings forgotten. Before it could change its mind, she reached into the sink and rescued them.

"Which still doesn't explain what you're doing in my *bathroom*," she told it, putting the earrings on: they were only a little damp, not slimy at all. "I don't think that was on the hotel prospectus, even for a suite this well appointed. How did you even get in here?"

It wasn't very big, either: the size of a half-grown kitten, small enough to fit easily into the basin. The European wellmonster, *Puteus incolens incolens*, seldom got larger than a human toddler—and unlike the New World species, *P. incolens brasiliensis*, which was equipped with large pointy teeth, had few dangerous characteristics. This one looked to be in reasonably good shape, if entirely inexplicable: how *had* it found its way into a fourth-floor hotel bathroom without anyone noticing?

Glup, it said, and wrapped itself tighter around her broken Bulova. Greta sighed again, and reached out to stroke it gently. "All right," she said, "you can keep that safe for me. *Depositum custodi.*"

The monster licked her hand.

*   *   *

"*I* don't know," she said that evening, looking into the same bathroom mirror as Edmund Ruthven pinned up her hair. "It was gone when I got back from the first session of the conference, taking my watch with it, I might add, and leaving no trace as to how the hell it got here in the first place—Ow."

"If you would hold *still*," said Ruthven, "this wouldn't hurt and would also take up far less time and energy. And I will buy you a new watch, as I have been threatening to do for months; I know perfectly well you were simply never going to get around to having that one repaired."

Greta made a face at him. She was wearing a black velvet dress she personally would not have picked out, but which she had to admit did quite remarkably nice things for both the bits of her it concealed and those it exposed. There was a certain Madame X air to the whole thing, especially when Ruthven finished with the pins and hairspray: her neck and shoulders were very white against the rich blackness, and he had somehow managed to get the majority of her hair into an elegant loose knot with several art-directed wisps escaping here and there.

The makeup was…effective. Ruthven had gone to quite a lot of trouble, and she looked not just dressed up, but something closer to transformed. He had used a whole variety of brushes to apply various things to her cheeks and eyelids, and then brought out an eyelash curler; despite her protestations that it looked like a torture instrument, she had to agree that it made something of a difference.

"I look like a high-priced courtesan," she said, meeting his eyes in the mirror. She and Ruthven were just about the same height, and Greta knew perfectly well nobody was going to look at *her* when he was present: he was much prettier than she was, delicate features, black hair, and big shiny white-silver eyes with dramatic dark rings around the iris. He rolled them now and glowered back at her, almost offensively perfect in a bespoke tuxedo with tiny ruby studs winking from the starched shirtfront.

"You look," he said, "like a very expensively soigné young woman. Which, all right, I'll admit there is some thematic overlap. Stop making faces and put your jewelry on, we haven't got much time, and remind me where the damn wellmonsters come from in the first place."

"They get summoned," she said, turning to get a look at the back of her head in the hand mirror. "By people who happen to need guardians for various shiny objects. It's what they're for: they protect treasure that's been entrusted to them. They do breed, but very rarely; mostly you have to muck about with chanting and runes and cobwebs and frog's blood to summon one, instead of capturing a wild specimen. The magic's not actually difficult once you've got the ingredients together."

"Cobwebs are easily come by," Ruthven agreed, "but frog phlebotomy strikes me as a lot of effort. So somebody summoned that creature?"

"Presumably. No way of knowing who or why, or how it got in here." The silly dress came with an even sillier purse, a tiny slip of a thing, and Greta eyed it dubiously before stuffing her wallet and phone and compact inside. She felt ridiculously naked despite the snug velvet and the matching wrap Ruthven offered her; she was used to hauling around a handbag the dimensions of a good-sized mop bucket and just about as elegant, stuffed full of everything from journal articles to mummy-bone-replacement castings, and not having that comforting weight on her shoulder was unsettling.

At least they'll mostly be looking at him, she told herself again, fastening the ruby drops Francis Varney had given her into each earlobe. *That's pressure off me. And it's* Don Giovanni, *I've always wanted to see that,* and *at the Palais Garnier.* Greta scowled at herself in the mirror. *So bloody well lighten up and have a nice time, Helsing, you deserve it for presenting a halfway decent supernatural-medicine conference paper on three days' notice.*

Ruthven straightened his tie in the mirror and offered her his arm. "'Madam, will you walk?'" he quoted, and she had to smile. It was something of a relief to have Ruthven here with her: not only was he good company, but he also spoke flawless French, and hers was somewhat more in the *le singe est sur la branche* stage.

He'd been at loose ends just recently, having completed some home repairs that had taken months to finish, and had begun to develop the signs Greta associated with profound and pathological boredom; he didn't go in for your standard-variety vampire angst, but he was prone to a kind of ennui that, if unchecked, was capable of developing into depression. When he'd volunteered to accompany her on this last-minute conference trip, wanting a change from London, she had accepted with alacrity.

"Yes," she said, quoting the song, "yes, sir, I will walk, I will talk, I will walk *and* talk with you."

Together they left the suite, and it was a good twenty minutes before something very hairy clambered in through the half-open window and went to hide under her bed.

The Grand Staircase of the Palais Garnier *should* have been an overwhelming, chaotic jumble of color and texture and shape. Every surface in the vast five-story atrium was either painted, gilded, inlaid, carved, or some combination thereof. Huge spiked candelabra jutted out from the four walls of the atrium and were thrust aloft by semi-nude bronze women posing on the newel posts of the staircase itself; the balustrades were dark red and green marble, the columns and pilasters of the atrium walls carved from two separate kinds of complicated veiny butter-colored stone, with layers of wrought-iron lacework forming balconies between them. High above, the ceiling was painted with dramatic scenes of allegories in saturated color. It *should* have been a cacophonous mess of design elements, and instead—somehow—it all *worked*. The over-the-top opulence offered the same kind of uninhibited, glittering cheer as a polished drag queen's performance.

It was at its best when thronged with people. In the golden light each surface glowed with rich warmth, polished stone and dark bronze providing a thoroughly complementary setting for the herd of humanity passing through. Glittering jewels, bare shoulders, snowy shirtfronts brilliant against black: a moving kaleidoscope of color, accompanied by the clamor of a great many people talking all at once, being seen in the act of seeing.

From the vantage point of a fifth-floor balcony, the people on the staircase were doll-size, inconsequential. Easily blocked out by the tip of a thumb held at arm's length.

Corvin leaned on the brass balcony railing, following the progress of two heads through the throng: one dark, one fair. The dark head was glossy, sleekly combed, with a part in it that might have been drawn with a ruler. He closed one eye a little, squinting, and gave his outstretched thumb a vicious little twist: the gesture of a man squashing some small and importunate insect.

The object of this pantomime paused for a moment on the landing, glancing around, as if Corvin's attention had somehow registered on his senses. He was short, very pale, impeccably dressed, and even from here, Corvin could see red fire wink from his ruby shirt studs, see the pale eyes flash as he looked around. They were remarkably pale, those eyes, almost silver-white. Corvin knew them very well.

The man's companion, a blonde in a black velvet number, had continued a few steps; now she turned to look back at him: *What's the matter?*

Corvin watched as the man shook his head, dismissing whatever had caught his attention, and offered the woman his arm once more. They passed on up the staircase out of sight, and Corvin was about to detach himself from the balcony and go to find his own seat when the man and woman reappeared on a second-floor balcony across the atrium, this time holding drinks.

They seemed to be enjoying themselves.

Corvin's fingers tightened on the railing, and there was a faint squealing sound as metal bent under his grip. Not tonight. Not tonight, but he was *going* to get his chance to talk to Edmund Ruthven *very close up indeed*—

"Ooo," said someone directly to his left. "Varda the omi palone."

Corvin jerked involuntarily in surprise, and swung around to glare at his lieutenant, who had silently appeared beside him, leaning on the parapet. He hated it when Grisaille did the silent-sneaking-up bit. He'd *said* so, multiple times. He also hated the stupid goddamn Polari gay slang, which Grisaille could turn on and off at will: not only did it sound dumb, it was four decades out of date, and it implied that he, Corvin, was *also* extremely gay.

"What the fuck are you doing up here?" he demanded. "You're supposed to be back at headquarters."

"Isn't he pretty, though," Grisaille said, nodding to the distant figure of Ruthven. "I can see why you want to pull his head off. It's a nice head."

"*Grisaille*," said Corvin.

"Devout and humblest apologies, dear leader." Grisaille sketched him a little salute. "Bad news, I'm afraid: it's Lilith, she is throwing yet another massive wobbler for reason or reasons unknown, and I've been sent to fetch you home to sort it out." He shrugged, returning his attention to Ruthven and the unknown woman on his arm. "Who's the dolly-bird with Mistress Bona?"

Corvin pinched the bridge of his nose. "Goddamnit," he said. "I told Lilith to lay off the junkies. And I don't know. Some human whore."

"Oh, not just *some* human whore. She must be special. Look, he's all into her, all solicitous and caring, such a gentleman. It's touching. In a *barbaric* sort of way." He paused, as if waiting for some particular response, and then sighed. "I don't suppose you saw what I did there."

Corvin ignored this. "You think she's important?"

"Could be, could be." Grisaille seesawed a hand in the air. "Shall I make inquiry?"

"Yeah. Do that, and—keep an eye on them, damn it. I suppose I have to go and see what's wrong with Lilith this time; I'm getting pretty tired of this shit."

"As you wish," said Grisaille with another little salute. "Don't worry, you're not missing much with this opera— spoiler warning, he ends up going to Hell at the end."

Corvin straightened up, ignoring the dents his fingers had left in the brass railing. "So do we all, Grisaille," he said. "So do we all."

When the curtain fell on the first act of *Don Giovanni*, Greta let out a breath she hadn't actually been aware of holding, and sat back in her chair. She'd spent most of the past hour leaning on the box's red velvet balcony edge, totally spellbound.

Ruthven was watching her, amused, a little smile curving his mouth. "Having a nice time?" he asked.

"Almost every single person in this opera," said Greta, "is behaving like a complete idiot, and I love it. Can I have more champagne?"

"The majority of opera plots would fall to bits if any one individual suddenly decided to act sensibly," said Ruthven, getting up. "Yes, of course. I'll be back in a minute. Amuse yourself by working out which one of the boxes belongs to the phantom."

"The what?" she asked, and then made a face. "*Is* there a phantom?"

"Very probably," he said, and patted her shoulder. "You're *going* to get ghosts in a place like this; it's like having rats, it's unavoidable. I shouldn't worry, though: nobody's disappeared through a trapdoor recently, and the chandelier appears to be secure."

She turned back to the hot, glittering open space of the auditorium, like a gilded cave—very aware of the huge brass-and-crystal wedding cake of a chandelier hanging from the middle of the ceiling—and tried to remember the book. She'd read it, of course, along with all the other classic horror novels, for research purposes—not that it was necessarily true. The account of Ruthven's own activities as portrayed by John Polidori were, as Ruthven was fond of pointing out, about ninety percent pure libel, and half of what was in Rymer and Prest's *Varney the Vampyre, or The Feast of Blood* was completely inaccurate. Nevertheless there were crumbs of truth in most of the classics, enough to make them worth the bother of reading, and Greta dredged up distant memories of paging through Leroux. It was First-Tier Box 5, wasn't it, that the ghost had required for his personal use?

Ruthven had secured Second-Tier Box 30 for them—the whole thing, at great expense; they weren't sharing the space with any other spectators, which she appreciated. They were facing almost directly across at the huge stone-and-gold columns flanking the boxes next to the stage on the left side. There was no one in the really stupendously over-the-top box with curtains, nor the one next to it; but she saw a flicker of movement in the next one along.

Whoever was in there had a carved stone column to their left, but was separated from the next box to the right only by the normal red brocade-and-velvet dividing wall.

Greta thought she could remember something about *the column*—someone hiding inside it, perhaps—and it certainly looked big enough to contain a person, if it happened to be hollow. That was it. That was First-Tier Box 5.

There was the flicker of movement again, and a man came into view, settling lazily into a chair at the front of the box. He wasn't wearing evening dress, like most of the patrons: his jacket was charcoal velvet and his shirt a deep blood-red.

Also, unlike most of the patrons, he had narrow silvering dreadlocks falling over his shoulders and halfway down his back. Greta decided that was why she was staring: that was some hair, all right, by Jove—

—but it wasn't just the man's *hair* that had caught her eye; and just as the thought crossed her mind, he turned, looked directly at Greta, eyes large and very bright in his dark face, and *winked*.

It was very quick. He returned his attention to the closed curtain, to the people moving in the auditorium below, but for a fraction of a moment he had looked right at her *as if he knew she would be there.*

Also, he was definitely a vampire. She couldn't tell the color of his eyes from this distance, but she hadn't needed to. The instant of eye contact had given her a familiar kind of mental tingle that Greta had long ago learned to recognize, a feeling like being momentarily and pleasantly drunk. It wasn't exactly thrall, but it said very clearly that the person looking at her was *capable* of thrall, should they choose to use it.

Encountering another classic draculine wasn't in itself all that surprising—it was a big city, there were bound to be some of them about, and attending the opera was such a *vampire* thing to do—but it felt somehow unsettling nonetheless.

Ruthven came back with two glasses of champagne, and frowned at her, sitting down. "What's the matter?"

"I think I know which box it is," she said, and pointed. "The one with the long-haired guy wearing a velvet jacket."

He followed her pointing finger, and for a moment he stiffened, as if unpleasantly surprised—the way he had earlier, on the staircase. Only for a moment.

"Spot on," he said. "The one containing a vampire. How very apt."

"He looked at me," said Greta, and took a swig of champagne. "Right at me, and winked. Do you *know* him?"

"Never seen him before in my life," Ruthven said, shrugging. "Remember you are being extremely beautiful at the moment, and thus should expect to have men winking at you; unfortunately we are no longer in a century where it is acceptable to assault them with your fan in response."

" 'La, sir,' " Greta deadpanned at him, and he grinned.

"Just so. Shh, they're getting ready to start again."

Greta leaned her shoulder against his, watching as the conductor reappeared and a hush began to spread over the auditorium. She was focusing her attention directly on the stage as the house lights faded to black—but couldn't quite stop herself glancing over to the darkened Box 5.

She was not entirely surprised to find there were two red pinpoints of light looking back at her, steadily, just for a moment—and then they vanished as he, too, turned to look at the stage.

"I thought the demons were very good," Greta said later in the hotel, "although I expect Fastitocalon would go on at length about stereotyping and the importance of remembering that not every demon actually possesses horns and leathery bat wings and a tail. How many pins did you put *in* here?"

She had taken off the Madame X gown, which had left pink marks all over her where various bones or seams had pressed, and was standing in her dressing gown undoing Ruthven's careful work on her hair.

"A sufficiency," said Ruthven, leaning in the bathroom doorway, still pristine in evening dress. "And yes, Fass would absolutely feel the need to lecture, which is why I wouldn't in a million years dream of taking him to an opera such as this one. I don't know if demons even *like* opera. Do they have them in Hell?"

"You know, I could make so *many* arts-and-culture jokes based on that question? Yes, there's an opera house in Dis, apparently, although he's never told me much about it. I hope he's having a nice time down there, even if being stuck at the health spa must be rather dull."

Fastitocalon was an old friend of Greta's family who happened to be mostly a demon, much the same way Ruthven was a friend who just happened to be a vampire, and had taken it upon himself to watch over Greta after her father's death. Banished from Hell in the sixteenth century due to a complex management shakeup in the infernal civil service, he had spent several hundred years in exile on Earth as a metaphysically defective creature—and in chronic ill-health, due to the banishment having stripped away much of his power and strength. However, an official *rapprochement* between Fastitocalon and Hell had been achieved the previous winter, and Greta had finally convinced him to stop being stubbornly self-destructive and bloody well take himself Below to the Lake Avernus spa and get himself properly all the way *fixed*. It had been difficult to adjust to not having the constant faint mental presence of Fass hanging around in the back of her mind, but at least she knew his absence was simply a function of being out of range. He'd scared her badly once by vanishing abruptly, and while she missed him, it was a small comfort to know he wasn't permanently gone.

"He's probably lying around doing algebraic geometry for fun," Ruthven said. "Or something equally impossible. All those multivalent polynomials and things. No one should be that good at math, even if they *are* a fiend from Hell."

"You're just bitter because you have to have somebody else do your taxes for you," Greta said mildly, finishing with the pins and beginning to brush the hairspray out. "Fass can't do latte art or use an eyelash curler worth a damn; let him keep the realm of truly alarming mathematics."

"I suppose," said Ruthven, and yawned ever so slightly ostentatiously. Greta got a good look at his teeth, and had to smile: yes, those *were* some impressive, if neat and proportionate, fangs.

Her hair was more or less back to normal; now she began to take off her makeup, which was rather a relief. With the hair down and without the foundation and contouring, she was beginning to look like herself again in the mirror, rather than the strange if undeniably beautiful other-self Ruthven had created.

He really did know makeup to a somewhat alarming degree. Greta wasn't completely ignorant of the art; she had to wear mascara to make her pale eyelashes visible, maybe a bit of shadow, concealer—more concealer if the sleep debt was really beginning to show—but that was about the extent of her experience. Ruthven, however, was *good*. She'd agreed to let him do this little mini-makeover for the evening, partly because he so clearly wanted to get a chance to play, and partly because she'd been kind of curious as to what he could actually achieve with the various specialized substances in his large black bag—but it was nice to get back to being herself.

It was almost midnight and she had to be at the Sorbonne at eight in the morning, awake and functional and caffeinated and dressed appropriately, and the extent to which Greta did not wish to do this was both significant and profound. This wasn't one of the conferences she had planned on attending—she hadn't even gone to this particular event in the past three years, and there were a hell of a lot of things at home she'd rather be doing than listening to her colleagues arguing about nomenclature. But there hadn't been anybody else around who *could* fill in for her friend on his conference panel on short notice, so here she was: preparing to give her own paper on osteoarthritis in the barrow-wight in place of the ailing Dr. Richard Byrne's.

Because I'm nice, she thought sourly, not at all pleased to find that the mascara was the waterproof kind and stubbornly resisted her attempts to remove it. At least she was only on the one panel, first thing in the morning; after that, all she had to do was pick and choose which of her colleagues' presentations she wanted to attend, which she might even enjoy, and do the obligatory round of professional social activities that were part and parcel of any conference, which she would not.

She'd have the hotel suite all to herself for two more nights; Ruthven was leaving for Scotland in the morning, to sort out something tiresome to do with the ancestral pile. He'd planned to stay throughout the conference, enjoying a nice little weekend holiday in Paris, but apparently another part of Huntingtower's roof had taken this particular moment to collapse and the agents had summoned him to come and deal with it.

"You need the oil-based remover for that, not the ordinary sort," Ruthven said after she'd spent several moments struggling with the recalcitrant mascara.

He sounded odd. Greta turned from the mirror to look at him, one eye partially denuded. "Great, now you tell me... look, are you all right? You were acting a bit strange earlier."

"Of course I wasn't," he said. There was a faint line of worry between his long inkstroke eyebrows.

"You were. On the stairs, when we got there, you just stopped dead for a moment and looked all faraway and preoccupied, like you'd just remembered you'd left the oven on or something, and then when we saw that other vampire with the long hair—are you *sure* you didn't recognize him?"

"Extremely sure. I would have remembered that one." There was a flicker of wry admiration in his voice. "I don't know, Greta. Something doesn't feel right here. It's not just the completely inexplicable monster in the sink, or the sense that I had on the stairs of being watched, or the handsome stranger winking at you. I can't put my finger on it and I do so hate to claim *vague forebodings* but I'm afraid that's what I've got just now..."

He paused, straightening up, and came into the bathroom. "Stand still and let me do that; you'll poke your eye out."

Greta gladly abandoned her attempts and shut her eyes for him; it felt kind of nice having someone else do it, little careful touches on her eyelids, the sense of someone's face close to her own. "You've had vague forebodings a lot recently, though," she said after a moment, picking up the thread of the conversation, eyes still shut. "And they almost never turn out to be justified. There was the time a month ago when you kept worrying about Things Happening to Cranswell for no reason, and the only Thing that actually Happened was he got a parking ticket, remember?"

"Vividly," said Ruthven. "There, you're done; wash your face and no trace will remain of the night's adventures. And—okay, fine, I admit you're probably right and it's nothing. I just hate to leave you alone here, Greta. Are you *sure* you have to do the rest of it?"

"Yes," she said, and bent over the basin. It took a minute or two for her to wash the oil from her face, and all the time she was conscious of Ruthven *looking* at her, silver eyes under black eyebrows, with that little worry-line that should not be there at all. When she straightened up again, she turned to him, leaning against the marble counter. "It's not that I'm super chuffed about spending the rest of the weekend doing this, either. I wasn't planning on coming to this thing at all, I've got so much going on at work, but now that I *am* here, I have to do what's expected of me. Richard absolutely owes me a drink, though."

She remembered how apologetic Richard had been on the phone, even though she could tell from his tone that he was in fact in quite a lot of pain. Diagnosis of appendicitis: surgery required at once; recovery period measured in weeks. Chance that patient would be traveling to, and presenting a paper at, an international conference in three days' time: nil. It hadn't been Richard's fault, but he still owed her one, and he'd been lucky she was available: there weren't all that many clinicians working with barrow-wights at all, let alone ones who could present on the topic.

"He does indeed," said Ruthven. "Many drinks. Just call me, will you, when you get a chance to? I will fret much less with reassurances."

"I will call you, and tell you enthusiastically in graphic detail about all the gruesome content of the papers being given, okay? I promise. And I've already told Varney I'd ring him up when I am not likely to be disturbed by people asking me for my opinion on lunar affective disorder in were-hedgehogs."

"Good lord," said Ruthven, but he was smiling a little. "I had no idea you were considered an expert in that particular specialization."

"World-class authority," Greta told him, straight-faced, and that got an actual laugh. "Written several pounds of literature on the subject, don't you know. Look, it's *okay*, Ruthven. I'm going to be just fine. I can take care of myself in the big scary foreign city for a couple of days without supervision."

"I didn't—that's—damn. Not what I meant. I know you can, you're perfectly capable, even if your French isn't exactly what one might call idiomatic. It's just my forebodings, that's all. I'll get over myself," said Ruthven, faintly flushed high on his cheekbones. "Sorry if—I'm being overbearing, aren't I?"

"No, you're being fretful and mother-hennish," Greta told him, and impulsively reached out to wrap her arms around him, pull him into a hug. "I'll be fine. I'll be in touch when I can, and I'll call you if anything goes wrong and I turn out to require assistance."

He hugged her back after a moment, and she could feel some of the tension in his shoulders relax. "And with that I shall be content," he said, and sighed, but the faint line of worry between his eyebrows had smoothed out a little. "I think I'll go out to eat. Leave the sitting room windows open a little for me when you go to bed, in case mine blow shut again?"

"Of course," she said. His bedroom was on the other side of the luxuriously appointed sitting room from her own. "I don't suppose you'd let me see you do the bat thing—"

"No."

"Worth a try," said Greta, smiling at him. "Good night, Ruthven. Have a nice dinner—and thank you, for tonight. For everything. I had a lovely time."

"So did I," he told her, and smiled back.

She'd taken her phone out of the silly clutch purse and returned it to her proper handbag when they got back, pleased with herself for remembering to do so, but had *not* remembered to get it out again and put it within easy reach for alarm clock purposes.

When it rang a little past two in the morning, it woke her

out of a sound sleep—but for a moment she couldn't work out why it was ringing on the *floor*, disoriented in the dark.

You left it in your bag, idiot, she thought, and sighed, rolling over to reach out an arm. Her fingers had just brushed the worn leather when *something warm and solid covered in hair* nudged itself firmly under her hand: something very like a head.

Greta's scream hit, and sustained, high C.

CHAPTER 2

By the time Ruthven—hair sleep-mussed, wearing charcoal silk pajamas and *still* somehow managing to look elegant—rushed into the room, she had the lights on and was kneeling down beside the bed to peer underneath it.

"Greta?" he demanded.

"Shh." She looked briefly over her shoulder at him and then returned her attention to the darkness beneath the bed. "It's okay, I'm sorry I scared you, that was very silly of me, wasn't it? Come on out, I promise it's safe, no one's going to hurt you."

She was using exactly the tone one might employ to coax a kitten out from hiding. This did not seem to mollify Ruthven in the slightest. "*Greta,*" he said, "what the *hell* is going on? If you're going to wake me up at half past two with blood-curdling shrieks when I'm already worried about you, at least have the decency to explain yourself. I gather that you are not in fact being murdered, but what *are* you doing?"

22

"Shh," Greta said again, reaching out a cautious hand under the bed. "Come here, sweetheart, it's okay, I promise..."

A dim humped shape moved tentatively toward her, and something soft and hairy touched her fingertips, sniffing. She held perfectly still for it, and a few moments later the hard curve of a skull came under her palm, nudging to be stroked. "There," she said gently, "that's right, come on out," and sat back on her heels.

What emerged from under the bed was not completely unlike a smallish dog. It was covered in long, soft, silky hair in a fetching shade of auburn, had four legs and no tail, and while it *did* have a head, it seemed to be rather lacking in the face department. There was just lots and lots of hair.

"Oh, good grief," said Ruthven, and dropped into a chair. The hairy thing startled, and Greta had to talk softly to it again for a few more moments before it climbed into her lap and settled down to be stroked.

It had been a long time since she'd seen a tricherpeton, commonly if unimaginatively known as *hairmonsters*. There was a very specific and small community within the supernatural and super-adjacent world that bred them, like pedigreed dogs, in lots of different varieties, although you *could* summon them individually via magic if you didn't have the patience or wherewithal to set up a breeding program. This one wouldn't have won any show awards for conformation or breed-specific traits; in fact, it looked like a complete mongrel—but the quality of the hair under Greta's hands was impressive nonetheless.

(There *were* sphynx varieties, but they were somewhat mercifully rare: a hairless *faceless* creature with nothing but a mouth was difficult to look at, even though their temperament was among the sweetest of the tricherpeton breeds.)

Once she was pretty sure the one in her lap wasn't likely to scuttle back under the bed in terror, she transferred some of her attention to Ruthven. "I'm sorry," she said, "I didn't intend to wake you like that, but it took me by surprise: someone rang me by mistake and the monster happened to be in the way when I reached for my bag, poor little thing."

"I don't suppose there are any other creatures hiding in here? Have you checked the wardrobe for bogeymen, by chance?"

"I have not. I don't think there's anything else here, but it's *weird*, Ruthven. First the wellmonster this morning and now this. Do I have—I don't know, monster-attracting pheromones all of a sudden?"

"Not that I'm aware of. You haven't changed your perfume lately?"

She gave him a look, and sighed. "I really am sorry. Go back to bed, all right? I've got this."

"Yes," he said, "you have, and I will in a minute, but perhaps I will raid the minibar *first*. For nerve-settling purposes."

The monster in Greta's lap gave a very doggy contented sigh, and a small pink tongue appeared amid the hair to lap at her fingers. Ruthven stared, running his hands through his own hair, then had to laugh at the absurdity of the entire situation—and came to kneel down beside her for a closer look. "I don't know what you're going to *do* with it, I'm sure," he said, reaching out a finger to stroke the silky hair. "You can't possibly adopt stray French monsters; wherever would you put it?"

"I have no idea," she said. "It doesn't appear to be in bad shape; honestly, I think someone's been taking at least basic care of it—no mats or snarls, it's a decent weight for its size, completely tame. It's not a thoroughbred, though, which means either it's an adopted stray or it's been *summoned*, which is a little odd. God knows why anyone would bother doing that kind of magic, but whatever—I suppose Parisian monster fanciers have to get their jollies somehow. I think it's come to visit, not to stow away in my suitcase."

"If this keeps up, you are going to be the most absurd Disney princess of all time," Ruthven told her. "Instead of happy little bluebirds perching on your finger to sing duets, you will be hung about with monsters like a tree with monkeys, and it will thoroughly complicate your personal life. You can't *talk* to them or anything, can you?"

Greta laughed. "No. You know perfectly well I have no *special abilities* whatsoever, I'm not even slightly clairvoyant, and a good twenty percent of the population has at least some degree of that, whether they realize it or not. I don't know why I seem to have acquired monsters all of a sudden, but poor old Richard is going to be terribly chagrined to have missed this experience."

"I expect so," Ruthven said. "It's objectively less unpleasant than having his appendix out, although I could do without the *middle of the night* part. Do you suppose it's worth trying to go back to sleep?"

"I'd better make the effort if I'm going to be sparkling and vivacious in the morning. Why is it always sparkling *and* vivacious? Can't one simply glitter?"

Ruthven quirked an eyebrow at her. "That's a loaded question to ask a vampire. I'm going to make us a drink, and then I'll attempt sleep—is that thing going to *let* you get back into bed?"

"I expect so," Greta said, looking down at her lapful. The hair really was beautiful; in sunlight it would be full of golden glints and deep red shadows, and she knew that underneath it, the tricherpeton's skin would be scattered with little coppery freckles. "I certainly intend to find out."

The green awnings of Paris's famous Les Deux Magots café glowed the expensive green of a banker's lampshade, in the clear light of midmorning. Across the way, the ancient church of Saint-Germain-des-Prés caught the light and held it, mellow stone pale and pleasing; it had stood exactly as it was for ten centuries, while the city around it ebbed and flowed and reinvented itself.

Gervase Brightside, remedial psychopomp, swirled his *pastis* and held it up to the light: louched pearl-yellow, the liquid was entirely opaque, but nonetheless he could see the church tower through it as clear as glass if he so chose. He could personally remember when the tower had been new; it, unlike several other items of his acquaintance, had aged gracefully.

"I can't believe you're swilling strong drink before ten a.m.," said his companion. Brightside took a sip and put the glass down, fixing him with a reptilian look.

"And I can't believe you're playing morality police," he said. "Doesn't suit you. Anyway, by our standards it is both all times and no times at once, so the sun is over the yardarm somewhere in eternity, hmm?"

"I hate it when you get philosophical," said Crepusculus Dammerung, grinning at him. "I think it means you're bilious. Pass me the paper?"

Brightside handed it over. Dammerung, like Brightside himself, was ageless—but appeared to be perhaps twenty-five, short and energetic, dark brown hair tumbling in untidy curls to his shoulders; he was wearing a T-shirt advertising Led Zeppelin and a leather jacket that seemed to have seen hard wear, and had a cigarette parked behind one ear. The overall impression was one of boundless, unsquashable cheer.

"Ta," said Crepusculus, refolding the copy of *Le Monde* and settling down to read about whatever atrocities the Americans had been up to recently. Brightside sipped his drink and watched the people come and go, and tried to ignore a faint, yet growing, unsettled feeling.

Crepusculus and Brightside—they did in fact have official business cards—were in the business of remedial psychopompery: in layman's terms, they helped the unquiet dead off to a peaceful afterlife. They'd been in that particular business approximately as long as humans had been around, and were in fact as old as creation itself, although Brightside appeared to be stuck in the mid-1970s and his partner would have fit right in at a Pearl Jam concert circa 1998. Nor were they directly affiliated with either Heaven or Hell; operating as independents, like the handful of others who performed this particular service, they went wherever they were needed. It had always been common enough for spirits of the departed to get hung up somewhere, caught between worlds, and Brightside and his partner simply came along and gave them a metaphorical tow.

The pair of them had been in Paris for a week now. The city's unofficial guardian, a large and amiable werewolf, had called them in to sort out an unexpected haunting some days back—and after dealing with the business at hand, they had decided what the hell, they could take a holiday. Paris was at its most beautiful in springtime, and it wasn't as if people were clamoring for their services anyway; the call had been their first job in weeks. They had settled into a routine: leisurely breakfast, largely in liquid form, at the café; people-watching; strolling around various points of interest.

The case that had brought them here had been a little odd, however. A whole host of ghosts—or *parts* of ghosts—had suddenly appeared in a group, in the square that had replaced the long-gone Cimetière des Innocents, confused and distressed: missing arms, legs, heads, milling about in a translucent crowd and demanding to be told where their vanished parts had gone. It hadn't been difficult to move them on, even though there were nearly thirty individuals, and Brightside *thought* he knew why they'd shown up in the first place: the desperately overcrowded cemetery's occupants had been transported piecemeal in the eighteenth century to what would become the Paris catacombs, and undoubtedly bits must have been left behind, causing their owners consternation and distress.

Why they'd suddenly shown up now, though. That was bothering him. Why now, after hundreds of years had passed since the removal?

There seemed to be an awful lot of coincidence going on; yesterday morning they'd been sitting here over coffee and pastries and watching people come and go, and whom should they spy strolling down the boulevard but Edmund Ruthven, accompanied by a blonde human woman. They knew the vampire socially—he'd never had recourse to their services, but they'd met several times over the past century or so, and it was a bit surprising to come across him in Paris: he didn't travel much outside Britain.

Brightside had considered calling out, or waving to him, but Ruthven and his companion had seemed to be talking fairly intently, and he had decided to let them enjoy the city on their own.

He drained the glass and waved over a waiter to order another. It was, in fact, half past nine in the morning, but Brightside was on holiday, damn it, and he was allowed the occasional flirt with sybaritism. In another couple of days they'd be back in London, their current base of operations, and it would be grey and rainy and ordinary, and the clear light on the church tower was too pleasant to ignore in favor of vague forebodings and disquiet.

"You think it's a timeslip?" said Crepusculus, out of nowhere. Brightside blinked at him. His partner was irritatingly good at reading Brightside's thoughts, even when he wasn't trying to. "Those ghosts suddenly showing up now, I mean. Could be one of those wrinkle-in-time things like we saw in Lyme Regis last year. Seems like there's been more and more of those lately."

"I don't know," said Brightside. "The thing in Lyme was—I'm pretty sure that was just the standard local wannabe necromancer meddling with things he oughtn't. Ghost smugglers landing a ghost cargo? That's classic self-contained disturbance-of-the-dead stuff; there wasn't any kind of ripple effect, no other weird temporal things going on. We would have noticed."

"Right, and nobody's disturbed these dead since seventeen-eighty-whatever," said Crepusculus, finishing his *café au lait*. "So why are they showing up complaining about it now? I mean, sure, the laid-back French approach is a thing, but that's several hundred years of lag time. It's weird, is what I'm saying."

"Why indeed? Perhaps some idiot urban explorer knocked over a bunch of bones somewhere in the catacombs and woke them up. It's over, Dammerung. We sorted it."

"So why are you still on edge?"

"I'm—" he began, and sighed, and was grateful for the waiter's return with a tray. "I'm not," he said once the drink had been set before him and the man had retreated once more. "I'm not on edge. I just would like to *know* what that was." He wasn't used to being less than certain.

"Maybe we'll find out," said Crepusculus. "I want one of those, come to think of it. Call him back over?"

Brightside sighed again and pushed the glass across the table toward him, trying to dismiss the lingering unease. "Be my guest. And then we should work out what we want to do today, other than wandering around feeding Gallic pigeons."

"Yeah," said Crepusculus, "the Gallic pigeons can take care of themselves; and I want to go look at Versailles while we're here."

"Versailles we can do," he said. "At least everyone there who's dead has the decency to stay dead."

"At least as far as we know."

Brightside found himself—unwillingly—returning his partner's grin.

Above the vast and colorful interior dome of the Opera, above the brass-and-crystal edifice of the chandelier, in a forgotten and dust-filled corner of the rehearsal room that occupied the next floor up, something peculiar was going on.

This was a part of the superstructure that had been modeled and remodeled multiple times over the years, and was now used by the corps de ballet: it had the vacant, somehow desolate air of all dance practice rooms when not in use, the long mirrored walls reflecting themselves into infinity. There was natural light from several of the circular windows in the curving wall; the room was approximately semicircular, taking up about half the interior space of this floor. To one side a locked cabinet stood tucked into a niche between support pillars, and beyond this cabinet, in the very far corner, unbeknownst to the people who used this space, was a strange dust-covered object.

It looked a little like a seismometer: a drum with a pen resting on it, tracing a faintly wavy line. The drum turned almost imperceptibly slowly—it would take a full week to complete one revolution—and the line was very nearly straight, although it was being drawn over several previous very similar lines. Whatever it was meant to measure seemed not to have been particularly active.

Now, however, a bluish glow, faint but present, surrounded the machine, and the pen trembled as if in the grip of two opposing and nearly equal forces; trembled, and then shot violently to one side and back again, drawing a wide jagged line. The whole machine shook. A smell like burned tin drifted from it, and a blue spark jumped to ground—and then, just as suddenly as it had begun, the transient came to an end. The pen returned to its neutral position. The blue glow vanished as if it had never been there at all. The machine was silent, still. The smell lingered for a few minutes before dissipating into the air completely.

The layer of dust on the machine would seem to suggest that whoever was meant to come and look at its tracings every now and then had not been doing so—which was a pity, because had they bothered to look, they would have seen that nineteen hours ago an identical transient had occurred: a sudden, powerful spike in the reading that lasted only a second before returning to baseline. Unrolling the paper from the drum to examine the recent readings would have shown two things: one, the machine had been drawing over its previous lines with each revolution because nobody had bothered to take away the completed week's recording, and two, these brief but violent anomalies had been occurring not just over the past week but over the past *month*, with increasing frequency.

When, in fact, the individual who ought to have been monitoring its readings finally came to look at it, he would be extremely alarmed at what he saw. Alarmed, and fascinated, and profoundly inclined to kick himself for thirty kinds of a lazy idiot.

The catacombs of Paris were a well-known tourist attraction: a curated series of passageways neatly lined with row upon row of skulls interspersed with femurs, the stacked V-shapes of their medial condyles forming a pattern reminiscent of rough knitting. There were some very big names down there— Danton, Robespierre, Camille and Lucile Desmoulins, among others—although it was now impossible to know which cranium was whose; *liberté, égalité, et fraternité* demonstrated in death if not in life.

Only a section of the catacombs was open to the public— which represented a very small fraction of the Parisian undercity. The tunnels themselves, chambers and passageways cut into the cream-pale rock, were the remains of subterranean quarries that once produced limestone and gypsum in vast quantities: the source of the phrase *plaster of Paris*. It was not until the late eighteenth century that they had been pressed into use as a place to store the city's dead, in response to overflowing cemeteries. Beyond the sections of the tunnel network serving as an ossuary, miles of passageways stretched into the darkness beneath Paris—forbidden territory, in which it was quite possible to lose oneself and be unable to find the way back out again. This was the realm of the *cataphiles*, a secretive strain of urban explorers who regularly went down into the dark for the thrill of it—who held parties underground, even at one point setting up a fully functional cinema—despite the dangers.

There were more dangers now than simply getting lost, or caught by the police. There were things down there now far more worrisome than the empty-eyed glare of a thousand nameless skulls, and one of them was currently paring his fingernails with the tip of a gem-encrusted stiletto and considering the relative merits of assorted methods of murder.

The vampire Corvin had chosen, for his lair, a section of the tunnels not so very far away from the Palais Garnier, in one of the old gypsum mines. He felt at home in the underworld, in the city's dark and ruined heart, and the aesthetic of the catacombs proper held a powerful appeal for him. ARRÊTE! said the inscription over the ossuary portal, C'EST ICI L'EMPIRE DE LA MORT. And Corvin thought it was *entirely* appropriate—although *undead* would technically be more to the point.

He stretched out his arm to admire the newly sharpened fingernails. They were about half an inch long and very pointy, and went well with the enormous heavy ruby ring on the third finger of his right hand—a ring which had begun its life adorning some fourteenth-century bishop, and which a museum in Germany would probably quite like to reclaim. Corvin had had it professionally desanctified, just to be sure;

and the underworld jeweler who had sized it down to fit had been paid by the simple expedient of having his neck broken afterward. Corvin liked to watch candlelight run and gleam in the depths of the stone, like a lump of solid anger, and thought it suited him very well: the red matched his eyes.

Corvin, who had been christened something rather different in a previous phase of his existence, *liked* red things. And expensive things. Most of his clothing was either black, or shades of red from burgundy to crimson, and he went heavily in for velvet and embroidery and leather. Where the walls of his lair were not stacked with bones, they were hung with red and violet silks and brocades, and his furniture tended toward the heavy, dark, and Victorian. Tonight he was in a fetching ensemble consisting of leather trousers and a dark red velvet shirt, accessorized with tall boots, and his black hair hung unbound halfway down his back. It was very black; he would need to have his roots touched up in the next week or so, but in the candlelight the contrast between the hair and his pale skin looked appropriately stark.

(Whether or not long hair *suited* him was not a question anyone wished to discuss, if they wanted to continue the even tenor of their ways.)

Satisfied with his nails, he sat back in his ebony chair and considered what little Grisaille had been able to tell him. The woman accompanying Edmund Ruthven was in fact apparently not just some human whore: she was of all things a *physician*, a human who made her living treating monsters, and from what Grisaille could make out, was a close friend of Ruthven's. They were staying together in one of the more expensive five-star hotels not far from the river.

Corvin closed his eyes, tapping the blade of the dagger gently against his teeth. One of them—the left upper canine— was made of platinum, set with a ruby, and it went *tink* as the blade made contact. He was picturing Ruthven on the staircase at the opera house, perfectly groomed and moving with the unconscious dancer's grace of a vampire, ruby shirt studs glittering, and as always when he let himself think very closely of Edmund St. James Ruthven, Corvin's mouth twisted subtly into a snarl.

He would *have* his revenge. Somehow, soon, he would have it. Ruthven had not defeated him the last time they had met: that had been . . . a setback, that was all. An inconvenient little setback. Anyway, he had regrouped. He had recovered, and regrouped, and gathered a new coven around himself, and traveled across Europe. He'd seen a lot; done a lot. He'd even been to Transylvania, which had been exciting, even if the people there tasted funny and didn't really agree with him; and up to Russia, where he'd had quite a nice time for a while, and eventually back to France. And when he'd been passing through Paris again, and felt a little voice inside him say, *Here, here is where you should be*, he had listened—and up until last night had been really enjoying himself, Lilith's stupid bullshit aside.

(Lilith. *There* was a problem, if you liked. She was dim even by Corvin's standards, and he did not exactly impose an intellectual requirement on his people, merely demanding their loyalty. She was dim but she was also determined in several counterproductive ways—she was particularly good at finding creative work-arounds to things Corvin had forbidden her to do, without directly disobeying his commands—and lately he'd had to spend much more time than he'd have liked in dealing with her overindulgence in junkie blood. More than once he'd wondered if this nonsense was worth it or if he should simply kick her to the curb and announce that the position of consort was open—but she was also *unbelievably* good in bed, and when she wasn't wasted, she was gorgeous, and looked just right on his arm, and at least she was mostly obedient and subservient and would do what he told her, most of the time, but ugh, Corvin wished things could be simple.)

At least her newest hobby with the monsters got her out of his hair: it was nice for her to have an interest, and she looked cute with the little baby creatures all cuddled in her lap and so on, even if Corvin wasn't sure it was such a hot idea to just...dump them in the sewers when they got too big to be adorable. Still, it was easier to deal with than her *other* habit of keeping humans as pets until she got tired of them or they died off; Corvin had never quite really liked the way she'd looked at her "beautiful boys," although he had avoided examining this reaction in any great detail.

He'd had a couple of fights with her about how many of the monster things she was keeping in the lair, however, and told her to go find somewhere else to do the stupid magic bullshit that wasn't right in the middle of his personal space, on account of he'd had enough of there being chalk circles and graveyard dirt all over the place. That whole business with the spells and chanting had weirded him out anyway, particularly the way the air felt while she was doing it—there were occasionally these kind of waves of pressure that made your ears pop, and the whole place smelled like thunderstorms for hours afterward.

It didn't matter now. Either she'd quit it, or she'd obeyed his order and moved her operations elsewhere; Corvin didn't care. It wasn't his problem.

Ruthven was his problem. He'd dreamed for so long of what he would say when he finally got the opportunity, and now it was so close he could almost taste it—

But the woman. The blonde woman. The human. She might be just what he'd been looking for. She might be *the way in*.

He got up, slipping the little dagger back into its jeweled sheath on his wrist, beneath the velvet sleeve, and made a decision. No sense wasting time. He would—

Corvin stopped, and looked down, and swore. Wrapped around his ankle was one of Lilith's monsters, a greyish lump about the size of a grapefruit. The goddamn things got everywhere. He'd *told* her not to let them roam around the lair all unsupervised; it was embarrassing. He shook his foot to try to dislodge the thing, but it just hung on tighter, wrapped around his boot with all four little limbs—and it looked up at him, blinking slowly, as if expecting him to do something.

Corvin's face hardened, and he slipped his hand into his

sleeve and brought the dagger out again, its blade winking in the candlelight, and bent to remove the impediment in his way.

Paris was at its loveliest in springtime, Greta reflected, and the lime trees in the Place de la Sorbonne were in full bloom, filling the air with their sweetness. It mostly made up for having to get up early, after her somewhat complicated night.

The tricherpeton had curled up and gone to sleep on the end of her bed, and was gone by the time Greta woke up; presumably it had left the way it had gotten in, via the window. It was almost possible to imagine that the whole thing had been a dream, except for the part where the bedspread was covered in long silky auburn hairs.

Ruthven had been somewhat hollow-eyed and irritable in the morning, but he'd insisted on taking the time to do her hair for her before having to leave for the airport. Greta missed him already, partly for the company and partly for the linguistic assistance. Standing in the bathroom, watching the deft white fingers in the mirror, remembering the care with which he'd touched her face, taking off the makeup—she'd thought briefly of what it might be like to have *Varney* there instead of Ruthven, Varney's long mobile hands in her hair, the easy intimacy of it, the calm competence. She'd seen him using those hands to play the piano once and never forgotten it; she imagined them cupped carefully to the curve of her skull—and then had shied away from the thought before her face could go an embarrassing shade of pink.

She had spent the morning after her panel listening to what turned out to be quite an interesting lecture on sarcoptic mange in bogeymen, complete with full-color slides, and then had gone to lunch with a couple of colleagues she hadn't seen in years. The story of her unexpected hotel visitors had raised some concern in the course of their discussion: someone must have summoned the specimen of *P. incolens* and then let it go, which was both irresponsible and unethical—in addition to which the subsequent appearance of the mixed-breed tricherpeton implied either a feral breeding population or *another* summoning-and-release.

That kind of magic wasn't exactly dangerous, the way a sharp knife wasn't dangerous in the controlled hands of someone who knew what they were doing, but summoning monsters and then releasing them suggested that whoever was responsible was—well, irresponsible, and might inadvertently do something that *was* dangerous to themselves or others.

Greta's colleagues had suggested that she look up the city's unofficial guardian, the werewolf St. Germain, and tell him what she'd seen. He ought to know about this, if he wasn't already aware.

He was, perhaps surprisingly, in the Paris phone book, or rather the online *annuaire téléphonique*; and now she had bought herself a latte and returned to the university, sitting in the shade—and fragrance—of the Place de la Sorbonne's lime trees, and got out her phone.

He picked up on the third ring, the French *allô* deep and not unfriendly. Haltingly she introduced herself as a friend of

Edmund Ruthven, and was spared having to work out how to explain wellmonster sightings with her limited vocabulary when he interrupted her in perfect, only slightly accented English. "Ah, yes, Dr. Helsing, I've heard your name before. A pleasure to speak with you; how can I be of service?"

It was a nice voice, she thought. "I'm sorry to just ring you up out of the blue, but I'm in town for a conference and I've seen a couple of peculiar things which you should probably know about. Do you have a minute?"

"Actually," he said, "I'm just on my way out, but if you're available later on, we could meet somewhere for drinks? Any friend of Ruthven's is most welcome to Paris."

She didn't have anything to do after the next lecture, other than show up to the obligatory formal dinner at eight; a drink or two beforehand would almost certainly render that experience less tedious, and this probably wasn't the kind of urgent that required a response right now; it could wait a few hours. "That would be lovely," she said. "Where shall I meet you?"

"There's a nice little bar called Bonvivant not far from the university," he said. "On Rue des Écoles. Shall we say six o'clock?"

"Perfect. Thank you so much," she said, smiling. Even if all she really had to say was *someone's summoning supernatural creatures, FYI*, it would be nice to get away from academia for a little while. Greta was a clinician, not a research academic: she was very fond of her colleagues, but one could have enough of them quite quickly.

"My pleasure. Until then, Doctor."

She hung up, and sipped her coffee, and scrolled through her contacts to the *V* section, still smiling. *V* for Varney the Vampyre-with-a-*y*, who had given her the earrings she'd worn to the opera *and* the ones the wellmonster in the sink had been hoarding, and also incidentally the aquamarine pair she had on right now to go with her neat conference-wear suit: he seemed to have settled on *jewelry* as an acceptable gift, and then decided it ought to happen quite frequently. She couldn't wear big fancy rings—she washed her hands all the time, which was bad for the stones, and wore gloves that could get torn on the setting; and she had never really been much for necklaces. Earrings, therefore, were the logical conclusion.

Varney liked logic, for a certain value thereof. She tucked her hair behind her ear, waiting for him to pick up: the double *brr brrr* ring went on and on until she'd almost decided to give up, when—

"Greta?" he said, sounding slightly out of breath and both surprised and pleased. "I'm so sorry, I'd left my phone all the way upstairs, I only just heard it. Are you still in Paris?"

"I am," she told him, "currently sitting just outside the Sorbonne watching tourists. And I take it *you* are not in town but in the country?"

Varney had spent quite a lot of the previous century in hibernation in the cellars of his decaying country manor, a huge pile with the unprepossessing name of Ratford Abbey— which was generally known to the locals as Dark Heart House, due to an avenue of copper beeches and a stand of them surrounding the house itself: dark reddish-purple leaves against pale stone. Greta had never seen it, but from Varney's description, it made her think of the House of Usher. It had an ornamental lake in which numerous people were said to have drowned over the years, and part of the roof had caved in while Varney slept the sleep of the dead in the wine cellar, down among the cobwebs and the nitre.

He had woken for the first time in thirty years the previous November, and come up to the city to slake his thirst and spend some time melancholically gazing into the river, weighing the merits of throwing himself into it. His plans had been drastically altered by the appearance of a sect of mad monks armed with vampire-slaying weaponry; following that unpleasant little episode, however, Varney's outlook on life had taken on a somewhat rosier hue, and he had recently decided to begin the work of repairing—well, *rebuilding* and redecorating—Dark Heart.

"I am indeed in the country," he said now, with a faint rueful edge to it. "Which contains rather more wildlife than one could strictly wish, and much of it seems to want to be *inside* the house rather than *outside*; there's a colony of what appear to be little brown bats that have taken over the room at the east end, which is still uninhabitable. I have tried persuading them that they'd be better off elsewhere, but so far it doesn't seem to be working."

She could picture him very easily: a tall spare figure with shoulder-length silvering hair, standing with his hands on his hips and looking up at bats roosting in the half-repaired coffered ceiling, addressing them in earnest and somewhat lawyerly tones. "Leave them for now?" she said. "They won't do very much harm, even if the floor will need to be cleaned, or possibly replaced, and they're useful creatures."

"Well, yes," Varney said, "of *course* I'm leaving them there. I'm not about to try to evict my first tenants in a hundred-something years until we build bat houses in the stables and the copse. I am not entirely without heart."

"You have rather more of it than me sometimes," Greta said with a swell of fondness. "I miss you. You'd find it desperately dull here, but—I miss you anyway."

She did. Once you got past the dour expression and the general air of melancholia, and the odd fact that the irises of his eyes were actually reflective, a dark grey with a metallic sheen like polished tin—he was excellent company; he enjoyed learning things, and there were so many he had missed out on, over the centuries. And Greta loved to teach. The thought of his hands in her hair came back, unbidden, very sharp and clear, and she closed her eyes for a moment.

"You *miss* me? Good heavens, really?" he asked, sounding taken aback.

"*Yes*," she said. "I'm coming home on Monday morning; I want to beg Nadezhda to run the clinic for me for a few more days, so I can come down and see these grand works of yours for myself. Including the bats."

"I think that could be arranged," he said, and his voice— the most beautiful thing about him, *mellifluous*—was very warm. One of the few things that penny dreadful by Rymer and Prest had managed to get right was their description of Varney's voice.

"Good. Oh, hell, I've got to go, I have another lecture to attend and tomorrow is packed, but I'll be home Monday on an early flight."

"Should—I come to meet you at the airport? Since Edmund's not here to play taxi driver?" He sounded as if he wasn't entirely sure the suggestion was appropriate.

"That would be lovely," she said, and even the prospect of the formal conference dinner ahead seemed suddenly less unpleasant.

In fact, the lecture wasn't too shabby, either: an overview of the various treatment modalities for tissue degeneration in Class A revenants, or in layman's terms, *how to stop bits falling off zombies.* The generally agreed-on therapeutic regimen had hitherto relied on chemical fixatives such as formaldehyde and glutaraldehyde, conveniently available in a variety of formulations from embalming supply companies—there was an ongoing argument on one of Greta's listservs over whether Kelco's Viscerol 30, Pierce's Cavicide, or Champion's Firmatone fluids were the superior choice—but today's lecture had covered the potential applicability of plastination as a permanent solution to the problem. It would, of course, be extremely unpleasant for the patient during the process, but afterward they could enjoy a greater quality of unlife without the constant concern over bodily integrity.

Greta had never had to treat any Class As herself, but it was fascinating to consider the challenges involved. She had ended up talking to the lecturer for fifteen minutes afterward, and only just remembered her appointment with St. Germain in time to tear herself away.

Locating the place he'd suggested wasn't difficult—it was just down the street, really, according to her phone; she wouldn't have to walk too far, and it was a lovely evening for a stroll.

She took a deep breath of the linden-scented air as she stepped out of the building. All in all, despite having had to get up early after very little sleep, it hadn't been a bad day whatsoever, which was why when someone behind her said in perfect English, "Excuse me, miss, I wonder if you could help me?" she turned at once, with a smile on her face—

—and was looking into scarlet, blood-colored eyes—a dark face—*the man from the opera*—no, the *vampire*—

—and had just enough time to think *Oh Ruthven you were right* before his thrall hit her like a freight train, and there was simply nothing left to think.

CHAPTER 3

Vampire thrall can perhaps most usefully be considered as a kind of hybrid of hypnotism and sedation. Its effects vary depending on the individual vampire involved, as well as the victim's susceptibility, but in general one can expect to experience analgesia, euphoria, diminishment or total loss of consciousness, and—afterward—total amnesia of the space of time between the initiation and withdrawal of influence.

And complete and utter obedience to any suggestion made while under that influence, of course. Someone under a vampire's thrall will happily walk off a building if instructed to do so by the vampire. Most often this facet finds its use in the replacement of memories lost during the event: *You will remember only that you left the club because you had a headache, and will return home as usual.*

For Greta, there was absolutely nothing between hearing the voice behind her—*Excuse me, miss, I wonder if you could help me*—and being on her knees, in some dim enclosed space, with her hands tied behind her and the unmistakable smell of blood heavy in the air. It was a mental jump cut, and she recognized it at once—she'd experienced it once or twice before, when she'd voluntarily undergone thralling.

This time she *hadn't* given consent.

Everything went cold and clear and slow, as it had done once before in the front seat of her Mini, with a poisoned knife held against her throat.

The chamber was some sort of cave, lit by hanging lamps that did not flicker, though made to look as if they should. They must be in the catacombs somewhere—this wasn't a cellar, this space was cut out of the living rock. The walls were hung with some kind of dark rich woven stuff. Underneath her knees the floor was covered with Turkish carpets layered on one another like the scales of a moth's wing.

And in front of her, on a huge, high, dark, carven chair—a chair clearly meant to resemble a throne—sat a vampire. He was very definitely a vampire. If the bright-red eyes hadn't given him away, the black flowing hair with a defined widow's peak would have, along with the pale hands steepled in front of him, their long colorless nails filed to a point. Or the way he smiled at her with his mouth slightly open, so that she could see the elongated canines resting on his lower lip. One of them gleamed silvery-bright.

Also, he sparkled.

It was just a little bit, here and there, high on his cheek-bones, the planes of his throat in the open V of his shirt collar, but he sparkled, and Greta—despite her daze—thought: *Body glitter?*

Other people registered in her peripheral vision. More vampires. More *sparkly* vampires; all of them were wearing fancy clothes, velvet and chiffon and leather and lace. None appeared to be older than their mid-twenties, which didn't actually mean much—but one of them, a girl with improbably red hair, couldn't have been more than a teenager when she was turned. There was a lot of jewelry. The smell of incense and perfume hung in the air, thick and cloying, underneath the coppery stink of blood.

The vampire on the throne leaned forward, looking at her over his steepled hands. A ruby ring the size of a kumquat glowed on his right ring finger. His leather trousers creaked.

"Dr. Greta Helsing, I presume?" he said in English. In slightly *accented* English.

"Who are you?" she said, and thought somewhat hysterically, *I am being held captive underground by a vampire wearing body glitter, with the remains of a Yorkshire accent and apparently no sense of irony at all.*

"I am Corvin," he said grandly. "And you are my guest. My *special* guest. It's a great honor. Isn't it, Lilith?"

He turned and beckoned, and a woman came out of the shadows to stand beside his throne and stare at Greta with undisguised dislike. She was stunning. Her hair was paler than Greta's own, a true platinum silver-blonde, and dressed in long, lush ringlets partly caught up in a knot that glowed with scattered jewels. Her skin was absolutely marble-white, under the faint iridescent touch of glitter, and there was a lot of it on display; her gown, a complicated and thoroughly engineered affair of black silk and lace, left her shoulders bare and her bosom—that was a *bosom*, no doubt about it—just barely on this side of decency; a necklace of rubies shone like vast drops of wine, or blood, around her snowy throat. In this light it was difficult to tell, but Greta thought she might be wearing purple contacts; her eyes were certainly made up with a great deal of care, and her mouth was a perfectly drawn masterpiece.

And then she opened that mouth and said in a kind of elongated whine, "Do we *have* to keep her here?"

A flicker of irritation crossed Corvin's face. "Of course," he said. "I let you keep your toys, don't I?"

"That's different," Lilith said. "My boys are *beautiful*. This one's ugly. I don't like her."

"We will discuss this *later*, Lilith," he said with an edge in his voice, the accent more pronounced, and Greta thought, *Sheffield?* "As I was saying," he continued, turning his attention back to Greta as if he had realized the scene was losing its dramatic focus, "you are my guest, and will remain my guest for as long as I choose to keep you here; and I am afraid your friends will find no trace of you, dear Doctor. No matter how hard they might try."

She was conscious of the hard hammering of blood in her ears, the fine sweat of adrenaline standing out on her skin. Everything was still cold and clear and slow, and she still had no idea why the hell she was down here.

"No words for me?" Corvin said, dripping with condescension. "Don't you appreciate my hospitality?"

"It's a bit different from the Hotel Le Meurice," she said, unable to stop herself, and then wondered if she was going to end the day by having her throat torn out by a bunch of idiots somewhere under Paris.

Corvin's face hardened. "Take her away, Grisaille, and see she is *accommodated* appropriately."

Strong, narrow hands closed around Greta's shoulders, and she was lifted effortlessly to her feet—and held, while her legs decided they wanted to try bearing her weight again. "As you command," her captor said, and she recognized the voice, well-mannered, accentless, *I wonder if you could help me*, and thought of red eyes in the dark.

"This way," he said, behind her, and she was actually grateful for the support of the hands around her upper arms as he propelled her along a corridor, away from Corvin's audience chamber. "I'm afraid we haven't got the *ensuite* marble bathrooms, madame, but one must expect certain privations whilst traveling in foreign parts."

"Who are you?" she asked.

"That would be telling," he said, and she heard in the voice a kind of amused self-mockery. It felt familiar; the phrase was a quote from some old TV show she'd watched with her father, wasn't it? *The Prisoner.* She was almost sure, and flying on adrenaline and lack of any useful options, she gave him another: a line she remembered from the show, but also a question she wanted answered.

"What do you want?"

He chuckled, turning them down another passageway, this one less brightly lit. There were ... bars, set into the wall. Bars and a door. It was a cell. An actual cell. He stopped; let go of her with one hand to turn a massive, ancient iron key in its lock; and dragged open the door.

Greta didn't try to pull free—for one thing, the hand around her other arm felt like iron itself, and for another, she had absolutely no idea which way to run. Not to mention that her hands were still tied behind her back.

He let go of her entirely, and then gave her a little push between the shoulder blades; she stumbled forward, into the cell, and turned to face him for the first time. It was the man from the Opera, all right; the dim light caught his dark silvering hair in a waterfall of narrow dreadlocks down his back, and she could see his scarlet eyeshine. If he was wearing glitter, it wasn't visible.

He pushed the door closed behind her. "Information," he said, and now it wasn't an answer, but simply quoting the scene.

"You won't get it," she said, meaning it in both senses, and she could see him smile without a great deal of humor.

"By hook or by crook," he said, almost regretfully, and turned the key with a screech of ancient metal, "we will."

At about the same time, a hundred feet above and a few miles away, Alceste St. Germain got up from the table he'd been sitting at for the past hour and a half, and walked out of the bar.

He was sufficiently tall and broad that very few people took the time to point out to him that *Alceste* was a girl's name. His mother had seen Molière's *Le Misanthrope* shortly after its premiere, and it had apparently left an impression; and the young St. Germain had very quickly attained a size and stature that dissuaded people from saying anything about it where he might overhear.

Born in a small village in the province of Gévaudan, he had, in fact, grown so large and strong that his parents had had him quickly apprenticed to the local blacksmith in hopes of channeling that strength into something more constructive than getting into an endless series of embarrassing scrapes. St. Germain had taken to the work at once. In the forge he was able to make things, not just useful things but *beautiful* things—although a properly balanced blade was a thing of beauty in its own right—and his masterpiece showed an uncommon facility for rendering a kind of delicacy in the medium of iron.

He had set up his own smithy in the neighboring town, and had enjoyed a career of about nineteen highly satisfactory years before, one night, encountering something in the woods that had yellow eyes and a great many teeth. The eyes—two lamps of yellow, in the dark—had been the only thing he'd remembered very clearly for months, while he tried to climb out of the hole of black madness that had followed the werewolf's bite; but he *had* climbed out, and he had learned, slowly, to be a person again.

A person with a tiresome but permanent condition. One

that meant he had to be very careful of certain metals and metal alloys, and that one week out of every month he had to be extremely cautious who laid eyes on him; but all in all, those were not such drastic or terrible handicaps. And he liked being the wolf. There was a certain profound and simple satisfaction in knowing that you could bite directly through somebody's femur without so much as loosening a tooth; and few people stopped to argue with an animal that stood about four foot six at the shoulder, with implacable amber eyes. It was also of use that he could, when he put a little effort into it, render himself nearly unnoticeable to ordinary human eyes—except in bright sunlight, when the shadow he cast remained visible.

St. Germain stalked through twilit Paris with his senses idling, not on alert. He could never switch off his nose: that was a constant, even in human form. The intense barrage of sensory input had been the hardest thing to learn to bear in the beginning, but now he could compartmentalize.

He knew every inch of this city—had been here for a few hundred years now, watched it change, watched parts of it rot, and burn, and fall, and rise again.

He had come to Paris just before everything really went to hell the first time, before Necker's dismissal and Camille Desmoulins's impromptu and incendiary speech on a café table; and he had been here ever since. Through the revolutions, through the famines, through the Commune and the wars and the occupations, St. Germain had been part of the city, taken it into his heart, spent his time walking its streets and *keeping an eye on things*—helping where he could, preventing harm where it was possible. Slowly the supernatural community of Paris had recognized in him both a resource and a protector, and these days he was known as the unofficial guardian of the city. Every big metropolis had at least one, even if he'd been a little distracted just recently by the manuscript he was working on, a popular history of Paris he'd been meaning to write for about thirty years and had finally begun.

Which was why, right now, he was in a foul mood. If the woman had decided she couldn't make it to their meeting, or didn't want to, for whatever reason, fine: but she could have had the basic courtesy to call St. Germain and tell him not to wait for her. He'd spent the evening sitting alone at a table and looking steadily more ridiculous as time went by, nursing a single beer; he could have been home *hours* ago and might even have finished the third chapter of the goddamn manuscript by now if Greta Helsing hadn't wasted his time.

Peculiar things you should probably know about, she'd said. It had been a phrase designed to capture his attention: he'd agreed at once to the meeting, which he might not have otherwise, not with the manuscript waiting for him at home. Peculiar, in the sense of *supernatural*, things were exactly what St. Germain needed to know about—although he supposed that rudely standing up a friend of a friend after requesting to meet them could be classified as *peculiar*. He'd called her back, half an hour after she was supposed to show up, and it had gone straight to voice mail—which he hadn't bothered leaving.

He crossed the river and headed west through the gathering darkness toward his flat in the 8th arrondissement, thinking about the part of the chapter where he'd left off earlier in the day, turning over phrases and imagery in his mind. He could still get some work done tonight, even if he'd had to waste several hours already; the night was still young.

By the time he passed the Tuileries, Greta Helsing and whatever her problems might be had completely faded from his mind.

"That was a werewolf in a nasty mood," said Crepusculus Dammerung, raising his eyebrows.

He and Brightside had been strolling along the edge of the river, discussing where to go for dinner and whose turn it was to pay for it, and had easily recognized the large man walking purposefully across the Pont Saint-Michel. The recent case wasn't the only time St. Germain had had recourse to their professional services over the years. Brightside liked him very much: he was *sensible*, which was a quality in short supply in general, and he always paid at once and in full.

And right now he didn't look like a well-satisfied client. At all. It wasn't like him; St. Germain's other distinguishing feature, besides being large and well endowed with common sense, was his good-natured amiability. At the moment he looked as if he might snap at anyone who got in his way.

"He's annoyed about something," Brightside said, leaning on the parapet with his elbows and watching St. Germain stride off into the distance. "Annoyed, or maybe worried. I wonder why." He couldn't quite help feeling a flicker of professional uncertainty—an unfamiliar and uneasy sensation in itself.

"We could always ask him," said Crepusculus.

"We could, but I think I'd rather have another look at that haunting location first."

As he said it, Brightside realized he'd made a decision of sorts: that morning, in the café, he'd been trying to convince himself there wasn't *actually* anything sufficiently strange about the haunting to warrant further investigation, but he couldn't get it to sit right in his head. Especially when coupled with the city guardian's visible displeasure. He needed to make sure they hadn't somehow made a hash of the job—and more than that, he needed to work out what if anything they had *missed*.

The mystery of why the ghosts should suddenly show up several hundred years after the initial disposition of their bones was—well, having considered it, he could think of a couple of answers to that one; people must be sneaking into the catacombs under the city all the time. It stood to reason that eventually someone would have disturbed some of the bones neatly stacked down there and triggered some kind of spectral response. What was odd, in fact, was not that the ghosts had shown up at all: it was that they hadn't *been* showing up regularly over the past couple hundred years. If nothing else, the reorganization of the catacombs and the decorative arrangement of the bones in the early nineteenth century should have resulted in any number of hauntings, and neither he nor Crepusculus could remember ever having been called in to deal with this particular issue before. It was possible that some of the other outfits who did similar work had handled the problem, but Brightside was fairly sure he would have heard *something* about it at the time.

"You want to go back there?" Crepusculus was asking, dubious.

"No, I don't particularly want to, but I think we ought. There's something I'm missing."

"What sort of something? Wait." Brightside watched him tap his fingers on the stone parapet, thinking. "There's got to be a *reason* they showed up now. Right? Some factor we didn't take into account?"

"It can't just be disturbance of the bones," Brightside said. "If that was the only cause, one or both of us would probably have been here several times by now. There has to be something else, something I didn't notice while we were working, and I don't *like* missing pieces."

As soon as the vampire's footsteps had died away, Greta pulled at the rope binding her wrists together, testing the tension. There was some give: not a lot, but probably enough; enough that she thought it was worth trying to get free.

She bent double, arms stretched behind her, straining the rope between her wrists as far as she could manage—and, fingers rapidly going numb, managed to get one foot and then the other backward over the rope. It hurt like hell, her shoulders and wrists on fire, but when she straightened up in the dimness, her hands were bound in front of her.

At least it wasn't completely dark in here.

She could have borne that for a while, but only a while. Now, with the faint light from the corridor falling into her cell, she was at least aware that the space around her was not closing in, that nothing was about to creep up on her in the blackness and tear off her head. At least, not without her getting a look at it first.

She peered at the knots in the dimness, once the pain had died down a little. Whoever had bound her wasn't going to win any prizes for their technique. She'd have at the very least used a surgeon's knot rather than a granny, or bothered to do a couple more throws; as it was, a few minutes of picking and twisting had the rope freed. Greta rubbed at her wrists, marked by red bracelets that were probably going to come up in spectacular bruise colors, and stretched, popping various things in her shoulders and back that had gone wooden-stiff. She hurt all over. The wrists were the worst of it, an ache like a rotten tooth.

How long was I under thrall? she thought. *How long have I been down here? What time is it?*

She had nothing in her pockets. Her handbag and phone were, of course, long gone, even if she could have found any signal underground. She couldn't even reach Fastitocalon for help: in Hell, he was far out of range of their tenuous connection. There was no way to contact *anyone*. She had, very effectively, been disappeared.

She was trying to think clearly, through the sour adrenaline and the background terror, and it wasn't working. Once before she had been lost in the darkness, with no one to find her, and it struck Greta as vaguely hilarious that she should be doing it all over again. At least this time there weren't mad monks with poisoned knives running around looking for her.

This time there was just a vampire coven.

She hadn't actually encountered one before; not like this. The sanguivores she'd treated tended to be singletons, for the very good reason that the larger the number of vampires in any given area, the greater the likelihood that someone would notice them. It was good sense to maintain a separation of territory, but the ones who had kidnapped her didn't seem to be long on *sensibility*.

That ridiculously oversized ring their leader was wearing, for example, and the body glitter. Really? And the leather pants. Unironically, leather pants, with a velvet shirt. Not to mention Lilith's whole Queen of the Undead outfit, which Greta thought you could probably buy online at the kind of shop that sold coffin-shaped handbags for fifty quid. And there must have been a good sixteen or seventeen vampires in that cave, which meant that Paris must be experiencing a noticeable rise in the incidence of acute idiopathic anemia. She was absolutely sure that this lot didn't go in for the conscientious catch-and-release kind of feeding, either. There had to have been deaths.

Greta thought again of St. Germain, and wondered what other problems he might be aware of, and how long he'd waited for her at the bar before realizing she wasn't going to show up.

He had her number, though. Her phone was probably in some storm drain somewhere, completely dead, but he had her number, and maybe when he couldn't reach her, he might try calling Ruthven; they were friends, she'd mentioned his name—

And the hotel, the hotel would *absolutely* try Ruthven,

assuming they could even reach him out in the wilds of Perth-shire; it was his black credit card that had reserved the suite for them. It would be his problem if his party failed to check out at the required hour, but that wouldn't be until Monday morn-ing; she was booked through the weekend. What time *was* it, how long had she been down here already, was it still Saturday night? Had she been out for a few hours, or more than a day?

Greta made herself take a deep breath, fighting off the first bubbles of panic. She knew the symptoms that would accom-pany having fasted for a significant length of time, and she didn't have them yet: no cold sweat, no watery weakness in the knees, no nausea or tremors, just a distant ordinary hun-ger. She *couldn't* have been out for very long.

The hotel would absolutely be able to reach Ruthven; it was simply a question of when. She could hope that St. Germain might try to get in touch with him first. It was possible. *Some-one* would get hold of Ruthven one way or another; and when they did, he would just as absolutely be on his way back over here to try to track her down. It was up to her to stay alive until he did.

She straightened up. She was good at staying alive. She'd had almost thirty-five years of practice. There was nothing to *do*, nothing useful she could achieve at the moment, except perhaps to get a better idea of where exactly she was being held.

Her eyes had adjusted to the dimness, and she could make out that it was a roughly rectangular chamber, deeper than it was wide. The side walls were carved right out of the white limestone, but at the back of the chamber—

The sound of footsteps startled her, and she turned, expecting to see the vampire with the dreadlocks coming back—he would undoubtedly tie her up again, and she had a feeling he'd be better at tying knots than whoever had done it the first time—but these were the sharp tap-tap of a woman's heels on stone.

Greta stayed where she was, watching; and it was a little surprising to recognize the youngest-looking of Corvin's coven. She could remember this one from when she'd woken up from thrall on her knees in front of Corvin's throne, with all the vampires standing around watching; she'd noticed her simply because of her apparent youth. *Can't have been more than eighteen or nineteen when she died*, Greta thought again, looking at the girl. *And when was that?*

She was wearing a black velvet mermaid skirt and vinyl corset, opera gloves, and more glitter than might strictly have been advised. Her hair was the particular shade of burgundy-red that you got out of a bottle, and her eye makeup called to mind Tutankhamun's golden mummy mask, only a bit less tasteful. And she was standing there, staring at Greta, shifting her weight from one patent leather platform six-inch heel to the other.

"Can I help you?" Greta said after a moment. At least it didn't appear that she was about to be tied up again. That was a small flicker of relief.

The girl went on staring at her for a little while longer before saying, too fast, all at once, "Are you really a doctor?"

Her accent wasn't Sheffield, but neither was it Parisian; she sounded like a thoroughly ordinary upper-middle-class Londoner. "I am," said Greta. "Why?"

"You're a *vampire* doctor?"

"Among other things. I treat anyone who needs my help, no matter what species they happen to be." Greta tilted her head, looking at the girl, her curiosity piqued—and thought to herself that she had seldom seen anyone look quite so uncomfortable in her life.

"Is—" the girl began, not meeting her eyes, very obviously making herself ask something she wasn't sure she had the nerve to ask, but just then both of them heard voices down the hall, and she took a sharp step back away from the bars.

"Sofiria?" said somebody. "What are you doing out here?"

"I came to look at the human," said the girl. "Lilith's right, she's terribly ugly."

"Come away from the nasty mortal, *chérie*, we have work to do; Corvin's asking for you."

Greta caught her very brief and fleeting glance, before she turned and stalked away down the tunnel, her boots clicking and tapping on the stone floor. *That one's new,* she thought to herself. *That one is very new.*

And perhaps still reachable. If I'm clever about it. If I'm careful.

She thought of Ruthven, bleak in the brightness of his kitchen back home in London, telling her about the baby vampires he'd found over the centuries, how he himself had been turned without the perpetrator sticking around to help him through the misery of the transition. How he'd been half mad with it, killing indiscriminately, and survived only by sheer luck and the kindness of strangers.

She imagined what he would say, having seen Sofiria and her eyeliner.

I have to try.

She had no idea how, or if she'd have an opportunity to make the attempt, and thinking about it threatened to bring on shaky hopeless despair—so Greta very firmly redirected her thoughts to her immediate surroundings. When there was no longer even an echo of footfalls, she turned again to the corner of the cell that had caught her attention.

Greta moved nearer, eyes wide, straining for every bit of light there was. She couldn't make out details, but the wall wasn't a solid face of rock. Running her fingers over the stone, she could trace the edges of individual blocks, irregular in shape, resting tightly on one another.

She bent closer to the stones, and could feel a very faint touch of air on her face. Cool air, damp and dank—there was a space behind this wall. The stones were not cemented together with mortar, just stacked, an underground dry-stone wall—*good fences make good neighbors*, her mind popped up, with a kind of unsteady amusement. If there was a space, that meant she might be able to get out of here—but what lay beyond was completely unknown, and she had no light, no way of *making* light, and who knew when the vampires were going to come back to find her digging away in the traditional and time-honored fashion of prisoners in durance vile? Greta was absolutely sure that Corvin would not look with favor on escape attempts.

She turned to rest her back against the wall and slid down it to sit on the floor, eyes shut, trying very hard not to despair. She could feel the edges of her self-control beginning to craze and splinter, threatening to bubble up with mindless acid panic, and made herself breathe deeply until she had some control back.

That faint breath of cool air touched her face again, and suddenly over the slowing thud of her own heartbeat, she could hear something else on the other side. Something like movement. Like *rattling*.

A hollow, scraping kind of sound, where no sound should be.

It slipped a finger of ice all the way down Greta's spine. She had thought she was too tired and sore and miserable to move quickly at all, but that faint hollow rattle coming from behind the wall was enough to get her on her feet and stumbling all the way across the cell to the farthest corner, near the door, where the light from the passageway actually fell on her face.

Greta tucked herself as tightly as she could into the corner, her back wedged against solid stone; drew her knees up, wrapped her arms around them, buried her face against the dusty fabric of her once-respectable conference-attendee suit. Whatever was behind the wall would have to come all the way over here to get her, into the light, and she thought it would probably take long enough to get through that she would have time to scream for help. She might even receive it.

That thought was enough to let her relax despite her physical discomfort, and she found herself falling helplessly, headlong, into shocked and exhausted sleep.

The Place Joachim-du-Bellay was ostensibly a perfectly normal city square, with two rows of trees planted at its edges and a monumental fountain tinkling away to itself in the center. Only the name of the fountain, and the name of one of the streets bordering it, hinted at the original use for the space: the Cimetière des Innocents, one of the most notorious hazards to public health in eighteenth-century Paris. It was the oldest cemetery in the city, dating from the twelfth century, and had been used for mass graves almost since its beginning; when they started running out of room to put dead people in, the bones of previously buried individuals were excavated and stored in charnel houses built along the cemetery's walls to free up space.

Conditions had steadily deteriorated, as one might expect with what amounted to a series of semi-open pits full of decomposing corpses, and businesses in the streets nearby had suffered as a result. There were accounts of dyed cloth changing color if exposed to the putrid air for prolonged periods; wine merchants' wares, stored in cellars close to the cemetery, turned to vinegar. Finally, after an unusually rainy spring in 1780, a cellar wall in an adjoining building collapsed and an unspeakable torrent of mud and decaying flesh filled the room. Later that year further burials in Les Innocents were forbidden—but it took another six years before remediation, in the form of exhuming bodies and moving the bones to the old disused gypsum mines under the city, took place.

Once it had been cleaned up, the space was paved over and used for a market; and today it was a pleasant, quiet place, the trees and fountain providing a restful atmosphere, with no hint of the horrors that had once festered there. No obvious hint, at least. Even the psychically sensitive didn't report perceiving any distress while present in the square, and—somewhat improbably—no recorded episodes of ectoplasmic manifestation were known to have occurred.

Until now.

Crepusculus and Brightside strolled around the perimeter of the square as the last of the twilight faded into full dark, the stars bright above them. Brightside was smoking a Dunhill in a holder, and the burning tip of the cigarette's glow and fade was like a slow-blinking orange eye. He didn't need light to see by; neither of them did. Nor were their presences remarked upon by any of the evening's human passersby; as soon as they'd stepped into the square, both of them had made themselves unnoticeable. The effect did not render them completely invisible—but nobody who did see them would be able to *remember* having done so. It was the most common of the tricks they used in passing through the ordinary world.

"They were over by the Rue Berger side last time," he said. When they were here last, the ghosts—there had been about thirty of them, all told, counting all the missing bits—had been milling around, plaintively demanding where their legs or arms or heads had gone; the lack of a head did not much incommode a ghost's ability to complain. Luckily it had been about three in the morning, and the few people who were out and about at that hour tended not to be in any frame of mind to give credence to occult manifestations.

"Yup," said Crepusculus. "Mostly. One of them was wandering around—or through, actually—the fountain. I had to go and fetch her separately, but that was an easy job. Hardly had to exert any energy at all, as I remember: I just sort of— nudged a bit, and they slipped right on through to the great beyond."

"I am wondering," said Brightside, "if it wasn't *too* easy." They didn't generally have to work very hard at their jobs, but he, too, remembered how little effort it had taken with each ghost: one by one, taking them in his arms, leaning on the cobweb-tangle of metaphysical field lines surrounding the dead until they parted and let the soul slip between planes. Sometimes the tangle was difficult to unsnarl. These...hadn't been.

And why now?

"That doesn't sound ominous in the least," said Crepusculus, and looked down at the stones under his feet, taking a deliberate step and then another one, and another—and stopping.

"What is it?" Brightside asked.

"Come here and feel this."

Brightside sighed and went to join him, and he, too, stopped suddenly. It was like walking into a cold room all of a sudden: the air felt *different*, and there was something like the faint creak and squeal of rock heard in a tunnel where the ground was uneasy, although Brightside wasn't exactly perceiving it with his ears.

"Sour ground," said Crepusculus. It was an apt descriptor, often used of places that had seen bad deaths and hasty burials; you got sour ground surrounding abandoned gallows, and patches of it all over battlefields. "This must have been the location of one of the mass graves," he went on, shivering. "I didn't notice it last time. Did you?"

"No. Emphatically not. I would have remembered." Brightside took another measured step forward, and the smell hit, unmistakable and familiar: rotting flesh. He made a face, but kept going, and after about eight more steps the smell and that uneasy faint squealing sound faded out again like a radio signal beyond its transmitter's range.

"This is weird," said Crepusculus. "Very weird. Let's see if there are more patches of it."

Over the next two hours, he and Brightside covered the entire space of the square. They discovered that there were several irregularly shaped areas of sour ground scattered around the space, which Brightside was absolutely sure had not been there a week ago when they'd first arrived to sort out the ghost problem.

"I bet you anything they correspond to the biggest of the mass grave pits," Crepusculus said. "Give me one of those Dunhills?"

Brightside took out his case and handed him a cigarette. Crepusculus lit it with the tip of his forefinger and blew out a pale plume of smoke. "Thin places," he said. "Between the living world and the next one. Right?"

"Or thin places in *time*," Brightside said, not liking the option one little bit. Temporal attenuation—or worse, temporal overlap—was almost always a sign of something larger and more difficult to repair than a simple haunting. "Old horrors showing through. Echoes of the past."

"Why are we getting echoes now, when we didn't during an actual manifestation episode? I could have sworn none of this was here a week ago."

"So could I, and I also can't think why these disturbances have only just begun; there's enough of a mess down there to have set up a chronic haunting all the way back to the end of the eighteenth century, and neither you nor I have heard of anything strange in this neighborhood until now." He rubbed the bridge of his nose. "There's got to be something else. Some catalyst, maybe. Another variable that wasn't in play until now."

"Something that's weakening the boundaries between planes," Crepusculus said. "What could do that?" He wrapped his arms around himself as if the mild spring air had dropped thirty degrees. "I mean, other than—oh, wizards fucking around with mystic artifacts stolen from the dead, or something."

"There was that thing last year in London," Brightside said slowly. "We heard about it afterward, remember? That wasn't a haunting; that was a remnant."

"A nasty one," Crepusculus agreed. "Which—hell, would

have had to bore a hole through the planes to get into this one and muck about with it, right?"

"That was taken care of, though." It had been a bad little episode as far as he could remember: a remnant, a shred of unwanted creation with a voracious hunger for fear and hatred, had taken up residence in some abandoned air raid shelter under the city, and made a serious nuisance of itself by taking over the minds of the susceptible and turning them into murderers. In the end, the Devil had had to sort it out in person, and presumably had mended the gap in reality that the thing had burrowed through, but the fact that it had happened at all was slightly worrisome. Interplanar boundaries were the sort of thing you did *not* want to have weakened; passing between them, between planes of reality—between worlds—was supposed to happen only in specific and controlled ways.

Brightside shivered, feeling chilly himself. "I think at this point we'd do well to talk to someone who might have more information about recent disturbances in reality. Who's the demon stationed here? There's always a demon."

"Irazek, I think. Either him or Chordeiles, and I think Chordeiles is in Lisbon these days."

"Let's go and bother Irazek in the morning, then," said Brightside. "I don't think we're likely to find out anything more at the site tonight, and right now I want a drink." The repeated immersion in sensory perception of decay had been quite unpleasant to experience, even for someone as used to it as they were—and the gathering suspicion that something larger was going wrong had unsettled them both.

"I want more than one," said Crepusculus, "and I spy with my little eye a bar not so very far away at all."

The vampires were having a party.

For the first time since seeing Ruthven on the Opera stairs, Corvin felt *satisfied*: truly and simply content about the state of the universe. He had Ruthven's human friend bottled up neatly in his dungeons, and perhaps he'd allow himself to sample her—although he couldn't take too much, a dead hostage was useless—well, perhaps. Perhaps later.

He sat on his throne and watched his people enjoying themselves. They were very beautiful, in their black and crimson finery, all alight with iridescent sparkle; the humans he'd had brought down to supply the festivities were also beautiful, even if one of them was already dead. An aesthetic object, even past its usefulness. He'd have someone go and dump the bodies before morning, like he always did.

The newest of them—of his *children*, he liked that, he was going to use it, *children*—was still more than a little awkward, but clearly willing to please, clearly loyal. So young: she would be barely nineteen for the rest of forever. And very lovely to look upon, with her hair freshly colored deep red, contrasting well with her alabaster skin. Corvin thought to himself, not for the first time, that if Lilith did simply become too much of a liability, he would not have to look very far to find her replacement. Not very far at all.

Corvin swirled the red liquid in his goblet, careful not to spill. It was a broad, shallow, almost oval bowl: creamy off-white, with a branching silver base and stem attached to it by tiny jeweled rivets. The individual who had made it had even sealed the faint squiggly lines where the individual pieces of bone fit into one another with clear varnish to prevent leaking. It was in every way a gorgeous object, and he was very proud of it, even if he hadn't personally been responsible for the death of its original owner; it stood for the skulls of his enemies, a symbolic representation.

He swirled the wine-and-blood mixture again, and took a sip. Delicious. He could *feel* the strength it was giving him. Soon Ruthven would come to him, attempting to rescue his little friend, and then Corvin would have satisfaction at long last. He let himself imagine those silver-white eyes widening in fear and understanding, that pale patrician face twisted in a grimace. Imagined him begging. *Please, I entreat you, spare me.*

Ruthven, of course, had been the cause of the platinum fang. It still hurt sometimes when the weather changed—his entire face hurt, old fracture lines in the bone aching dully. He could remember with excruciating clarity the last time they'd come face-to-face, back in London, years and years ago now, and the look of resigned, condescending irritation on the face of the older vampire would probably never quite leave Corvin's mind. He'd ruined everything. Back then, Corvin and his coven had really been enjoying themselves, taking whatever they wanted, drinking from the city's cup with gleeful abandon, stalking the night streets in a short but glorious reign of terror and intrigue and really stylish haircuts, and fucking *Ruthven* had popped up to spoil all Corvin's fun and instruct him not to kill people.

But you're one of the Kindred, Corvin had said, staring at him. *You're above the humans.*

Ruthven had said a lot of extremely offensive and ignorant things, and then he had hit Corvin so hard in the face that he'd broken not only his cheekbone but three of his teeth— one of which had had to be replaced completely, and hadn't *that* just been a lovely little experience, six hours of work in a French underworld dentist's surgery for which he'd had to be largely conscious—and thrown them out of London. To say that Corvin resented this treatment with profound vigor would be somewhat of an understatement.

He thought again of Ruthven begging for his life, and half closed his eyes in pleasure. "Not a chance in hell," he said under his breath. Beside him Grisaille, who had been leaning against the wall with his arms folded, watching the celebrations, straightened up.

"What was that?" he asked. Corvin scowled.

"Nothing. I was talking to myself. Why don't you go join the party; you're kind of bringing me down just standing there—what, isn't this scene hot enough for your taste?"

The sneer in his voice was almost as good as the one on his face, and he was pleased to see Grisaille flinch. That was better. His lieutenant had been insufficiently subordinate of late.

"Sorry," Grisaille said, and detached himself from the wall. "*Fantabulosa* party, Corvin. Like yours always are."

Was he imagining things, or had there been just the faintest hint of sarcasm in that last statement? Corvin scowled. "Go away," he said, "and tell Lilith to stop doing body shots off that body, I desire her presence right here and now."

Grisaille simply nodded, and slipped away into the crowd; and Corvin sat back on his throne, with his goblet in his hand, and thought again, *Soon, Ruthven. Soon.*

It took Grisaille two attempts to get Lilith's attention over the music—Corvin was into techno these days, turned up far enough to get the occasional shower of bits of stone to fall from the ceiling—but eventually, pouting and unsteady on her feet, she was persuaded to rejoin Corvin. Grisaille watched as she climbed into his lap, straddling him on the throne, and covered his face with somewhat inexact kisses.

What a good thing somebody invented indelible lipstick, Grisaille thought, turning away from this edifying sight, and went to get himself a drink. Three of the humans were still alive, he was relieved to see; dead blood had a particular aftertaste that some vampires enjoyed, but he found it unpleasantly metallic.

They'd draped the naked victims over dining tables, groggy both with thrall and with a sizable hit of something euphoric to prevent them from struggling, and Corvin's people were enjoying the buffet. Black and red and violet silk rustled, leather creaked, lace whispered as they wandered from table to table, biting indiscriminately in between dancing to the pounding beat and feeling one another up in alcoves.

At the last table Grisaille found a young man with pale wavy hair and very long eyelashes, curves of gold catching the light where they rested against his cheeks. He was lying curled on his side, face slack and peaceful, as if he'd simply fallen asleep. This one had been given a good going-over, judging by the number of bite marks, but Grisaille felt for the pulse and thought there was probably enough left in there for one more.

Without a lot of delicacy, he lifted the young man's wrist and bit it, sharp and quick, and rested it over a goblet to catch the blood. If he'd been out hunting alone, he would have enjoyed the process of drinking directly from the vein—there was something profoundly satisfying in the feeling of warm skin against your lips, *life*, brief and brilliant and fragile, a pleasant little memory—but he didn't much go for being watched while he fed, and so Grisaille waited for the young man's slowing heart to fill his glass.

When he'd finished, he lifted the wrist again and held it to his mouth, pressing the tip of his tongue against the wound he'd made until he could taste the change as the clotting agent he was secreting went to work. Most of the others hadn't bothered to put the stopper back in after they'd had their fill, but Grisaille disliked wasting resources, even if the human was already nearly dead.

He added a splash of vodka from the forest of bottles on a side table and went to lean against the wall and watch the party. The newest vampire was faring a little better this time than she had at the last of Corvin's celebrations, when she'd made a right mess out of one of the victim's necks— embarrassing not only herself but the vampire who'd actually made her. Now she'd clearly gotten the hang of biting cleanly, even if she still looked awkward as hell and not even slightly confident.

Someone must have actually bothered to teach her something, he thought, *and about damn time*.

He didn't much like the way the entire business with the kid had been handled. Nineteen was just *too* young to turn someone; they hadn't finished learning how to be a person the first time around, and making them into something else just got you an unstable and unhappy vampire who needed a great deal of supervision, which this one had not been get-ting. He could clearly remember the week right after she'd been brought down here, when she'd done a lot of screaming; one of them would have to thrall her practically every hour to get her to calm down. *Not smart, ducky*, he'd told her maker, a tiresome creature called Yves, at the time. *Not smart at all*. And nobody, to Grisaille's knowledge, had volunteered to take the responsibility of actually teaching the girl how to vampire.

You could have, said a nasty little voice in the back of Gri-saille's head. It was technically correct: if he hadn't minded breaking every single unwritten rule in Corvin's rarefied version of society, if he hadn't minded the consequences of establish-ing a highly inappropriate teacher-pupil relationship between the leader's second-in-command and the lowest-ranking of the entire coven, he could have done it. He could have done it quite well, if briefly; that kind of thing would have served as a highly efficient method of getting himself killed. But he *could* have done it.

And I didn't, so how about that? he told the little voice.

You're good at not doing things, aren't you? Got a lot of practice.

Grisaille took a swig of his drink, trying to ignore the voice, and closed his eyes for a moment as the heady richness of spiked blood warmed him from the inside out. It wasn't as good as hunting, but it was pretty damn pleasant all the same. There was a kind of cold shaking weakness that came on after you hadn't had anyone to eat for much too long, and that first sip of blood breaking the fast always felt like swallowing sweet fire, racing through your veins, driving back the chill—which was, of course, nothing more than the natural chill of a dead body. The first taste of blood tonight felt a little like that reawakening, and Grisaille concentrated on it, trying not to think about the past.

What a lot of things there were that you could have done, over the years, said the voice, matter-of-fact, implacable, *and chose not to. Victor, for example. You could have stopped Victor from doing unspeakable things; he might have listened to you when he wouldn't hear anybody else, and guess what, you did nothing, and look what happened, how well that turned out for all parties involved! How very responsible of you.*

Sod off, he thought wearily. *I'm not supposed to be the one responsible. I'm not the one in charge. I'm Number Two.*

That you are, said the voice, and of course it was his own voice; of course it was, he knew that, even as he reached for the vodka bottle to top up his glass. It had always been his own voice, even back when he'd been alive, and it had chased him across countries, across continents, oceans, carried along with him wherever he went.

In the abandoned hotel suite, something very hairy clambered in through the window, as it had done once before. It liked people who smelled right, and the woman who had first screamed at it and then stopped screaming and petted it properly had smelled right. Most people didn't.

It stopped, sniffing the air, and then the faceless head bent to snuffle at the carpet, following a trail to the bed—it hopped up on the bed, yes, this was where it had slept, all right, but there was now no warm body in the bed for it to curl up against. There didn't seem to be *anyone* there at all, not even the cold man who had been there last night with the woman.

The night breeze sent the curtains flaring and rippling. It was cold in here now, with the window open, and the hairy thing whined softly: something wasn't right. When it had first climbed into the room, nobody had been there, either, but there were lots of things that suggested they'd be coming back. There had been a big, complicated, stuffed-full-of-*things* handbag, which it had quite enjoyed investigating: all kinds of smells were in there, some of which it had never encountered before.

Now, when it jumped down to the floor and set about sniffing intently, all it could find was a closed suitcase, and in the other room where the cold man had been, there wasn't even that.

It whined again, pushing its non-face against the suitcase. That belonged to the woman, it could tell, it had her scent on it—the things inside smelled of her, too. But nothing else was there.

Eventually it curled up on top of the suitcase, in an almost round knot of limbs, and went to sleep; and when a knock on the door in the morning roused it, all the maid found when she came into the room was a scatter of long, inexplicable, silky auburn hairs.

CHAPTER 4

The first thing Greta was aware of, out of the darkness, was a clutching weight around one ankle, and a faint but present smell of mold.

She came awake suddenly and entirely, sure that whatever had been rattling behind that wall had come out to say hello—and her terror stuttered, sliding sideways, when she opened her eyes to find nothing horrible bending over her.

Nothing at all. Only…

…there was that weight around her ankle, and several smaller weights pressed against her feet. She looked down, and as the mindless terror retreated, she thought, *Oh God, someone really has been summoning them, these can't be more than a few weeks old—*

Clinging to her ankle was a wellmonster about the size of a turnip: a grey lump, with narrow little arms and legs that gripped her pant leg with surprising strength. As she watched, it began very slowly but determinedly to climb up her leg—she was reminded of the deliberate slowness of chameleons, of sloths.

She looked down. There were—God, five of them, ranging in size from the biggest one watching her a few feet away to the one climbing her ankle, small grey hand over small grey hand, to the tiniest damp creature sitting on her foot. She couldn't help reaching down to scoop that one into her hands, even as the largest crawled over and pressed its clammy face against her, radiating its characteristic mildewy smell.

These were *very* new. The wellmonster she held was the size of a large frog, and when it wrapped its hands around her fingers and licked her thoughtfully, she wasn't quite able to stifle a squeak.

"That's intensely adorable," someone said quite nearby, and she looked up to find the vampire with dreadlocks watching her. He was leaning against the wall on the far side of the corridor, arms folded, exuding the typical effortless vampire style; today's outfit featured a faintly iridescent dark grey shirt under a fitted leather blazer. One or two of the narrow silvering locks falling over his shoulders had tiny jeweled bands around them, glittering red as he moved. She couldn't help noticing that it was the only thing on him that sparkled: this one apparently really didn't go in for nineties nightclub body glitter.

Greta was extremely aware of the fact that she had on yesterday's clothes, crumpled and filthy, and that her hair very badly needed a comb. And that she had managed to get free of the rope around her wrists, which she should not have been able to do.

She glared at him. "What do you want?"

He opened his eyes wide in a *who, me?* expression. "I've come to escort you to the facilities," he said. "Unless, of course, you'd rather a bucket?"

She could feel her face going red. The question had occurred to her more than once, and in point of fact, she was rather in need of *facilities*. "Oh," she said. "No. I mean—"

The vampire turned the key in her cell door. She had tried, of course, to reach it herself, once she'd gotten her hands free; but whoever had designed the door had clearly taken this into consideration, and the lock was set into a flat expanse of metal much too wide for anyone to reach the key from inside. "Come on out then," he said. "If you can bear to detach yourself from your admirers."

It was, in fact, difficult to unpeel the monsters. The little one climbing her leg required less effort; the one clinging to her fingers *glupped* unhappily as she loosened its grip. "They're very young," she said. "Very...new."

"They are indeed. You should see the hairy things, too; they shed everywhere."

"You have tricherpetons down here, too?"

"Is that what they're called? Yes. *Many.*" He sounded as if he could have done without them. "Come along."

Getting up hurt: she was stiff all over, and in fact, he had to steady her with a cold hand on her elbow while she tried to get her knees to work. He picked up the discarded length of rope with which her wrists had been tied, coiling it up with the air of someone tidying a disorganized room; Greta expected him to say something about it, or just tie her up again, but he simply slipped the coil of rope over his wrist like a bracelet and took a firmer grip on her arm. The little group of monsters looked up at her with expressionless coppery eyes as he led her away.

She had not known what to expect—had no idea how extensive Corvin's lair was, or how sophisticated his household infrastructure—but in fact, they had quite a luxurious bathroom, even featuring the kind of expensive free-standing bathtub that was currently in fashion. *Someone*, she thought, staring at her haggard and filthy self in the mirror over the sink, *someone has done a great deal of work to make this place habitable, and I bet it wasn't Corvin.*

When she emerged, still smelling powerfully of wellmonster but feeling rather a lot better as well as less covered in dust, the vampire straightened up from the wall he'd been leaning against. The coil of rope was nowhere to be seen. "Now what?" she asked. "What does he *want*?"

"Now you toddle on back to your bijou maisonette," he said, "and enjoy catered brunch. I've found it does not do to ask questions about Corvin's motive or intention, as a general rule."

I've found, she thought. *Interesting choice of phrase there.*

The grip on her arm was not ungentle, but Greta had no illusions regarding the possibility of escape despite the lack of restraints: that hand was as firm and insistent as iron, and she let him walk her back along the passageways. The bathroom was at the end of a much wider, more brightly lit corridor than the one leading to her cell, and as they passed several other openings, she could glimpse more luxurious furniture as well as rather a lot of decorative bone arrangements, and did her best to mark each one in her memory.

The wellmonsters were still there when he returned her to the cell, blinking up at them; and when she sat down again, they returned to investigate. Without further comment, the vampire left her alone with them, and she had to wonder what he'd meant by *catered brunch*—crusts of bread and a jug of water?

It turned out to be a large coffee and a chocolate croissant still in its white pastry bag; and while Greta was still attempting to assimilate the remarkable nature of this development, the vampire—whose name she still didn't know—simply gave her a pointed if not unfriendly smile, and said, "Enjoy. It could be worse, you know. He does want you alive."

It was not until he had gone away again, until she had half finished the pastry, feeding tiny bits of flaky crust to the monsters, that Greta remembered the line from *The Prisoner*. She'd got it wrong, last night. It wasn't *who are you* that was answered *that would be telling*.

It was *whose side are you on*.

Alceste St. Germain's apartment on the Avenue George V faced almost due west. From his fourth-floor windows, the sun wasn't directly visible until it had climbed quite a long way up the sky; instead, each morning, his bedroom was filled with reflected brightness from the dawn-lit stonework of the other side of the street. From deep shadow the tide of light would catch the chimney tops first, then the blue-grey of the slate roof, creamy limestone, gleam of glass, black lacework of wrought-iron balconies, slipping farther and farther down the facade as the sun's angle changed. He enjoyed lying in bed and watching the line between light and dark steadily advancing, pushing back the remains of the night. It was not lost on St. Germain that moonlight, which figured so largely in his personal experience, was nothing more than reflected sunlight itself; the thematic continuity amused him.

This particular morning he was in no mood to appreciate the beauty of sunlit stonework, however. This morning he had woken early, after a disturbed and restless night, full of a vague crawling sensation that something *wasn't right*; that he had somehow forgotten to do some task that he ought to have done a long time ago, and something therefore was about to go very badly wrong indeed.

The feeling hadn't gone away once he'd gotten out of bed. It was with him while he showered and shaved—this time of the month he could get away with shaving only twice a day, if he didn't mind looking somewhat stubbly—and it was with him while he made coffee, barefoot on the kitchen tiles, wrapped in a bathrobe precisely the shade of grey that didn't show the worst of the wolf hair unavoidably clinging to it.

He'd spent the previous evening solidly working on the book, after returning from his fruitless errand, and he thought he was really getting somewhere on it, and...

...and he couldn't stop thinking of Edmund Ruthven the last time they'd talked, sometime last spring it must have been, and the warmth in the vampire's voice as he discussed his human friend with the peculiar medical practice. Ruthven was *kind*, yes, but he also didn't have an enormous amount of patience with stupidity or bad manners, and St. Germain was having an increasingly difficult time making the faultlessly polite woman's voice on the phone match with the image of a person who'd talk about *peculiar things you should probably know about* and then casually stand someone up.

Maybe something had happened to her.

Maybe she had been unable to keep the appointment, rather than choosing not to.

He stood there for a few minutes, amber eyes expressionless, before cursing and going to fetch his phone. Trying her number got him nowhere: straight to voice mail, just like before.

She's quite remarkable, Ruthven had said. *Doesn't give up in the face of adversity—you should see the things she does with what I'd consider absolutely hopeless mummy cases, practically rebuilds the poor creatures from scratch.*

St. Germain went back to his phone's contact list, scrolling down to *Ruthven, E. St J.* This would be embarrassing if it turned out she was perfectly all right, but still—

"Your call cannot be completed as dialed," said a recorded female voice, sounding somewhat smug about it. *"Please check the number and dial again."*

It hadn't even rung. Carefully St. Germain dialed the numbers one by one, pressed *Send*. Immediately, not a single ring:

"Your call cannot be completed as dialed. Please check the number and—"

He hung up on the robot and bounced the phone thoughtfully in the palm of his hand. One person not answering their phone, well, there could be a thousand reasons for that. Two people not answering—and one of them not even ringing, like there was something wrong with the number itself—was enough to make St. Germain's vague feeling of unease solidify into a cold finger at the base of his spine.

He wanted to talk to some people about this. Some very specific people, who only came out at night—

And all at once he was entirely and completely aware of what he had forgotten to do, and when he had forgotten to do it; the knowledge dropped into his mind like blood into water, uncurling, spreading tendrils of mordant guilt.

What he hadn't been doing was *his job*, in effect. He hadn't been *a little* distracted by the book, as he'd vaguely considered it. He'd been almost totally distracted: so focused on this stupid project, finally doing a thing he'd been thinking of doing for so long, that he had spent less and less time patrolling the city; less and less time keeping an eye out for anything unusual. Less time *paying attention*, keeping people safe, knowing what was going on.

St. Germain dropped into a chair, covering his face with his hands. He should have been out every night—or at least *most* nights of the week—instead of sitting here in his cozy apartment with a glass of cognac trying to make words into sentences into paragraphs the way he had once made bars of metal into delicate and beautiful scrollwork. He should have kept some semblance of balance, instead of forgetting a duty in pursuit of a challenge, and the thought of what might have been going on, all those nights he hadn't been on the streets, was nearly unbearable.

So was the fact that he would have to wait until darkness before making that self-appointed round. The people he needed to talk to were other supernaturals who for obvious reasons could not let their presence be widely recognized by the human population, and therefore St. Germain could do nothing *useful* until nightfall—

No, he thought, taking his hands away from his eyes. *No, I can at least try to track her, even if neither she nor Ruthven are picking up the phone. I know where she was when we spoke—or where she said she was. There might be something still there to find.*

Something that might tell me what happened to her, or where she might have gone. What she might have meant to tell me. And tonight—tonight I am going to catch up with what I've missed.

St. Germain got up, moving fast now, trying to waste no more time than he already had; and by the time the light on the houses opposite had slid halfway down the facade, he was dressed and on his way back to the Place de la Sorbonne, the last place he knew Greta Helsing had been before her disappearance; he needed to be *out*, in the city, feel it around him, settle it back into his senses the way he should have been doing for *weeks*—

I'm here now, he thought, heading south, making his way

easily between the herds of pedestrians, moving with purpose. *I should have been here all this time, but I'm here now. At this time, in this place. Better late than not at all.*

St. Germain walked a little faster.

Greta had the smallest of the wellmonsters tucked into the hollow of her collarbone, hanging on to her lapel with both little grey hands, and wished like hell she had a tennis ball to bounce against the far wall of her cell. Anything. *Anything*, to pass the time, to take her mind off the situation.

She heard the footsteps quite a while before anyone came into view, and actually welcomed the sound—maybe it was the one with the dreadlocks back again. He was at least entertaining to talk to, even if he was one of them, and he was apparently the person tasked with bringing her improbable pastries. But the sound was too sharp: the sound was the click-tap of steel boot heels, and she thought she could remember hearing that particular pair of boots before.

She was right. The youngest-looking of the vampires had her hair in elaborate ringlets today, and the body glitter was a fetching iridescent shade of lavender, although Greta would have suggested more subtlety in its application: she must have put the stuff on with a palette knife. She was wearing the same opera gloves and velvet mermaid skirt, but the top was in purple brocade with black lace overlay, rather than shiny vinyl.

"Hi," said Greta, since the girl didn't seem inclined to start a conversation.

"…Hi," she said. Again Greta was struck by how completely ordinary she sounded. Somehow the getup and general aesthetic suggested an excitingly foreign if geographically imprecise vampire accent, instead of Estuary English. "Can I ask you something?"

"Of course," said Greta. After a moment, as she watched, the girl glanced down the corridor as if making sure nobody was there to see her. Presumably nobody was, because she took a few steps forward and sat down all at once on the floor outside the cell. Her velvet skirt trailed in the pale rock dust of the floor, and Greta was slightly impressed by how little she seemed either to notice or to care.

"Is—so, like, is there any way to, um, *de-vampirize* a person? Like, is it curable?"

Oh, thought Greta, and a spike of absolute furious loathing for this group of terrible people and their irresponsible behavior arrowed through her. She thought again of Ruthven talking about this, any number of times—talking about the vicious stupidity of vampires who turned people for the hell of it, without preparing them beforehand, without informed consent. It was the worst thing, he had told her over and over again, the worst thing that could be done to somebody—and Greta could remember, too, how much Varney hated thinking about the people he himself had turned back in the bad years.

Oh, Christ, she thought. *You poor kid.* Out loud she said, "No, but there are several things you can do to make it easier to deal with. How long ago did it happen? And what's your name?"

"Sofiria," said the girl with a slight but telling pause. Greta tried to remember where she'd heard that name before, and then sighed. *Sofiria* was the name of Dracula's wife, the Countess Dolingen—*sought and found death 1801*, Greta thought, *the dead travel fast*—and she would bet a great deal of money it wasn't the name this child had been given at birth.

"Sofiria," she repeated without letting the skepticism into her voice. "Do you want to tell me about it?"

"No," said the girl honestly, and Greta had to smile a little. "I don't, I just—there's—it's permanent, then? I can't—it can't be fixed?"

"The condition is permanent," said Greta, "but how you deal with it is up to you. I expect they've told you a lot about how the Kindred are superior to the humans, haven't they?"

Sofiria blinked at her. It wasn't that it was *bad* eyeliner, Greta thought. There was just a great deal too much of it. "...Yeah," she said. "I mean. Corvin's—he takes care of us. He's a good leader."

"He's a pillock," said Greta with precision. "And somebody ought to tell him to get a bloody haircut."

The girl let out a startled laugh, and covered her mouth with her gloved hands, glancing again down the hallway to make sure nobody was coming. She swallowed hard. "He takes care of us," she said again.

"For a certain value of 'care,'" said Greta. "Tell me what happened? You're not from here."

"I'm not," she agreed. "I was with some friends—we'd finished our exams, and we wanted to come over here and hang out and go to clubs, like people *do*—we rented a flat together, we were here for, like, a week. That was supposed to be it."

Greta thought she could fill in the rest of it, but simply sat there, listening, occasionally stroking the little monster clinging to her neck. Sofiria was looking down at her hands clasped in her lap, and talking fast, as if once she had begun, she couldn't actually stop.

"...and so I'm having a great time, right, and we're all dancing at this club one night, it's called Rise, really nice place, hard to get into, you have to know somebody who knows somebody, and I'm—kind of wasted, but *good* wasted, you know? And this ridiculously hot guy just comes up to me and starts talking to me and it's weirdly nice to hear someone else speak English, and also he's gorgeous, and we end up in a booth together way in the back of the club and he buys me drinks and gives me these pills, I don't know what they were but they were brilliant, and I don't remember anything after that until when I woke up here."

Greta's desire to see something extremely unpleasant happen to Corvin rose another several points. To Corvin, and to his people; this was exactly the kind of stupid, vicious, irresponsible predatory behavior that gave the entire sanguivorous community such a shit name.

"And I was, like...okay, did he rape me?" Sofiria said, and looked up at Greta, her kohl-lined eyes huge and terribly young. "Because everything hurt. Like I'd been beaten up or something, *everything* hurt, and I felt really sick and thirsty at the same time, and my vision was all weird, and that was when I realized I was lying in an actual coffin, and I freaked out."

"No wonder," said Greta. "They left you alone in a god-damn coffin after the change with nobody there to help, that's thirty kinds of *not okay*, Sofiria. You should never have had to go through any of this, you should never have been turned without consent in the first place, but the least they could do having done the thing to you is to provide a single solitary crumb of reassurance or support. I'm so sorry."

Sofiria stared at her, looking rather heartbreakingly confused. "You are?"

"Yes. I've met a lot of vampires, and this kind of bullshit is roundly condemned among the sensible members of that community. Turning someone without their active and enthusiastic consent is just not done, except in a life-or-death situation, and even then it's iffy. And leaving you alone afterward—even a voluntarily turned vampire needs help after the change; there are so many physiological effects that you have to get used to, so many things that need to be explained, things you need to be taught. Corvin should be tied up in knots and roasted."

The girl let out a startled laugh. "It wasn't him who—did it to me, actually; it was one of the others. Yves. He has this amazing asymmetrical haircut?"

"I expand my statement to include Corvin *and* his goons," said Greta, "haircut and all. Tell me what happened after you woke up."

"I didn't know where I was," she said, "just that I was in some kind of underground chamber, in a coffin, and I freaked out and screamed and then somebody did come, one of the other women, and she did something with her eyes and that kind of chilled me out, I don't know how it works—can *I* do that now? Is that something I can do?"

"Yes," said Greta. "It's called thrall, and every vampire has some capability for it. Varies with the individual and with the subspecies, but you're pretty much guaranteed to have that power."

"Okay, that's…actually cool," she said, sounding a little surprised. "What other stuff can I do?"

"I'll tell you in a minute," said Greta, "but I want to know what they did after that. Did you get officially inducted or something, or did they just say, *You're a vampire now, oh, and here's your lord and master, do what he says?*"

"Kind of both? It's pretty hazy, to be honest. I just felt so gross and everything hurt, my bones hurt, and I kept having these…panic attacks, or something, and then one of the others would do the eye thing and that made me feel better for a while. I don't know how long that actually took before I kind of…got over it."

"Did they make you go hunting with them?"

"Yeah. Well, first they brought some…some humans, that's so weird to say, *humans*, like a category…some *people* down and showed me how to, um. How to bite them. Like where to bite, that kind of stuff. They had to do the eye thing on me—what's it called again?—before I could deal with that, but once I started, it got easier."

"Thrall," said Greta. "And I'm not surprised, either at the

difficulty or the easiness: you have physical instincts now which will help you do the things you need to do."

"Sometimes it's like I just know what to do," Sofiria agreed. "Other times I'm, like, *what the fuck am I supposed to be doing here*, and then I feel really dumb for not getting it. There's... can I ask you a gross question?" Very faint color was shading her cheeks palest pink under the glitter.

"Of course," Greta said. *I am going to inject Corvin with a syringeful of distilled allicin*, she thought, *and I don't care if that equates to straight-up murder, he's caused God knows how many deaths and his people have stolen this child's life.* Out loud she said, "I've heard loads of gross things in my time, don't worry."

Sofiria looked away, still pale pink. "So I kind of don't have to go to the bathroom anymore. I did at first, but then it just kind of got less and less. Sometimes if I drink a *lot*, I'll have to go, but it's never much. Is—like, is that normal or is there something wrong with me?"

"That's perfectly normal," Greta said. "The type of vampire you've become is known as the classic draculine in modern terminology, after the obvious example of Vlad Țepeș. This subspecies—"

"There's species?" Sofiria interrupted. "And Dracula is real?"

"Very real, but he's a recluse; he and his wife rarely leave their castle. And yes: three main subspecies, the classic draculine like you, the lunar sensitive, and the nosferatu."

"Have you met him?"

"I have not. I know a vampire who did meet him, ages ago now, but I doubt I'll ever get to encounter Dracula in person. I gather he no longer rides around town putting babies on spikes, however."

Sofiria gave that startled laugh again. "Okay, wow. Um. So I'm this classic kind?"

"Yes. I can tell for two reasons: one, your teeth and eyes, and two, you've almost certainly drunk blood from non-virgins and not had a violent negative reaction."

The girl's eyes widened. "Wait, what? That's a thing?"

"It is a very well-documented thing. The lunar sensitive vampire is actually spelled with a *y*, *vampyre*, and they need to feed much less frequently, but they can't drink from any-one but a virgin unless they want to spend several hours being extraordinarily sick. They can, however, be revived by moon-light if they get killed, and moonlight helps them recover from illness or injury. You, on the other hand, should probably try to avoid looking at the full moon: it won't hurt you but it may sort of hypnotize you into standing there and staring at it. Incidentally, your eyes have gone silver-white—it's either that or red, generally—and only your upper canines have length-ened; if you'd been a lunar sensitive, the eyes would have been metallic grey and the upper lateral incisors would be lengthened along with the canines."

Greta was conscious of a kind of bone-deep relief, like put-ting down something incredibly heavy: it was so very pleas-ant to be *herself* again, even temporarily, to be who and what she was, to be a doctor instead of a prisoner, a woman locked up in an underground cell. To be useful. To have a purpose, other than simply staying alive.

"I kind of want to take notes," said Sofiria. "Nobody told me any of this."

"That's because they're terrible. About the bathroom thing: your digestion has radically altered itself to suit your new dietary requirements, and your stomach is capable of breaking down blood extremely efficiently, so much so that there's little if any residue. Your intestines are basically off duty at this point. Your kidneys do still work, but there's much less for them to do: you're not producing anywhere near as much by way of toxic metabolites that need filtering out. When you drink a great deal all at once, your circulating blood volume increases, and the kidneys filter out the excess fluid, so you have to urinate—rarely, and never very much."

"How do I still have a heartbeat and kidneys and stuff if I'm dead?"

"You're technically dead in that you have died," Greta said. "That was a temporary state you passed through on your way from mortal human to near-immortal vampire. Don't ask me about the magic aspects of it, that's beyond my frame of reference—but you are *differently alive*, if it helps to think of it that way. Your body's still functioning, it's just doing it differently now."

"Can I still eat stuff?"

"I wouldn't recommend it. You can have liquids—coffee, tea, fizzy drinks, alcohol are all fine in moderation, although you will need to pee after that because of the extra chemicals you're taking in. Solids you pretty much can't digest, and you'll just feel terrible until you throw up and get rid of whatever it is. You *can* take most drugs, which is handy, but your tolerance has been drastically altered, so they won't actually do all that much good except in truly enormous doses. What you absolutely cannot do is consume garlic or garlic compounds."

"What happens if I eat garlic?"

"Not just eat: *touch*, inhale fumes, *get close to*. You'll go into anaphylaxis. You now have an extremely severe allergy, which you are going to have to take seriously, and it will be difficult at first to predict what is likely to have garlic or garlic products in it. Do you know anyone who has a serious nut allergy?"

"One of my cousins can't have peanuts," Sofiria said. "At all, like, he can't touch anything someone else has touched if they just ate a peanut. He has to carry one of those stabby pen things in case he has a reaction."

"The pen thing is a dose of adrenaline, which makes the reaction ease off. In humans, anaphylactic shock can be fatal; in sanguivores, it's less dangerous but still extraordinarily unpleasant. Garlic is to you as peanuts are to your cousin; I cannot overemphasize the importance of this—and it's not just garlic, it's several other members of the allium family to lesser extents."

"France is *full* of garlic," said Sofiria, looking resentful. "What's a sang-whatever?"

"Sanguivore just means 'eater of blood,'" Greta told her. "The older term was *hemophagous*, but these days all creatures who feed on blood are known as *sanguivorous*."

"What about crosses, or religious stuff? Does that do bad things?"

"To some extent. The crucifix on its own won't do much to you just by looking at it, although there's mention in the literature of the ankh giving vampires a nasty headache. Don't touch anything that's been recently blessed; you'll get a mild burn, as if you've touched something hot or caustic."

Sofiria sat back on her heels. "How do you know all this stuff?"

"I've studied it," said Greta. "There's a whole discipline of supernatural medicine which most people do not and should not know about—that's another thing, you have to *not be noticed*. This is one of the things Corvin is doing wrong. Running around killing people is the kind of thing that gets you noticed, and when you get noticed, you get people after you with stakes and garlic and so on. It puts the rest of the supernatural community in jeopardy. Stay secret for your own sake and for everybody else's. Ruthven gets extremely cross about this sort of behavior."

"Ruthven is that guy Corvin's obsessed with, right?"

"Is he? First I've heard of it," Greta said. "But if Corvin's been doing this sort of thing where Ruthven could see it, he'd definitely have stepped in to put a stop to the whole mess."

"What's he like?"

Greta leaned her head back against the wall, ran a hand through her hair. "What's Ruthven like," she repeated. "Let me tell you about Edmund Ruthven."

"Are you guys friends?"

"We are," she said. "Ruthven is a *helper*. I think Mister Rogers once said that: after any disaster, look for the helpers, look for the people who step in to try to make things better. I owe a lot of my clinic equipment to his generosity. He's extremely rich, and extremely hospitable, and something like four hundred and sixty years old. And he used to drive a Volvo, which I find illogically charming."

Sofiria looked as if she could not conceive of a situation in which vampires and Volvos could coincide. "Does he— um." She looked down at herself, shedding glitter. "Does he sparkle?"

Greta had to laugh, and it felt surprisingly good; the little monster clinging to her shoulder *glupped* as it had to hang on tight against the sudden jolting. "Oh God. No, he doesn't sparkle. Vampires don't, you know. Not naturally."

"I thought they did," said Sofiria. "Like—I wasn't sparkly because I was too new or something, so I kind of cheated?"

"The rest of them are cheating, too," Greta told her. "I guarantee it. Nobody down here glitters without the aid of something from a tube, and—I would suggest easing off on it a little."

"It looks dumb," said the girl, and sighed. "This whole thing is just so *stupid*."

"It is incredibly stupid and you should never have had to experience any of it," said Greta. "It was not your fault that you were out at the club having a nice time and caught the eye of some unscrupulous scumbag with sharp teeth; nothing you did means that you deserve this. You deserved to be able to enjoy yourself safely without being attacked by vampires."

Sofiria didn't reply, and Greta looked at her more closely,

and was a little appalled to see her eyes brimming with red-tinged tears.

This must be the first time anybody's told her that, she realized, *since it happened; she must have been thinking that it* was *her fault.* Aloud she said, "This should not have happened to you, and I'm sorry that it did, but—you don't have to deal with it like this, down here among the edgelords and the murderers. You can leave, Sofiria, you can escape from Corvin, you can get help and support and shelter from someone who's competent and not a complete twit. There *are* sensible vampires out there. I know several of them."

"Emily," said the girl, almost too softly to hear.

"What?"

"My name's Emily," she said, and a tear brimmed over and spilled down one cheek. "They changed it, when I—when I got here."

Greta detached herself from the wall, pulling herself close to the bars, and reached between them to touch the girl's shoulder, a little encouraged when she didn't pull away. "Emily," she said. "That's a much better name. Listen—next time they take you topside to hunt, tell them you want to do it on your own, you want to prove to Corvin you are a vicious and capable hunter all by yourself, some rubbish like that, and then leg it. Get as far away as you can."

"They'll catch me," she said. "They'll come after me and catch me and then I'll be—either in a cell like you, or dead. Properly dead, for good. I don't know what to *do* on my own; I can't make it without these guys."

"Not necessarily," said Greta. "You're a lot stronger than you think you are, and Paris is not without resources. Find a phone and call a man named Alceste St. Germain. He's a werewolf, a friend of Ruthven's, and he will help you." She sighed. "And possibly rescue me."

"I can't," said Emily, sounding miserable. "I *can't*, I'm too scared—shit, someone's coming…" She wiped at her face. "Is my eyeliner smudged?"

"No. Just smoky," Greta said. "You look fine."

Now she could hear voices from down the corridor, and Emily got to her feet in a hurry, brushing rock dust from her velvet skirt. The effort with which she slid back into the vampire sneer was evident, but once she'd got there, it was thoroughly convincing—even when she said, quickly and quietly, "Thank you—I'm sorry—thank you—" and turned to stalk away.

It was both facile and useless, after the fact, to say things like *I knew something was wrong* or *I had a feeling something was going to happen*, when in fact he hadn't: he'd been blithely unaware of the gathering shadows underneath the city. Even if he *had* been paying more attention, St. Germain was just a wolf, not a clairvoyant or a metatemporal perceptive. It also didn't help to dwell on the fact that he *could* have rescheduled the appointment for which he'd been about to leave when Greta Helsing had called him. He could kick himself now for not having taken the time to speak with her properly; she might have been safe and sound right now if he'd stopped to listen to what she had to say.

She'd mentioned *a couple of peculiar things* she'd seen. *Peculiar things I'm told you ought to be informed about.*

And she still wasn't answering her phone.

He had gone back to the place where Greta Helsing had claimed to be calling him from, yesterday afternoon. He'd spent quite a long time sniffing around the Place de la Sorbonne, and nothing out of the ordinary had pinged any of his senses. Thousands of people had come and gone, their scents overlaying one another in his nasal vision, trails crisscrossing one another, brighter here and there with the sharpness that meant emotional intensity, but nothing St. Germain could really consider out of the ordinary. There'd been a hint of vampire, faintly, lingering on the air, but *which* vampire he couldn't tell, and there were at least two relatively blameless sanguivores known to St. Germain personally who might well have passed through this space in the past twenty-four hours. And no blood. That he wouldn't have been able to miss if he'd been trying: blood was vivid and unmistakable even after considerable time had gone by.

Peculiar things, she had said.

After coming up with nothing in the immediate vicinity, he'd begun to circle wider and wider as the afternoon dragged on, trying to catch the scent of anything untoward. Anything *peculiar.*

Eventually St. Germain had given up the hope of finding answers on his own, and gone to kill some time in one of his usual haunts, an old café in the Place Saint-Michel, while night drew in. As soon as it was dark enough to be safe, he'd ventured forth again and spent most of the night patrolling Paris, doing the job he should have been doing properly for some time now. Visiting his friends and informants; catching up on gossip; asking questions about anything *peculiar* people might have seen in their perambulations around and under the city.

He had learned a great many things, among them the fact that his own efficiency as a protector had, for the past couple of months, been practically nil. He'd been distracted, yes—the work he was doing on the book had taken up so much of his attention—but that wasn't an excuse.

There had been deaths. He'd seen that in the paper, at least. Bodies pulled out of the river—the Sûreté was being cagey regarding the details of the actual cause of death, but St. Germain had now spent half an hour talking with the grey and sharp-boned melusine who lived under the Pont au Change, who had told him quite offhandedly that none of the bodies *she* had seen contained a single drop of blood. She'd had rather a lot of words to say on the subject of people polluting her river by dumping dead bodies into it—the changes in nitrogen and oxygen levels in the water as a result of decomposing corpses were not to her liking—but the means by which these unfortunate individuals had met their end was for her a matter of supreme indifference, expressed with a very Gallic shrug of one thin shoulder.

A brief discussion with a ghoul chieftain in the quartier du Petit-Montrouge had revealed that the ghouls had had to relocate several of their underground lairs recently after multiple near-encounters with intruders—in parts of the catacombs where no intruders should be, carrying no light with them. "Smell like meat," the chieftain had said, or rather hissed. "Too fresh. Like blood—and *astrkhk*. Too much *astrkhk*." He had wrinkled his face up in a remarkably unpleasant expression of disgust. It was the ghouls' word for *plants*, or *things that grow*: they didn't have much cause to differentiate between types of vegetation, living underground, but St. Germain thought he understood.

"Flowers?" he'd asked, and the ghoul nodded. "Blood and flowers. Perfume."

"Too much," the ghoul had repeated. "They come three, four time. If they come again"—he sighed—"we must move our home." And then, almost an afterthought: "Not just the man-creatures. There are other things under the city that are new."

"What other things?" St. Germain's attention refocused sharply.

"My people call them *hakh-nir*," said the ghoul. "Guardians of treasure. We see them sometimes in old places, but not here, not in this undercity, before. They are small, these *hakh-nir*. They smell new."

"Guardians of treasure," St. Germain had repeated. "About so big, grey, sort of like a frog?"

"Smaller," said the ghoul, nodding.

That had to be a wellmonster, and a fairly recently summoned one at that. He had no idea why anyone would be summoning wellmonsters in this day and age; most people kept their valuables in safes, not halfway down abandoned wells, and relied on codes and PINs to maintain security. It made no sense—and that bothered him almost as much as the evidence of vampires.

He should have known. He'd grown complacent, that was it, so long since anything more than minor evil crossed his path that he'd settled into thinking it couldn't, that there was no urgent need to keep the watch he'd charged himself to keep; he'd gotten distracted with his stupid project, failed to pay attention, and now there were people dying, and—

St. Germain made himself shelve the self-recrimination, with an effort. There had been that faint trace of vampire scent in the Place de la Sorbonne earlier. It *could* have been someone new; it could just as easily have been one of the Paris vamps he had encountered many times.

They were pretty calm, to his knowledge: much too sensible, and too old, to be running around killing people in a profligate sort of way—let alone dumping the bodies in the river to be easily found. That was a *young* vampire's characteristic mistake. Like—well, like wearing unnecessary evening dress and much too much perfume.

The other stupid thing young vampires did which often got them killed was forming groups, rather than maintaining an individual territory. The natural group size of vampires in a self-sustaining closed environment was basically *one*; they didn't do well for very long in larger numbers, especially if they went in for the pile-of-bodies bit. A few centuries ago, they would have self-selected right out of the food chain, as a string of greedy exsanguinations would invariably lead to discovery by angry townspeople or a determined hunter, and then there would be the pitchforks and torches, the stake and garlic and burial at the crossroads, and silence long enough for people to forget.

Now, though. Now they could get away with a little bit more than that. In an age where few people paid attention anymore, and fewer believed—an age where fear was focused on death from the air, determined madmen in desert caves and in political office grinding the world on toward mutually assured destruction—things that went bump in the night held little actual terror. Perhaps, he thought, the underdwellers missed it; perhaps they were trying to *manufacture* it, and positively enjoying the collateral damage.

New vampires. In his city. Somewhere, in his city. And he hadn't known; hadn't stopped them when they started killing. He'd let it happen.

And the wellmonsters. That wasn't as bad as the vampires, but it made no sense: where the hell had they come from and why?

And somebody who'd planned to tell St. Germain about *peculiar things* he ought to know about had disappeared—or been disappeared—before she'd had a chance to pass on that information.

Whatever had happened to Greta Helsing had not involved exsanguination. Not here, anyway. There was no blood, not even a trace of it, in the Place de la Sorbonne. Still, he couldn't shake the conviction that the vanishing doctor and the evidence of new vampire activity were connected.

Young vampires, preying on the citizens of Paris. That in itself he could have taken care of easily, ages ago, if he'd bothered to notice.

There had been other signs that something was wrong, as well. Signs he simply hadn't paid enough attention to. The herd of confused and unhappy ghosts—or parts of ghosts, missing legs, heads, arms—that had appeared in the Place Joachim-du-Bellay last week.

Young vampires, and disappearances, and unexpected supernatural creatures wandering the undercity, and unexpected hauntings. The psychopomps he'd hired to take care of that particular problem hadn't seemed all that concerned at the time—although Brightside had been rather quieter than usual, St. Germain thought belatedly. They'd said the haunting must be due to the fact that the bones had been relocated from Les Innocents to the catacombs, accepted their payment, and taken their leave.

Things going rotten, underneath his city. Inexplicable creatures in the catacombs. It was like pulling on a single weed stem and realizing you'd got hold of only the edge of a vast underground network of branching roots, deeper and deeper. What else had he missed?

And what *else* might be going wrong?

Lilith's boudoir was a symphony of violet and black, lace and ruched satin, silver and jet. On her dressing table a black coffin-shaped purse did the duty of a makeup box, spilling a scatter of expensive lipsticks in various shades of shimmery black. She had selected every piece of furniture from a catalog, circling the item number with a black gel pen that left faint sparkles in the darkness of its ink, and she was thoroughly proud of the effect she had achieved.

Mostly she spent the nights with Corvin, in his massive scarlet bed, but this was her personal retreat, and in here everything was exactly to her taste. Her perfume—violets and vanilla—hung sweet and heavy in the air. No one dared disturb Lilith in her boudoir but Corvin, and he was busy doing something else; she wasn't sure what, nor did she much care. Right now she had other things on her mind.

She sat crosslegged on the violet counterpane of her bed, framed by the heavy tassel-trimmed curtains, bent over something cupped in her hands: a small, sleek creature, brindled brown-and-black, that wriggled and squeaked faintly and licked at her fingers with a tiny pink tongue.

It was very new—as was the tiny grey creature sitting on her knee, its miniature hands clinging to the velvet of her skirts. She had only summoned these last night—it was easy now, she knew all the words and she was getting so good at it, the strange *sucking* feeling didn't bother her at all, not like the first couple of times—and she thought the brindled hair-monsterlet was definitely her favorite of all. The grey creatures were called something weird in the book she'd found, Lilith wasn't sure how to pronounce it, but they were supposed to guard treasures, so she had just been calling them her little guardians. One of them had been very naughty, near the beginning, and stolen Lilith's black chandelier earrings with the marcasite and rubies in them, and Corvin had—well, he'd been really not happy about that. But she'd been more careful afterward. That was all. She just had to be careful.

Lilith lifted the hairmonsterlet to her face, nuzzled its soft belly. She was definitely getting better at it. This time she hadn't even had to look at the book at all before drawing her circle. Soon she wouldn't need the book, and it could go away again, she could get rid of it, or maybe have someone take it back to the weird little shop where she'd found it to begin with. She didn't really like the book all that much—it smelled funny, and the leather cover always felt a little strange, sticky, as if it was covered in something that hadn't quite dried; she always found herself wiping her hands on her skirt after she'd touched it, even though there was never anything left on her palms.

It would be nice to get rid of it. Soon. As soon as she was sure she could remember *everything*.

It had been a long time since Greta had worn a watch. The one she'd given to the wellmonster, back in the hotel, had been broken for months—she really had meant to get it repaired, at some point, but simply never seemed to get around to it. Checking the time on her phone had become habit the way glancing at her wrist had been, and now, bereft of phone and watch, she had no idea what time it was; only that it *felt* like late evening. Her diurnal rhythm had not so much altered as disappeared altogether.

She could also wish Corvin's design concept for his cells had included furniture. Presumably the lack of any such items was due to his well-developed sense of paranoia—what if a prisoner were to break the leg off a bed frame and use it as a stake, for example—but whatever the reason, the result was profoundly demoralizing. Trying to sleep lying on the floor with her jacket rolled up as a pitiful attempt at a pillow was bloody difficult, but she was exhausted enough to consider making the attempt.

She had spent some time earlier playing with the monsters before the forced inactivity became unbearable, and had done a few push-ups and sit-ups to make herself feel virtuous; at one point, one of the other vampires had escorted her to the facilities, and there had been another coffee and pastry delivery. Beyond that, and the conversation with the girl—Emily—she hadn't seen a single other person all day.

This mattered rather more than Greta thought it should. She *enjoyed* solitude, ordinarily. Not having to talk to anybody for a while wasn't something she expected to mind—but there was a difference, wasn't there, between solitude you had *chosen* and the kind she was experiencing now. For one thing, it was so miserably boring.

Talking to Emily had been both invigorating and heart-breaking; the fact that they'd turned her without consent was unspeakable in itself, and their subsequent refusal to provide any support or reassurance or comfort after the fact was almost as bad. That brief period of being herself again, being a doctor, a scientist, imparting information, had made the return to miserable boredom even worse. Greta hated being useless more than almost anything, and here she had no choice in the matter at all.

She curled up on her side, feeling every pebble and lump of the floor where it bit into her shoulder, her hip, her thigh, thinking about the pattern of the bruises it would leave, thinking of what she would make of a similar pattern if presented with it in a clinical situation. That thought slid unbidden into a mental image of her clinic—the blessedly familiar *ordinary* mismatched waiting room furniture, the bright cheerful white plastic of her equipment, the stainless steel and enamel of instruments and basins, the well-beloved faces of her friends—and her closed eyes stung with tears.

I want to go home, she thought. *Oh God, I want to go home so much.*

Greta had not cried in a long time; had not cried at all since this whole nightmare had begun, but now she could not stop the tears, hot and awful. She cried almost silently, exhaustion and misery squeezing her chest in long spasms like waves on a beach, her breath coming in little judders between them, her eyes shut tight, for a long time.

Somewhere along the line, eventually, she fell into uneasy sleep; when a hand touched her shoulder, she jerked sharply, for a moment unsure where the hell she was before it all came back to her. She had no idea how much time had passed, but the tears soaked into her makeshift pillow were dry; it felt like the middle of the night.

Greta sat up, wincing. Every inch of her was sore and stiff.

The little monsters were gone. And kneeling outside the cell, her arm stretched through the bars, was Emily.

Emily and someone else, as well.

She knew her face must be a blotchy, tearstained mess, and part of her cringed in embarrassment at being seen in this condition, but the sight of the other figure pushed that entirely out of her mind. He was tall and thin; his bleached-white hair was cut in a thoroughly edgy asymmetrical style; and he was leaning against the wall, slumped over, pressing his hands to his midsection.

"You're a doctor, you have to help him," Emily hissed. "*Fix* him."

"What happened?" she asked, eyeing the way the other vampire was shivering.

Emily glanced down the hallway. "It doesn't matter, just fix him, okay?"

"I can try," Greta said. "If you bring me what I need."

"Anything, I'll get it for you, please, just fix him."

"Either let me out or bring him in here," she said. Presumably there was some reason, or reasons, that this needed to be dealt with in a furtive and clandestine manner: right now Greta didn't actually care. In the dim light the indisposed vampire was a very unpleasant color indeed.

Emily glanced down the corridor again, and turned the key in the lock.

The sound of the tumblers falling into place made her heart beat faster, despite herself. She stood aside as Emily pulled the door open and helped her companion into the cell.

"Sit down," Greta told him. "I regret I have nothing but the floor to offer you, but my jacket's better than no pillow at all. Tell me what happened."

"Can't," he said through his teeth—but he did as she said, with a stifled groan, and when Greta gently pulled his hands away from his stomach, he didn't resist. She unbuttoned his shirt to find a devoré velvet scarf wrapped haphazardly around his torso, holding in place a pad of some dark shiny fabric that was darker in the middle, glistening wet.

Vampires healed *fast* under normal circumstances. Wounds that would take a human days to recover from posed a few hours' inconvenience to a healthy sanguivore. This didn't look right in the slightest, and she thought of the last time she'd seen a vampire—vampyre, in fact—failing to heal from a minor injury. That instance had been due to a particularly unpleasant poison on the weapon that had inflicted the wound.

"Em—*Sofiria*," she said, catching herself just in time, "help me unwind this. What's your name, anyway?" she added, to her patient.

"Yves. He's Yves," Emily said before he could reply. Greta remembered her saying, *It was one of the others who did it to me, he has this amazing asymmetrical haircut?* and fought down a sudden and vicious surge of enmity. This creature had turned a child—

And now he needed help, and that was what mattered. The *only* thing that mattered right now. He needed help, and she was trained to give it. She'd told Varney that, last year, when he asked her why she did this: because it needed to be done.

She got the makeshift bandage unwrapped, wondering whose scarf it was and if they'd ever want it back, and as gently as she could, she lifted the pad of cloth away from the wound.

Wounds, plural. It was difficult to tell with all the blood, but she thought there were at least three separate lacerations. Greta bent closer, peering in the dim light, looking at the shape of them—two appeared to be diagonal slashes about six inches long with ragged edges, but the third was different. The third was a wider, deeper tear, with what looked like a half-circle of small but deep puncture wounds at its apex.

She recognized that pattern. She'd have recognized it anywhere, and suddenly the rest of the clinical picture made sense, with the familiar satisfactory sense of pieces falling into their proper place. Sitting back on her heels, Greta twisted around to look up at Emily. "Ghouls," she said, ignoring the little gasp from her patient. "These were made by ghoul teeth and claws. No wonder he's not healing; I have to get them clean right away. I need water and clean bandages that aren't made of burgundy polyester velvet with fringe on it, and you almost certainly don't have antiseptic on hand so bring me the highest-proof alcohol you can find. And light. I need light."

"Is—are they poisonous?" Emily asked, eyes wide.

"Ghouls? No. Not exactly. They just carry around an astonishingly unpleasant and extensive collection of assorted bacteria in their mouths, and their claws aren't much cleaner. Humans who get bitten by ghouls end up losing limbs to the resulting infection. Yves, on the other hand, is *trying* to heal, but his body is dealing with a hell of a lot of pathogens all at once as well as the physical insult of the wounds themselves. Can I have that water, please?"

"Oh. Sorry. Yes," said Emily.

It was a hell of a lot easier to do her job when she could *see*. Emily had brought back everything Greta had asked for—it took her a while to collect it all, looking over her shoulder the whole time in case someone came home early and caught her at it. Corvin and his inner circle, it appeared, were all out hunting; they were entirely nocturnal, which didn't surprise Greta in the least. It stood to reason that someone so thoroughly committed to the vampire aesthetic would spend his nights roving abroad on the dark tide of the mortal city and his days in undead slumber far from the burning eye of the sun. Possibly in a coffin. Possibly in a coffin on a bier, covered with a black velvet pall; she wouldn't put it past him to have stacks of lilies lying around the place as well.

The fact that this entire business had to be kept a secret from Corvin also did not exactly surprise her. She'd gotten very little detail out of Yves regarding what had happened, but the gist of it seemed to be that he'd run into some ghouls while on an errand for Corvin and they had viciously attacked him without the slightest provocation. (Greta took this to mean that he had wandered into a section of the undercity near a ghoul lair and they had very firmly seen off the intruder, but she kept this to herself.) Apparently Corvin's patience regarding mistakes or failure of any kind on the part of his underlings was not so much limited as nonexistent; as Emily explained it, if he found out that Yves had been ignominiously defeated by common ghouls *and* failed to carry out the errand he'd been sent on, the repercussions would be dire. Coming back empty-handed was bad enough; coming back fucked-up and empty-handed was unacceptable.

He had stumbled back to the lair, bleeding and in considerable pain, and encountered Sofiria/Emily, who had volunteered to stay behind as a lookout while the rest of the coven went out for dinner. After her amateur first aid had failed to deal with his injuries, Emily had decided to seek professional help.

Greta could picture Yves trying to keep his untreated condition secret from his leader. She was fairly sure Emily wouldn't have brought him to her for attention if Greta hadn't had that conversation with her about the nature of vampire physiology. *I've probably saved his unlife*, she thought, *at least by proxy.*

That's a good thing, right?

He had recovered enough while she cleaned his wounds to start complaining, which she took as a positive sign, but the skin around the lacerations was red and ever so slightly warm to the touch; she wasn't finished yet. "I'm going to have to disinfect these now," she told him, quiet and sympathetic but firm. "It's going to hurt quite badly for a short time. Do you want something to bite on?"

She supposed vampires didn't get asked that very often. Yves looked up at her—red eyes, he'd started off with brown irises—and then over at Emily, who was kneeling nearby to watch. He reached out to her, and Emily hesitated only a little before holding out her arm.

"That's not what I meant," said Greta sharply, but the girl shook her head. Yves was holding her forearm in his hands much as a man might hold an ear of corn he was about to bite into. Before she could protest further, Emily said, "Please. We don't have much time," and Yves rasped, "Get *on* with it if you're going to."

Get on with it, she repeated to herself, and spun the cap off the bottle of grain spirits.

The next few minutes were thoroughly unpleasant for everyone present, and Greta worked as fast as she could, grimly ignoring the muffled sounds of pain from two directions at once; but when it was over, she sat back on her heels and could already see the beginnings of improvement.

"You'll start to heal properly now," she said. "I'd estimate in about twelve hours these should be nothing but scars. I'll put a dressing on which won't be visible underneath a clean shirt, and you should rest as much as you can."

What he really ought to do was drink some nice reinvigorating blood, but Greta was not about to recommend this particular restorative when she herself was the only readily available source. Yves sat up and she began to wrap his midsection in bandages that were not, in fact, made out of burgundy polyester velvet: they were what appeared to be strips torn from a very nice bedsheet that happened to be jet black.

When she had finished, he had some color back in his face, and the relative ease with which Greta and Emily helped him to his feet demonstrated an improvement. He looked down at Greta—quite a long way down; she thought he must be six foot six at least—and sneered. Presumably he was feeling well enough to sneer.

"Don't expect me to thank you," he said. "I didn't *need* your help. It was simply convenient."

Beside him Emily stiffened, holding her wounded arm. Greta ignored her. "I wouldn't dream of expecting thanks," she said politely. "Not from one of the Kindred."

"Well, good," he said, looking slightly confused for a minute, as if he were working out what she had actually meant. "Come, Sofiria. Bring all these things away."

Greta helped Emily collect the supplies she had brought, including the lantern, which she was going to miss rather badly once it was gone. The girl looked as if she wanted to say something else, but glanced over her shoulder at Yves and sighed instead.

As they left her cell and turned the key in the lock once more, Greta watched Emily mouth the words *thank you*, and nodded. She stood at the bars for a long time, after the brighter light of the lantern had died away, staring into the distance of the empty corridor where the two of them had gone. She thought of the blank fear in the girl's eyes earlier, when she'd said, *Run*, when she'd said, *Find a phone and call a man named*

Alceste St. Germain. He's a werewolf, a friend of Ruthven's, and he will help you. And possibly rescue me. And the flat negation: *I'm too scared to escape.*

It was going to be up to Greta to get out of here. It was always bloody well up to Greta to do *what must be done*, however she could do it; she knew that, she'd always known it, that had never not been the case, but sometimes—God, sometimes it was *hard*.

CHAPTER 5

S ir Francis Varney was what might be termed a late adopter of modern conveniences; but having accepted the inevitability of things such as mobile phones and the Internet and online banking, he had relatively little trouble using technology. He simply complained about it all the time.

On the phone, Greta had failed to mention the fairly crucial point of which flight she intended to take to Heathrow this particular morning, and Varney had failed to remember to ask; and she had said she was busy attending lectures, so he hadn't quite felt comfortable calling her back to make sure.

He still wasn't quite certain of—well, of many things regarding Greta Helsing, nor did he have the experience or confidence to ask the right kind of questions to *make* things more certain; worse still, he was acutely aware of this lack. It simply wasn't something he had any practice with. His previous interactions with the fairer sex had been more along the lines of *the vampyre is at his hideous repast*, rather than *can I buy you a drink*, and it continued to amaze him when Greta seemed legitimately to enjoy his company, and desire more of it.

He hadn't actually tried to do anything as forward and improper as kiss her, but more and more over the past several months, the thought had occurred to him that he might, and that she might not immediately retreat in horror and disgust.

I want to see these grand works of yours for myself, she had said, and this morning—sitting in his bedroom in the refurbished wing of Dark Heart House, with an extremely expensive computer in his lap and dawn dripping misty light through the windows—Varney had felt the stirrings of an unfamiliar kind of pride in his achievements.

There were several Paris-to-London departures that might fit her vague description of an early flight, and Varney had decided—with the kind of impulsiveness that had characterized a great many of his decisions over the centuries—simply to drive up to London and wait for her at the airport, and see what happened.

That had been several hours ago. The 6:55 Transavia, 7:10 Vueling, and two Easyjet flights from Charles de Gaulle had landed on time, disgorged their passengers, and departed once more, and there was no sign of Greta. Varney had waited for her to call him, and waited a little longer for her to call him, and finally bitten his lip and called her, and got voice mail. Twice.

Of course she's thought better of it, he told himself. *Why would she want* you *to pick her up at the airport, she's changed her mind, she's coming in later on or something*, and as the minutes went by and the single peach-colored rose he'd bought her began to droop on its stem, Varney fought a strong desire to simply get in his car and go back down to the country, to his falling-down estate with its ornamental lake that probably contained a drowned skeleton or two, back to the gloom and decay where he belonged—

I miss you, she had said, and even over the phone he'd heard the warmth in her voice.

His mouth thinned, and he looked down at the uncommunicative screen of his phone: *Call ended.*

No, he thought. *No, this isn't right.*

Varney tapped the screen to clear it, and then dialed a different number.

This time he didn't have to wait: Ruthven picked up on the second ring. "Hello?" he said, and Varney could hear the edges of the Scots back in his voice—it always crept back in when he had to spend any time up north, despite his efforts to the contrary.

"Edmund," he said, "has Greta been in touch with you?"

"Not since I left Paris," Ruthven said, and his voice had sharpened. "Why?"

"Did she say what flight she'd be on?"

"No. What's wrong, Varney? You are not being reassuring in the least."

"We spoke on Saturday afternoon," Varney said, "and I offered to pick her up at Heathrow on Monday, and she said that would be"—he couldn't quite quote her *that would be lovely* phrasing, not to Ruthven, not over the phone—"that would be acceptable, and I forgot to ask which flight, like an idiot, and I'm here, and she's not. And she isn't answering her phone."

"Shit," said Ruthven, delicate and sharp and clear as ice. "I *knew* something wasn't right. She said she'd call me; I just assumed she was caught up in the wonders of were-hedgehog medicine and had forgotten. Look—stay there for now, okay, I'm going to make some calls—oh Christ, what now, hang on, Varney, the other line's ringing."

"All right," Varney said, a little nonplussed, and there was a *click* and silence.

He looked down at the rose in his other hand, its neck drooping like a tubercular heroine's, and felt abruptly and horribly sorry for it: for the fact that it had been grown somewhere, fed and watered and nurtured, and cut and brought all the way here to this airport to be bought and given to someone, to make them smile, and here it was with him instead, dying in his hand. Thwarted of its purpose. Its small brief life all wasted.

He could feel the weight of melancholy that had been keeping its distance over the past half a year threatening to descend upon him all at once, a precarious balance ready to collapse in crushing, sharp-edged rockfall—and had in fact turned away from the arrivals board to walk back to the car park when Ruthven's voice was suddenly back in his ear.

"...sorry about that," Ruthven was saying, still sounding sharp and focused with concern. "That was the hotel in

Paris calling to ask why my party hasn't checked out by the specified time. She hasn't been back there, Varney. She's not answering my calls, either; no one can get hold of her. I *knew* something was wrong."

"What do you mean you *knew*," Varney said, his own unhappiness banished from the active center of his mind. "Did something happen while you were there with her?"

"No. Not—not really. I felt bloody strange at the Opera, and there was another vampire there I didn't recognize who was apparently paying close attention to us, and there were these monsters—"

He sounded uncharacteristically unsure of himself. "What monsters?" Varney demanded.

"It's a long story, but—I had a feeling something was going to happen, and she told me not to worry about dire forebodings and get on with the task at hand. So now the task at hand is to get over there as soon as possible and start looking. I can try to get a flight to London from here but it's probably simpler for us to just meet in Paris, to save time."

Varney blinked. He still didn't quite expect anyone to want him to be *part* of things. "You—I—that is, yes, all right, I can manage that."

"Good. I'm going to call an old friend of mine who lives there and have him meet us at the airport. I'll text you the details. Talk soon."

Varney took the phone away from his ear and stared at it for a moment or two. He straightened up. Slipped the phone into his pocket. Looked again at the drooping stem of the rose—and with another of those impulsive choices, cut the stem off short with a slice of his thumbnail, and tucked it into the buttonhole of his lapel. Against the dark grey of his suit, its bright peach-coral petals looked undeniably, absurdly brave.

He dropped the rest of the rose stem into a wastebin, on his way to the ticketing desks; and the tiny wounds its thorns had left in his thumb and fingertip healed to faint white scars as he walked.

Crepusculus and Brightside had sat up quite a long time talking—and drinking—after the expedition to the site of Les Innocents. It was late morning before they emerged from their hotel and found their way to a building on the corner of the Rue du Temple and Rue Pastourelle.

Brightside peered at the list of tenants' names over the doorbell-intercom button. Everything had seemed rather less alarming by the light of day, and while he wanted to know what was causing the strange manifestations, he felt less of the unease that had threatened him the night before. They would get some answers out of Irazek, at least—or possibly get him to have a word with somebody in Hell who could investigate, and then Brightside could stop worrying.

" 'Isaac, Z,' " he read, and pushed the button. "They're just not all that creative, are they?"

"Hello?" said a puzzled voice after a while, crackling over the intercom.

"Irazek, of the Department of Monitoring and Evaluation?"

Brightside asked, brisk. "My colleague and I would appreciate a minute of your time."

There was a pause, while Irazek presumably worked out that anybody who knew his real name and his infernal departmental affiliation was probably someone to whom he should be polite, and then the door unlocked with a buzz. "Please come up," said the staticky voice. "It's the third floor. Mind the floor in the entryway; it's just been waxed."

Brightside held the door open for Crepusculus, and paused in the hallway. "We should be wearing identical dark suits," he said. "And possibly pretentious sunglasses."

Crepusculus eyed him. "You're having too much fun, Gervase, are you coming down with something? I prefer to blend in."

"Tattered jeans and a leather jacket are blending?"

"It's a lot better than the silk-turtleneck-with-a-blazer thing. Granted, that makes a statement, but the statement is 'I am stuck in 1975.'"

Brightside rolled his eyes. "You have *never* had any taste. Come on, let's go and ask Mr. Irazek some questions."

Demons came in all shapes and sizes. This one turned out to be short, earnest-looking, with hair that was not so much ginger as orange. He was wearing an apron and had a tea towel draped over one shoulder, and when he let them into the apartment, the smell of fresh croissants suggested he'd spent the morning in the kitchen. "Hello," he said, looking at them. "Er. What exactly can I do for you?"

"We have some questions about haunting," said Brightside, and then sighed. "I'm terribly sorry, allow me to introduce

myself: Gervase Brightside, and this is Crepusculus Dammerung. Have a card."

He liked the cards. They were heavy cream-colored stock
with slightly raised, dark silver lettering: DAMMERUNG &
BRIGHTSIDE, REMEDIAL PSYCHOPOMPS. Below that, in much
smaller letters: NO JOB TOO IMPROBABLE.

Irazek took it with slightly floury fingers, and then looked
back at the pair of them, and swallowed hard. "Would—
either of you like a croissant?" he asked. "There's coffee."

"I'd love one," said Crepusculus with a broad grin.

It turned out that demons could, in fact, bake remarkably
decent pastries, and once they were settled around Irazek's
kitchen table with coffee and croissants and homemade straw-
berry jam, the tension in the atmosphere had defused a lot.
Brightside let Crepusculus do the talking to begin with: how
they'd been called in to see to an unexpected sudden attack
of ghosts, how they'd dealt with it quite easily, and decided to
stick around and enjoy Paris for a few days, and how despite
the uneventful resolution of the haunting, it hadn't quite felt
right—why now, and not before—and then their adventure
last night in the Place Joachim-du-Bellay.

"So what we want to know," Brightside put in, "is what
the essograph traces look like for the past week and a half—if
there's been any unexpected planar incursions other than the
one we were called in to handle. Could you pull those for us,
by any chance?"

Essographs—literally, *thing-writers*, named after the esson,
the reality particle—measured fluctuations in the standing

magical, or mirabilic, field. Any travel between planes of existence would cause a disturbance in the field, and the magnitude of that disturbance corresponded to the size or power of whatever had come through. Hauntings were generally a very mild blip on the essograph trace, unless there was some serious psychic trauma involved. Every major city and location of mirabilic significance had several essograph placements, installed by a division of Hell's bureaucracy charged with keeping an eye on interplanar travel, and monitored by a surface operative—in this case, Irazek. Heaven was generally assumed to be running a similar operation, although they were extremely cagey about it. The point was to keep an eye on things going and coming between the planes in order to maintain a *balance* between Heaven and Hell.

Brightside watched Irazek, who had gone first pink and then white and then pink again and dropped his gaze to the tabletop: something was wrong. He should have been able to produce the weekly records with no hesitation at all.

"Um," said Crepusculus. "Irazek? Is there a problem with the traces?"

"Ye-ess," Irazek said, still looking firmly down at his plate. "I mean. No. They should be just fine. I just—didn't get around to collecting this week's yet, that's all."

Crepusculus and Brightside shared a look. "Didn't get around to it?" Brightside repeated.

"I know, it's dreadfully irresponsible," said Irazek wretchedly. "I've just—I got caught up in other things and I simply forgot to go out yesterday and change the tapes."

"Can you take us to go and look at them now?" said Brightside.

"Better late than never," Crepusculus added, not unkindly, and the demon looked up at them both. Some of the stricken look faded from his face.

"Of course," he said. "Yes, of course I can take you to see them—that's no trouble at all—let me just tidy up and I'll get my coat."

Brightside glanced at Crepusculus again while Irazek cleared the table, and neither of them had to say anything out loud: it was rather painfully evident that Paris's surface monitoring protocol was substandard at best, and who knew what important events might already have been missed?

What else might have come through, and why? Brightside thought. The sense of unease he'd felt the night before was back, stronger than ever.

"Right," said Irazek, returning to them with a determinedly cheerful expression. "Let's go and check out some essographs, shall we?"

"Lead on," Brightside said, thinking privately that whoever was responsible for matching assignments to operatives—or selecting candidates for surface-op duty—might need to pay a little more attention to their job.

In a city the size of Paris, multiple essograph installations were required to cover the various loci of particular interest to M&E. And at least one of them was broken.

Brightside watched Irazek peering disconsolately into the

innards of what was obviously an ex-machine—its magically concealed location on top of the Arc de Triomphe had perhaps not been the safest of all possible installation spots, as it appeared to have been recently struck by lightning. The roll of paper on which the mirabilic field fluctuations would have been recorded was so much charred ash.

He remembered a storm a couple of nights earlier, a brief but violent affair that had walked and talked and flared the sky blank white-violet with sheets of lightning for about ten minutes before passing off; and he tried not to think, *If Irazek had done his bloody job right and changed out the machine's roll when he was supposed to, we'd still have whatever this thing's been recording.*

He and Crepusculus were making themselves unnoticeable, and so was Irazek, using a variant on the mirabilic influence laid on the essograph itself; nobody was paying any attention to the three of them. There were a couple of tourists at the other end of the huge platform that was the top of the arch, exclaiming and taking photographs, but Irazek, Crepusculus, and Brightside were effectively invisible, casting no shadows at all.

They had already visited two of the other installations, and successfully retrieved the paper rolls with the red-ink trace of the recordings on them—and what they had shown had made Irazek go white all over again, the spray of freckles across the bridge of his nose standing out stark as sepia ink drops. Both the Bastille and the Sorbonne essographs demonstrated a repeated pattern of brief disturbances interspersed with unremarkable background readings; to Brightside, it looked not unlike a heartbeat on an EKG trace. Certainly it didn't show any major incursions of the sort that'd really worry anyone, but Irazek looked pretty damned worried all the same— and that was enough to send a cold finger of unease down Brightside's back. Demons—even fairly ineffective demons— weren't supposed to look at esso traces like that.

Or to put it another way, esso traces weren't supposed to *make* demons look at them with that sort of expression.

All at once, the sensation he'd felt last night at Les Innocents was back: a feeling of something going very badly wrong, just out of sight, too distant to be easily recognized.

"What does that pattern mean?" Crepusculus asked a moment or two later, when it was obvious Irazek wasn't going to explain on his own.

"It means I *still* need a third reading," Irazek told them unhelpfully, standing up. "There's—oh, no, there *is* another one, I just—haven't looked at it in ages—hopefully it still works..."

Brightside couldn't prevent himself from glancing at Crepusculus, and had seen the same thought on his partner's face: *How did M&E's Department of Operative Training and Placement ever decide to pick* this *particular demon to do this job?*

It wasn't *like* Hell to be inefficient. And now Irazek looked so miserable, staring at the wreck of his lightning-struck essograph, that Brightside had to sigh and pat him on the shoulder, despite his gathering sense of unease. "Where is it? The last installation?"

"In the Opera," said Irazek. "In the Palais Garnier, all the way up inside the dome. I'll have to flip us; it'd take too long to walk. Hang on to me."

He and Crepusculus were both perfectly capable of translocation themselves, but they didn't have Irazek's clear mental image of the destination; it was easier to take hold of him and hang on through the disorienting wrench as Irazek flipped all three of them. When Brightside's vision cleared from the brief white blankness, he saw that they were in an oddly shaped room, almost semicircular, with ornate round windows set into the curving wall—and jumped a little to realize that there were in fact huge mirrors all along the straight wall, reflecting the three of them without doing anybody any favors.

Brightside had never liked mirrors. He looked away, and watched as Irazek reached into a dusty corner and pulled out another of the seismograph-looking things. This one at least didn't appear to have undergone structural damage, but Irazek blew enough dust off it to make them all cough.

Underneath the dust, the red-ink trace showed the same pattern: flatline and spike, flatline and spike. This one had the spikes quite a lot closer together than the others Brightside had seen.

"Could you please explain what it is we're looking at?" Brightside said with slightly forced patience. "I don't think I quite understand."

"Interference," said Irazek. "Interference patterns. These are peaks. Nodes. I need to get back and do some calculations, I'm afraid. I can't tell you more than that until I've worked out the numbers for each of these locations."

Brightside looked at Crepusculus, mouth drawn into a thin line. "I see," he said. "Is there anything we can do to help?"

"Yes," said the demon, sounding a little surprised. "Yes, actually there is. I—you can talk to ghosts, right?"

"One way of describing it," said Crepusculus. "Why?"

"Could you go to one of the cemeteries—Père Lachaise is probably the best bet—and ask the ghosts there if they've noticed anything out of the ordinary in the past couple of months?"

He sounded sharper, more businesslike, than they'd yet heard him; it was evident that, having failed so far to do his job properly, he meant to make up for lost time.

"There are ghosts haunting the cemeteries?" said Crepusculus. "Just hanging out? They aren't causing any trouble?"

"Several of them. They seem to be quite happy staying there, rather than venturing out into the city. I need to know if they've seen or heard of anything like—oh, necromancers, people grubbing around for graveyard dirt or doing any sort of ceremony that might possibly have an actual result. There's been magic done, but I don't quite know what *kind* yet, and it matters."

"These spike readings," said Crepusculus. "Are they ripples, from something coming through?"

"I think so. Nothing really huge or powerful, just multiple minor incursions, but the effect on reality is cumulative— it could have set up a standing wave, that'll shake things to pieces—no, I'm catastrophizing." He pushed his hands through his carroty-orange hair, leaving a smudge of dust on his forehead. Brightside felt slightly sick; *catastrophizing* wasn't the kind of word one wanted to associate with demons. Whatever was wrong was more wrong than he knew what to do with, and it was clear that the authorities who ought to have been keeping an eye on the situation had not been—and he wondered again what else might have been missed.

Irazek straightened up. "I have to get back and start on these calculations, I'm terribly sorry—but if you could go and talk to the ghosts, I'd be much obliged to you both."

"We can do that," said Crepusculus, glancing at Brightside, and a moment later they both winced at the tiny thunderclap as the air collapsed in on the space where Irazek had been standing. The faint electric smell of mirabilic discharge dissipated after a few seconds, but Brightside's profound sense of unease remained.

"I don't suppose this will all turn out to be a hilarious misunderstanding," said Crepusculus. "Ha ha, incompetent demon is incompetent, news at eleven?"

"No," said Brightside.

"No. Well. Let's go, shall we? This place gives me the creeps. And that's a professional opinion—"

Abruptly, without any warning, the room around them flared brilliant white, shutterflash brightness, the violet-white of lightning strikes, of arc flash, of released energy jumping to ground: a stutter of actinic light like a projector running empty with the douser open. Brightside was aware of an awful *sliding* sensation as his solid presence in a steady timestream suddenly lost stability—for creatures like him, temporal dislocation produced intense vertigo—and had just about enough time to reach for Crepusculus's hand, but not to find it, before everything around him *changed*—

—all around them the walls of the poky little dance studio first flickered and then faded away, drawing down from the ceiling like a film played backward, an outgoing tide—

—a sudden clamor of noises, shouting of men at work, the thud and chug of steam machinery, clang of iron on iron, a man's voice in French: *It's no use, the water's back again—tell them to turn the pumps back on and pull everyone out, we can't lay a foundation in a goddamn lake*—

—falling, Brightside was falling, through a space that changed around him even as he fell: open air with pitiless white winter skies above, black half-constructed iron girder-work below, the city all around him—and then he was enclosed once more, a mad spider's web of ropes all around him like the rigging of a ship, vast winches like horizontal capstans arrayed in long rows, the musty closeness of a space shut up when not in use—glimmers of gaslight, butterfly-flames in dim glass prisons—

—and now he was falling farther and farther down, into cellar after cellar, passing through stone and dark air with equal helplessness—and into icy water, shocking and painful, closing over his head—

—through the shock, all around him, there was a sound like faint sweet singing, poison-sweet, seductive, and a bell ringing, and a man's voice: *You've been here for twenty-four hours. You're bothering me, and I warn you this is going to end badly—if Erik's secrets do not remain Erik's secrets, it will be too bad for many members of the human race—*

—a beautiful voice, which did not at all match the words it spoke: *Remember that grasshoppers jump, and they jump very high—*

—and now suddenly Brightside was rising up again, rising as if drawn by those endless forests of rope up through the layers of dark and busy cellars, into sudden brilliant light and open air—the heat of burning gas jets lifting his hair, bank after bank of them focusing on Brightside as he stood on a raked stage—beyond the lights the huge waiting hollow silence of a darkened space—and farther down the rake, with others nearby but clearly cast into the background: a woman in white raising her arms, glorious golden hair tumbling over her shoulders, caught frozen for a moment before the image began to move again and sound came back, shocking him into stillness with the force and sweetness and pure, golden, crystal clarity of her voice—

Anges purs, anges radieux, she sang, *portez mon âme au sein des cieux*—and beyond her there was a dead hush and then a gathering murmur that exploded into a roar, voices and applause raised together—Brightside *knew* this opera, this was Gounod's *Faust*, she had just sung the final trio in *Faust*, and now in an instant, the woman was gone, vanished from the wide-open space of the stage upon which she had just triumphed—

—and just as suddenly he was not on the stage at all but in a box, one of the expensive ones near the stage, looking down at a different woman, horrorstruck in the middle of a line at the terrible sound that had just come out of her mouth—there was a voice in Brightside's ear, laughing a poisoned laugh, *the way she's singing tonight she'll bring down the chandelier*—knowing before he even looked up at the huge brilliant brass-and-crystal confection that it was beginning to fall—*five hundred thousand kilos on a concierge's head*, in the papers the next day—God, he *knew* this, he'd *seen* some of it before—

—and the vivid images dwindled away as suddenly as they had begun, drawing away from Brightside like the picture in an old television, shrinking to a point of light and then gone entirely.

He blinked hard to clear his vision, finding himself on his hands and knees on the polished wood floor of the dancers' practice room, dizzy and sick. Nearby Crepusculus lay curled on his side, clutching at his head, and a stab of worry registered even through Brightside's own distress.

The quality of the light had changed appreciably, the angles of shadows on the floor visibly different. How long had they spent caught in—whatever the hell that had been?

"Dammerung," he said, not liking the shaky sound of his own voice, and was extremely glad when Crepusculus uncurled and sat up, rubbing at his face with both hands. "Dammerung, are you all right?"

"No," said Crepusculus hoarsely. "You?"

"Not really. Did you—did you see all that, the building being *built* and the lake underneath it—all those cellars—"

"And the girl disappearing from the stage," Crepusculus

finished. "And the lights. I think that *happened*, Brightside. I think we saw it happen. Timeslips."

"A series of them," he said. He'd been through a couple of timeslips before, in his long and storied career, but they had been brief instants of disorientation, not a kind of unfolding poorly cut-together immersive film. "That's—not right. Not even slightly right. I think we should get out of here before it happens again." He didn't know why it had happened in the first place, but Brightside was absolutely one hundred percent sure he never wanted to experience anything like that again.

"This building's *wrong*," Crepusculus agreed. "And—shit. I don't know what to do about it, and I don't think I trust Irazek to know, either—what do you say we go to the university library and look it up ourselves? It's old enough; there's bound to be some interesting source materials in there."

"I think that's the best idea I've heard in days," said Brightside, wincing. The dizziness had faded finally, leaving behind a nasty throbbing headache behind one eye. "If nothing else, we can do a bit of historical research about the construction of this place. It *feels* odd to me, like it's got supernatural conductivity inside every structural member."

"I'm trying not to imagine what happens if lightning strikes the goddamn lyre on top. Do we get walking armies of opera ghosts all singing at once?"

"Let's not stick around to find out."

CHAPTER 6

Francis Varney had not traveled outside the country in over a hundred years, and it had not occurred to him during his more recent interactions with the world that along with an ordinary driver's license he ought to get himself a passport.

This became a problem almost at once, and it was really only due to the urgency of the situation that he didn't hesitate at all before fixing the ticket agent with the full force of his metallic eyes and dropping half a ton of thrall on her. He was aware that he would have to spend rather a lot of effort over the next several hours doing just that to various officials in various positions of authority, and the thought came to him with bitter clarity: *One can always do what one must.*

After that, actually purchasing a first-class ticket on the next BA flight to Paris had been easy. So had the process of making his way to the gate and trooping down a narrow rectangular corridor that ended in a concertina of rubber pressed against the curving wall of an airplane; actually stepping through the door let into that curving wall had been much more difficult. He had to duck his head slightly; straightening up inside, surrounded by bright artificial light and the smell of plastic, he had been assailed with a powerful sense of claustrophobia. The last time he'd really been going to and fro about the world or walking up and down in it for any length of time, aviation had been a pipe dream. Varney had slept through the early days, through the introduction of the first passenger aircraft, through the evolution of flight from an exciting and luxurious experience into an unpleasant and exhausting necessity for modern life, and the inside of an A320 looked to him like a narrow coffin lined with row upon row of squashed-together armchairs.

Greta, he thought, and just before the uniformed flight attendant had to ask him a second time for his seat number, he forced himself to smile and apologize for his moment of inattention.

The seats had been exactly as uncomfortable as they looked, although up here in the front they were a bit bigger and set farther apart than the ones he could see down the aisle. He settled into one of them next to the curving wall, peering out through a thick window at a world that looked already alien in its distance. Peculiar vehicles of various shape and size, whose purpose Varney could not begin to imagine, scurried around the tarmac.

The flight attendant's little lecture on disaster preparation had left him clutching the armrests and wondering why in God's name he hadn't just taken a *train*, they could do that now, somebody had built a tunnel under the Channel so you didn't have to bear the awful, awful sea passage—like most sanguivores, Varney was afflicted with crippling seasickness—was it too late to get out now—they were moving, damn it all—

Greta, he thought again, and looked down at the rose in his buttonhole.

When, a few minutes later, the plane began its takeoff roll, a vast invisible hand pressed Varney back into his seat harder and then harder and harder, the sound of the engines waking a kind of idiot trapped-animal terror in him. It seemed to go on forever—surely this couldn't be right, some disaster was befalling them—and then with a giddy vertiginous ease *the world outside his window dropped away.*

It was the strangest thing he could remember experiencing in a very long time. His stomach seemed to have been left far behind them on the ground; he was very much aware of being *heavy* still, pressed back into the seat by an invisible force—but as the world grew smaller and smaller underneath them, as the plane tilted to show him London as a tiny model of itself, a perfect dollhouse reproduction, Varney found himself staring in total fascination.

And then they'd offered him a drink, with faultless courtesy, exactly as if he'd been sitting in the Savoy; and he had spent the next forty minutes sipping quite decent brandy at what he was told afterward was something like four hundred miles an hour. It was surreal. It was almost enough to take his mind off the gnawing worry about Greta, who didn't *do* things like fail to answer her phone. Or disappear. She didn't do that, either.

Now, standing in the arrivals hall at Charles de Gaulle and trying not to have a headache after thralling three different customs officials into believing they'd seen a nonexistent but perfectly unremarkable UK passport, all that worry came back to him. It was a relief to see the familiar figure of Edmund Ruthven threading his way through the crowds, wearing a very stylish coat and an expression of determination.

"Varney," Ruthven said, stopping beside him and looking around. "You got here."

This was not something Varney felt required a response. He'd found the business of *existing in the world*, of managing the logistics of travel, while tiring, less difficult than he'd expected. He watched Ruthven's pale eyes tracking through the tangle of people coming and going, carrying suitcases or rolling them along like obedient gun dogs trotting at their masters' heels. It was obvious that Ruthven was not only worried as hell, he was angry; Varney thought of him saying, *I knew something was wrong*, and wondered how much of that was hindsight and how much was actually true.

"There he is," Ruthven said, and waved; after a moment Varney saw a man striding toward them who was very definitely not a man, although he passed without question among the humans thronging the hall.

He was *large*. Varney put him at about six foot six, broad-shouldered, thickly muscled, moving with the easy grace of someone who keeps themselves in excellent physical condition. The hair pulled back into a loose queue at the back of his neck was wavy, thick, dark gold, streaked and grizzled with grey. To vampire—or vampyre—eyes, however, he stood out from the rest of the crowd because he appeared to be lit subtly differently: like a person in full color against washed-out, desaturated surroundings.

Weres always looked like that: slightly but noticeably brighter. As soon as he got close enough, Varney could see his eyes were amber-yellow. He looked not exactly grim but determined, entirely focused on the task at hand.

"Edmund," he said, holding out his hand to Ruthven, who shook it. "I'm so sorry."

"Yes, well," said Ruthven. "Alceste St. Germain, meet Sir Francis Varney; Varney, St. Germain. Local werewolf, keeps an eye on the city."

St. Germain winced. "And hasn't been doing so brilliantly at that. Pleased to meet you, Sir Francis. Do you have any bags?"

"We do not," said Ruthven. "My plan is to go straight to the hotel and collect Greta's things."

The werewolf nodded. "Once I have her scent, I can be of some actual use, I hope," he said. "This way, gentlemen."

Paris had changed much the way London had, to Varney's eyes. The city he'd visited before, so very long ago, was still there—the bones of it—only now thickly encrusted around the edges with new construction, layers of humanity building on itself. They took the train from the airport, and as it passed through the outer industrial sections of the city and grew nearer its core, Varney felt himself increasingly glad to be here—it was strange, inexpressibly strange to be traveling again, particularly for such an awful reason, but it was also oddly exhilarating. They passed underground at the Gare du Nord, and the next time Varney saw the sky, it was in the heart of the old and beautiful center of Paris.

It was the kind of overcast grey day that meant neither he nor Ruthven needed to worry terribly much about sunscreen and hats, but Varney was glad when they got to the hotel nonetheless: even diffused sunlight had a cumulative effect, and his headache wasn't getting any better. Thralling the customs officials had been a little bit like lifting weights with his mind.

He had very deliberately not been thinking about Ruthven sharing a hotel suite with Greta Helsing, but actually entering the rooms made the thought impossible to ignore. He knew perfectly well Greta and Ruthven had absolutely no feelings toward one another than friendship, but Varney couldn't avoid picturing what it would have been like if *he* had been here instead—staying with her, in a five-star hotel, overlooking the Tuileries, in arguably Europe's most romantic city—

He was glad of the dimness of the suite, the curtains half-drawn: he had to turn away, his face briefly hot, and pretend to be busy inspecting the knickknacks on the mantelpiece. Ruthven and St. Germain were going through Greta's things, and that brought another wave of heat to Varney's cheeks. Her clothes. Her *things*, which she had touched—

For Christ's sake, he told himself viciously. *You're supposed to be helping, not dissolving into embarrassingly clichéd emotion like some idiot teenager. You stopped doing that centuries ago after Flora Bannerworth, bloody well get a grip.*

When he came to join the others in the room Greta had occupied, he was mostly all right again; perhaps a little flushed, a little bright around the eyes, but in control. Ruthven was zipping up Greta's suitcase, and Varney was profoundly grateful that he hadn't witnessed the werewolf getting a good sniff of her scent.

"We'll take her luggage back to my apartment," said St. Germain, giving Varney a slightly curious look. "For safekeeping. And then—"

"Then we search," said Ruthven, getting up. For a moment Varney could see the weariness in him, the worry, before the smooth facade slipped back into place. He had a brief flicker of memory—last winter, after the business under the city, carrying an unconscious Ruthven over his shoulder, all the urbane polish gone to tatters of exhaustion, and thought: *This isn't any good for him, either.*

"We search," Varney repeated, as if something other than the three of them were there to hear.

After Yves and Emily had left, Greta had curled up again and tried to sleep; this time there were dreams, confusing fragments of imagery—ghouls, not the ones that had attacked Yves but *her* ghouls, the London tribes whose leader she knew well, passing through low tunnels that were not the ones she remembered from her brief sojourn underneath that city. In the dream there was a sense of urgency, but no clear purpose or danger, and eventually it faded out altogether.

She woke stiff and aching, but could tell by the level of her own hunger that she must have managed several hours of mediocre rest; when one of the vampires came to take her to the bathroom and provide her with food, she devoured the pastry despite how bored she was getting of chocolate croissants.

How long have I been down here? she thought, licking her fingers. *Three times they've brought me food; does that mean it's Monday in the world?*

She was supposed to check out of the hotel on Monday morning, and when she didn't show up, they would have to do something—contact Ruthven at the very least—and she'd be *missed*. Someone would know to look for her, although by now, Greta thought there were going to be damn few clues for anyone to find.

But they'd probably try. It wasn't as comforting a thought as Greta could wish.

She couldn't help wondering what was going on with Emily and Yves, either. Her patch job on the vampire's wounds had been the best she could manage given the situation, but she didn't have much confidence in her patient's common sense—or his ability to keep the entire business a secret. Greta didn't know what was likely to befall a prisoner convicted of providing unauthorized and secret medical care against the local dictator's wishes, but it wasn't going to be *good*.

She spent some time pacing across the cell, turning over assorted dire repercussions in her mind, expecting to hear footsteps at any moment; sitting down, getting up again, unable to settle, as time passed without the benefit of measure.

Eventually, though, she ran out of imagination. Nothing had happened; perhaps nothing was *going* to happen, and she would simply be left here forever, forgotten about. That wasn't much fun to contemplate, either, but at least it didn't involve having her throat torn out, and she slid down the wall to sit wearily on the cell floor and stare at the opposite wall.

She didn't know how long she had been sitting there when the monsterlets reappeared. Silently clambering through the bars of her cell, the little group of them were the friendliest things she'd seen in a long time, and she was profoundly grateful for their company.

Even if they only gave her a perfunctory sniffing before ignoring her completely and crawling toward the back corner of her cell.

Hm. That was interesting.

They were, in fact, gathering in the corner where the flat rock wall gave way to stonework—the walled-up space behind which, that first night, she had distinctly heard something move. At the thought, all the little hairs on Greta's arms stood up at once in a long wave of chill.

"I wouldn't go near that if I were you," she said, standing in the middle of the cell, arms wrapped around herself. "I don't know what's behind it."

Glup, said one of the monsters—the medium-sized one—and

as Greta watched, it actually climbed on top of the largest of its friends-and-relations with the deliberate slowness that characterized the species. It seemed to be very interested in the stonework, and it reached with small grey hands to feel the chinks between the bits of limestone.

She shivered. "I really don't think you ought to be messing with that," she said, and this time didn't even get a *glup* in response: something about the wall was apparently much more fascinating than she was.

They liked enclosed spaces, of course. They were often set in such spaces to guard things—the classic example, of course, being a treasure hidden in a secret alcove in the stonework of an abandoned well, thus the colloquial name for the species. The unwise adventurer who tracked down such a treasure and went down the well to retrieve it would find themselves taking hold of a large heavy leathery baglike object, which, when pulled out of the secret hiding place, *wrapped its arms around their neck and hung on tight*. At this point in the story the adventurer would invariably describe a horrible smell of mold and the sensation of a cold face pressed against their own, and one could hardly blame them for being somewhat upset thereby, but Greta tended to think that people who went after buried treasure were greedy little twerps who probably deserved whatever curse they might invoke. She felt much the same about people who broke into mummies' tombs, with or without university affiliation to back them up.

She watched the monsters. They were all working their fingers into the cracks between the stonework now. There was an awful kind of inexorability about it: slow, inefficient, but endlessly patient.

They wanted to get through. They wanted whatever was on the other side.

Greta shivered again. If she didn't stop them, they'd eventually manage, and she absolutely did not want to know what it was they thought they were after. Something about that rattling sound had badly frightened her, even if she had no idea what it might actually *be*.

She retreated to the far corner of the cell again, and sat down, arms still wrapped around herself. After a few minutes the smallest wellmonster left off picking crumbs of stone out of the wall and made its slow toadlike way across the floor to her; she scooped it into her hands, lifted it up to get a closer look. "What are you so interested in?" she asked it.

Glup. It wrapped its hands around her thumb and chewed on it thoughtfully—well, *gummed* was more accurate; the European wellmonster didn't have any teeth—and this was distracting enough to take her mind off whatever might be behind the wall.

They weren't bright, but they were what you might call *canny*: they had a strong sense of self-preservation, as befitted a creature whose purpose was to guard valuable treasure. They could see very well in almost lightless conditions, with those huge eyes, and their vomeronasal organs were highly sensitive—the generally accepted explanation for the characteristic *P. incolens* odor of mold or mildew was pheromonal—and, Greta thought as the specimen in her hand went on gumming her fingers, they were capable of detecting *danger* with a fairly high level of specificity.

Which meant that whatever was behind that stone wall, they didn't think it was dangerous to them, at least. And they wanted it.

What wellmonsters wanted was—treasure.

And what was most often walled up in cellars, other than mad wives, pregnant nuns, or importunate ex-friends? *Valuable objects.*

Greta could feel the curiosity surfacing through the dread, and resented it. She didn't want to know what was in there, and—yes, okay, fine, she *did*, she wasn't going to be able to ignore it. She knew better than to indulge curiosity; of course she did—there was an actual ghost story titled *A Warning to the Curious*—but sufficient levels of boredom were apparently capable of overriding even her fairly solid common sense. She sat there for a little longer, debating with herself, before finally getting up and going to have a look.

They had picked out a lot of the smaller chips of stone wedged between the blocks, and that faint breath of cold air was stronger now. The monster in her hand reached out toward the wall, and Greta held it closer—and watched as it stuck one tiny arm into a crack, as far as it could reach. *Glup*, it said, with clear overtones of *want*.

That cold air. Like a long, invisible finger touching her face.

"Oh-kay," she said on a sigh. "It can't be worse than edgelord vampires from fucking Yorkshire, whatever's behind there," and she set the littlest wellmonster gently down and began to pull pieces of stone out of the wall with both hands.

It was hard work. Despite the cave-chill in the air, Greta took off her suit jacket and rolled up the sleeves of her blouse. She had broken two nails and scraped the skin off several knuckles by the time she had loosened the fill enough to start wiggling one small block of stone free. It came loose in her hands after an initial resistance, revealing a square of complete blackness through which chilly air flowed in a steady stream.

Funny how captivity changes your perspective, she thought. When the vampire with the dreadlocks had first brought her to the cell, she'd been too scared even to attempt investigating the integrity of this part of the wall lest someone catch her trying to escape; her risk tolerance had gone up considerably with the interminable hours of enforced boredom.

There didn't seem to be any ravening horrors in the darkness, at least. Nothing was looking back at her with little yellow eyes, or reaching a claw through the hole to pull her head off. Greta set down the block of stone and pulled its neighbor free, conscious of a shift in the rest of the stonework: she couldn't take more out without risking the collapse of the entire wall. Maybe she wouldn't need to.

As soon as the hole was revealed, the wellmonsters gathered around it, and Greta wasn't quite in time to catch the smallest one before it clambered into the opening. "Hey—" she said, "don't—you don't know what's back there—" but the monster didn't even give her a look before hopping, like a toad, into the space behind the wall.

There was a thud, as of something hitting a flat surface, and then the rattle came again. The same noise that had sent Greta scrabbling across the cell to the farthest point from the wall. It was—metallic. Something metal, rattling as it moved over stone.

The other wellmonsters were still clustered around the opening. They were *glupping* to one another in a combination of tones that Greta would, under other circumstances, have been fascinated to listen to—no one knew much about how *P. incolens* communicated—but they did not seem alarmed by the disappearance of the smallest monster, even after several minutes had gone by.

God, I wish I had my penlight, Greta thought uselessly. She wished she had her bag, with all its myriad useful contents. Wished she had her phone. Wished she weren't *here*.

She was still engaged in this pointless activity when the rattle came again, closer now, and after a moment or two the smallest wellmonster appeared out of the darkness, dragging something with it. A metal object.

A tube, about four inches long, which appeared to be of considerable age. There was an inscription down one side, almost illegible under the tarnish: QUIS EST ISTE QUI VENIT.

Greta stared at it—at the monster clutching it, looking terribly satisfied with itself—and sat back on her heels, pushing hair out of her face. "I'll be damned," she said, an enormous tide of relief washing over her. "Is that all it was? A summoning whistle?"

Egredior sibilus, colloquially the whistle-monster, or simply "whistler," was a fascinating creature. It was a classic object-linked apparition, which had at one point been considered nothing more than the partial manifestation of a larger curse, but in the early twentieth century further research had determined it to possess individual agency.

They were completely invisible by themselves, but they manifested by inhabiting large pieces of fabric—bedsheets were ideal, but curtains would do, or even towels—whereupon they could manipulate physical objects. Summoning one was easy: all you had to do was blow its whistle.

(There were the inevitable *You know how to whistle, don't you? Just put your lips together and blow* jokes in almost every single write-up of *E. sibilus*, and sometimes Greta despaired of the lugubrious sense of humor common to academicians.) As long as you possessed the whistle, the monster would stay with you once summoned, whether you liked it or not.

The wellmonster in her hand, still clutching the whistle with all four little limbs, blinked slowly up at her.

You know how to whistle, don't you, she thought. And then: *I could use some help here.* She'd be missed by now in the world above, but she couldn't count on anyone actually *finding* her.

Sometimes you have to make your own luck.

Gently setting the monster down in her lap, Greta felt at her ears—thank God, the aquamarine drops she'd put in Saturday morning, a hundred years ago, were still there. She took them out, and—as she had before, back in the hotel, offered to trade the wellmonster's treasure for a shinier object. This time it took a little longer to convince the monster to relinquish its prize, but eventually it did unwrap itself from the silver whistle and grab for her earrings, clutching them tight in small grey hands, and Greta slipped the whistle into her pocket—

And heard, coming down the corridor, unmistakably, footsteps.

She had just enough time to wedge the stones back into the wall and settle down again, manufacturing a bored expression, before the vampire with the dreadlocks appeared.

Who are you, she thought again. The answer to that in the old TV show intro was *the new Number Two*, and Greta imagined that much to be fairly accurate: Corvin's lieutenant, his second-in-command.

"Getting comfortable?" he inquired, looking at her rolled-up shirtsleeves. The medium-sized monster was clinging to her knee, and the smallest one sat in her hands, gumming one of her aquamarine earrings industriously. "He'll be so pleased. Your presence is required at dinner; I've been sent to dress you up in suitably gildy clobber."

Greta stared at him, and renewed cold dread dropped into her guts, the brief gains of the past half an hour completely forgotten. "He's . . . going to eat me," she said, not a question.

He smiled a little, a flash of white teeth. "No. An easy conclusion, I agree, but in fact you're off the menu for tonight. He simply wishes to extend his hospitality to his much-valued guest."

"Hostage."

"Semantics," said the vampire, seesawing a hand in the air. "And that outfit is *completely,* but *completely* naff, my dear. You can't possibly show up to Corvin's table dressed like that. What size ballgown do you wear?"

It was different for St. Germain, trying to track a missing person, with the chemical signature of Greta Helsing's scent fixed in his mind. Less hopeless. He thought he would be able to follow that particular scent even after considerable time had passed.

She smelled of L'Occitâne hotel soap, some kind of faint old-fashioned green-sharp perfume St. Germain identified after a moment as Ma Griffe, bad coffee, and a variant on the concerto of chemicals that was human sweat—nobody's scent was a single note but a particular *combination* of notes, contingent on their emotional and physical health and what they'd been up to, and the development and change of that combination as time went by left a pretty good temporal record of how long it had been since the person had left the trace.

St. Germain couldn't stand perfume counters in shops, the chaotic barrage of combined scents all at once tended to hit him like a blast of migraine static, but he had read rather a lot of literature on the process by which humans developed individual commercial fragrances. The descriptions of the multiple elements of a perfume crossed over fairly well to werewolf olfactory experience. Top notes, heart notes, base notes: it felt a little easier to talk about his perceptions in a terminology already understood. The synesthetic aspect was a lot more difficult to explain: sometimes scents were sharply colored in his mind, but not consistently.

From the hotel they had gone straight to the Sorbonne, where she'd last been located according to Varney's and St. Germain's phone conversations with her; he hadn't found anything the first time he'd searched the Place de la Sorbonne, but he had her scent now, and St. Germain had left the others standing out of the way while he made a slow careful circuit—and picked up something almost at once.

Traces. Faint but present traces. It was clearest and strongest near the building itself, where she would have come and gone multiple times per day, but—

"I can't get more than traces unless I change," he said, tight and apologetic. "There's no spike in the traces that indicates anything like fear or anxiety, but the wolf has better nasal acuity."

"*Can* you? During the day, in public?" said Ruthven, paler than usual, dark under the eyes. He was fiddling with the lapel of his coat, and the stink of *anxious vampire* was threatening to blank out St. Germain's nose completely. In stereo: the other vamp, the one he'd not met before, taller than Ruthven and cadaverously thin, radiating social awkwardness on a wide bandwidth, was just as anxious about Greta Helsing—in a subtly different way.

Sits the wind in that quarter, thought St. Germain, registering a particular sequence of chemical signatures, and sighed. *He's not just gone for her, he has no idea what to do about it.*

"Yes," he said, "I can, just—it'd be easier if you went over to the other side of the square and had a noisy argument, or something equally distracting, while I find a convenient alleyway."

Ruthven looked at Varney, who nodded, and the two of them set off toward the benches on one side of the square, beginning to talk loudly in English about something to do with the financing of some house refurbishment or other; St. Germain neither knew nor cared. He took advantage of the distraction by slipping into the Rue Champollion, narrow and shadowed as the afternoon drew into evening, and found a convenient doorway to shelter in while he did what needed to be done.

You never really got *used* to it, the change. You just stopped minding how much it hurt. St. Germain had heard it described as a full-body sneeze; for him it was what he imagined a brief but powerful convulsion might feel like, an instant of flaring pain as his bones changed shape and the tendons and ligaments and muscles re-formed themselves accordingly. During his *time* he couldn't control the change at all if he was exposed to moonlight, nor could he change back to his bipedal form as long as that silver light was touching him. It was mostly a voluntary decision for the rest of the month, except in situations of extreme stress, when his body would shift into the less vulnerable of its two available options.

He had never quite understood the process by which his clothing seemed to stay with the one form while he changed to the other, but that was the kind of metaphysical stuff that gave him a headache; he didn't spend a lot of time thinking about it. Now, in the shelter of the doorway, St. Germain hunched over and *leaned* on an internal switch, and felt the stretching somehow *fibrous* pain as the change began.

About three minutes later, a wolf that stood approximately four foot five at the shoulder trotted out of the Rue Champollion, yellow eyes bright in the gathering dusk—and appeared to the humans present as simply a very large dog, possibly a husky mix, that had unaccountably lost its collar. In this form the nasal chaos that had been perceptible before was almost overwhelming until he managed to step down his mental gain—but he could definitely perceive the traces of Helsing's scent much more clearly.

He rejoined Ruthven and Varney, sitting down like a well-trained service animal, and said without opening his mouth all the way, "I think I have something. Follow me—one of you ought to look like my handler for appearance's sake. Edmund, you're shorter and more delicate-looking, you do it. Keep a hand in my ruff as if I'm leading you."

"Thank you, I'm sure," said Ruthven, faintly pink for a moment, and glanced over at Varney, who shrugged. St. Germain could pick up the anxiety plus the emotional lability even more in this form, but Varney simply fell in behind them without a word. Ruthven's pale fingers worked their way into the heavy fur at St. Germain's shoulder—steady, even through the stress hormones coming off him like faint curls of steam.

St. Germain led the vampires in the direction that Helsing's signature felt strongest. It was a pale greenish-blue, like aquamarine, faint but present, sharp-acrid-sweet all at once. She'd left the Place de la Sorbonne, he thought, padding along with his nose close to the ground, head swaying side to side as he sniffed.

She'd been on her way to come and meet with him. This was the easiest way from the Sorbonne to the bar he'd suggested. There were still clear if fading marks of her, tracks he could follow on the pavement now that his nose was close enough to make out details. She'd been on her way, and—

Ruthven's fingers tightened in his ruff as St. Germain stopped. "What is it?" he demanded.

"It ends," St. Germain said. "Ends right here. She's still incredibly faintly in the air but I have nothing on the ground at all: she's—either vanished completely, or something has picked her up and is now carrying her."

"What kind of something?" Varney said, sharp.

"Not sure. There are vampire tracks here, but they've faded, and—no offense, but fresh vampire scent tends to block out older vampire traces that might have been present."

"So what do we do?" Varney asked.

"I wish I knew," said St. Germain with a doggy sigh. "I don't. I think—maybe we ought to ask for help."

"From whom?" That was Ruthven.

"From Hell, of course," said St. Germain, and shook himself so that silvery hairs raftered everywhere. "The obvious last resort."

Corvin's soirées were famous for good reason. Usually, Lilith thoroughly looked forward to the opportunity to wear her loveliest gowns and graciously welcome her subjects, sitting at her lord's right hand—welcome them, and also their guests, hand-picked humans of particular beauty and appeal. It was a charming little game, playing host and hostess, everyone on their most sophisticated and polite behavior, just as if they were humans themselves at a formal dinner party, as if they *weren't* about to fall upon their living companions with teeth bared and drink them dry; and Lilith particularly enjoyed the part *after* the dinner party, when the clothes came off and the music was turned all the way up. This time, though...

This time, she couldn't *stop* thinking of how much she'd rather be in her circle, in her secret place, alone with the words and the candle flames and the acrid smell like burned metal that seemed to be the scent of magic. This time, it was with uncharacteristic impatience that she went through her beauty rituals, knowing perfectly well that she wouldn't have a chance to go back to her spells until the following night.

Lilith swept violet glitter shadow over her eyelids, shading to silver in the inner corners; blended smoky black into the crease; drew a perfect even wing with black eyeliner along one lash line and then the other, businesslike and quick. Usually she spent at least an hour lovingly painting her face before one of these parties, and another hour on her hair; this time it took her no more than forty-five minutes to finish both. The *impatience* was unfamiliar, a little uneasy; the idea that she'd rather be doing something else than making herself beautiful was not native to Lilith's worldview.

Much earlier than usual, she left her boudoir—she was

almost always ready just when Corvin called for her to join him—and nearly ran into Yves's newest acquisition in the hallway. The girl shrank away—God, she couldn't even *move* right, she had no grace at all—and Lilith glared at her. And then *stared* at her.

She'd apparently put her makeup on in the dark, or possibly tried using her toes to apply it. The red shadow was uneven, with a drift of fallout smudging her cheek; one eyeliner's wing wobbled and the other was twice as thick. And she looked as if she was about to burst into tears, which would emphatically not improve the situation.

"What the fuck is wrong with you?" Lilith demanded. "You can't intend to show up to Corvin's party with your face looking like *that*. Tell me you're not that stupid, what's-your-name."

"Sofiria?" said the girl, looking as if she'd had to remember it herself. "I'm sorry, Lilith, I don't know what's wrong with me, I just—can't get the eyeliner right tonight?"

"Don't be so *wet*," snapped Lilith, and grabbed her wrist, ignoring Sofiria's startled yelp. She half-dragged the girl into her own boudoir, propelled her across the room, and sat her down on the satin stool facing the dressing table. "I cannot stand pathetic baby vampires. It's not your fault that useless idiot Yves turned you and then didn't bother to teach you the first bloody thing, but you could take some *initiative* about it, couldn't you? Hold still and close your eyes."

She soaked a cotton ball in makeup remover and took Sofiria's wretched attempt at eyeliner off with a few brisk ungentle strokes. It flaked and smudged in a way Lilith hadn't seen in a long time, not since she'd had to buy the cheap stuff, and that was exasperating as well: didn't this kid know they could take whatever they wanted?

"You're not normally this bad at doing makeup," she said, leaning back to get a better look at Sofiria's face. "I'd have noticed. I mean, you're not *good*, you're never good, but you're usually not terrible."

"I know," said Sofiria miserably. She looked at Lilith with wide silver eyes, and Lilith noticed how dark the circles underneath them were, and that the hands gripping each other tightly in her lap were shaking. "I just…"

"This is your first big dinner party, isn't it," Lilith said in a slightly different tone. "You weren't here yet the last time he had one."

Sofiria nodded, looking down. The dye job wasn't all that great, either, Lilith noticed: whoever had done the girl's hair for her hadn't gotten all the roots evenly, and a little patch of brown was visible underneath the red.

I could be in my circle right now, *instead of doing this*, she thought, and took a deep breath. "It's not that bad. You'll probably have a good time, even. You just have to—not let him know that you're nervous, okay? That, like, annoys him *instantly*. Close your eyes again and don't move."

The immediate obedience was pleasing. Lilith sorted through her makeup box and found the palettes she wanted, shades of rose and gold that would go better with the girl's skin tone and hair, and tilted her chin with a long-nailed fingertip to get a clearer angle. "I can teach you how to do this right," she said. "When I have time." *When I'm not busy with my babies.*

"Thank you," said Sofiria, biting her lip. "It's—it's really nice of you, Lilith."

"No it's not," she said. "I told you, I can't stand pathetic baby vampires, and I *really* can't stand pathetic baby vampires with awful makeup, and if Yves can't tell you how to get your fucking eyeliner on straight, *somebody's* going to have to."

Thank you wasn't something Lilith heard all that often. It seemed to echo in her head while she painted the girl's face and rearranged her hair to hide the little brown patch underneath a jeweled comb; it went on echoing after she had dismissed Sofiria and gone to join Corvin in his own chambers; it went on, in fact, until she swept into the richly decorated cavern that served as their dining room and saw the seating arrangements Corvin had ordered to be made, and then it— and everything else—was drowned out in a surge of simple outrage.

This time the vampire with the silvery dreadlocks led Greta not to the pleasantly appointed bathroom but the other way, down the corridor, and she could tell at once they were in the more domestic and central section of Corvin's lair. Not for the first time she very deliberately tried to set her mind to record the details, fixing each opening they passed, each new tunnel leading off somewhere into the dark, trying to memorize the layout of the space. The intense level of observation was a slightly rusty skill, a holdover from her childhood, when her father had made a game out of very deliberately teaching her to observe scenes for short periods of time and remember as much as possible of what she had seen. Until she got to medical school and found herself having to memorize enormous amounts of information very quickly, Greta hadn't quite understood the value of the game, and now she thanked Wilfert Helsing all over again for those long-ago lessons.

The thought occurred, unbidden, of a video she'd seen online of people pouring molten metal into ant nests or termite mounds and then excavating the incredibly complex solid cast of the insects' tunnels and chambers once the metal had cooled. Some of the casts had been beautiful, branching, treelike; all had looked intensely alien, and Greta thought now of the network of tunnels that must underlie most of the city: what would *this* tangle of passageways look like rendered solid and three-dimensional? What kinds of patterns did humans, or human-shaped creatures, instinctively make?

They passed a couple of vampires in black lace and velvet, chatting to one another in French; Greta got a curious look from one of them, but the other averted his eyes from Corvin's prisoner as if he couldn't bear the sight of her. The hand on her arm tightened ever so slightly at that, but her escort made no sound; and a moment later they came out into a wider chamber, hollowed-out from the rock, in which long carpets had been laid. Someone had gone to some considerable effort and expense to fit this place out for its inhabitants: there were actual doors in door frames set into the walls, and she could see the paler marks where the rock had been chiseled into shape to receive them. It was to one of these doors that the vampire led her; and when he opened it and ushered her through, the light was so dim compared to the brighter chamber outside that she could see nothing at all for several moments.

He's going to kill me after all, she thought. *This is how everything ends, he won't wait for Corvin to bite my neck, he's going to kill me himself*—and then her eyes finished adjusting, and she looked around to find herself in a space quite unlike the rooms of the lair she'd seen so far.

There was nothing of the layered, over-the-top drapery or carpeting she remembered from Corvin's throne room; this chamber contained a bed, a desk with books on it that looked as if they had been chosen for content rather than color-matching spines, a wardrobe, and a dresser with a beveled-glass mirror atop it. As she got used to the dimness—the lamps had dark green shades that made her think of banker's desk lights—it was also a bit of a relief after the sudden brightness of the corridors.

The door closed with a click, and she turned to find the vampire looking thoughtfully at her. His eyeshine was visible, as it had been at the Opera. She'd never quite gotten used to that particular manifestation of vampire physiology: it seemed that some deep hindbrain sense would never quite manage to feel comfortable watching people's pupils glowing red.

"Don't worry," he said. "I don't intend either to ravish you or to suck out all your blood. I thought you were probably around a size 34, right?"

Greta blinked at him, and he gave the little self-mocking eyeroll of someone who's forgotten something obvious. "Eight, in the UK. Wasn't sure, because that truly dreadful outfit you have on could hide a multitude of sins, but you look like a 34 to me."

She hadn't answered his previous inquiry as to her dress size; clearly he hadn't needed her to tell him in the first place. He nodded at the bed, where she now noticed a dress in some dark material had been laid out. "Try it on. I'll even turn my back like a proper little gentleman, I promise."

Still feeling as if she'd somehow slid into a completely different situation by accident—from prisoner of vampires to contestant on twisted sartorial reality show—Greta moved to the bed and picked up the gown lying across the covers. All she'd been able to make out was that it was black, but the moment her fingers touched the fabric, she pushed it away with a stifled curse.

"What's the matter? I thought you looked quite good in black velvet the other night."

Black velvet, and Ruthven there with her, Ruthven with his well-beloved big silver eyes and offensively perfect shirtfront, Ruthven who had underwritten the refit of her clinic, Ruthven who was *safe and ordinary and not horrible*—in a world that still made sense, where she was free to walk under the sky—

"I'd rather not," she said, and her voice sounded priggish even to herself, clipped little tones. "If you don't mind."

"Suit yourself," said the vampire, eyebrow raised. He picked up the black velvet gown. "I'll see what else the wardrobe department has that might better please madame's sophisticated taste."

He locked her in; when he came back a few minutes later with a quite different dress over his arm, Greta had not moved at all. She was standing in the middle of the dimly lit room with her arms wrapped tight around herself.

I will not cry, she was thinking in a monotonous loop, *I will not let him see me cry, I will not, I will not, I will not.*

Afterward Greta would remember that dinner at Corvin's table as a kind of endless, hazy dream—the unpleasant, self-referential, looping kind where everything was not quite in the real world, the kind that accompanied the stuporous heat of fever. Even so, it had been better than looking at herself in the mirror and seeing a vampire who wasn't Edmund Ruthven putting up her hair.

The gown he'd brought back with him had been dark red taffeta, unflattering in the extreme, and Greta had put it on and let him zip it up the back, had gritted her teeth and made it through the part where he had his fingers in her hair, thinking all over again, *I will not cry.*

She'd been imagining the fleeting concern in those red eyes, meeting hers in the mirror; she had to have been imagining it. He had almost offered her his arm, and presumably she had looked even more stricken at the prospect, because he had simply dropped it again and gestured for her to precede him—and then there had been the candlelit chamber, reeking of perfume and incense: a long table brilliant with crystal and silver, people seated along each side, their skin sparkling, wearing velvet and lace and leather in all the shades of black there might have been in all the world, iridescent like a raven's wing—Emily, porcelain-pale apart from her lipstick and the rose-gold shimmer on her eyelids, and a few places farther down the table Yves in ruffles, holding himself ever so slightly unnaturally—

And Corvin, resplendent in royal scarlet, at the end of it, waiting for her—with the seat at his right hand empty, where Lilith should have been. And Lilith herself, down the other end of the table, staring poisoned daggers at her.

The vampire's gaze felt like a physical attack, drilling into Greta's mind so hard that she half fell into the seat with her vision gone to sparkles for a good thirty seconds before it cleared, thinking, *He's done this on purpose, he's—put me in her seat, he's* playing games *for some reason of his own—*

Corvin was talking. Something about celebration and honor and manners. She couldn't quite follow it, because she was too busy trying to figure out what the hell he was up to. She was also surprised to find that she was not, in fact, the only human present. Two men and one woman, all startlingly beautiful, and all listing subtly to one side in their seats with the glazed expression of the profoundly high.

Greta found it in herself to wonder what with, and then there was a hand like cold marble on her wrist and she looked down to see Corvin's fingers. The candlelight caught and glowed in the ruby of his ring.

"Won't you smile for us," he said, "you are so much more beautiful when you smile," and the fingers around her wrist tightened slightly. This close, she could see the slight change in color at the very edge of his hairline, where the new growth had begun to show; he'd need his roots touched up in another few days. His breath smelled powerfully of blood and wine.

Oh, Ruthven, she thought again, *Ruthven, you were right about forebodings,* and she smiled, as brightly and believably as she could manage; smiled until her face ached, until he was apparently satisfied and the hand around her wrist let go. "A toast!" Corvin called. "To my most honored guest, and to the final satisfaction that lies now within my grasp."

Around the table, glasses were raised, and after a moment Greta raised hers, too: it was full of some dark red liquid, beaded with pink bubbles at the brim. She avoided looking down the table at Lilith, watching the other humans take a sip from their own glasses before she tried the stuff and found it to be a perfectly serviceable merlot—and took another, larger swallow. If it was drugged, well. She might mind whatever was going to happen to her *less.*

That was when things began to grow hazy, dreamlike. She wasn't sure if it was just wine, or something *in* the wine, that was to blame—and the heavy sweet stink of burning incense seemed to fill the whole world, perfumed smoke sending her a little farther away from herself with every breath. There was solid food, for the humans—delicate platters of fruit, little cakes— and she was the only one who ate much of it, while the wine-glasses were filled again and again by Corvin's people.

She'd glanced across at Emily; despite the perfect makeup, her bearing spoke of just how nervous she felt. It was evident that nobody had bothered to teach her how to conceal emotions, among all the other things she hadn't been properly taught. Greta noticed that she kept glancing over at Corvin, as if expecting him to suddenly turn and snap at her, wondering if he had found out about the business with Yves—who looked somewhat faraway.

He'd turned a child, and Greta had fixed him nonetheless. She thought again of Ruthven in his kitchen, talking about people turned without consent, about people who needed help to learn how to be what they had been made to be; thought about the girl asking her questions, *what's wrong with me*, bringing her obnoxious creator to Greta for help, at personal risk; and somewhere inside all the haze, she thought again, *I have to try.*

At one point Greta noticed that Corvin was, in fact, drinking out of what appeared to be a goblet made from the calvaria of somebody's skull, and wondered who had had the presence of mind to leak-proof the cranial sutures for him, because she was damn sure he wouldn't have thought of it himself. The conversation came and went around her in waves of sound she did not have to pay attention to, and so she didn't try, and had no real idea how much time had passed when something warm and soft and silky underneath the table rested its chin upon her knee.

It was due to the wine that she didn't yelp, or recoil from the touch; she merely blinked hard, and slipped a hand under the table to feel whatever it was, and got her fingers unexpectedly licked.

Tricherpeton, she thought. The vampire with dreadlocks— she'd been told his name but she couldn't remember it, something with a G—had told her they had hairmonsters down here, but she hadn't encountered one until now.

There was a faintly doggy sigh from underneath the table, and the weight on her knee was joined by a weight on her foot. More than one, then, and pretty big. Had the one in her hotel room been an escapee from Corvin's lair, and if so, could she somehow use them to get a message to the surface—

Greta put down the wineglass. The movement shifted the underpinnings of her bodice, and she felt the hard and unyielding whistle press against her ribs. *That* was more useful than a tricherpeton, if she was clever with it. She'd taken it out of her pocket and tucked it into her dress when he'd turned his back to let her change clothes, and she was pretty sure the vampires didn't know of its existence.

She was still absently stroking the creature leaning against her knee, thinking as hard as she could through the haze of incense and alcohol, when Corvin beside her tapped a glass for silence. Belatedly Greta realized that the other three humans at the table were slumped over in their chairs, either unconscious or close to it, and she wondered again what they had been given, and why *she* hadn't had it, too.

"I believe it is time for the evening's proper entertainment to commence," Corvin said. Greta hadn't noticed until now that not only was one of his fangs made of metal, it had a jewel inlaid in it. In the heavy, thick air of the chamber, it caught the light in slow glinting flakes. "My dear," he went on, turning to look at her with a wave of unsubtle thrall—good God, that felt like being struck, a heavy thud of a blow—and reached out to tip up her chin with one long-nailed finger. "I regret to inform you that tonight's festivities will not be to your taste. It's time for you to go back to your luxury suite. Grisaille, take her away."

A slim dark hand inserted itself into her somewhat blurry field of view, and she took it, and let herself be pulled to her feet. They had to pass by Lilith on the way, and despite her hazy vision, Greta had no difficulty whatsoever recognizing the visceral hatred in the other woman's face. The room rocked and swirled around her; she was glad of the iron grip on her arm as Grisaille walked her out.

Grisaille, she thought, with effort, through the dizziness. *Shades of grey.*

Grisaille had been watching the doctor throughout the evening's ostentatious little pantomime. The fact that it *was* evening didn't help his mood; otherwise nocturnal, Corvin occasionally decided to hold his gatherings at perverse hours, midday or evening, for no reason that Grisaille could see other than to fuck with his people and remind them who was boss.

He did this sort of dinner party thing every few months, often enough that Grisaille was used to it: Corvin liked play-acting as a gracious host, only this time, for whatever reason, Lilith hadn't been cast as hostess. Judging by the poisonous looks she'd been sending down the table, there would almost certainly be *repercussions*.

She wasn't bright but she was cunning, and Grisaille knew she was capable of holding on to grudges. In this case, it hadn't been Helsing's fault that Corvin had given her Lilith's place, but Lilith was undoubtedly going to do something creatively nasty to her the moment she got a chance. He thought to himself that the doctor probably knew that, too.

She was odd. He couldn't work out what it had been that had made her react like that to the black velvet dress, which frankly would have suited her much better than what she had on; neither could he identify what about having somebody pin up her hair should have resulted in that grey-pale, stricken look. She'd covered it quickly, but Grisaille had seen enough to know that her distress was genuine.

Then again, he thought drily, *she's not exactly in a pleasant situation to begin with*, and wondered what Corvin did plan on doing with her. Not that there was really very much doubt on that particular score.

Corvin's people went out to eat most nights, but when they ordered in, somebody had to dispose of the leftovers. More than once, Grisaille himself had been tasked with hauling bodies; the undercity was honeycombed with tunnels and passageways, and they had long ago found a way into the ancient sewer system from the quarry network useful for disposing of remains. He had a sudden very vivid mental image of pale hair disappearing into the darkness, black noisome water closing over a pointed, intense little face.

Grisaille shivered once, hard, and reapplied his gently mocking half-smile, which had slipped off his face entirely. He had escorted the doctor back to her cell and locked her safely inside, and it was not his problem; nothing, in fact, was his problem other than following Corvin's orders, and that was how it ought to be. Grisaille had no desire to be the one in charge. That came with *far* too much responsibility.

Or at least it should, he thought, *if the leader is one who's actually worth following. I should know; I wasn't.*

The only good thing that had come out of his own brief abortive attempt to gather a small group of vampires under his command was the sure and certain lesson that he wasn't cut out for it; but Grisaille had never been any good at being alone for very long, even when he'd been alive. Even a sub-optimal position in an organization like Corvin's was better than facing the world on his own; at least here he had a role, things to *do*, commands to follow, instead of having to make all his own decisions.

He took a long, deep breath before returning to the party; and when he got there, he drank four Bloody Marys in rapid succession, heavy on the vodka and light on the blood.

The scene was already fairly well advanced: one of the humans was dead, and the other two would be joining her shortly. Grisaille watched with some distaste, noticing the youngest of their little group fastened on to one of the victims, and looked away—and saw Lilith with three others busily at work on a second. There was something repellent about a flock of vampires all feeding from the same victim at once, two from the throat, one from the wrist, one from the femoral artery. It reminded him of the clusters of rubbery parasites attached to the legs of a leech-gatherer: something Grisaille hadn't had cause to think about in nearly two hundred years.

As he watched, Lilith—who had gone for the right side of the throat, as usual, her favorite site—raised her face to snarl at the others. She said something he didn't catch, but the import was clear; reluctantly they disengaged, leaving Lilith with the human all to herself. She pulled the naked body into her lap. It was one of the young men, her preferred type of snack, and there wasn't much left in him, but Grisaille saw him move a little with a faint choked moan.

He wondered how much dope they'd given him. All three of the humans had been pretty much drugged insensible.

Not my problem, Grisaille thought again, and made himself another drink.

Varney had forgotten exactly how long it had been since he'd done any sleeping. It *felt* like days, but he checked his phone and found it was still the same day—or the night of the same day—he'd begun by waking early to get to the airport to meet Greta. There had just been rather a lot happening between then and now.

After St. Germain had led them around the Paris streets in a widening gyre beginning in the Place de la Sorbonne, finding only that Greta had been there at some point and that her tracks abruptly ended with no clear explanation of where she had subsequently vanished to—after that, the werewolf had said with what Varney considered an unnecessary level of drama that he was going to ring up Hell to ask for further instructions.

Varney had leaned against a convenient wall while St. Germain, once again bipedal and only slightly disheveled, talked on his phone; it turned out that the particular demon he was asking for assistance was located north of the river, and they'd have to either walk or take a cab. Tiredness washed over him in low, long comber-rolls like a tide beginning to come in—

"Varney?" Ruthven was saying at his elbow. "Varney, are you all right?"

He looked down at the rose in his buttonhole, drooped in an art-nouveau curve. "I don't know," he said honestly, and then straightened up. "But I will have to be; so lead on."

Ruthven gave him an uncertain look but didn't protest further; and the three of them walked on two legs each across the Pont au Change, pausing only briefly in the center of the span because of a brief chilly sensation Varney associated with ghosts.

Who died there? he thought, following the others. *Who died there, that in dying left a stain on reality?*

It was probably for the best, given Varney's already upset state of mind, that he did not look back from the Place du Châtelet to see a figure in a dark blue greatcoat and an official hat climb to the parapet of the bridge and stare down into the river, particularly since this figure faded back out of existence just at the moment when he took that first heavy-booted step out into nothingness, accompanied by a faint and unplaceable snatch of bright music.

Varney didn't remember a great deal of that brief walk; at some point St. Germain led them to a building on the corner between two streets, leaned on the buzzer and talked rapidly in French to someone on the other end, and then shepherded him and Ruthven up three flights of stairs. That exertion was enough to shake Varney out of his vagueness, and he was blinking but present once again when a short orange-haired individual opened the apartment door to let them in.

"Alceste," said this person, looking up at St. Germain. "I'm so very glad you've come. Can I possibly offer you dinner?"

"This isn't a social call," said St. Germain. "Irazek, what's going on? These gentlemen are trying to locate a friend of theirs who's mysteriously gone missing, and I've had reports of all sorts of uncanny things—"

"I know," said Irazek wretchedly. Varney noticed that he actually did have a pair of tiny horns, as carroty-orange as his hair. They resembled carrots, in fact. "I do know. There's— I have to do so many calculations—the esso traces—I don't know where Mr. Brightside and his friend are, I haven't seen them since this afternoon, I do hope nothing's happened to them—"

He looked from St. Germain to Varney and Ruthven, apparently noticing them for the first time. "Can I offer *you* dinner?" he said, and then went a shade of pink that clashed with his hair. "I mean. I can't—quite—I don't have proper, um, supplies for your specific—I'm sorry—"

Ruthven had clearly been overcome by the same wave of contact embarrassment that had just engulfed Varney, and almost in unison the sanguivores offered two variants on "Please don't go to any trouble, it's quite all right, we'd love to stay, a little red wine is quite sufficient."

"Are you sure?" asked Irazek, looking uncertain.

"Quite sure. Although I should love to see your kitchen if that would be all right. I'm still remodeling mine—it's so difficult to work out *which* built-ins I absolutely can't do without," said Ruthven smoothly, stepping forward. Varney envied him the ease and speed with which he'd recovered from the embarrassment. "Show me?"

If he hadn't been so tired and cross and miserable, Varney might have been touched at the simple, guileless, sheer pleasure on Irazek's face. He stood aside so that Ruthven could follow Irazek into his kitchen and rhapsodize about equipment, or space, or whatever it was people who cooked actual food liked to have available to them.

He looked up at St. Germain, who gave him a look that communicated quite clearly his own lack of clues on the subject. "Um," he said.

"Would you like a drink?" asked the werewolf. "It's too bad of me to commandeer Irazek's whiskey but I think we might both be due a little something."

Varney hadn't had anything at all since the glass of brandy on the flight over, and he really *ought* to protest, but the idea of a little bit of something to take his mind off the universe was awfully tempting. "My thanks," he said. "I'm—going to use my status as a stranger in a strange land to bypass the usual *tempora et mores*."

That made St. Germain smile, a sudden and intensely warm expression that lit his eyes, made him look years younger. "Well said. Here."

Varney took the cut-crystal glass with a shallow amber flare in its depths and, for the first time since he'd discovered Greta was missing, felt somewhat as if things might possibly be all right after all.

CHAPTER 7

The Scotch had helped; having something to *do* helped more.

They'd discussed the situation, in Irazek's kitchen, and Varney and Ruthven had been delegated to go out into the city and talk with the established vampires while Irazek and St. Germain looked at the strips of paper marked with squiggly lines, which apparently had some particular significance. He wasn't entirely clear on what the squiggles indicated, only that it was worrisome, and Varney had never been very good at sitting around patiently while people discussed something he couldn't understand.

Some of the fatigue had lifted, or perhaps he had simply stopped noticing it so much; the moonlight helped a little, and the night air was pleasantly cool against his face.

He had no idea what to expect. St. Germain had told them that Lucia and Élise were as much fixtures of Paris as he himself; they'd been in the city for several hundred years now, behaving themselves, keeping under the radar. If there *had* been a recent uptick in vampire activity, they were almost certainly not to blame for it—but they might know more than St. Germain had been able to find out thus far.

The address was in the Avenue Montaigne. Varney didn't have a good handle on property values in Paris, but even he could tell that this was seven- or eight-figure territory; the ground floors of the buildings were taken up with Versace and Chanel boutiques, Harry Winston diamond showrooms, the kind of restaurant that styled its name in lowercase sans serif. It reminded him of Mayfair—only the people window-shopping or stalking along on their own business had the sort of style that Varney had come to identify as innately Parisian. *Everyone* looked as if they'd just stepped out of a magazine editorial, except Varney himself; Ruthven fit in much more easily.

He stood watching the traffic come and go while Ruthven rang the bell of an *immeuble* sandwiched between Chanel and Ferragamo storefronts. There was a pause, and a woman's voice said, "*Allô?*"

"Mademoiselle de Favand?" Ruthven said, his accent pitch-perfect Parisian. "So sorry to bother you, but I'm a friend of Alceste St. Germain and he suggested you might be kind enough to lend us a few minutes of your time."

Another pause, and then the voice, sounding amused: "It's Madame, in fact; and tell Alceste we are *capable* of operating the telephone; he could simply have called us rather than sending his friends on quests through the Paris streets. Do come up, Monsieur...?"

"Ruthven," said Ruthven. "And my colleague Sir Francis Varney."

"*Lord* Ruthven?"

"I'm afraid so," he said, glancing sideways at Varney.

"Our household is honored," said the voice, and a moment later the door unlocked itself with a click.

Inside, the building was classic Deco. The elevator had been modernized, but everything else looked to Varney as if it had been preserved perfectly in its original form. "You don't *know* these people, do you?" he asked Ruthven on the way up.

"Not as far as I'm aware," said Ruthven. "It's entirely possible they might have read that godawful Polidori book; in which case this will be extremely embarrassing."

"Not as embarrassing as *Varney the Vampyre, or The Feast of Blood*," said Varney drily. "Practically nothing is as embarrassing as that. Polidori at least wasn't being paid by the word."

Ruthven sighed as the elevator came to a halt. The apartment was on the sixth floor. "Let's get this over with," he said. "I have no idea what to expect."

Neither did Varney. The vision that greeted them in the doorway was impressive: a tall woman, as tall as Varney himself, wearing something draped out of chestnut satin, a long cigarette holder poised between her fingers. Her hair was cut in a short twenties-style bob, so deep a red it looked almost black, stark against her marble pallor; it matched her lipstick.

She looked them up and down for a long moment, pale eyes giving nothing away, and then the dark red lips curved in an amused little smile, as if she had come to some conclusion. "Welcome to Paris, gentlemen," she said. "I'm Lucia de Favand. Won't you come in?"

Varney and Ruthven exchanged a glance—there was a certain undeniable *step into my parlor, said the spider to the fly* aspect to the situation. She moved aside to let them pass, and Varney thought about the old vampire trope of needing to be *invited* in order to enter a dwelling.

Inside, the apartment was gorgeous even by Parisian standards. Lucia took them into an elegant living room overlooking the avenue, three tall windows opening to a balcony that ran the entire width of the building. He could see the Eiffel Tower on the other side of the river; the same angle as the London Eye seen from Ruthven's home on the Embankment. "Do sit down," she said. "Élise will be along shortly; I'm afraid we're extremely late risers."

"I'm terribly sorry—" Ruthven began, but she waved the cigarette holder at him.

"Nonsense. Always a pleasure to make the acquaintance of nobility."

Varney watched Ruthven go faintly pink for a moment. He was sensitive about the *Lord* thing, which Varney had never been able to understand: his own title was simply a part of his name, his history, nothing he had to be particularly proud of or embarrassed by. "This is a beautiful apartment," he said, moved by an obscure urge to take the woman's attention off Ruthven for a moment or two: it felt a little bit like a searchlight when Lucia turned to him.

"And you would be Sir Francis Varney," she purred. "A

vampyre. How fascinating; I don't believe I've met one in half a century. May we offer you some refreshment?"

"Please don't trouble yourself," he said. He could hear the leaden weight of his accent, although his French vocabulary had come back without a great deal of difficulty. "We won't take up much of your time, Mademoiselle—"

"Madame," she corrected again, and turned to look over her shoulder, where another woman had just come into the room. This one made Varney think immediately of an 1851 Cordier bronze bust he'd seen once: a young woman with tightly curled hair in a short waterfall of locks, the burnished planes and angles of her face, neck, and shoulders both defiant and graceful. *African Venus*, it had been called, and although this woman was wearing a silk robe and slippers rather than a strapless gown and half a ton of jewels, the effect was just the same.

Lucia held out a hand to her, and the woman's patrician face warmed in a smile as she came forward into the room, perching on the arm of Lucia's chair. "My wife, Élise," said Lucia, smiling up at her, and Varney *knew* he was staring and found it extremely difficult to stop.

"*Enchanté*," said Ruthven beside him—his self-possession had come back with that odd frictionless ease. "Madame and Madame. I am truly sorry for bothering you so early in the night."

"It's quite all right," said Élise. "Has Lucia offered you a drink?"

"Of course I did. These gentlemen are friends of Alceste's;

he's sent them over here to talk to us about something terribly mysterious."

"What does Alceste have on his mind that's so particularly pressing?"

"Well," Ruthven began. He was entirely over his embarrassment, Varney saw; he was doing the slightly infuriating ineffable-style thing once more, completely at home in these surroundings. "He thinks there may be a new vampire group in town. A—*coven*."

The distaste with which he pronounced the word would have amused Varney in other circumstances. He was still trying not to stare at the women—Élise had her hand on Lucia's shoulder, casual easy intimacy—and redirected his gaze at the collection of extremely beautiful celadon ware on the coffee table instead. "There have been deaths," Ruthven continued, "bodies drained of blood floating in the Seine, and apparently a strange vampire was sniffing around in ghoul territory— and a friend of ours has disappeared. St. Germain suggested we ask you for help."

"A *coven*," repeated Lucia, evidently amused. "Is *that* what they're calling themselves. Well. Poor Alceste, he's been so distracted just recently—he's writing a book, did you know, of all the things—it's no wonder he hasn't had time to keep a closer eye on the baby-vamps."

"Then there is a group?" Varney said.

"Oh, absolutely. They've been here for—how long, darling? Several months at least."

"We think they're hiding in somebody's wine cellar," Élise

said, just as amused. "And coming out to make a nuisance of themselves."

"Have you met them?" Ruthven demanded.

"Not to say *meet*," Lucia said. "They're not the sort of people one cares to acknowledge socially, you understand."

"I do," he said, "although I don't believe we have much choice, not if our friend is involved. Can you tell me where they are?"

"Where they're *staying*, I've no idea," said Lucia. "But they *hunt* in Pigalle. Up and down and to and fro, in among the sex shops and the tourist tat. No class at all, I'm afraid; not the slightest flicker of taste. I shouldn't bother with them if I were you, *chéri*. Come out with us instead."

"We can show you a much nicer time," said Élise, and she and Lucia exchanged glances, laughing. "You're one of *us*, after all. And you, too, of course, monsieur," she added, looking at Varney. "Most welcome."

"Under other circumstances," said Ruthven, and Varney was a little surprised at how warm his voice was, "under other circumstances I should be *most* pleased to accept; but at the moment I'm afraid we really do have to be going. Thank you so much for your time."

"Look us up when you're finished enacting justice," said Lucia. "Our door is always open, metaphorically speaking. And Alceste does have our phone number, if he can be bothered to remember it."

She got up and walked Varney and Ruthven to the door,

and Varney was not surprised when she gave Ruthven the three cheek-kisses of acquaintance, nor when she turned to Varney himself with a smile and offered him her hand. Some kind of—understanding—had clearly passed between the two of them, which Varney had failed to follow.

"One thing," said Lucia, standing in the doorway as they set off down the hall. "They're making more of themselves, we're almost sure. Young ones. *Very* young."

She closed the door behind her with a final *click*, leaving Varney and Ruthven staring at one another with almost-identical expressions of horror.

Vampires do dream. The sleep patterns of any given individual vary based on a number of factors; some of them make a point of sleeping *like the dead*, sometimes actually in a coffin, sometimes in proper beds. And they dream of many things.

Grisaille had had this one before. He was somewhere complicated and terribly cold, with the stink of death all around him, and while he had no clear understanding of why he was there, he felt a powerful sense of oppression—of something terrible drawing nearer and nearer, and no idea which way to run. When the screaming started, he thought for a long moment that it was part of the dream; so many of his included screams, one way or another.

He sat up, blinking in the darkness of his rock-cut bedroom, disoriented. The party had gone on for long enough that Grisaille had completely lost track of time, and had no idea how long he'd been passed out. As the last of the dream faded, the sound was still going on: something between screaming and laughter, jagged peals of it, ringing in the corridor outside.

He was already out of bed and tying the belt of his dressing gown when he heard the unmistakable voice of Corvin bellowing "*Grisaille!*"

"I'm coming, I'm coming," he muttered, not bothering to turn on the lights. In the corridor some of the others had already emerged from their rooms, roused by the screaming; alarmed and dazed, still half-drunk from their earlier revelry.

The last time the group had been startled by unexpected screaming had been when the kid first woke up after being turned, and that had been an entirely different kind of scream: this one came from much closer at hand, and was laced through with a kind of hysterical laughter that was a lot worse than simple screaming might have been.

Grisaille hurried to the ornate carved door of Corvin's chambers, pretty sure what he was going to see before he saw it.

Corvin was on his feet, red silk sleepwear disarranged, looking both frantic and disgusted. Lilith was writhing on the bed, shrieking, clutching at the sheets with hands curled into claws. "Grisaille," he said, "*do* something, Christ, make it *stop*, make her *stop*—"

He'd never seen Lilith this bad. Once or twice before, she'd had a kind of fit, after unwise indulgence, but this was worse than anything Grisaille had seen before: there was blood on her mouth where she'd bitten her lips, and her eyes were rolled back in her head so far that only a rim of iris showed.

He made a decision. This was beyond his own extremely limited experience or skill, and they had someone at hand who almost certainly knew more than he did.

There was a certain weary flicker of relief at the thought: having someone there who *knew what they were doing*—who could give accurate instructions—was something Grisaille hadn't enjoyed in decades.

Ignoring Corvin's demands to be told what the fuck he thought he was doing, Grisaille stepped out of the bedchamber into the hallway, where five or six vampires were milling around uncertainly, and snapped his fingers at the nearest of them. "You," he said, "go and get the human, right now, and bring her to me."

The tricherpetons had followed Greta when she was escorted back to her cell—two of them, gorgeous things, one glossy black and one a deep mahogany brown in loose curls. They and the collection of wellmonsters had apparently decided the cell was where they wanted to be.

It felt like the small hours of the morning. Earlier, when Grisaille had brought her back from the party, logy with the haze of wine and whatever that incense had had in it, Greta hadn't felt capable of doing much of anything other than sitting very still and waiting for the room to stop spinning; she'd drifted off, briefly, and had woken with a vicious headache and an equally vicious determination that she wasn't going to spend any more time under Corvin's roof. Ceiling. Whatever. If she was going to get out, she was going to get out *now*.

Everything hinged on the whistle. If it worked—and she had no reason to believe it wouldn't—blowing it would summon the creature; once summoned, it had to manifest in some type of cloth, and she planned to rip up the voluminous skirts of her stupid ballgown to oblige. It was a *very* stupid ballgown, and it made Greta look like a cabbage, and it must have cost a truly ridiculous amount of money; tearing it to bits would be satisfying on several levels at once.

After that, she'd have to trust sheer luck, but maybe she was due some of that by now, after her recent string of misfortunes. She stood in the middle of the cell, bouncing the whistle in the palm of her hand, trying to get up the nerve to actually set the plan in motion.

It was only because the tricherpetons both suddenly got up and started growling that she had enough time to shove the whistle back into her bodice before running footsteps in the corridor approached, and an out-of-breath vampire turned the key in the cell door's lock. Greta vaguely remembered this one—she had purple wavy hair and went in for teal frosted lipstick and cobweb-patterned lace frills down her bodice—but right now she looked *scared*, which was not something Greta had seen on a vampire all that often. She grabbed Greta by the wrist and yanked her out of the cell without a word. "What's happening?" Greta demanded.

"Grisaille wants you," said the vampire, and broke into a trot, spike heels or no spike heels, pulling Greta along. She realized she could hear something in the distance, something like faint screams, growing rapidly louder as they ran.

She was being taken the same way Grisaille had escorted her on the way to his own rooms, through the same corridors, and when they got to the rock-cut chamber with the doors set into it, a different one of them was open. Whatever was screaming was in there.

The purple-haired vampire gave her a shove and she half stumbled forward, into the room, and got a good look at what was going on; the remainder of the haze from the wine she'd drunk earlier went away in a hurry.

Grisaille, in a dark grey dressing gown, was bending over a huge, scarlet-hung bed in which Lilith lay, quite a lot of pearl-white skin revealed. His hands were on Lilith's shoulders, trying to hold her still while she writhed and clawed at him, arching her back; her heels drummed against the tangled sheets. A little distance from the bed, Corvin stood in red silk pajamas that to Greta's brief glance appeared to be encrusted with jewels at collar and cuffs, his face screwed up in an expression of disgust which she was sure he didn't know was intensely unattractive.

Greta pushed past Corvin and crossed the room to the bed, taffeta skirts rustling. She took one of Lilith's flailing wrists. "What was it?" she asked Grisaille. "In the victims tonight. The humans. What were they full of?"

"Heroin."

"That shouldn't do this, especially not with a delayed onset. Did she just wake up like this?" Greta asked Corvin sharply, turning to look at him. The stink of Lilith's perfume, artificial vanilla and violets, sickly-sweet, was almost overpowering this close up.

"All I know is she woke *me* up because she's suddenly screaming and flailing around," he said, sounding petulant rather than grand. "She *kicked* me."

"It's not just the heroin; she must have taken something else as well—can you thrall her?" she asked Grisaille. "I need to know what's going on in there."

"I can try," he said, not sounding particularly confident, and she moved aside so he could get a better angle. Her foot touched something under the bed that rolled away with a faint glassy clink.

It was always odd *watching* a vampire thrall somebody. The rhythmic pulsing of the irises, expanding and contracting, was unnerving even if the force they exerted wasn't directed at you. Grisaille stared intently at Lilith, his eyes working hard, for only a few seconds before he winced away and straightened up again, pressing his hands to his face. In the dark grey silk gown he looked both stark and oddly stylized, his long fingers the deep brown of patinaed bronze.

"What is it?" she said. "What's wrong—are you all right?"

"I will be," he said, muffled behind his hands. "That's a goddamn mess—she's seeing monsters, and I don't mean the cutesy kind, things with claws and teeth and burning yellow eyes—the walls are liquid—"

"Acute hallucinogenic delirium," Greta said. "She had to have taken something else—wait. Hang on."

Grisaille dragged his hands down his face, ashy undertones visible in his skin, as she knelt down and felt under the bed. It didn't take her long to close her fingers around an empty bottle: the thing she'd heard rolling away a few minutes back. Greta brought it out into the light. One look was enough to tell her exactly what was going on, and she went cold all over.

"Shit," she said with exquisite clarity. "She's only sunk a bottle of undiluted absinthe; no bloody *wonder* she's hallucinating. We have to get it out of her, now, before there's permanent damage. Can one of you stick your fingers down her throat, please, because she'd bite my hand clean off if I tried." She looked up at the pair of them, Grisaille and Corvin, everything still very cold and clear and bright.

Absinthe was generally held to be very mildly hallucinogenic to humans, due to the presence of the chemical compound thujone, but no real research results could back that up. In sanguivores, however, it was *extremely* effective; one glassful of prepared, diluted absinthe could send a typical vampire witch-walking for hours, and Lilith had drunk God only knew how much of the stuff neat, on top of a heavy dose of heroin-laced blood: far more than any vampire's accelerated healing could accommodate. Greta had no idea if she'd had enough to cause permanent neurological effects, but they had to get whatever remained out of Lilith in a hurry, and here she was without a goddamn ounce of ipecac to her name. "*Now*," she repeated. "Help me, if you want her to get through this."

Corvin backed away. "This is disgusting," he said. "*She's* disgusting. I can't deal with any more of it. I should have gotten rid of her weeks ago—"

He turned on his heel and left them alone in the bedchamber. Greta looked up at Grisaille, who was still an unpleasant color, and was about to say something else along the lines of *are you going to help me do this or not* when he straightened up, taking a long breath.

"This is going to be awful, isn't it?" he said.

"Yes."

"I'll go and fetch a bucket."

It was, in fact, awful. Grisaille had done a great many unpleasant things in his couple of centuries, but this experience would rank very near the top of that list: once they'd got Lilith to start vomiting, she seemed thoroughly disinclined to stop. The doctor—Helsing—was sitting behind her on the bed, one arm wrapped around Lilith to support her and the other hand cupping her forehead over the bowl in her lap; the shrieking and flailing had dwindled into moans and shudders. The incongruity of the red taffeta ballgown in this particular tableau was not lost on Grisaille.

Both of them were liberally spattered, and the bed was a disaster. "Try thralling her again," Helsing said, grimly hanging on to Lilith through another wave of retching. "See if you can get through to her—she's not fighting me anymore but I need you to try calming her down. What's her real name anyway?"

"I'm not supposed to know that," said Grisaille, "and you

absolutely aren't, but she's really a Samantha. Hold her still for a second."

He reached for Lilith's mind—still a swirling mess of confused misery, but less terrified. Through her eyes he was no longer a faceless monster with huge claws, which was an improvement, and he could tell she at least knew where she was. He leaned a little, pushing *calm* and *reassurance* at her, and she relaxed slightly in Helsing's arms.

"That's better," said the doctor. "You're going to be all right, Lilith, I know it's awful but you're doing wonderfully; just get it all up and you'll feel much better afterward."

The tone of voice was just about as bizarre, in this situation, as the ballgown: she sounded brisk and sympathetic and confident, ordinary, exactly as if she weren't being held captive underground by a bunch of vampires. Grisaille was having difficulty parsing it—and aware, too, of that little flicker of sheer relief at being *told what to do* by somebody competent. The comfort of authority. How *long* it had been since he'd been given orders by someone he could actually trust. How much of a difference it made.

"She's not hallucinating anymore," he said to distract himself. "Or not as badly. I think she'll recover."

"Of course she will," said Helsing. "I imagine she'll have a nasty day or so while she gets this out of her system, but she'll do. Thank you, by the way. You're being extremely helpful."

"It's not exactly the first time I've been called upon to sort out someone in extremis."

"I was going to say, have you had medical training?" She

looked up at him, apparently genuinely interested. Her hair was still partly caught in the updo he'd arranged what felt like a century ago.

"Not exactly," he said, aware again of the sense of oppression he'd felt waking from the dream. "Not proper training, anyway. I never finished my studies."

"Where were you?"

"Ingolstadt," he said without meaning to. "A long time ago."

—and it was all back, all at once, memories he hadn't thought about in years: snow, the acid smell of it sharp and clear in his nose, the cold kisses of snowflakes against his face as he and Victor lurched back from the tavern, laughing at nothing, leaning on one another while the ground tried to tip them off their feet—and later standing looking out at that same snow, days later, wondering what he could have done differently, *knowing* what he could have done—simply left, told Victor he was mad, that the things he'd been considering were not things to be considered beyond brief blurting horror in the small hours of the morning—knowing, *knowing* he was complicit, that whatever Victor achieved or failed to achieve he, Grisaille, would never be free of the stain of it—and finding his old friend collapsed on the floor of that charnel house of a laboratory, burning with fever, clutching at Grisaille's sleeve with shaking hands and whispering, *I did it, I did it, it can't be undone—*

"Grisaille?" Helsing was saying, and she reached out as if to touch his arm and then apparently thought better of it, given the state of her hands. "What is it? Are you all right?"

There was actual concern in her voice, and somewhere beyond the sickening slide of memories, he could find it in himself to be amused at that; and he pulled himself together, with effort, and gave her the slightly maddening little half-smile he'd perfected over the centuries. "I'm dead, my dear Doctor," he said. "I hardly think the term applies."

"You are infuriating, is what you are," Helsing said, and his smile turned real.

"One tries, you know. One does one's best. In fact I did try, a very long time ago, to train as a doctor, back when I was alive—but it didn't suit me."

He wasn't sure why he was talking, only that nothing felt quite real, just at the moment; that the three of them had somehow slipped out of time, that perhaps it didn't matter what he said in this strange lacuna of reality. He found himself telling her about Ingolstadt, about the classes in the freezing lecture halls, about the one kid from Switzerland who was apparently determined to do everything better than everybody else.

"We had one of those," said Greta. "I will never forget the day he sort of tried to lecture the professor in the middle of grand rounds; it was the *well, actually* trope in its purest and most crystalline form. I have to admit I really enjoyed watching him be taken apart in the office later."

"Ours never got taken apart by professors, which I think would have done him a great deal of good in the long run," said Grisaille. "He came to a sticky but appropriate end. It's probably some form of irony that he spent all that time trying to work out a way to defeat death, and he's stayed dead for, oh, coming up on two centuries now—and here's me, who didn't try anything of the kind, still going after all this time."

"Defeat death?" said Greta, making a face. "Ours just wanted everyone to tell him how clever he was, but the delusions of grandeur had a limit." She looked down at Lilith; the active eruptions seemed to have passed for the moment. "I think she's over the worst of this. Can you get me a clean bowl of water and something to wash her face with?"

"I think I can oblige." Grisaille got to his feet, aware of his joints aching a little—he was very much older now than he had been that winter in Ingolstadt—and thought again about Victor and the dogged visceral *stupidity* of that brilliant mind. Perhaps only someone with that kind of arc-flash intelligence could have not only come up with, but put into action, such an idiotic concept; perhaps only someone whose mind was trained to focus on the task at hand to the exclusion of all else could have failed to notice the horror of what he was actually working on. That it had come as a surprise to Victor—Grisaille had heard it all, in Victor's delirium, in the weeks following his collapse, the whole story, over and over again, the terrible idea and the terrible execution, the long descent into madness during the construction of the experiment—still, even now, made him pointlessly angry. There was so much hubris in the entire business. Why should Victor have thought that *he*, of all people ever to have been born, should be the one to work out how to resurrect the dead?

And why didn't you stop him? Grisaille's mind piped up again, and he pushed the thought away with conscious effort.

By the time he'd fetched the water and some towels from the bathroom, he was more or less in control of his own memories again. He even found the smile and reapplied it, handing the basin to Helsing, and then without meaning to said, "Why do you *do* this?"

She looked for a moment desperately unhappy, and Grisaille found it in himself to feel vicious distaste for the universe and everything in it, particularly him.

"You aren't the first sanguivore to ask me that," she said. "The answer is extremely simple: because it needs doing. Help me get her changed, will you?"

Helsing was bathing Lilith's face. Now that the vomiting had stopped, she appeared to be semiconscious and totally exhausted, responding to questions in a slurred, vague voice. That was the comedown from the absinthe, Grisaille thought, plus the amount of opioids she'd consumed earlier probably still circulating in her blood.

He went to find some clean clothes for her—the wardrobe was a symphony in black, with black accents, black detailing, and the odd flash of purple—and together he and Helsing peeled Lilith out of her unspeakable nightgown and cleaned her up with the wet towel.

Grisaille had no concerns about his own ability to deal with handling the naked body of a woman who happened to be his superior's consort: Lilith was emphatically not his type, and he had cultivated a certain detachment over the time he had spent with Corvin which he leaned on now, and which served him well. He was struck, however, by the way Helsing touched her: impersonal, efficient but gentle, with a care he knew damn well Lilith had done nothing to deserve.

He was also slightly impressed, and tried not to be, by the way Helsing stripped the bed down and remade it with clean sheets—she had to be told where they were, of course, but she didn't even ask him to help her with any of it. He watched, sitting on the arm of the chair they had deposited Lilith in, and realized for the first time in some hours how tired he was. It had to be early morning, at least.

"There," said Helsing, and piled the clean pillows up against the headboard. "In you get, Lilith. Can you—ah, thanks," she added to Grisaille, who was already lifting Lilith in his arms to replace her in the bed. "She'll do; she'll probably sleep the clock around and wake up with the world's worst and most richly deserved headache, but she'll be all right, you can tell Corvin."

Grisaille was sure Corvin didn't give even half a fuck, but nodded. Helsing tucked the covers over Lilith, put her hands on the small of her back, and stretched to the accompaniment of a series of cracks—and then looked up at him.

"Thank you," she said. "You were...very helpful. I appreciate it."

Grisaille bit down on what he'd been going to say and simply nodded, thinking again: *Why didn't you stop him?* "You're welcome," he said, and his mouth was filled with the old familiar taste of self-loathing, a taste like the bitterness of snow.

CHAPTER 8

At the balcony of a hotel suite not so very far away from the one in which Greta Helsing had first encountered a wellmonster, Crepusculus Dammerung stood leaning on the iron railing and looking out at the Jardin des Tuileries across the street. The midmorning light was gorgeous, with that oddly powdery clarity that comes with spring, and beyond the gardens the river glinted like a sheet of electrum.

He was still wrapped in the hotel's bathrobe, his hair damp from the shower, listening behind him for the tapping on the door that would mean breakfast had arrived. In the other bedroom, Brightside hadn't yet shown any sign of stirring, and Crepusculus hoped the room-service knock wouldn't wake him.

They'd come straight back from the university library the previous night without going to ask any questions whatsoever of any ghosts; Crepusculus had made the decision that whatever was happening to the fabric of reality was probably not going to mind waiting one more night, and Brightside had been half-blind with one of his rare but vicious headaches. Crepusculus had put his foot down, carefully, and insisted that they return to the hotel. It had been a testament to just how bad Brightside had been feeling that he hadn't offered any argument.

After the experience in the Opera—they'd lost about twenty minutes of real time, Crepusculus calculated, while they flipped between periods in history like a kid hunting for a reference in a dictionary—they had gone looking for some answers.

The afternoon had started looking up when they'd found out that the majority of the Bibliothèque-Musée de l'Opéra National de Paris collection had been temporarily moved to the Sorbonne library while the part of the Opera building that normally housed it underwent renovation. Neither of them had been too terribly keen on spending any more time in the Palais Garnier than absolutely necessary—the awful vertigo of sliding out of time, of temporal dislocation, had been bad enough that neither Brightside nor Crepusculus had been able to face the possibility of a second experience just now. Having access to those records without having to set foot in the place was an unexpected stroke of luck.

Getting into the university had been remarkably easy: Crepusculus supposed they resembled a professor and a postdoc closely enough that nobody cared very much what they were up to, and in fact they had found quite a lot of information about the history of the building and the somewhat complicated process of its construction. Charles Garnier's single-minded purpose had felt more than slightly suspect to both of them, and they had spent the entire afternoon and evening buried in primary sources. It really did seem as if something thoroughly out-of-the-ordinary had been built into the structure from the very beginning; a significant proportion of the ironwork girders that supported it had been specially made to order, using a specific alloy, and the long list of stones that had been chosen for the interior decoration included a noticeable number of minerals that held specific occult meaning. The kind of crystal-healing enthusiast who spelled magic with a *k* would have a field day with the masonry manifest.

On a three-dimensional map of reality, Crepusculus thought, the Opera would be analogous to a heavy weight on the rubber sheet of space-time—and Hell should have *known* that, honestly, how had they just glossed over it, why hadn't there been a more intense monitoring presence? Crepusculus had been to other major loci of mirabilic significance from time to time—Stonehenge, Hagia Sophia, Cluny, however many else—and there had been at least two surface operatives per site detailed to keep an eye on things, and you'd better believe the esso traces were kept up to date. Something else was wrong here, profoundly wrong: something other than the problem of the reality incursions themselves.

It was only because they'd been asked to leave so that the library could close that Crepusculus and Brightside had stopped working—and Crepusculus had surfaced from his own concentration to find that his partner should have given up hours ago. It was easy to tell when Brightside had one of his bad headaches—there was a particular shade of greenish-grey that crept into his complexion, and he went very quiet. Crepusculus didn't blame him: the effects of that multiple timeslip had been pretty damn horrible, and he hadn't precisely been feeling his very best and brightest, either, truth be told.

Now he sighed, looking down at the tourists trundling along the Rue de Rivoli. He and Brightside hadn't contacted Irazek with the information they had found, partly because when they got back to the room, all either of them wanted to do was collapse, and partly because they didn't have a hell of a lot of confidence in the demon's ability to *use* that information. Today, he thought, they'd probably have to go over there, and they could also have a go at talking to the ghosts tonight if that still seemed worth the bother.

Tap-tap, discreet, on the door behind him. Crepusculus turned from the balcony and went to let the waiter in. He intended to let Brightside sleep as long as he could, but, well. Fresh croissants were fresh croissants, after all.

(He could remember so many other strange mornings, over the centuries. Saigon at dawn, the air already flannel-thick and drowning-hot, how *green* everything had been, how green and how lush, and the blank helpless awareness of just how *many* souls there were to escort home. A field in Guyana, patchwork-bright with a carpet of bodies lying facedown amid the rising song of flies, like a bow drawn across strings; blue and red and white and pink and yellow and green, clothes tight over swelling bodies; a horrible cacophony of voices no ears could hear but theirs, hundreds of people, all frightened, all wanting to go *home*. Tuol Sleng, unspeakable: that one they could not possibly hope to remedy, not all the way, pieces of people's souls irrevocably soaked into checkered linoleum, bonded, *welded* to this world due to the means by which they'd left it. Tuam Care Home, in Ireland, and Smyllum in Scotland, so many others, mass graves of babies and children, orphans left in care and killed instead. And back, back, back through the centuries, over and over, the same story—but this one was different, wasn't it, this one was not man's inhumanity to man but something much larger, much more frightening, the underlying machinery of reality itself...)

Stop it, Crepusculus told himself, closing his eyes. *Stop it: you're here to help, that's it, that's all that you can do.*

"At least I have the grace to have my horrors somewhere *other* than the breakfast table," said a voice, and he blinked, looking up. Brightside was leaning in the doorway, his own hotel robe neat and white and somehow vaguely monastic. He smiled, and as always it lit up his face, transformed him briefly. Crepusculus had to smile back, the memories receding.

"I was going to let you sleep," he said.

"You didn't take into account how good fresh coffee smells," said Brightside, coming forward into the sitting room. He looked better than he had the night before, still somewhat worn but entirely back on his game. "We'll—do what we can, Dammerung. Whatever that might be. Tonight when it gets dark, we'll go over to the cemetery, like we said we would, and have a chat with whatever happens to walk there in the night. Today we can try to get a better idea of what's been going on with that wretched building. We'll do what we can to help this situation, and the rest isn't up to us."

"I hate it when you're right," Crepusculus told him.

"I know. Pass the croissants, there's a good eternal, hmm?"

Grisaille stared up at the ceiling of his bedchamber, the darkness relieved only by the faint red light of his eyes; he didn't need the lamps lit to see by. He knew it was getting on for midday in the world above, but sleep did not seem to be a thing that was happening to him.

After returning the doctor to her cell—and hadn't that just been *awkward*, really—Grisaille had taken the time to wash very thoroughly and change into something that wasn't liberally spattered with the evidence of Lilith's indisposition; but he still felt soiled.

The stain is on the inside, he thought, *where no soap can reach it, and . . . good lord I must be in bad shape; I'm thinking in the worst kind of clichés.*

He got like this sometimes. Once he'd heard a miner describe what they called attacks of *the weight*: an occasional sudden and visceral awareness of the sheer mass of stone over their head, the heaviness of all that rock pressing down on them, the weight of it driving them into something like a panic attack. You got it a lot when you were new to the job, the miner had told him. Experienced miners, old hands, rarely felt *the weight*—but it was always there. For Grisaille, the thing that occasionally threatened to squash him flat was not physical weight but *memory*, two hundred years of it stacked up and teetering unsteadily, a precarious balance.

He had never found a method for forgetting things that really worked. Getting blind drunk, or sufficiently fucked up on some other substance to induce brief periods of amnesia, yes, sure, but he couldn't spend his entire unlife in a state of profound inebriation; there wasn't enough vodka in the *world*. The problem was that he had done things—or *not* done things—and that he remembered doing or not doing those things, and most of the time he was able to file those memories away in *not now* space but occasionally—like right now—the file storage overflowed.

Victor, and the thing in the snow, with its wet yellow eyes, misbegotten and tragic; he could have stopped that, perhaps, or at least done something to try to prevent it. Bitter cold and that sharp acid smell of snow over the lower, deeper reek of decay: he remembered that.

And fleeing west, after that dreadful little episode; pawning everything he could to buy passage to America, as far away from his old life as he could go. And, one night in New York, walking down the wrong alley. The one that had a vampire at the end of it.

That had been something he didn't want to remember in any detail, but it was still quite clear in his mind—the pain of it, the frantic confusion after the change, the adjustment period while he got used to his new abilities and limitations. For the first time since Victor, however, he'd found himself among—well, *friends* was a bit much, but friendly new acquaintances, who had helped him understand what he'd become, and that had made things easier to bear.

Working his way across the country, as time passed. Leaving a trail of unexplained cases of anemia that could probably have been followed without too much difficulty, if anyone had been trying. Finding himself eventually in Seattle, and staying there for long enough that people began to comment on his apparent lack of aging. He'd liked the Pacific Northwest. It was very much not like Ingolstadt, and he *did* have friends, some of whom were human; and one of them even came with Grisaille when eventually he ran out of explanations and had to conveniently disappear.

They left the States for England on the request of Grisaille's companion, who was of the British persuasion. Crossing the continent back to New York had been all right, but oh, gods and monsters, did he *not want* to remember the eight days of unending misery that followed embarking the ship for Southampton; he hadn't realized that one of the side effects of the change was a tendency to crippling seasickness. He was sure he'd come close to turning all the way inside out.

It's in the legends, his friend had told him, one interminable afternoon in their cabin, looking excited at having Worked Something Out. *They—you—can't cross running water. I don't really think the ocean is* running *water, but—*

Grisaille's reply had not been verbal. Now, lying on his back, he rested an arm over his eyes and wished the visceral memory of that experience and the much more recent Lilith episode did not match up quite so well with one another.

At least dealing with Lilith he'd been assisting someone who knew what they were doing, rather than having to rely on his own limited and long-ago training to handle the situation. Grisaille had never wanted to be the one at the very top, the master of all and maker of decisions; he was one of Nature's seconds-in-command, at his happiest when following the directions of a person he could actually trust, and . . . it had been a long time, hadn't it, since he had been happy.

It was stupid, but he *liked* the doctor—possibly because competence in any field was always nice to observe, and possibly because she was easy to talk to.

And she'd watched *The Prisoner*. There was that to consider.

He let himself imagine what it might be like to sit outside her cell and have a conversation, like people, and knew that any such encounter would end his tenuous ability to ignore the bars of the cell, and that would mean he'd simply have to let her out, and *that* would mean . . .

No, he thought, arm still pressed over his closed eyes. *Not that.*

Greta was getting used to waking without any idea of how much time had passed since the last time she'd paid attention. It had stopped being disturbing; all she had to go on was the physiological level of her own hunger, and that was deranged by things like being taken to a vampire dinner party and then being woken up some unknowable length of time later to deal with an OD-in-progress.

After Grisaille had taken her back to the cell, she'd tried very hard not to wonder if she could still somehow convince him to let her go; had gone over her own memory of the past few hours and tried to find any chink, any weakness that she could possibly lever into an advantage—and, still trying, had fallen into a restless sleep. At some point in the following hours, the tricherpetons had found her again, and Greta woke with her head pillowed on the warm, moving ribs of something soft and very much alive.

They were all around her. Warm bodies, soft and determined, nudged into the small of her back; others lay over her legs, her feet, lending her their heat. She drifted off again, something close to comfortable for the first time in days; when she woke properly, only two of them were left, mewing and crawling into her lap when she sat up, trying to nurse on her fingers.

They're very new, she thought, petting the earless silky heads with a fingertip. *So new. Like the wellmonsters. Someone must have been summoning them—or breeding them.*

Why, though? What on earth would a bunch of urban Goth vampires want with hairmonsters? She hadn't really thought Corvin would be into the monster-breeding hobby. That was more the kind of thing that old-money aristocrats went in for, people with nicknames like Muffy who owned country houses—

The mental image of Sir Francis Varney sitting in the library at Dark Heart House with a couple of thoroughbred tricherpetons lying at his feet occurred suddenly and vividly to Greta. *That* was where these creatures belonged, sprawled elegantly on the hearthrug, or trotting along behind Varney as he walked in the house's rolling parkland. Not down here in the caves underneath Paris.

The ones in her lap gave her fingers a last lick before stretching enormously and making their way between the bars of the cell, padding silently on the rock floor. She watched them go, not without a certain regret: it had been pleasant to hold something soft and warm and friendly.

Someone had brought her another pastry and coffee while she slept. She got up, crumpled taffeta ballgown swishing around her feet, and snagged the cup and bag sitting outside the cell: both stone cold now. It didn't matter. She settled down to eat hungrily enough that she managed to get a bite of greaseproof paper along with the croissant: calories, gorgeous much-needed calories, and she could feel her blood sugar rising back up to something bearable.

After she'd eaten, she balled up the wrappers and put them neatly into the empty coffee cup, still sitting barefoot beside the bars in her horrible ballgown. She'd taken off the matching red Louboutin stiletto sandals Grisaille had pressed on her the night before: no reason to wear them in here, and if she had to run, if she'd ever have the *chance* to run, barefoot was better than four-inch heels. At some point while she slept, the hairmonsters had found the Louboutins, and one of them had been gnawed fairly thoroughly, which afforded Greta a measure of mean satisfaction.

The warm hardness of the whistle pressed against her ribs, and she took it out, rolling the silver cylinder on her palm. *You know how to whistle, don't you,* she thought again, staring at the tarnished silver of the object so recently freed from its imprisonment behind the wall.

It looked...perfectly ordinary. It held around it no dark and ominous impressions; it felt just like plain sterling silver in her hand, warmed to her blood-heat from its long sojourn inside her bodice. It could have been simply a whistle, a thing to make noise with, and nothing more.

She knew better. QUIS EST ISTE QUI VENIT, the inscription read: *Who is this who is coming?* Or—not who, but *what.* There was a reason it had been walled up in a niche for God only knew how long: these things could be dangerous. There were cases in the literature of people who had been literally frightened into heart attacks by an unintentionally summoned whistler. The old cliché of the ghost wearing a sheet and gibbering had some basis in reality.

I have to get out of here, she thought, feeling her heartbeat in her temples, the roots of her teeth. *No matter what, I have to get out of here, I'm not spending any more time in this cell waiting for Corvin to get bored and rip my head off.*

Greta still didn't know *why* he'd had her captured. Emily had said something about Ruthven, *that guy Corvin's obsessed with,* but the terms of that obsession were still unclear. Presumably they knew each other, or knew *of* each other, and she couldn't imagine Ruthven looking with kindness on the kind of antics Corvin displayed—but that didn't tell Greta enough

214

about Corvin's intentions toward her. Whether she was of more use to him alive or dead.

I'm not sticking around to find out.

Something touched her hand, and she jumped, looking down. Greta hadn't realized that the smallest of the well-monsters was still there; it had been sitting in the corner and resembling a small grey stone, but now it had come over to her and determinedly began to climb up her arm with cold little hands and feet. It tickled; she held as still as she could while it made its slow ascent and attached itself very firmly to her bare shoulder.

I'm going to have to take it with me, she thought, stroking the wellmonster, as the tiny grey hands clung to her neck. *It'll slow me down, but it can't be helped.*

She padded to the cell bars, leaned out, tried to see down the corridor.

What the hell time was it? Enough time had passed since the coffee and pastry had been left outside the cell that both had been completely cold when she had woken—but the croissant was still soft and flaky in the middle, not yet stale. That meant, she was almost sure, that it was far enough past daybreak—late afternoon, in the other world, maybe early evening—that most of the nocturnal vampires must be asleep, especially after their debauch; but that they wouldn't neces-sarily *stay* asleep for all that much longer. It had to be now. If she was going to do this, it had to be now.

Okay, she thought. Still in her somewhat-befouled red taf-feta ballgown, with the tiny monster attached to her shoulder like the world's least elegant accessory, Greta stood in the middle of her cell and closed her fingers around the whistle lying on her palm. She was about to lift the whistle to her lips when she thought, *You idiot, it has to manifest* in *something, and having it inhabiting your skirts while you are also still inside them is not going to be one of the world's greatest experiences.*

Also, fuck this dress.

She put the whistle back into her bodice and—with a sense of enjoyment that was the first positive emotion she'd felt in days—grabbed two handfuls of the vast rustling skirt and pulled. The fabric ripped with a satisfying noise.

She tore most of the overskirt off, leaving herself enough of the underlayers to maintain at least a little decency, and spread the panel of fabric on the floor: that would have to do.

Now, she thought again. *It has to be now.*

Greta drew a deep breath, deep enough that the boning of her bodice creaked, put the warm silver to her lips, and blew: a long, strangely sweet note that seemed to echo much longer than it should have.

There was nothing for a minute—three—five, and then a soft gust of wind blew itself into her cell: a wind out of nowhere, which rippled the taffeta panel on the floor and then died away.

And the fabric moved. Humped up, as if something underneath it was growing. The surface of the taffeta wrinkled up and clung to a developing shape as it rose: a head, two arms, hanging in the air. It held still for a long moment, only the blind head turning this way and that as if to work out where it was—or where *Greta* was—and gave the impression of listening very intently for the slightest sound.

She'd never actually seen a whistler manifest before.

She'd read about it, of course, but written accounts hadn't quite conveyed the intense and visceral horror it produced, like a physical blow, draining all the strength from her at once, her knees threatening to give out and spill her to the floor. It was with considerable difficulty that Greta managed to make herself speak out loud, a single word: "Hello."

Instantly the thing's head turned to her, and then it was *right there*, a face made out of wrinkled fabric thrust close to her own, and she was not going to scream, she was *not going to scream*, she was going to shut her eyes tight to block out that awful crumpled face and breathe like a sensible person—

The little monster clinging to her neck *glupped* unhappily, and with that small noise, Greta's horror snapped, draining away all at once. She had summoned this thing; she knew how they worked. She could do this.

She looked the creature straight in the eyes it didn't have and said, "Thank you for coming. I need your help."

This obviously was not what it had had in mind. It tilted its head a little, the rudimentary expression shifting from one of leering menace to one of puzzlement. Her confidence was flooding back now, a warm tide. "I'll make you a deal," she told it. "You help me get out of here, and when I'm free, I'll take your whistle and put it anywhere you want to haunt."

Egredior sibilus wasn't among the brighter of the object-linked apparitions. It seemed to take a while to consider her proposal, during which time Greta stroked the wellmonster's flat little head with a fingertip. *It's too dry*, she thought, *poor thing, nobody's actually caring for them down here, they need proper moisture to keep their skin in good condition. When I get out, I'm going to...*

Going to what? she wondered. *Come back down here again armed with a bunch of stakes to dispatch the vampires, rescue this irresponsibly summoned menagerie, and incidentally try to get that one kid out of here?*

Why not?

At which point the thing hanging in the air in front of her gave a decisive nod, and reached out one of its arms toward her face.

Greta stayed quite still while the crumpled fabric ghosted over her skin, a light touch that sent goosebumps flaring all down her arms and legs. There was an unexpected sense of *wonder* in that touch, as if it had never before actually had a chance to investigate a human like this, without all the terror and screaming and carrying-on. She wondered how long its whistle had spent walled up inside that niche, and who had put it there—and how.

It took a minute or two before the whistler was satisfied. When it took its arm away, there was a subtle difference in the way it held itself in the air: a straightening of its rudimentary shoulders, a kind of readiness for action.

"I can't reach the key on the other side of the door," Greta said, tucking the whistle back inside her bodice. "They've left it in the lock but I can't reach it. I need you to slip out there and turn it for me. Can you do that?"

She wasn't actually sure it could: this was a small whistler, there wasn't much of her skirt for it to manifest in, and the key would require strength to turn. Nonetheless it turned and swooped through the bars as easily as a piece of paper blown on the breeze. There was a faint sound as it took hold of the key, and then a grinding of metal on metal. It took so long that Greta had begun to feel the edges of despair rising in her throat when all at once the key turned. The lock's tumblers fell into place with a clank so loud she thought it must have alerted the vampires—she held her breath, heart hammering, listening for the distant sound of footsteps—

Nothing. Just silence, and her blood roaring in her ears.

But the lock was open. She closed her hands around the bars, very aware of the chill of the metal, the prickle of rust-flakes against her palms; pushed, hard and then harder. Reluctantly the door swung on its hinges, silent and well-oiled, and Greta was *out*.

The whistler, in its taffeta drapery, was hovering in the corridor with a definite air of satisfaction in a job well done. "Thank you," she told it. "Thank you so much, you did wonderfully—and now I think I know which way is out."

On her various excursions to different parts of Corvin's lair, she'd built up a pretty decent mental map of where the tunnels ran, and she had definitely seen one that went off in the opposite direction from the main complex—one that she might have overlooked but for the marks in the dust on the floor, marks as if something heavy had been towed along without much regard for its comfort, accompanied here and there by drops of dried-up blood. *That's the way they take the bodies when they're done with them*, she had thought, fixing it in her mind as Grisaille hurried her along. *Taking out the trash, like civilized creatures.*

She looked back for the last time at the rectangular rock-cut room she'd grown to know so terribly well over the past few days—every inch of it familiar—relatively *safe*, compared to whatever might be waiting for her outside. It was surprisingly difficult to turn away from that familiar known environment; she had to steel herself, taking a deep breath.

Go, she thought, and set off down the corridor at a trot, her bare feet making no sound on the tunnel's floor.

The most dangerous phases of any cycle are not the extremes, but the point halfway through the cycle: where things are balanced precisely between those two extremes, where matters could tip either way with equal ease. The edges are sharpest, right there where the balance-point lies, and the vast potential energy of either extreme hangs waiting.

This is why magic done at dawn and twilight is easier, and more dangerous, than at other times—and why the half-moon, neither crescent nor full, holds the most power of any phase. Crepusculus and Brightside had arrived at Père Lachaise cemetery under a rising half-moon, in that strange uncanny twilight when the edges of everything seem indistinct, and both of them could feel that balanced potential as the moon rose in the sky.

They'd spent the day back in the library, and while they had discovered more information about the Opera's potential significance as a locus of mirabilic force, they had found few answers as to why, or what was going on. Now, under cover of darkness, they were fulfilling Irazek's request of the previous day, whether or not he might be able to do much with the information.

Ask them if they've seen—oh, necromancers, people grubbing around for graveyard dirt, Irazek had said. Now, at least, they had some more specific questions to pose of the cemetery's inhabitants, other than *have you seen anything strange lately.*

Not for the first time Brightside wondered about the process whereby Hell trained and tested their potential surface operator candidates, and what would possess a demon to want this particular job, to want to live on Earth—in Irazek's case, apparently, it was the opportunity to teach himself the art of *pâtisserie,* which Brightside appreciated for its intrinsic merit but considered somewhat divergent from the main job description, i.e., *watching the bloody monitors.* At least he had seemed to be fairly focused on the patterns they had discovered in the essograph traces, even if he should by rights have noticed them before. Nor did it make much sense to Brightside that one single solitary operative had been assigned to Paris, with something as complex as the Palais Garnier to keep an eye on. The problems here went deeper than Irazek, but he was all they had: neither Brightside nor Dammerung had the ability to contact Hell and say *what are you doing*, exactly. They had to make do with Irazek.

Maybe he'd even know what to do with the information they'd found in the library. What would be *ideal*, of course, was if Irazek could be convinced to give Hell a ring and ask for backup from somebody who *did* know what they were doing, but that kind of admission of incompetence probably didn't look too shiny on one's permanent record.

"Hey," said Crepusculus beside him. They were walking along one of the cemetery's narrow little lanes; it was laid out like a miniature city of the dead, cobbled streets flanked with neat little mausolea like tiny houses, some decorated with statues, some starkly plain. In the moon's half-light everything was touched with silver. "Chopin's in here, isn't he?"

"And Jim Morrison," Brightside said. "And Oscar Wilde. Édith Piaf. Maria Callas. Loads of famous people."

"Mm. Look," said Crepusculus, and pointed: in the distance, up a little hill, a pale greenish light had begun to glimmer between the tombs. "How much do you want to bet they're having a *soirée?*"

Brightside realized he could hear faint music, a ripple of liquid piano notes, almost too distant to make out. It sounded a little like wind chimes, and a little like the Étude no. 3, and along with it he thought he could hear singing—

A sound like the singing of the dead, he thought, without knowing quite why the phrase rose fully formed into his mind. They stopped walking, tilting their heads to listen, and the song came to an end in what sounded like distant laughter.

The ghosts were having a party. It was just about absurd enough to fit into the strangeness of the last several days; why *shouldn't* the dead be carousing in the early-morning hours in Paris's most famous necropolis?

Crepusculus looked up at him. "They sound like they're having a good time," he said. "Nice to know that *somebody* is."

"You want to crash it, don't you?"

"I totally want to crash it," said Crepusculus, grinning. It was the grin that defined him, bright and cheerful and irrepressible, and Brightside felt a wave of fondness for the simple familiarity. Everything else might be going off the rails, but Crepusculus Dammerung's enthusiasm endured.

"Very well," said Brightside, "let's go and say hello."

The cold greenish light grew as they climbed up the hill, but the owners of the voices had chosen a kind of square surrounded by high-walled tombs for their get-together, and it wasn't until they were almost upon them that Crepusculus and Brightside saw who was doing the talking.

They'd...manifested *furniture*. There was a translucent piano, its lid open, all its strings visible in pale green light; there was a vast curvy Second Empire chaise longue and several chairs, and what looked to Brightside like a spectral *narghile*, a tall water-pipe with several hoses, standing in the center of the space.

The ghosts themselves were of slightly different colors, some paler shading to white, some greenish, some almost blue, but all of them translucent—their features recognizable, finely drawn, their eyes dark hollows surrounding points of cold light. Brightside had seen innumerable ghosts on his journeys through time and space, and these were absolutely classic.

One of them, a man whose dark hair was outlined by faint pale flames—that was a good effect, Brightside thought, nicely conceived—sat at the half-visible piano; he had stopped playing when the psychopomps appeared, and was now glaring at them instead. On the chaise longue another ghost, this one holding a lily and wearing an embroidered dressing gown made out of dim white light, looked up. Several other men and women, wearing clothes from a variety of centuries, followed suit.

"Hi," said Crepusculus with a little wave. "You, uh. Having a good time?"

"Who is it?" said one of the women.

"It's the *living*," said the man at the piano, the way one might say "the taxman."

"They're not living, darling," the occupant of the chaise longue corrected in a drawl, "they're *eternals*, and they're here to meddle. Aren't you?"

Crepusculus glanced up at Brightside, who sighed. "We're here to ask you a few questions about the Opera," he said, "and determine if any of you happened to have noticed anything going on recently that's magic-related."

There was general derisive laughter. "The Opera?" said another ghost, a shirtless young man with long wavy hair, smoking a faintly green-glowing translucent joint. "I'd stay away from that place, man. It's *haunted*."

A striking woman with dark hair nodded, trying not to

laugh. "There's a phantom in residence. All the singers know about it; the managers just pretend otherwise."

Crepusculus folded his arms. "Anyone know why it apparently got built with all kinds of arcane symbolism hidden in the blueprints, and half the materials chosen for occult significance? Was the architect trying to bring about the Second Coming, or some magical transformation, or what?"

"Who knows how architects think?" said the shirtless man, and blew a glowing smoke ring. "There something specific you had in mind?"

"What about the magic thing?" Crepusculus wanted to know. "Who's been doing magic, and has that got anything to do with the Opera?"

"*Magic*, he says," drawled the chaise longue's occupant. "Magic. Do you mean like the stupid little tart digging up graves by moonlight? We know about all that, don't we, Freddie my love."

"Oscar, you said you wouldn't call me that in front of *people*," said the man at the piano, and pushed back his dramatic hair.

"What tart?" Crepusculus asked, redirecting his attention with some effort.

"The one with the tits and the teeth, dear boy." He gave an extraordinarily expressive little gesture, indicating that the lady had been well endowed with tracts of land. "Nasty sharp pointy teeth and a voice like a whining kettle. Smelled like a downmarket whorehouse. Whoever she belongs to, I devoutly wish him joy of her."

"A vampire," Brightside said, unwillingly distracted from the question of the Opera. "A vampire's been digging up graveyard earth?"

"Mm. Bearing it off rejoicing, to be used in eldritch ritual and unholy rite, I shouldn't wonder. Possibly even *in* the opera house, although that place is a bit classy for the likes of her, bizarre though it may seem."

"When was this?" Brightside demanded.

"Oh, she comes back regularly to top up. Must be going through the stuff at quite a rate. Up to no good, just you mark my words."

Crepusculus and Brightside looked at one another. "That would explain the incursions Irazek mentioned," said Crepusculus. "Repeated summoning. Even if each individual incident was minor, doing it over and over again *could* set up a standing wave, couldn't it?"

"And weaken that already-thin spot on the plane," Brightside agreed. "That and the mirabilic weight of the Opera together might be enough to do some serious damage."

"Splendid," said the Second Empire chaise longue's occupant, waving his lily at them. "Do carry on."

"Look, this is *serious*. What's happening could quite possibly rip reality apart," Brightside snapped at him, hoping he was exaggerating. "It's dangerous, it's stupid, and it has to be stopped before anything *else* goes wrong, do you understand?"

"Yeah, this isn't okay," said Crepusculus, as close to serious as he ever got. "Maybe not the best time to throw parties right now."

"Oh please," said the ghost of Oscar Wilde, lying back against the cushions of his chaise longue. "I hate the cheap severity of abstract ethics, I really do. Sod off, won't you, there's a nice couple of eternal beings, you're interfering with the expression of *art*."

Corvin woke with an ironclad certainty: he had had enough.

No sex, even mind-blowingly good sex, was worth dealing with a girlfriend—*consort*—who regularly got so fucked up on various substances that she woke you up screaming like a goddamn banshee and throwing a fit.

And he was going to have words with Grisaille about making unilateral decisions right in front of him—who did he think he was, taking over like that, and who said Corvin wanted the bloody human involved in this, it was—embarrassing, and now that the human *had* seen that little performance, Corvin was basically going to have to tear her throat out, because no way was he going to risk her telling anybody about it.

And the human had given him, Corvin, *orders*, expected him to *do what she said*, and to—ugh, he just couldn't handle this situation any longer; it was more than he could be expected to put up with. He'd been far more patient with Lilith and her habits than she deserved, and it was long past time to get rid of her.

Probably time to get rid of Grisaille, too. He didn't like the way his lieutenant had been acting recently, even before all this started. Culling both Lilith and Grisaille would throw a healthy dose of fear into the rest of his people—his *children*,

Corvin thought, his *subjects*. The new little vampire would do nicely in Lilith's place, at least for now.

Still in his gorgeous, embroidered red silk pajamas, his raven hair slipping over his shoulders in a waterfall of midnight-black, Corvin stalked through the passageways of his lair. Those few of his subjects who were awake this early in the evening flattened themselves against the walls as he went by, fear bright and vivid in their eyes. When Corvin was angry, everybody knew it, and the ones who were bright enough to stay out of his way were the ones who tended to survive.

The opulence of his bedchamber was restored, but to Corvin's eyes, even the clean sheets were irretrievably sullied; he decided everything would have to be replaced, furniture and all.

Lilith lay sleeping in the high carved bed, propped on pillows, her face pale grey, bruised stains under her eyes. Her crystal-silver hair spread over the black silk of the bedclothes like lace. Her lips were bloodless, slightly parted in a rose-petal curve. He could see the darkness of her eyes through the delicate vein-traced eyelids; the lush sweep of her eyelashes looked too dark and heavy to be real. She breathed slowly, shallowly, a faint tide drawn in and out like waves on a far shore.

Corvin stood looking down at her for a long moment before he reached down to cup her face very gently between his hands; her lashes fluttered and parted, and she gazed up at him with huge, brilliant eyes—and smiled a little, hazy, half-asleep. Without the purple contacts they were silvery-pale.

He waited until the look in those eyes changed; waited

until he saw the truth begin to dawn, waited until she took a breath to say something; and then he tightened his hands and gave a sharp and vicious little twist.

There was a bitter snap, like a branch breaking under a weight of winter ice; and a moment later Corvin straightened up. One less little difficulty to take care of.

He had at least ninety-nine problems, but a particular bitch was no longer among them, and now he could turn his attention to the newest of his subjects. The girl—Sofiria, such a suitable name—needed breaking in properly. He'd been meaning to exercise his *droit de seigneur* in that direction for some time now; it was understood that Corvin could, and did, take anyone he wanted into his bed at any time he pleased, and that this honor was something only the fortunate and special received, but he hadn't gotten around to her yet. Something to look forward to.

He stood back from the bed. She looked better like this: death became her. Nonetheless it was untidy to leave bodies lying around, human *or* Kindred, and Corvin thought he had one last task to demand of Grisaille before the latter's enforced retirement from duty: clean up this mess.

It was his job to take care of small matters so Corvin didn't have to think about them, after all. Somebody else would have to take out the trash once he was gone, but for right now this was entirely Grisaille's problem.

Corvin smiled unpleasantly, and went to summon his domestic help.

CHAPTER 9

Varney woke with the disquieting sensation of having no idea where the hell he was. The last time that had happened, he'd been in Ruthven's spare bedroom with a square of white gauze taped over a hole in his shoulder, and things had rapidly gone downhill from there.

He sat up, and it all came back in a rush: Paris. The demon's flat in Paris. He was alone in the living room, stretched out on a rather boxy old-fashioned sofa; it, and the matching armchairs, were in a shade of avocado he himself would not have picked out, and the rug under the plastic coffee table was a deep-piled shag. It looked very much like a set for a 1970s period piece.

Demons were *weird*, Varney thought. The only other one he had ever encountered, Fastitocalon, went around dressed rather like Edward R. Murrow, pinstriped suits and perfectly-parted 1950s hair and all. On the whole, Varney preferred the latter aesthetic to Irazek's, even if he didn't understand the motivation.

He had no idea what time it was; the windowpanes were black mirrors in the light cast by a floor lamp. Nighttime, but *which* night, or which time of night, Varney wasn't sure.

He could remember now coming back to Irazek's with Ruthven after that strange little interview with the vampire ladies, quite late, and the exhaustion hitting him like a wave. Ordinarily he could go much longer without sleeping, but in the recent past he'd had to thrall several people very hard for quite some time, which always took a lot out of him—and the sheer force of worry in itself was a source of fatigue. Irazek had offered him the sofa and Varney hadn't tried to protest that it was unnecessary.

Presumably the others were somewhere close by: he could hear faint voices. Varney swung his legs off the sofa and stood up, stiff and aching but at least less miserably tired, and went to see what was happening.

They were in the kitchen, sitting at the table together, and looked up as he came in. The clock on the wall read nearly eleven; he must have slept all day and well into the night. *No wonder my back hurts*, he thought, and then, *Has anyone else gotten any rest?* Ruthven was more than a little heavy-eyed himself, and St. Germain looked more rumpled than usual.

"*There* you are," said Ruthven. "We were beginning to wonder if you'd slipped into hibernation by mistake. Have some wine."

He pushed the bottle across the table. Without blood, red wine was the best Irazek could do for them—better than nothing, it offered vampires at least a little energy. Varney sat down, trying not to wince, and took a long swig; somewhere along the line, the nicety of his manners seemed to have lost its edge. "What's going on?" he asked.

"Irazek is telling us about the essographs," said St. Germain. "Which are not even slightly reassuring."

Irazek went faintly pink for a moment, looking apologetic. Spread on the table in front of the demon were three wide strips of graph-ruled paper with a red line traced down the middle of them, and a notebook full of calculations lay open at his elbow.

"I'd forgotten all about the essograph at the Opera," he said, tapping one of the strips with a forefinger. Varney looked closer; all three of them showed a spike in the red-ink trace at regular intervals, like the regular peaks of a heartbeat, but the intensity of the spikes and the length of the interval varied between the three readings. The one Irazek was talking about had the shortest interval of the three. "I *know* I ought to have remembered to check them all regularly, but it's tricky to get to most of them and there just didn't seem to be such a crucial need for multipoint monitoring of planar incursions. I'm going to get shouted at very loudly for a long time about this."

Varney thought he'd roundly deserve it. "What does this actually mean, though," he asked. "These readings. What conclusions can be drawn?"

"Well, it's—these are interference patterns, when the reading spikes," said Irazek. "Whenever something comes through from another plane, it sends out ripples in the background mirabilic field, and they move outward in all directions in a series of spherical wavefronts." Irazek turned the page in his notebook and drew what looked a little bit like a bull's-eye target. "If there's only one incursion, one point source, you don't get these interference patterns, but if there's two close to one another, the ripples intersect and you get constructive interference..." And he drew a second bull's-eye next to the first, tapping the pen on each place where the concentric sets of rings crossed one another. "Nodes and antinodes. Here and here and here. They show up on the esso as a series of regular spikes."

"Why do you need three of these recordings?" said Varney, who was feeling a little pleased with himself for following this at all.

"To determine the location of the incursion points. The frequency of the spikes on each reading show me how far away the location is from that individual essograph, and with three of them to triangulate with, I can work out where the point sources have to be." Irazek sighed and ran his hands through his hair. "I wish I had any idea what could be *causing* it."

Grisaille had slept—must have slept, because Corvin's voice woke him: that bellow he thought his leader probably considered a stentorian roar but which actually brought to mind a suburbanite shouting at the newspaper delivery boy for tossing a paper into the hedge.

He got up, still fully clothed, and went to go see what the matter was. Corvin hadn't changed out of his thrice-gorgeous crimson silk sleepwear, and the dyed-black hair falling over his shoulders, meant to evoke Antonio Banderas in the Anne Rice film, needed some work.

"Fuck, *there* you are," Corvin said, looking slightly up at him. "I have a job for you."

"Anything," said Grisaille, with no inflection whatsoever. Corvin narrowed his eyes.

"What's that supposed to mean?"

"Anything you command," he said. "What's on your mind?"

"Come with me." He spun on his heel and crossed the empty chamber to the door of his own bedroom, and Grisaille thought he knew—no, *knew* he knew, with a sinking certainty—what he would see when Corvin threw the door open wide.

Lilith lay in the bed as he and Helsing had last seen her, only her head was tilted at an unnatural angle and her eyes, open, were glazed dull. There was a faint expression of horror in those perfect features.

"Clean up this mess," said Corvin. "And then come to see me. I need to discuss certain matters with you in private."

For a moment, only a moment, Grisaille saw himself turning on his leader and closing his hands around Corvin's throat, the way Corvin had closed his own around Lilith's white neck: the dead did not bruise easily while they were still up and around and walking, but there were vivid dark handprints on that snow-white skin.

He saw a flicker of something in Corvin's eyes that might have been fear or apprehension, but only a flicker. "As you wish," he told him, and Corvin spat.

"Take the remains to—oh, where you always get rid of

them, it's not my job to consider disposition. Just get her out of here and then have someone remove the furniture; I'll want an all-new suite."

"As you wish," Grisaille repeated, and slipped past Corvin into the room. It had not been so many hours ago that he and the human had worked here together to try to preserve what of Lilith's existence might be worth the bother, and here was all that work, all those hours of disgusting, thankless, miserable work, wasted with one sharp twist.

She looked younger, dead. Younger and more vulnerable, without the sneer she habitually wore, without her makeup. He remembered Helsing gently unpeeling the fake lashes from her eyelids, loosened by tears; remembered washing this face himself, dabbing away the dark stains of mascara and eyeliner, the smear of lipstick.

"Well?" demanded Corvin from the doorway. "I gave you an order, Grisaille. Get on with it."

He looked up, and something about his face must have given Corvin pause, because the latter blinked hard and drew himself up to his full height and said, "Fucking move, all right?" before stalking away. For a moment Grisaille let himself enjoy that brief change in expression; then the flicker of pleasure drained away again. It didn't matter. He wasn't entirely sure if anything did.

Grisaille bent over the bed, slipped his arms under Lilith, gathered her up as he had done once already in the past night and day. She was heavy now with the total gracelessness of death, her head rolling at an unbecoming angle on her broken neck. He could vividly remember holding her through shuddering spasms of misery, helping Helsing keep her upright and stable, trying to give her some comfort or at least some ease with the power of his own thrall.

Looking down into the beautiful, stupid face, he made a decision, as he had also done once already. He could not carry this one to the breach in the tunnel wall communicating with the *cloaca* and let the sewer current take her where it would. Not like this. Not now.

Grisaille looked around the room for a last time, not at all sure he'd ever see it again, and then carried Lilith out into the tunnels, into the warrens of old mine-drifts under the city, the ancient honeycomb cut into the stone. He knew where he was going; it was a bit of a walk, but Lilith was not heavy, and he wanted rather badly to be far away from Corvin and his works.

In fact, it took him only about three-quarters of an hour before he came to the surface. It was extremely evident that someone had come and gone along this particular tunnel many times in the recent past, tracks of a woman's high-heeled shoes visible in the dirt and rubble of the floor, and he recognized this particular violet-and-vanilla perfume.

What were you up to? he thought, looking down at the woman in his arms. *What did you want with this particular place?*

Stepping out of the tunnel mouth into the small enclosed space of a mausoleum was briefly claustrophobic, but Grisaille leaned against the stone door slab and it opened easily on the blue-black quiet of a peaceful spring night. He stepped out into the air, Lilith cradled against his chest. All around him were acres of tiny houses of the dead: Paris's largest and most famous necropolis, the Père Lachaise cemetery, with its narrow cobbled streets, spreading trees, and prestigious inhabitants—and its crematorium, at the top of the hill, neo-Byzantine grandeur with two stark chimneys rising above the stonework.

One of the jobs Grisaille had done, in his long, long not-quite-life, was run the retorts in the small hours of the night at a crematorium in London. It was easy work, they paid reasonably well, didn't mind that he was largely nocturnal—it fit the hours—and nobody asked any inconvenient questions. That had been about ten years ago, but he thought he'd probably be able to work out how French crematory retorts were operated. And fire was better than—so much better than—the black sewer water. Fire was... *clean.*

No one else was around. He could do this, and *then* think about his next move. It wouldn't take long; there wasn't much of her. Two hours, maybe, and then—well. Then he'd have to make a few more decisions.

Grisaille loped easily up the cobbled street toward the white building, glimmering through the trees, and had absolutely no difficulty whatsoever in gaining entry without setting off alarms. By now he had a sixth, seventh, and eighth sense for where cameras were likely to be, and he shoved enough energy into *not being seen* that visible-light sensors couldn't pick him up; infrared, of course, would show him only as a very slightly increased patch of room temperature.

He was in luck. The company that had built the Père Lachaise retorts was one he knew.

Grisaille didn't bother with the cardboard container; he set Lilith's body down on the gurney exactly as it was, still clad in the nightgown he and Helsing had put her into not so long ago. He lit the burners, and—before he slid her into the firebrick-arched enclosure of the retort, silent except for the faint roar of almost colorless gas flame—bent to kiss her forehead, just once. She hadn't deserved this.

Most of them hadn't. Not all, but most.

He could remember, when he'd first woken to a subtly different consciousness after the change, mourning for the things he had suddenly lost. For a life left behind, a lifetime's worth of presence in the world, closed up and ended. He could remember weeping a little at the thought of everything lost and wasted, everything gone beyond his reach. He could even almost remember what it had been like to understand for the first time, truly understand, that there *was* no going back; that there was no *back* to go to.

That was a long time ago, he thought, closing his eyes. It did no good; he could still see much too clearly with his mind's eye.

One gets used to it. With practice.

He looked down again at Lilith's face for a long moment; and then sent her into the retort in a single smooth motion.

The door descended slowly enough that he could clearly see the faint blue burning jets splash into bright gold fire as they found her, as they began to feed.

Crepusculus was more subdued than Brightside had seen him in years as they turned to leave the ghosts' little soiree; subdued, and that was wrong, that was yet another indication that the world was spinning off its accustomed bearings, heading toward something unpleasant and yet not quite entirely understood. This morning he'd been remembering things Brightside hadn't thought about in decades.

"You all right?" said Brightside uselessly as they walked down the narrow cobbled street.

"Fine," said Crepusculus. He paused to light a cigarette, and then stiffened, staring back the way they'd come.

"What is it?" Brightside asked, already turning himself; he saw it at once, pale wisps of smoke where no smoke should be, rising from the stack of the cemetery's crematorium. Someone was burning bodies at an hour when no respectable person should even be present inside these gates.

Bodies, or something else.

He and Crepusculus looked at one another, and then the latter threw down his cigarette, stepped on it, and nodded back up the hill. Brightside didn't have to say a word; neither of them did. This was at least something easier to think about than the potential destabilization of the fabric of the universe.

It didn't take them long to climb the hill to the cremato-rium. The building was dark except for the faint pale smoke coming out of the right stack; of course, the retort chamber wouldn't have windows for the curious to peer through.

"We should go in," said Crepusculus, as if he wanted to be reassured.

"We should."

Together they concentrated briefly and proceeded to walk directly through the wall—it felt a little bit like passing through a dull cold waterfall—and found themselves in a thoroughly utilitarian chamber containing two large metal monoliths, each with a rectangular door stained black with soot, each sur-mounted by a massive exhaust chimney, each equipped with a control panel with a whole Christmas tree's worth of telltale lights. One of these was lit up; there was a roaring like a distant gale, heavy in the air, and a smell of burning matter.

And sitting beside the oven that was running: a vampire in a folding chair, bent over with his head in his hands, who took a good thirty seconds to react to their appearance.

"Who the hell are you?" he said in French—sounding, Brightside thought, less surprised than resigned, as if the night had already offered him sufficient surprises to render the sud-den appearance of two strangers relatively uninteresting.

"Could ask you the same question, sir," said Crepusculus. The ghosts had described vampires, or *a* vampire, actively excavating graveyard dirt, but by no means could the one sitting on the folding chair by the oven be described as voluptuous—or *female* of any description. He had died in

240

what looked like his early thirties, and the only thing even vaguely feminine about him was the length of the silvering hair falling over his shoulders. "You haven't by any chance been digging up people's graves and taking bits away with you?" Crepusculus continued.

"What?" said the vampire, and both of them could tell the irritated confusion was genuine. He had no idea what they were talking about. "No. I'm—who *are* you? What are you doing here?"

"Investigating," said Brightside. "Who's in the retort, and how exactly did they come to be in there?" He nodded at the oven still busily roaring away.

They watched as his face went greyish for a moment, the confused look hardening into a profoundly grim expression. "Her name was Samantha, but she went by Lilith," he said, "and she deserved a bit better than simply being dumped into the drains like all the rest of them. Who *are* you?"

"Brightside and Dammerung, remedial psychopomps," said Crepusculus. Brightside thought: *All the rest of whom?* "We've had a report of vampires, or a vampire, disturbing some graves on a regular basis. You wouldn't know anything about that, Mr...?"

"Grisaille," said the vampire. "Remedial *psychopomps*? You— what, go around tidying up after people who didn't get shuffled off to the afterlife properly the first time?"

Brightside raised an eyebrow, glancing over at his partner, who looked equally nonplussed. "Most people need a bit more explanation than that," he said. "Yes. And there's something going very badly wrong with the world, or at least this particular bit of it: something to do with that incredibly gaudy opera house, to go by what we've seen already, and it might involve grave-robbing by voluptuous lady vampires."

"I have no idea what you're talking about," said Grisaille, and looked back at the door of the crematory retort. "All I know is that I spent several hours quite recently helping to pull this one through a particularly nasty OD, which I can tell you was not the most joyous and pleasant of experiences—only to find that her charming boyfriend had subsequently snapped her neck and wasted all our hard work and time, and why I am telling you gentlemen this is beyond my comprehension—"

He broke off and pressed his hands to his face, and both of them watched as he forced himself back to something approaching calm. "His last instruction to me was 'clean up this mess,' and here I am cleaning it up, all nice and neat and environmentally conscious and aboveboard, like a good little lieutenant." The words dripped acid.

Brightside looked from him to Crepusculus and back again. "I see," he said after a long moment. "I'm—sorry for your loss."

"Oh, she's not my loss," he said. "Frankly I couldn't stand her; but—all that work, all that *effort*, and then he simply switched her off like a toy he'd had enough of, and I—don't think I can see myself going back for more of that. I really don't."

"Who's *he*?" Crepusculus said.

"Our great and fearless leader? Corvin. King of the fucking vampires."

"How many of you are there?"

"Sixteen—no, seventeen now with the kid. *Sixteen* without Lilith. Fifteen without me."

Crepusculus and Brightside exchanged another glance. "You know," said Brightside, "there's someone you should probably talk to about this. Someone who might be able to give you some advice about what to do next."

"Oh yeah?" said Grisaille with a sneer. "Vampire oracle of Paris, step right up and receive your fortune?"

"Not quite. His name is Irazek and he's a demon—and he should probably know about gangs of vampires running around the city. St. Germain's really the one to talk to, but he's been distracted recently; Irazek might be your best bet for reporting this. If you do mean to leave the group."

"I already have," said Grisaille bleakly. "I'm not going back. Fuck it. I might as well go tattle on the rest of them. Look— you're—if you're really psychopomps—I don't know if she has any kind of soul left, if there's much in there at all, but if there *is*, could you..."

He trailed off, scrubbing his hands over his face again, took a deep breath. "Could you maybe stay to make sure whatever's left of her gets to where it's going? She wasn't a prize specimen of humanity when she was alive and she was damned annoying as a vampire but—she deserves some peace, if she can get there."

Brightside nodded. "Yes," he said. "Yes, of course. We'll take her home, if there's anything to take."

"Thank you," said Grisaille, and stood up. He was taller than Brightside had thought, slender, dressed in grey and black. "I don't know what you're talking about, with grave-robbing, but it's not exactly out of character for Corvin's lot."

"Tell Irazek that, too," said Brightside. "He lives at 126 Rue du Temple, third floor. Give him this." He handed Grisaille a card, which the latter stared at for a moment before pocketing. "And—good luck."

"In my experience, there's no such thing," said the vampire, sighing. "You have to make your own luck. But...thanks for helping Lilith, if there's anything there to be helped."

They watched him stalk out of the room, and turned to one another. Brightside held out his hand, and Crepusculus took it, squeezing firmly.

"Time to go play in the fire," he said. "I think there *is* something in there, Gervase, a little bit of soul left: I can feel it, but it's very faint."

"Me too," said Brightside. "No time like the present, eh?"

Hand in hand, they stepped forward, and walked *into* the stainless steel facing of the oven; through the refractory firebrick, through the roaring of the gas jets, until they could close their arms around the wavering faint image of a woman's body invisible to human eyes; flickering and trembling, it was barely present at all until their arms closed around her.

—who are you—

A tiny thread of a voice, terrified and lost.

We're friends, said Crepusculus. *It's okay, Samantha. It's over now. It's time to come home.*

I have had enough of stumbling through underground passageways, thought Greta Helsing, *to last me any number of lifetimes, and yet here we are again: lost under Paris, lost in the dark.*

The tunnel leading away from Corvin's lair had undergone several twists and turns, leaving the electric light of the inhabited passageways behind, and it was only because the little turnip-sized wellmonster huddled against her neck had quite unexpectedly begun to glimmer palely with a cold unnatural light that she was able to find her way at all. *When I get out of this*, she told herself, eyes wide in the near-complete darkness, *I am so writing a paper on these creatures. I don't think I've ever heard of them bioluminescing, but I'm jolly glad they do.* Its eyes were two small pale lamps, brighter than the glowing skin around them.

But even by monsterlight, Greta could make out only a few feet in front of her, and she walked along with one hand trailing against the tunnel wall to keep her bearings, moving as fast as she dared. She had no idea how long it would take for the vampires to discover her absence, and she knew very well—and wished she didn't—how sensitive their sense of smell was: they'd have no problem tracking her—

She stumbled over a rougher patch in the floor and stopped to clutch at her foot, toes stinging in pain. Maybe she should have kept the stupid shoes Grisaille had made her wear. Four-inch spiked heels might at least have offered some protection from sharp objects underfoot, and if worse came to worst, she could have tried using one as a weapon.

The whistler had been following her a few feet behind her left shoulder, and now she felt the soft brush of fabric as it got close enough to touch. It was oddly comforting, despite the actual nature of the thing manifesting inside the fabric, a small affirmation: *You may be lost in the dark, but you're not lost in the dark alone.*

Limping a little, she got moving again. Soon the nature of the tunnel itself underwent a change: instead of a rough-walled quarry passage, it was lined with masonry, a thing built rather than simply dug out of the living rock. A breath of dank, chilly air from the darkness up ahead touched Greta's face, and she paused for a moment with her fingertips on the cold stone of the wall while another wave of dread washed through her: what was up ahead, what was she walking into, *whose lair might this be?*

Can't be much worse than what's behind me, she thought determinedly, and turned to face the hovering specter of the whistler. In the pale greenish light, the taffeta looked brown-purple, the color of dried blood. "Can you go on up ahead," she said, "and listen for danger?" She'd been about to say "see what you can see," but of course it couldn't: *E. sibilus* was completely blind, navigating only by hearing and touch.

This one touched her shoulder again, with that oddly gentle touch, as if it was still so curious about what kind of creature she might be—and then turned and floated away into the darkness of the passageway.

Greta, left alone with the small wellmonster, discovered that her hand was damp from leaning against the stone wall. She moved closer and saw in the dimness a faint reflection, a trickle of water making its way out from between two stones. Cupping her hand against the wall, she gathered a scant palmful of water and offered it to the monster—which promptly let go of her neck, finally, and hopped straight into the hollow of her hand with a splash.

"You really *are* thirsty, aren't you," she said, and held it close to the trickle running down the wall. If she hadn't been quite so desperately exhausted and strung out and terrified in general, she would probably have squeaked at the sheer adorability of watching a tiny monster giving itself a bath after lapping up quite a lot of water with a small grey leaflike tongue. As it was, she simply leaned against the wall and let her eyes close for a long moment or two, breathing. The metallic tang of exhaustion in the back of her throat was stronger now.

And suddenly she was *somewhere else*, the cold stone gone into a dizzying swirl of confusion, like being spun unexpectedly in some huge off-kilter machine—still dark, in the dark, somewhere in the dark and—

—enveloping her all at once, sinking into her, sharp and vivid emotion: *fear, raw fear, heart-pounding sickening fear and somewhere nearby music playing, titanic, vast, furious music, an organ giving voice to notes both glorious and terrible, feverish, scarlet*—

Something touched her face.

Greta jerked out of the—dream, that had to have been a

dream, there was no music and no fury here: only the hollow dripping of water onto stone, and the slowing of her own heart from its frantic speed.

The whistler tilted its head at her, with what looked like concern. Greta straightened up and returned the little creature in her hand to its perch on her shoulder, where it continued to wash itself not unlike a very small cat. "I'm all right," she said, scrubbing at her face, remembering too late that one hand was regrettably covered in wellmonster smell. "Is it safe up ahead?"

A nod, in the dimness, and then it reached out one of its arms to her. After a moment Greta held out her hand, and the taffeta wrapped itself around her fingers, feeling like a small hand inside a mitten. *I wonder what their physical form actually is,* she thought disjointedly, and then, as it tugged on her hand, she simply let herself be led.

The passageway twisted and turned. She had a horrible idea that they were doubling back on themselves, that this was all just a maze Corvin had had installed to toy with escaping prisoners—and then she thought: *No, that's too clever for him, too clever by half.* They were going *somewhere.* She only wished she knew where.

Greta had no idea how much time had passed when she began to smell the unmistakable high-sulfur reek of sewers, and for a nasty moment she was back in a church in London staring at the wreck of what had been a man, a creature that used the sewers under London as its highways and byways on its journeys around the metropolis. *I can't*, she thought, *I can't go into the sewer.* She made herself think of Jean Valjean, pacing through the *cloaca* with an unconscious idiot slung over his shoulder, but it didn't help.

The whistler tugged at her hand, and Greta kept walking, into a thicker and thicker stench. She was expecting at any moment to pass through some kind of archway into a round tunnel knee-deep in human waste, and tried not to think of her nice clean cell back in Corvin's lair, with all mod cons, even if she did have to be taken to and from them under guard—

—*blaring, deafening music, an attack on the ears and the mind, music written by a madman who had already tasted the heady brew of murder and now could not satisfy his thirst—red, scarlet, crimson notes, and around her, smooth glass walls in the blackness, smooth glass that met at a precise angle, that offered no purchase to her scrabbling fingers, and she could not reach the trapdoor that had dropped her into the monster's killing bottle, it was too far, and oh but when the music stopped, that was so much worse, that meant he was* there, *right outside, and who knew if he had heard her fall, if he knew she was there, if the tortures would start automatically—he had secret ways, he was the lover of trapdoors—*

This time Greta knew it wasn't a dream: she'd been wide awake when that one flashed over her, an incredibly vivid snatch of someone else's memory. She came back to herself finding the whistler squeezing her hand almost painfully tight—*okay, they* are *pretty strong,* she thought, *note to self*—and squeezed back, just as hard.

She wasn't hallucinating.

She hadn't ingested anything that could do that to her, and vampire thrall simply didn't cause hallucinations, either immediate or delayed.

It didn't *feel* like a hallucination, either: she knew what those were like, she'd had a couple of bad reactions to some medicine or other as a child, and she would have recognized the physical symptoms long before the point of seeing stuff that wasn't there. This was different. This felt like the patchy fading in and out of a radio station just on the edge of its range, static occasionally washing through the sound, interspersed with clear reception.

It's not me, she thought. *It's this place. I'm—moving through patches of something that isn't right.*

And it was so familiar. She couldn't remember where she'd seen—or heard—about any such thing, but it was sickeningly familiar all the same: mad music, trapped inside glass walls.

Greta had never been even slightly capable of metatemporal perception, or in fact any supernatural ability at all, as she'd told Ruthven in the hotel a thousand years ago: she was an entirely bog-standard ordinary human, and therefore the fact that she *was* perceiving this, while lucid and of relatively sound mind, meant something was badly wrong. Something very much larger than herself.

The whistler tugged at her hand again: *Come on.* Still a little dazed, she stumbled after it, and only noticed afterward that they'd passed a black opening in the tunnel to one side, following which the smell of human waste began immediately to decrease. They weren't going into the sewers, after all. They were going . . . somewhere else.

—the torture chamber, this is the torture chamber, he had showed her how it works, six-sided mirrored walls and the drums with images on them that reflect into eternity, the illusion of a forest in the Congo, the iron tree in one corner with its painted leaves and dangling Punjab lasso—

Greta shook her head as if she could somehow dislodge the flickering scraps of sound and vision, still trying to work out where the hell she'd seen or read about something like it before; she squeezed the whistler's unseen hand, and walked faster into the dark.

Twice more in the passageway she saw and felt things that were not there, but with varying levels of clarity: interspersed with the vivid images and awareness of her surroundings there was a kind of formless, visceral, atavistic terror. After the second time, there had been a pause, and she had begun to hope that maybe they were fading out, that she was passing beyond whatever sphere of influence was responsible for the effects, when the third hit like a physical blow.

—drowning, she was drowning in the dark, like a rat in a trap, the water swirling all around her, cold pressure against the crevices of her body, whirling in the rising tide like a piece of wreckage— the tree, the iron tree, under her reaching fingers—how much

space was there between the iron tree and the domed ceiling of the torture chamber?—the air rushing away as the black water rose— she cried out, Erik, Erik, I saved your life, you were doomed and I opened the gates of life to you, Erik, *but there was nothing in all the world but the gurgle and roar of water, nothing at all, but a faint echo of some unseen voice:* barrels, barrels, any barrels to sell?—*before the world closed like a fan in darkness—*

Hard stone, damp and cold, pressed into her knees and the palms of her hands. The dark around her had changed: it was no longer black water surrounding her, but air, and the faint glow of the monster still clinging to her shoulder was enough for her to see a little by. Her hair hung in her face, swaying as she panted.

"Jesus Christ," she said in a little strengthless voice. "Jesus Christ, I *remember* this."

She hadn't liked *Phantom of the Opera* at all, really, other than the lovingly detailed descriptions of the Palais Garnier and the bit at the end where the boring vicomte was suddenly plunged into an *adventure* with the Persian, the only interesting character other than the phantom himself. That part of the book she'd paid more attention to, and now she could remember reading about what she'd just experienced. It had felt real: the terror of drowning in the dark, in the monster's mirrored torture chamber, had felt as real as you like.

So why, she thought now, *why is that story suddenly happening to me?*

Maybe Leroux hadn't been making it up. Maybe the book *was* actually faithful, unlike the rest of classic horror lit.

Maybe there really *had* been a lover-of-trapdoors who called the Palais Garnier his home.

Wonder about it somewhere else, she told herself, and got to her feet. She didn't have time for this—the vampires might already have discovered she was missing; she couldn't hang around all night waiting to be found, story or no story.

The whistler, which had been hovering awkwardly a little way away, came back over to her. She was probably confusing the hell out of it with her behavior, poor thing. Greta reached out her hand and felt the firm grip of its narrow hand inside the taffeta. "Let's go," she said. "I'll try not to fall over again, I'm sorry about that."

The chill of the imagined water was still with her, and she shivered in the remains of the stupid ballgown as she hurried along. The passageway narrowed, growing damper: water dripped from the rock above her head and ran down the uneven stone of the walls. They had been descending for a little while, she thought, and was dimly aware that the water table under this part of the city was very high indeed, and then tried not to think about it. The whistler was leading her *somewhere*, and it was probably not directly to certain death.

When the passage dead-ended in neatly mortared masonry, much neater than the stone walls of the passageway, she blinked at it, and at the metal pressure door that had been set into the stone as if into some ship or submarine's interior. It was the kind of door that locked with a central crank wheel, ancient and corroded.

Greta closed her fingers around the wheel, and expected a

terrible rusty shriek when she gave it a turn—but the wheel spun smoothly, well greased, and the door swung open on a subtly different darkness.

She knew where she was now. With the light of the tiny creature sitting on her shoulder to guide her, with the hard little hand of wrinkled taffeta in hers, Greta stepped over the threshold of another kind of monster's home.

CHAPTER 10

The knock on the door startled St. Germain—startled all of them, in fact. Irazek broke off mid-sentence and looked up, blinking. They'd moved from the kitchen to the living room, but the discussion of interference points and their significance for the fabric of reality had continued.

"Who on earth is *that* this time of night?" Ruthven said. "Do you have a particularly busy social life?"

"Not even slightly," said the demon, getting up. "Nobody's rung the bell to be let in downstairs; it must be someone with access to the building—or maybe Mr. Brightside and Mr. Dammerung, but I would have thought they'd call. I do hope nothing's *happened* to them; it's been ages."

"Those can't possibly be real names," said Ruthven. St. Germain had noticed before that fatigue and worry tended to erode the vampire's usual shell of patience and understanding; he wasn't usually quite so sharply acerbic. " 'Mr. Brightside'? I—"

He broke off, looking past St. Germain at the door, and all the faint color drained out of his face, leaving him wax-white and *staring*. St. Germain turned to see a stranger standing in the doorway and was hit all at once with a wave of scent he recognized.

"*You* were the one I smelled at the Sorbonne," he said. "I knew it was a vampire, but not *which*—"

St. Germain broke off, only just in time to grab Ruthven by the arm before the latter could lunge out of his chair. He'd never seen him look quite so inhuman. "Edmund," he began. Ruthven ignored him.

"I know you," he snarled at the newcomer. "I saw you at the Opera. Before all this began. You *winked* at her. If you are behind this, I swear to all the gods I will *dismember you*— Alceste, let *go*—"

St. Germain had to exert considerable force to hang on to him. "Edmund," he said again, aware that Francis Varney had also gone dead-white. "Let's at least ask him a few questions."

He had been watching the strange vampire's face. Tall and slim, dark, his long hair in narrow locks, wearing an expression of slightly superior and cynical amusement—but just for a moment there had been both weariness and a drawing kind of misery in those red eyes. He hid it well, but nothing could lie to a werewolf's nose: whoever this was, he was not even slightly all right.

"It's a whole *party*," he said, drawling not just with his voice but his expression. St. Germain had heard that kind of drawl before; it was specifically designed to elicit a strong desire to hit the drawler. "Here's me being told to go and have a natter with a demon, and what do I find but a little *congregation*. So terribly sorry for interrupting the fun."

"Who are you?" said Varney, grinding out the words, keeping control of himself with visible effort.

"The name's Grisaille. And *you* are a vampyre and *you* are a werewolf and *you*, my dear, are Lord Ruthven, famed in song and story; *très* bona to varda your particular eek, and haven't I just got *such* a lot of things to tell you."

Behind him, Irazek looked apologetic. "Um," he said. "He's—I had to let him in—Dammerung and Brightside sent him to see me, something's going on—"

"Where's Greta?" Ruthven's voice cracked like a whip.

"Safe underground, as far as I know."

"*As far as you know*," repeated Varney. "That's not good enough."

"He wants her alive." The drawl had dropped almost completely, and St. Germain could see the effort with which he got it back again. "She's still useful, don't you know."

He'd clearly meant *useful* to be mocking, but it slid into vicious, and St. Germain thought the cutting edge of it was directed at Grisaille himself, sharp and acid. He wondered why.

"Who is *he*?" Ruthven demanded.

"His name is Neil Geoffrey Higgins, which is why he's calling himself 'Corvin.' He's originally from Sheffield. He's behind the series of bodies in the river drained of all their blood, and also the theft of several hundred thousand euros'

worth of wine and spirits from the cellars of various unsus-
pecting citizens into which he has caused tunnels to be dug.
He murders people when he gets bored with them, deco-
rates his lair with stolen bones, and dyes his hair black with
L'Oréal box color. Up until a couple of hours ago, I was his
second-in-command."

Grisaille's voice had been steadily losing the affected tone,
and underneath it, there was nothing but stark and exhausted
bitterness. When he'd finished reciting the list, he covered his
face with his hands and took a deep unsteady breath.

"Are you all right?" said Irazek after a moment.

"No," said Grisaille behind his hands, "although I hoped
you wouldn't notice."

"Sit down," St. Germain said firmly, and recognized the
flicker of *relief* in Grisaille's scent: gratitude for being told
what to do. Obedience.

He kept his hand wrapped around Ruthven's arm, in case
Ruthven was still feeling actively murderous, but the tense
dangerous energy had gone out of him; expressionlessly he
watched Grisaille sink into a chair as if a string holding him
up had just been cut, and St. Germain thought the immediate
danger of bloody violence was past.

"I think," said Varney, "you had better tell us everything,
quite rapidly." The iron control was still there in his voice, the
effort it was taking him to remain calm and collected.

Grisaille nodded, his eyes shut. "If I have to remember
everything," he said, "I'd like to remember doing something
right for a change."

Still that bitterness, and still the flicker of gratitude for being given an order to follow. *I was his second-in-command*, he'd said.

St. Germain wondered what that had been like. And then thought, as he got up and went to fetch a glass of Irazek's whiskey, that he didn't actually want to know.

Ruthven, too, had had recourse to Irazek's drinks trolley. In fact, all of them had: the story Grisaille told was the sort of thing that went much better with something to take the immediate edge off.

His arm hurt a little where St. Germain had grabbed him; he knew there would be brief red marks on his skin in the shape of the werewolf's fingers, and was glad now of St. Germain's quick reflexes. The shock of seeing the stranger from the Opera again—the one who'd winked at Greta, the one she'd pointed out—had blanked out half his higher brain functions, leaving only the uncivilized desire to rend and maim; and that sort of thing simply wasn't *done*.

Ruthven didn't go in for vicious murder, as a habit. And truth be told, as soon as Grisaille started telling his story, the flat blank hate had drained out of Ruthven's mind, to be replaced with a weary, familiar kind of misery. The world was, as several of his kind had taken pains to point out, a terrible old vale of tears in which unspeakable things occurred with depressing regularity.

And under that misery, of course, the need to *fix this situation*. And the guilt: he should have made sure of this particular vampire coven leader the last time they'd met, ages ago now, back in London. He could clearly recall the crunch of that face underneath his fist, the way Corvin's people had held him up by his arms, choking and sobbing through the blood that poured from his nose; could remember telling the lot of them to get the fuck out of his city and try to grow up, if they could manage it. He'd thought that had been the end.

The litany of things that Corvin had done since then—had bragged of doing—was more than enough to send red rage-mist clouding Ruthven's vision all over again, but he did his best to compartmentalize: he needed to hear what this person had to say.

"I've only been with his group for a couple of years," Gri-saille was saying now, sitting forward in the demon's period piece avocado-green armchair, forearms resting on his thighs, looking into the amber depths of his glass rather than meeting anybody's gaze. "He'd already had the hate-on for you, Lord Ruthven, long before I joined up. I think he's been thinking about it ever since that incident in London, and waiting for a chance to get revenge, and your friend Dr. Helsing sim-ply happened to be in the wrong place at the wrong time: he chanced to see her with you, wondered who she was, and told me to find out. And I found out, and—told him. And he had me snatch her as bait to capture you."

Another flare and fade of intense, furious anger; this time Ruthven was in control of it, and set down his glass with deliberate care before it shattered in his hand. He was feeling slightly sick.

Grisaille hurried on, still not meeting anyone's gaze: "Before that—he traveled. I know he's been to Russia, at least, and possibly to some of the other bits of Eastern Europe. Wouldn't put it past him to have gone looking for old Dracula's castle, in the hopes that he could set up his headquarters in such a storied site."

"He'd have a bloody difficult time of it," said Ruthven, without actually meaning to. "The Voivode doesn't take kindly to outside intrusion, no matter who's intruding, dead or alive. He and his lady wife keep themselves very much to themselves."

Grisaille looked up at him, the scarlet eyes dilated, huge black pupils eating up all but a thin ring of red. "He's real, too?"

"Oh yes," said Ruthven. "He's real. And actually I think he'd absolutely want to host your Corvin, if by 'host,' you mean 'throw into the oubliette and leave him there for a century or two.'"

"He's not *my* Corvin," Grisaille said, and rubbed at his face again. "I'm—look. Can we by any chance perhaps pretend that we've already *established* how bloody awful I feel about my part in the current situation, and move on to what the hell to do about it? Is that a thing we could do?"

Beside Ruthven, Varney stiffened slightly, and Ruthven knew his expressionless expression would have cracked a bit to let the menace through. "Perhaps. If you care to provide a single solitary reason for us to believe you're really here to be of use, tell us exactly how we are to get inside this person's lair," he said, enunciating with silken, deliberate clarity.

Ruthven thought again how much his voice balanced out the rest of him: Varney could have had any career he liked on radio or as an orator, and almost certainly as a professional singer. He lacked the easy unintentional style and grace of the classic dra-culine species—but that *voice* made up for so very much.

"The four of us ought to be enough to deal with whatever we find down there," said St. Germain, and Ruthven glanced over at him, a little glad to be distracted. "Fifteen vampires, most if not all of which will be asleep during daylight hours, of varying levels of competence, against *us*."

Grisaille blinked at him, and looked at Varney and Ruth-ven, his expression much too clear; Ruthven was sure he didn't know how transparent he looked. "You *want* me to come with you?"

"Of course we do," Ruthven said, sharp. "We need a guide. And you might prove useful."

He hadn't meant it as a barb, but the word *useful* made Grisaille flinch ever so slightly. "Yes," he said, "of course, I'll take you in the back way, most of them don't know about it—you'd trust me?"

"I don't think we've got a lot of choice right now," said Ruthven, and then deliberately reaching for his own memo-ries of Polari slang, "*ducky*."

That, an intentional jab, went home far harder than he'd intended. Grisaille flushed dark mahogany, instinctively jerk-ing back a little as if he'd been physically struck. "Yeah, all right," he muttered, sounding entirely like a tired and miser-able person not trying to pretend to be anything else at all.

"You—" Ruthven began, but just then Irazek dropped his pen and said, "Oh, *no.*"

Everyone else turned to stare at him; he was sitting at the table with his head in his hands, staring at a map of Paris on which he had drawn several red lines converging on two points quite close to one another.

Ruthven came over to peer at the map. One of the crosses was located not very far from the Moulin Rouge, about where Grisaille had said the lair's main entrance and exit lay. The other was directly over the Palais Garnier.

"They aren't just murdering people," said Irazek, looking up at Grisaille. "I mean, that would be bad enough. But whatever they're up to is affecting reality itself. This is where those incursions happened, and because one's in the Opera, which is—like a kind of magical echo chamber, it augments whatever's done in there—every time they do whatever they're doing, it's weakening the fabric of reality. Something's been *repeatedly* summoned, over and over, far more often than any such spell is supposed to be invoked. It's a bit like—oh, I don't know, hitting a thick glass window over and over and over with a tiny mallet; each individual blow isn't that hard but over time the cracks just... well, *spread,* until the whole thing gives."

"Do you know," said Grisaille, sounding slightly unhinged, "I would bet money that Lilith had *no idea* she was doing that with her little hobby?"

"What *was* she doing, other than orgiastic murder parties?" Ruthven said.

"Well, other than orgiastic murder parties in which she

abused multiple substances and had a lot of very noisy public sex with Corvin, I'm pretty sure she spent her time making monsters. Or—I suppose *summoning*, if that's the word we've decided to use."

"She what?" Varney demanded, blinking.

"Monsters. I never saw it happen, but she's got—" He broke off, took a swallow of his drink, coughed. "She *had*. I keep having to remind myself that she's dead, that he killed her. She *had* this—charm-circle thing, with all sorts of squiggly runes, and candles, and she did something every now and then, some kind of magic, and afterward there were *more* of the creatures. There's two kinds: a hairy kind and a sort of grey froggy sort that smells terrible, and there are *lots* of them."

He looked at the others, the frank puzzlement impossible to mistake. "Corvin threw a fit a while ago, told her to cut it out or take it elsewhere; he didn't like all the magic bullshit cluttering up the place. Not that she'll be doing it now. How bad of a problem is this?"

"How long had this been going on?" Irazek asked.

"Months," said Grisaille. "I think, anyway. She seemed to like doing it. At first it was just one or two, but she'd been doing it more recently. Or they've been breeding. Or both. I don't know which."

St. Germain snapped his fingers. "*That's* where they came from, then. The ghoul chieftain I talked to mentioned them, but didn't make any sense—I couldn't work out why anyone would be making them. And that has to be why the ghosts at Les Innocents showed up *now*. That's damaged reality enough to allow easy timeslips—before, there wasn't such a straight-forward route through the planes for them to manifest."

Irazek nodded. "And if it's not stopped—and patched—we're just going to see more and more of that, and it will get worse."

"How much worse?" Grisaille asked.

"You do not wish to know." Irazek ran his hands through his hair again, and for the first time, Ruthven realized that he had a tiny, neat pair of horns hidden among the curls—hidden very well, because they were exactly the same carroty-orange as his hair.

"Can you patch it?" Ruthven asked him. "More importantly, is it an immediate threat right now?"

"Well—yes and no, I mean—not right this second, but if anything *else* comes through, I can't promise you reality won't totally fracture—it has to get fixed and *I* can't do it. I have to call someone who can. Your friend—"

"Needs to get out of there," said Varney, clipped and neat, and probably no one who didn't know him would have been able to tell quite how murderously angry he was. Ruthven moved a little closer to him, instinctive. "Now," Varney added. "And once we've got her safely out of this creature's clutches, you and whatever less-incompetent friends you've unaccount-ably managed to make can get on with papering over the hole in the world at your personal leisure."

"That's not how it works," said Irazek, squeezing his eyes shut. "That's not how any of this works—but go, get her out of there, before anything *else* starts to go very badly wrong."

* * *

Not very far away at all, Greta Helsing paused in a subtly different darkness: too wide and open for the faint glow of the little creature on her shoulder to make much of a difference. Even without sight she could tell that she was in a room rather than a tunnel—a room with ordinary walls, straight and vertical rather than roughly cut out of the rock or arched in masonry overhead.

There was a very strong smell of mildew—no, of mold, a specific kind of rot. *Wellmonsters*, Greta thought. *Lots of them.* Very carefully she took another step into the room, one hand clasped in the wrinkled taffeta grip of her whistler, and was not entirely surprised when the metal door swung shut behind her with a final sort of clang.

The sound had sent a shock through the unseen room, and the floating whistler let go of her hand. One by one, a constellation of little points of greenish light appeared in the dark, all around her. In pairs. Little pale cold lamps, watching her, unblinking. Wellmonster eyes.

The one on her shoulder gave a series of *glup*s that Greta really wished she could interpret. There were a *lot* of them. Rather more than one might comfortably wish to see in one place, especially alone in the dark in a ruined underground lair.

Well. Mostly alone. The whistler in its taffeta drapery had drifted a little way away from her, invisible in the darkness, and she wished she still had the negligible comfort of its hard little hand in hers.

Glup, said her shoulder monster, and whatever that meant

appeared to be convincing: slowly the room lightened around her, details becoming visible, as the monsters' skin began to glow almost as brightly as their eyes.

I am *going to have to write a paper on bioluminescence in P. incolens,* she thought again, in the part of her mind not actively engaged in observation. The revealed surroundings were...surreal. She was standing in what must have been at one point a rather upsettingly ordinary sitting room, complete with Louis Philippe couch and armchair, the remains of knickknacks still sitting on a stone mantelpiece. Everything looked green and black with rot in the wellmonsters' light; satin-striped wallpaper hung down in wet tatters; the carpet underneath her bare feet squelched with unpleasant slime.

Her whistler drifted along the mantelpiece, apparently sniffing at what it found there, and then ascended to hover just beneath the ceiling, intent on something. Greta looked up at it, wondering what it was looking at, and went cold again all over.

To her left, high on the wall, was a little curtain half-rotted from its rod, the small rectangular window behind it opening on complete darkness. A ladder led up to it. Greta thought she knew what was on the other side of that window—

—drowning, drowning in the dark like a rat in a trap, the water swirling all around her, nothing but flat cold mirror glass and then the tree, the iron tree, under her reaching fingers—

She knew exactly where she was now. She was in the house of the phantom, the house of Erik, built directly into the double wall of the Opera foundation. If the book was accurate after all—and so far it seemed to be matching up exactly—she knew that beyond one of the black-gaping doorways would lie a decaying bed on which a dim if talented young woman had once slept, and that beyond the other almost certainly would be the remains of a pipe organ, and a red-lined coffin on a bier. So far it had been practically word-by-word, at least as closely as she could remember Leroux.

Corvin would like this, she thought to herself. *It's just his terrible style, only much too much of a mess.*

And the monsters were *everywhere*. Lurking in corners, settled in groups on the remains of the furniture. One clung upside-down, like a tiny grey sloth, to the sagging brass curve of a gaslight fixture. They were all very, very new.

The largest she could make out was barely the size of a half-grown kitten, six months old at most. The rest of them ranged in size from days to weeks old. Someone had been summoning them as recently as—*Christ*, she thought, *some of these were probably made while I've been kept prisoner down here, what on earth are they thinking, who could possibly want this many wellmonsters?*

It's got to be the vampires, who else *is down here, but why would they be making monsters at this rate, or at all?*

They were watching her, glow-pale eyes steady and unwavering. There had to be forty or fifty of them at least. She was glad when the whistler drifted down to take up its position just behind her left shoulder; the touch was slightly comforting, odd as it seemed.

"Hello," Greta said out loud, slightly surprised at how unconcerned she sounded. "I'm...a friend. I won't harm you."

She had no idea how good they were at human languages, but it was worth a try, and although she did get the feeling that the one on her shoulder had pretty much convinced them she wasn't a threat, this many wellmonsters could actually be dangerous to a human if they decided to work together.

Her announcement was met with a slow wave of blinking, the creatures' eyes slipping closed and open again, like a cloud passing in front of stars. *At least these ones aren't dehydrated,* she thought; this place was the ideal temperature and humidity level for wellmonsters to thrive. Whoever was making them had at least taken that into consideration.

No, she thought after a moment, *I'm pretty sure that was coincidental; whoever's behind this isn't exactly well versed in responsible monster husbandry.*

Glup, said the one on her shoulder again, which apparently translated to *show us where to go*: the entire constellation of monsters began a slow but inexorable process toward the door on the far side of the room, the one she thought would lead into Erik's music chamber. She could vaguely remember a description of black hangings with white musical notes on them and thought again how much Corvin would have appreciated the opera ghost's I-am-made-of-death aesthetic. *The original edgelord.* She was so tired of it. Of everything. The silver whistle was very heavy in her bodice; she thought it had probably printed itself in bruise colors over her ribs, and she could not remember a time in her life when she had felt more exhausted.

Too bad. There's still a lot of miles to go before I sleep.

She followed the tide of monsters through the doorway—and stopped still.

There *were* black hangings on the wall, but these weren't a hundred-forty-something years old, not the rotting remains of a long-dead creature's decor: they were a very familiar spiderweb-patterned netting. And while there was a jumble of tubes and piping that might once have been an organ shoved unceremoniously into a corner, the only thing in here capable of making music was what looked in the dim light like a 1980s-vintage boombox, battered silver plastic, with a stack of cassette tapes beside it. On the floor in the center of the room was—

Greta stared. It was a summoning circle, all right, with the candles at each star point, but it had been drawn in what looked like iridescent violet lipstick.

This was still turning over in the forefront of her mind while a rather more practical part of it pointed out *candles*, and then *matches, in a box, by the tapes, light a goddamn candle* and *curse the darkness so you can see what you're* doing, *woman*.

She stepped carefully around the circle—even poorly drawn in lipstick, with the runes misshapen, it still held potential power—and picked up the box of matches. Even with her eyes closed, the shock of light when she struck a match was painful after so long in near-darkness, and Greta was dazzled by it almost long enough for the flame to burn down to her fingertips. With another hissed expletive, she bent over to light two of the candles, and slowly the room brightened into being all around her; the wellmonsters' luminescence faded out as the candle flames grew, leaving them just the familiar dappled grey she recognized.

Along with the black cobweb drapery and purple lipstick spell circle, there were definite signs that this room had been occupied recently, and Greta was pretty sure she knew whose lair this was. Even above the generalized background reek of rot and damp and mildew—and monsters—she could make out a particular and familiar scent: sickly-sweet artificial vanilla and violets. Greta had spent a couple of solid hours surrounded by that particular perfume while she and Grisaille worked over Lilith; the woman must *bathe* in the stuff.

In the corner not taken up by the wreck of the organ, a damp beanbag chair covered in purple velvet bore the imprint of an occupant. It was difficult to tell in the flickering uncertain candlelight, but Greta thought she could make out a faint sparkle: body glitter.

There was no doubt about the forest of bottles beside the chair: mostly vodka, a couple of absinthe, one still half-full of *crème de menthe*—apparently even Lilith hadn't been able to stomach much of that cloying sweetness—but the rest of them were empty. And—

Greta took another step around the rim of the summoning circle, careful of the little monsters who had gathered all around it, and squatted down to get a closer look. The wellmonster that had been riding on her shoulder climbed down and hopped to the floor to join its fellows; the floating taffeta ghost of her whistler had already gone to investigate the ruined organ. Tucked down beside the edge of the chair, barely visible, was something whitish and bedraggled. She reached out to touch it—damp plush, soft under her fingertips—and pulled it out into the candlelight, and again stopped perfectly still to stare.

Dangling from her hands was an ancient and disintegrating stuffed white rabbit, one button eye missing, half its seams coming apart, most of its plush worn down to nothing. The fake vanilla scent was very strong.

She looked closer. The seams *were* coming apart, but someone had repaired them before. Repaired them many times, with varying levels of success, in different-colored thread.

She sat back on her heels and looked from the elderly rabbit to the boombox, and the tapes beside it, and recognized even in the dimness a couple of the albums. *Bon Jovi*, she thought. *Bon Jovi and U2 and Debbie Gibson, here, alone in the dark, her place, the only safe place she could find, where these things might be kept away from prying eyes.*

Greta thought of Lilith in her ridiculous Bride of Dracula outfits kneeling beside this circle, drawn in lipstick according to whatever spellbook she'd been able to find; Lilith buzzed on vodka and blood, listening to the familiar worn-thin tapes she must have taken with her from her first life, must have kept with her all this time through who knew how many moves over the decades; Lilith alone, and chanting words in the dancing candle-lit dimness to call creatures into being, small silent company but—perhaps—sometimes preferable to the clamor of the glitterati at their celebrations. Lilith with her ancient stuffed bunny. *Samantha*, Greta thought. *Her real name is Samantha.*

And Emily. Emily, looking at her with those huge kohl-rimmed eyes, saying, *It's permanent, then? Like I can't—it can't be fixed?*

Her eyes prickled. Greta could remember five months ago, in a different abandoned room under a different city, on her knees, crying for grief but also for everything lost, everything stolen, everything thrown away, wasted, unwanted; and she felt those same tears threaten now.

Underneath the city, in the mine galleries and passageways that had been abandoned for hundreds of years, lights glimmered: here and then gone, a flickering unsteady glow, several of them at once appearing, moving through the tunnels at head height before winking out again. Along with the lights came sound, a dim clink and shuffle of hammer and pick on stone, the susurrus of distant voices, fading in and out as if borne on an unfelt breeze.

Only a few of Corvin's people had seen the moving lamp flames in the distance, the yellowish cast of oil-lights where no lights ought to be, and none of them had reported it for fear of being laughed at for superstitious idiots. Now—as the sky in the world above began to pale in the east—the lights bobbed and flickered in a rock chamber whose barred door stood ajar, hovering around a hole that gaped in the far corner of one wall. In the dim uncertain moving illumination they provided, shadows seemed to hunch and sway inside the hole, as if something in there was trying to get out.

Corvin saw them, saw them very well, but his vision was suffused scarlet with fury, and he could not spare a thought for the provenance of mysterious moving lights inside his cell block: everything else was eclipsed in the roaring blaze of anger at the *empty cell*, where was the *human*, where was the goddamn *human* he'd had safely tucked away, where was his *bait*—

Yes, okay, he'd meant to murder her, bait or not, after that unspeakable little scene in the bedchamber. That didn't matter; she was *his* to do with as he chose, bait or personal indulgence, it was *his right*—and where was his *lieutenant*, where was Grisaille? He'd never taken *this long* to arrive when Corvin yelled his name. It couldn't have taken him more than half an hour to dump the body at the absolute outside, why hadn't he come *back*—

His hands closed on the bars of the cell—useless bars, they hadn't stopped her getting out because *someone had opened the fucking door for her*, and all of a sudden Corvin was pretty sure who that might have been.

Who knew what the two of them had talked about while they'd been messing with Lilith, who knew what kind of treachery they had plotted together, Grisaille and the human, oh, he was going to kill them both, he was going to *kill them both*, slowly, creatively, when he caught up with them—

The iron of the cell bars tore in his grip with a shriek of tortured metal, echoed by Corvin's own scream of pure fury, and it rang and rang again in the rock-cut passageways of the undercity, echoing and re-echoing into the dank chill of the webwork of tunnels, into the darkness left after the flickering lights—all at once, a wrinkle in time smoothing itself— went out.

CHAPTER 11

It had been such a long time since Varney had been the bat.

You never really forgot how to do it, a kind of disorienting shiver while you changed shape and size, but after a while even the familiar sensations drew away into strangeness, like old neighbors you had not seen in a long time. His chest and shoulder muscles were already aching from the unaccustomed strain of flight.

He and Ruthven—and between them, so they both could keep an ear on him, Grisaille—flew through the breaking dawn, the rose-gold light barely registering in his limited vision but the city beneath them spread out in strobe flashes of sound. Several hundred feet below, St. Germain was running at a steady pace on all fours, keeping up with effortless ease.

It didn't take them very long to get from Irazek's apartment in the Marais to the 9th arrondissement: flight and wolf-gait were much faster than they could have managed in their ordinary forms. The huge massif of the Opera was visible from

quite some distance, set like a jewel in the center of the diamond pattern of its four adjoining streets, the early light gild-
ing Apollo's lyre atop the dome and beginning to slide down
the shallow gables of the flyloft roof.

Between Varney and Ruthven, the silvery-dark bat that was
Grisaille drew ahead and dipped a wing, banking left. Neither
of them honestly expected him to make a break for it, but
both banked sharply with him, following quite close through
the descent, until he landed in the shelter of a kind of alcove
formed by two intersecting walls of the Opera facing the Rue
Scribe.

At this hour there were very few people around, and nobody
witnessed the spectacle that was three specimens of *Desmodus
rotundus* changing—in a rather briefly horrible manner—into
three strange-eyed men. The arrival a minute or two later of
a large wolf registered no more interest; St. Germain shook
himself and sat down.

"This is the Rue Scribe," said Ruthven, hands on hips.
"They park *coaches* here. You're not telling me there's a door
into your underground lair right here in plain view?"

"You haven't read your background lit," said Grisaille with
a rather unsuccessful smile. "Don't you know there's a secret
passage from the Rue Scribe to the underground lake? *Everybody* knows that. It's so well known, in fact, that nobody actually bothers to look for it. Here."

He gestured toward an iron grating let into the wall which
Varney had thought simply another basement window
grating—and then stopped, because St. Germain's black nose

had neatly slid into the space between him and the metal. Varney was a little impressed at how silently the wolf moved.

"Hold," said St. Germain, very soft. "I smell something."

"That's not—" Grisaille began, and a sharp elbow in the ribs from Ruthven shut him up. The wolf bent closer to the grating, hooked a paw into the cross of iron bars, and pulled gently: there was a brief unpleasant sound of tortured metal and the grating came free.

"It's her," said St. Germain. "Her, very strongly."

"Should we go in?" Ruthven said, blinking at him.

"I rather think we wait for the lady to come out," St. Germain said, and backed away several steps, sitting down with his tail wrapped over his feet. Varney glanced at Ruthven, at the dark hole in the building, and had decided St. Germain was entirely wrong—had, in fact, ducked under the stone lintel— when a movement in the darkness froze him entirely still.

Something *was* there. Something, coming toward them.

After a moment Varney could make out a pale shape, and then a face, and he made a little helpless sound he could not in the least suppress: wordless gratitude. He didn't know what to *do* with the alarming, unfamiliar sensation of his own rib cage trying to expand despite itself, containing a gathering, spreading, growing heat; he'd never experienced anything like it before. It was tempered with a gloss of fear: she'd been down there for days now, and God only knew what they had done to her, would she be *she*, would she be Greta, would she *remember him at all*—

And then he saw her face change—saw the change come

over her all at once, completely—saw her pick up what was left of the ragged skirts of the dress she wore and not just climb the remaining steps up to the world but *run* up them, emerging into the daylight all at once and flinging herself at Varney, throwing her arms around his neck.

The scrim of fear holding back his gladness shattered all at once, and he was more than a little afraid of the sheer volume and force of it, a flood of bright hot gold. He wrapped his arms around her, held her close: stroked the planes and angles of her back. Too sharp, the bones too near the skin—what had they *done* to her, oh, he was going to kill somebody, he was going to—never mind, it didn't matter now. The inexpressible sweetness of her face against his shoulder. He could have died a thousand times over if he only knew *this* could be waiting at the end of it.

She was filthy, covered in various sorts of mud and slime, and the dress she was wearing had at one point been a strapless red taffeta ballgown but was now something out of nightmare, and she had a thing clinging to her neck, a creature that opened coppery froglike eyes at Varney, stared at him with what he considered impertinence, and went *glup*.

Nothing seemed to matter very much, grey froggy creatures notwithstanding, because Greta was back with him; the presence of the others signified not at all, he didn't care that they were watching, didn't care that they were there. When her knees gave out, he caught her; lifted her gently in his arms, cradled against his chest, and leaned down to kiss her forehead very lightly.

It was the first time Sir Francis Varney had kissed anyone in far, far longer than he could clearly remember. He could have died all over again for the faint little sigh she gave as unconsciousness rose up to claim her. No one, even when he'd been alive the first time, just a man and not a monster, had ever trusted Varney quite this much.

Like a lot of the classic horror literature Greta had read, it turned out that Leroux's novel *had* been partly accurate—much more so than she had expected—but not all the way. There was, in fact, a body of water underneath the deepest cellar of Garnier's gold-and-marble confection—a feature that hadn't been included in the original plans—but it did not have a shore along which one could stroll.

When the foundations for the Opera had been dug, Garnier and his colleagues and construction workers had been thoroughly dismayed to find an underground waterway passing right through the bit of ground he'd intended to put the building on. Huge steam pumps running day and night could not dry things out sufficiently for construction to go ahead as originally planned. The solution Garnier came up with was elegant in its simplicity: to resist the pressure of the surrounding groundwater on the foundations of the building, he created a vast underground water tank—a cistern—the pressure of which pushing outward on the foundation walls would counteract the groundwater pressure coming the other way and stabilize the entire structure.

And one of his contractors, in the process—a remarkable

individual in many ways—had built himself a little house inside the cistern wall. Which also did not appear on the official plans. A house with certain peculiarities originally imagined and built by this particular architect at the Persian court, in the period known as the Rosy Hours of Mazenderan, to please the little sultana's desire for amusing forms of death.

A secret house. Like a few other little alterations made to Garnier's plans by the same individual, to allow him to move throughout the vast empire of the building without ever being seen unless he chose to be.

Greta opened the front door of Erik's house on almost utter darkness. In front of her, two steps down, a dead-still surface reflected her candle's flickering glow like a black glass mirror. The lake. There was no way to tell how deep it was, or what lay under the surface.

She knew there had to be a way out to the interior of the Opera itself from here—surely the caretakers had to come down now and again to check on the water levels, or something—but she had no idea where it could be, or if it was accessible from the water itself. Paralyzed by indecision, she stood at the top of the water stairs and stared into the darkness, so thick and black it felt as if it carried physical weight.

The tiny wellmonster was back on her shoulder, which had come as some surprise; she had been pretty sure it was happy to rejoin its fellow monsters in the dark and slimy ruins of the house, but as soon as she got to her feet, it had given an ungainly hop and clung to her ankle—feeling exactly like the cold wet nose of a dog pressed against her bare skin—and begun laboriously to climb up her leg, so she had let it. There was something pleasant, in a weird way, about being *wanted*, even by a thoroughly improbable little supernatural creature.

Her whistler, whom Greta was thinking of more and more fondly as *Winston*, after a poltergeist she'd once encountered with a similar rough charm, had swept past her shoulder as soon as she opened the door on the lake and was now presumably enjoying itself zooming around in the pitch darkness where she couldn't follow its maneuvers. It couldn't go *very* far, because its whistle was still firmly shoved down Greta's bodice, but it had a full range of perhaps a couple of miles from that anchor.

What the hell do I do now? she thought, trying to see past the candle and managing only to ruin what visual purple she'd managed to build up. *Now what?*

Far behind her, she heard a faint clang, and a sudden brief wind blew past her, lifting the remains of her skirt and snuffing the candle out completely.

Someone, somewhere back in the tunnels, was moving. It was probably her imagination that the clang had been accompanied by a distant shriek of rage.

Greta stared wildly into the darkness, clutching the dead candle in one hand, and when a ripple of water and a hollow *bonk* sound of wood on stone came out of nowhere to her left, she let out a tiny little scream, almost voiceless: *what else was down here with her*, what was going to reach out of the dark and grab her and—

A hard little hand made out of crumpled taffeta curled

around her fingers and tugged her forward, tipping her off balance, and in the faint light of her shoulder monster, she could just make out the curving gunwale of a small rowboat before she fell into it, scraping the skin off one knee in the process.

Greta lay sprawled in the bottom of the boat, which rocked only a little before settling, and reached dazedly for the creature on her shoulder; it was still there, hanging on very tight, apparently unhurt. She could feel motion. They were being towed.

Winston had found a *boat* for her, of all the improbable things. And now Winston was pulling her along in said boat, in a businesslike fashion, silent except for the liquid babble of water lapping along the sides. It was a very small boat, large enough for one rower and perhaps a passenger, if they didn't mind close quarters. The wood was dark with age but still apparently sound—

And at this point Greta realized she could *see* the grain in the planks. Could see her hands in front of her face, see the fluttering shape of the whistler towing them along on a rope tied to the bow, and the light was brightening all the time—a diffuse, blue-tinged light, from somewhere up ahead, somewhere in the ceiling.

She tried to think through the fog of exhaustion and residual stress hormones, reaching for her memories of the book. There had been a way to get from the underground lake to the Rue Scribe, hadn't there? Another secret passage in and out of the building, by which the lover of trapdoors could come and go at his discretion—

—music, faint but present, all around her; whispered singing in the dark, achingly sweet, so beautiful that all she wanted was to go on listening; music that seemed to come out of the air— no, out of the water itself, a song rising like the faint pale mist of dawn from the dark water—tantalizingly far away, and she wanted more than anything to hear it clearly—

—leaning over the edge of the boat, leaning down toward the lake—

—a pair of arms bursting from the surface, seizing her by the shoulders in a grip like iron, pulling her headfirst into the shock-cold of the water—

Greta thrust herself back from the edge of the boat so violently that it rocked, splashing faintly. Her heart was racing. *That's him*, she thought, *that's—him, that's Erik, playing the lake-guardian siren to prevent unwanted visitors to his horrible little house, it's in the book, I'm still in the* book, *I've been in the book for hours now—it's like some kind of strange possession—*

Or like a haunting.

The whistler had paused to look back at her over one taffeta shoulder when she'd jerked away from the gunwale. She tucked back her hair and tried to smile for him, wondering again where the hell he was actually taking her, knowing that she had no choice but to trust him. He'd got her out of the cell. And he had guided her this far.

Greta sat in the very center of the boat, the candle end lying forgotten beside her, and strained to see through the brightening gloom—holding on tight to both worn wooden sides. There was never any warning with the flickers, which made them worse—it was bad enough that they were *happening,* that they were somehow possible for someone like herself with no supernatural powers whatsoever to perceive; were hauntings ever *like* this, glitches in time, rather than the unquiet dead hanging about and bothering the people on this side of breath? It was the kind of strange she could not understand because she did not have the necessary information, and *not understanding* was almost worse than the fear.

They passed under another set of arches and the source of the light suddenly came into view: a grating in the curved roof of the chamber, iron bars crisscrossing a square opening, through which broad rays of light fell to the surface of the water. Through the surface. Greta realized it was crystal clear, and only about four feet deep; there went all her worries about unspeakable bottomless black waters populated by creatures hungry for human meat.

That was daylight she was seeing. Daylight. The first natural light she had seen in—she didn't know how long. The real world was so close now. So close.

They passed under the grating, and the light falling on her head and shoulders, her hands, felt like a blessing; then it fell away behind them, and she wondered again what the whistler was doing.

She closed her eyes, leaden-heavy, and had no idea if it was a minute or ten minutes that passed before the boat abruptly bumped into something solid with that hollow *bonk,* and jarred her all the way back to consciousness again.

Water stairs. Leading up to a dark archway in the wall with

more stairs beyond it, bending to the right as they climbed upward.

It was the right direction, at least. And Winston was hovering in the archway, looking impatient, if a tattered bit of taffeta could look impatient.

Greta cupped her hand to her shoulder monster for a moment, and then reached for the stone edge of the steps and hauled herself ashore.

There are probably vampires waiting up there to recapture me, and right now I don't know if I can actually make myself care. If I can do much of anything at all.

She was all out of *can*.

Climbing the stairs felt like the summit push to Everest. Greta was aware, intensely aware, of the muscles in her thighs being made to do work: that grew to take over most of the world, she was not so much a person as a *thing that climbs*, she would be climbing forever, and possibly at the end of the stairs there would be a locked iron grate, and if there was a locked iron grate, she would simply sit down on the top stone step and close her eyes and wait for Corvin's goons to come and find her—

Someone was talking, up ahead. Someone with a deep voice she thought she'd heard before, and a moment later another voice answering them.

That was a voice she *did* know, and in fact it turned out she did have the strength not just to climb the rest of the stairs but *run* up them, and there was not an iron grate, there was just a brilliant square opening with a tall thin figure outlined against the brightness, and Greta made it up the last steps and flung herself into light and air and vast, enormous *space*—and into Sir Francis Varney's arms.

He held her close, *tight*, heedless of her filthy ragged state, and she felt him stroke her hair, dizzy with sudden reaction. Everything was sliding, confused.

Behind Varney, that deep voice chuckled briefly. "A very belated welcome to Paris, Doctor," it said, and she looked up long enough to register a wolf the size of a Volkswagen sitting on its haunches and observing the two of them with warm yellow eyes—and beyond him, Ruthven, pinched and focused, and a shock of familiarity as she recognized *Grisaille*. "I do so apologize for the way it's been treating you thus far," said the wolf.

It *was* a voice she knew: she'd made a date with the owner of this voice to meet at a bar and talk about peculiar happenings, approximately a thousand years ago. Greta would have liked to put together some kind of apology for that entire business, but she was drunk on fatigue poisons and the sheer relief of being held. Nor could she think about Grisaille, or why he should be out here with the others; her mind was skipping like a scratched record, locked in the *Varney's here, I'm safe, I'm safe, I'm out, I've gotten out, Varney's here* feedback loop.

Varney squeezed her a little tighter, and she clung to him, shaking in long helpless tremors. "*I*, for my part, am so sorry it has taken us this long to find and rescue you," he said, and with her ear against his chest, she could both hear and feel his voice. "Only you seem to be largely self-rescuing, which does not in fact surprise me in the least. Also you appear to have a passenger," he added as the wellmonsterlet on her shoulder *glupped* at him.

"Please feel free to do it anyway," she said, muffled in his suit jacket. "The rescuing. I don't—think I can stand up for very much longer, actually—"

She didn't have to finish the sentence: Varney simply bent to slip his arm under her knees and lifted her off her feet with no apparent effort whatsoever. It felt absurdly nice just to be held, to be *someone else's problem* for a while, and Greta leaned against his chest and let herself think of nothing.

Well, no. One thing. "There's a whistle-monster," she said, sounding very far away even to herself. "I don't know where he went—I've got his whistle, I owe him a very large number of favors, he's been extraordinarily helpful—"

"I expect he'll turn up," said St. Germain. "For right now I'm taking you all back to my flat, where it is safe, and you can get some proper rest and decent food."

"And a bath," said Greta, nearly asleep. "Possibly several baths. And can I borrow something else to wear?"

"I don't believe burgundy taffeta is very *you*," said Varney. "We've got your things from the hotel; don't worry." And she felt a brief cool touch on her forehead that might have been the faintest brush of lips; she took that sensation—the shock of it, deep and terrible and sweet—down with her into the dark.

The demon Irazek had had a fairly terrible night—well, day and night—well, actually he didn't quite recall how long it had been; he'd lost track somewhere in the impromptu house party while he'd been scrambling to do the calculations to triangulate where all this wretched business had begun. That Brightside and Dammerung were still around was a little bit of a relief, although Irazek could have wished they'd bloody well been in touch with him themselves rather than retreating into complete radio silence and then sending him a discontented vampire to pump for information.

At least said vampire had *had* some information. Irazek could very clearly tell that Edmund Ruthven wanted to pull his head off, and that Francis Varney had similar but rather more violent desires—but after Grisaille had told them his story, both the vampires had seemed to calm down from active murder into organizational mode.

They and St. Germain had left with Grisaille some time ago to rescue the missing Dr. Helsing. Irazek had stayed behind, ostensibly to work out what was to be done next, but in point of fact he was simply stalling: he *knew* what was to be done next, and a significant aspect of that was going to be *losing his job.*

At least, he thought, looking around his familiar and beloved apartment, he could do it with a bit of class. Somewhere that wasn't here.

He put on his coat. The dawn had run a pale lemon-colored flood of light up the eastern sky while he was dithering; now it was day properly, even if the only people abroad at this hour were the deeply industrious, the crepuscular, or the kind of libertines who rarely went to bed.

Irazek walked through the streets, *aware* of Paris in a way he wasn't normally. Trying to register the city, imprint it on his memory, storing up recollections for the time when he'd be stuck back down in Hell. There wasn't really a gigantic hurry, he told himself. The weak spot in reality had been there for ages now: surely it could wait a little longer, couldn't it? Just a little longer, and *then* Irazek would be properly chastised.

The delicate light, shading from powder-pale into clear, slipping down the facades of the city, seemed more beautiful this morning than it ever had before. He wondered, walking along with his hands in his coat pockets, looking up, if it had really always been that lovely and he simply had not bothered to notice until now.

Irazek stopped at the base of the long, long hill of Montmartre, with its classic steps. In the new day's light the white confection of Sacré-Coeur atop the hill glowed against the sky: a church wrought of perfect meringue, crisp and weightless and snowy-white, breathing sweetness into the morning.

Here's as good as anywhere, he thought, and began to climb the stairs.

He was going to miss it, living here. Going to miss the colors of early morning, like today: dew-damp green leaves in window boxes, the blue and dove-grey of the city before the sun found its way up the sky. Going to miss small things, like the tiny perfection of those new leaves, vivid jade-green, soft and delicate before they grew into sturdy dark green architecture: a constant sweet pleasure in the perception of *life*, of growth. Going to miss the way croissant dough folded back on itself in layer after layer, puffing up in the oven to a delicate flaky melting-light golden brown. So many things he hadn't paid enough attention to, one way or another.

He'd been here for two years. Long enough to fall in love with the place in ways he hadn't even slightly anticipated, during the surface-op training: M&E had told them to expect a period of adjustment, but not the kind of weirdly unfolding *pleasure* Irazek had felt walking through the streets of his newly assigned city. Parts of Paris were enough like parts of the city of Dis—the gloriously overdone architecture of the Opera, for example, the Palais Garnier and the Pandemonium Conservatory could have switched places with barely anybody noticing—that he had found the adjustment remarkably painless.

He didn't know why they had never bothered to send up a second agent to assist him with monitoring the essographs. When he'd volunteered for the Paris job, it had been with the understanding that he'd almost certainly be sharing the duties with another operative, and the days and then weeks and then months had just gone by without a single message from Below, so he'd…got on with it, and found himself really enjoying the work. And since Hell clearly hadn't been paying terribly close attention, he had gradually slipped into something like complacency.

And now it was almost certainly going to be over.

Standing on the steps just below Sacré-Coeur, Irazek took a narrow flat glass object out of his pocket, distinguishable from a smartphone by the fact that it was mostly transparent except for a few iridescent sigils floating inside the glass itself, and touched it here and there in a particular sequence. The sigils glowed briefly as his finger made contact, and then faded.

Audible only to the demon, a faint chime of sound came and went several times. Four. Five. He was beginning to wonder if he'd placed the request-to-contact correctly when a tired, somewhat irritable voice resonated inside his head.

"*Yes?*" it said.

"Um." Irazek was not entirely sure he *had* made the right call. "Is this Monitoring and Evaluation?" He'd been expecting one of Asmodeus's lower-level functionaries, and he didn't think this voice belonged to any of them.

"*Yes, it is, we're a little busy just at the moment*"—it paused, as if accessing data—"*Irazek; what is it you need?*"

"Um," he said again. "There's—been a problem up here. In Paris. The—there's been some repeated incursions from the P3 plane and the—fabric of reality is a little bit—"

"*What? How many incursions? When?*"

"I'm not…entirely sure," said Irazek wretchedly. "But enough to weaken reality, and it's—I can't repair it on my own, I'm afraid."

"*You aren't sure,*" said the voice, delicate. "*Could you perhaps hazard a guess as to how long this has been going on?*"

"About a month and a half," he said, "maybe a bit longer. I take full responsibility for the failure to recognize the severity of the situation. I abjectly and humbly abase myself before the just and justified displeasure of my lord Asmodeus, before whom I am but a—"

"*Can we dispense with the forehead-knocking, it gives me a pain*," said the voice, "*and—let me see, you're in Paris—damn, Paris, I'd meant to do something about that before now. I haven't got anyone I can send at the moment, either; everyone's already occupied. I suppose I'll have to do it myself.*"

"Yourself?" said Irazek, profoundly puzzled. "I—may I have the pleasure of knowing with whom I speak?"

"*Hang on*," said the voice. "*I'll be there shortly. Don't do anything to reality until I get there.*"

"Who—" Irazek began, but there was flat silence in his head once more. He rubbed at his temples, where a headache was beginning to throb, and wished not for the first time that he had never put his name in for the surface-ops training curriculum. Whoever it was would—hopefully—be able to fix this mess, but what happened next, Irazek had absolutely no way to predict.

Maybe they'd let him make pastries back in Hell, once he was demoted. If there was anything left of him after this situation was resolved.

Safety—the lack of immediate, visceral *need to do something*—felt absurd right now. Sitting in St. Germain's rather pleasant living room with a glass of red wine between his palms—he was getting tired of wine, but it was better than nothing—Varney was conscious of the weight of fatigue held at bay only by an effort of will.

It was so difficult to think, and he didn't know what to do with this new kind of worry: not that Greta was somewhere in the clutches of monsters, but that she *had been* in the clutches of monsters, and that the things they had done and said to her might mean she was not quite the woman he had known, or had grown to know a little. He understood very well the ways in which trauma could leave a mark on somebody, *change* them, and the thought of her being thus changed was...awful.

What had happened to her down there, and what did it mean, and what could he *do* about it, about any of it—

Varney tried again to push away the thought, and let the blank tiredness close over it again. He was staring vaguely ahead of him, not seeing the werewolf's furniture or the brightening windows—it must be seven or eight in the morning, the sun climbing the sky—and he was inexpressibly grateful when St. Germain himself arrived with a steaming cup of coffee and sat down across from him: something else to focus on other than the inside of his own head.

"She's still sleeping," St. Germain told Varney. Greta had taken a shower lasting about half an hour when they'd returned to his flat, and subsequently curled up in the werewolf's spare bedroom and passed out completely. St. Germain had pulled the blankets over her and left her to it while he made coffee and got Varney his wine. "I want to let her sleep as long as possible—but we have to do something about these people. I don't completely trust Grisaille, but we need him to get in there and to show us the way, and for what it's worth, he *smells* as if he's telling the truth rather than waiting for an opportunity to betray us."

When they'd gotten back to St. Germain's apartment,

Ruthven had taken Grisaille aside to talk to him, and Varney was entirely content to let him handle that situation; he was better at extracting information than Varney himself, and now that he'd gotten over his initial response, he was probably capable of greater patience as well.

"What about Irazek?" Varney asked.

"Irazek is in the wrong job, I think, although he's undoubtedly off trying to do it as best he can. But I'm honestly less worried about ripples in the fabric of reality right now than I am about a murderous group of baby vampires infesting the undercity, which is probably not the most farsightful or balanced thing I've ever said—but they *offend* me."

He had taken the tie out of his hair again and it fell in a tumble of grizzled gold waves to his shoulders: Varney watched as he scrubbed his hands through it, an oddly human gesture. "I know that sounds a little strange."

"Not at all," said Varney, and meant it. He thought of Lucia and Élise, in their exquisite apartment, saying, *They're not the sort of people one cares to acknowledge socially, you understand… no class at all, I'm afraid; not the slightest flicker of taste.* "They are—distasteful," he said, echoing the memory. "Meddling with the proper order of things."

"That's it exactly. They're *wrong*, and they're an embarrassment. I should have noticed them earlier; it's partly my fault that things have gotten so bad, but I can worry about that after I've rid Paris of them properly."

"I have a personal desire to remove this Corvin's horrible little head myself," said Varney.

"Not if I get there first," said St. Germain, sounding hard as iron for a moment, and then sighed. "Do you know what to do with the wellmonster, by any chance? It's in the bathroom now, sitting in the sink, wrapped around a sort of tarnished silver thing."

"I'm afraid not," said Varney. "She seemed to be concerned about another monster, too, something to do with a whistle?"

"Oh, good grief, I'd forgotten." St. Germain pushed his hands through his hair again, sitting up. "I haven't seen one of those in ages. Well, I'll leave a window open for it—that silver thing must be the whistle. It'll be back sooner or later, as long as that object's still present." He sighed. "I'm going to go find out what the hell Edmund's talking about with our guest."

Varney nodded. When St. Germain had gone, he sat there for a few minutes before hauling himself off the couch and getting himself some coffee. Wine was all very well, but he needed caffeine.

The kitchen was, like Ruthven's, a space designed by a person who enjoyed both cooking and entertaining. Where Ruthven's was all blue tile and stainless steel and blonde wood, the warm rose-gold of polished copper, St. Germain's kitchen was in shades of clear grey and pale green. There were shallots in a green glass bowl on the countertop, but no garlic was in evidence—no garlic in a French kitchen, Varney was a little impressed—and a wide turned-maple plate on the table held fresh fruit. The wine bottle stood beside it on a glass coaster. An expensive coffee machine sat and steamed to itself beside the sink.

Glass, and ceramic, and wood, and stone. No silver. No

silver*ware*: all the knives and forks that Varney knew would be neatly stacked in one of these drawers were undoubtedly polished stainless steel. It was fascinating seeing someone else's limitations, and the ways in which they got around those limitations, from inside; it was fascinating, too, to be aware of the little ways in which they had made a *home* for themselves. Despite Varney's fatigue and the profound need to murder Corvin, he found himself thinking again about his own house, and what he wanted it to look like; what he wanted it to become, when all the work was done.

What it had been, for so long, was—a lair, a decaying bolt-hole to which he'd retreated time and again from the pursuit of the living, after each iterative failure to live in the world with any grace. Ratford Abbey even in its first youth had been haphazardly decorated, full of the kinds of luxury that Varney imagined a living nobleman should possess, arranged without much thought or care. With the passage of time, he had tried and failed over and over to keep the interior *au courant* with fashion, until—mired in the black despair that characterized so many of his interactions with the world—he had finally given the house up to the ravages of age and weather, and retreated to the cellars to sleep.

Bringing it back piece by piece—beginning to bring it back, anyway—had given Varney something closer to satisfaction than he had felt in a very long time. Overseeing structural repairs and imagining how the house's rooms would look when they were finally complete felt like a *purpose*, in an existence that had hitherto notably lacked in such. He had been pleased with it even before all this had begun, and now—well, over the past several days he'd done more *living* than he had in decades, in other people's houses, and he thought with a certainty unfamiliar to him that he wanted to keep on doing that; wanted to have a kitchen of his own in which people could be comfortable, wanted not just to repair the ruin of his house, make it beautiful again, but to make it into a *home*.

If we get through this, he thought to himself, *if we get through this and safely back to England, I am going to put some serious work into Dark Heart.* Greta had said it on the phone, before everything went to hell: *I want to see your grand works for myself.*

He could see her in the green drawing room, restored to the beauty he could only half remember, the cool green silk of the wallpaper and the banded malachite of the mantelpiece rendering her luminous by comparison. He could see her walking through the long gallery, passing through the bands of light and shadow thrown by the great windows across parquet floors polished to a mirror shine. He could see her in the library, curled in an armchair before the fire, surrounded by mellow rosewood and the scent of age, the variegated gold-stamped spines of his book collection stretching up to the ceiling all around her, warm light on her hair.

He realized he was looking forward to that rather a great deal.

Gervase Brightside hadn't ever seen his partner quite this *un-*cheerful, at least in recent memory. Being cheeked by a bunch of ghosts wasn't entirely unheard of, but being cheeked by a bunch of ghosts *while* discovering that in fact the fabric of reality was in considerably worse shape than previously understood was a little daunting.

It had at least helped a little to deal with the vampire afterward. Both of them always felt rather better for doing their jobs, doing the thing they were *for*, and assisting the last vestige of the creature that had been called Lilith to a final peace was perhaps the first time in days they'd managed to be useful. There wasn't much of her soul left, but there had been enough to hold, to comfort; they had shown her the way home, and left the retort cooling from white heat, empty again, its work completed. One thread neatly wound up; one less loose end.

They had not spoken since leaving the crematorium, walking together through the narrow winding streets of the necropolis; they had nearly reached the cemetery gates when both of them stopped, struck by a mental wave of pressure like a distant explosion. They looked at one another.

"Did you—" Crepusculus began.

"I did," Brightside told him, fingers pressing his temples. "That was a significant incursion." Something important had come through. Something big enough for them to *feel*—and how many more incursions could the fabric of reality take, if it was as frayed as he was beginning to fear?

Crepusculus closed his eyes for a moment, turning a little as if to follow a rolling echo of sound, and pointed. "That way. It's—I think it's from Hell, I can't be sure—"

"Irazek," said Brightside. Crepusculus shut up and looked

at him with wide dark eyes. Both of them were thinking the same thing: the situation had escalated, and now someone with rather more of the *vis vires diaboli* than Irazek had taken over. Which didn't bode particularly well for the latter.

"We'd better go and see," he said, and a moment later both he and Crepusculus vanished with two small thunder-claps as the air collapsed in on the space where they'd been standing—and reappeared, near-instantaneously, about four miles away on the steps of Montmartre. And blinked.

There was Irazek, all right, but he didn't appear to be in imminent danger of anything dire; he was sitting on the steps talking animatedly to a tall man in a pale pearl-grey pinstripe suit that matched his complexion rather well.

Crepusculus and Brightside looked at one another again—they seemed to be doing a lot of that just recently—and Brightside said, "Fastitocalon?"

The man in the suit had looked up as soon as they popped into existence. It had been several decades since they'd encountered this particular individual, back in London, but he hadn't changed all that much. He was thin, but not cadav-erously so, and appeared to be in his mid-fifties, ruler-straight parted hair and all, and the only thing about him that belied his actual nature was the interesting point that his skin was, in fact, ever so slightly grey. He looked in some lights as if he had a mild case of argyria.

He was also a demon. Or—Brightside thought back—had *been* one, until there was some sort of complicated business in the 1600s and he'd been exiled to Earth; Brightside couldn't quite remember the details. There was no doubt that he'd just now arrived from Hell, however. His spectral signature was unmistakably infernal.

He looked more than a little irritated, as well. "Ah," he said, "Brightside and Dammerung, it's been a while, hasn't it, but I'm afraid I'm rather in the middle of something right now."

"The incursions," said Crepusculus. Irazek was looking from them to Fastitocalon with a rather dazed expression, and Brightside didn't blame Fass for being somewhat irritable with him. *Come on*, he thought, *keep up, Irazek, make a bloody effort.*

"Yes," said Fastitocalon. "I'm gathering that there have been rather a *lot* of them recently—have you two been involved in this?"

"Peripherally," said Brightside. "We were here to sort out some ghosts, but then we sort of got curious and hung around."

"They came to visit me," said Irazek, with the air of someone wanting to make a contribution.

"Mm," Fastitocalon said. "What can you tell me about the situation?"

"That a vampire had been grubbing around in a graveyard collecting spell components," said Brightside, "we assume for summoning purposes, and had been doing so for some little time according to a group of ghosts we interviewed—she's dead now, killed by someone calling himself the 'king of the vampires,' but presumably the damage has been done."

"Well. We can't have *that*," said Fastitocalon, looking suddenly preoccupied. "You don't happen to know a woman called Greta Helsing, do you, either of you?"

Beside them, Irazek opened his mouth as if to say something, but subsided anxiously. "Nope," said Crepusculus. "Any relation to the famous one?"

"Descendant. Damn. I have a feeling something's gone wrong—hang on—"

He got up, pacing a little way up the stairs from the three of them, and appeared to be having a conversation inside his own head. Crepusculus and Brightside looked at Irazek, who shrugged. "He's—apparently he's the interim director of M&E, which is weird—I thought he was in Budget and Finance, or had been a couple hundred years ago, but something weird's going on with staffing Below?"

"Good old Fass, making his way up in the world," said Crepusculus, "or possibly down, depending on your viewpoint. *I* thought he was an accountant."

"I don't know," said Irazek. "I called for help, because— well, unfortunately, I can't actually fix this on my own. And I was expecting to get someone from Asmodeus's staff basically saying, *You're fired, and also we're going to turn you into something nasty for a set period of time*, but instead it was him. Not that I'm complaining, mind you," he added hastily. "He hasn't done much shouting. Yet."

Brightside looked back at Fastitocalon, still evidently intent on his internal conversation. The demon did look *better* than he remembered from years ago, less unhealthily thin, without that raspy little cough he'd never seemed to be able to shake.

More determined. "You think he'll have the power to fix this, whatever needs to be done?" he said. "I don't really remember him being particularly strong, last time we met, but that was a while ago. Things might have changed."

Irazek shrugged. "I bloody well hope so," he said. "Otherwise we're all going to be in *real* trouble."

"Amen to that," said Crepusculus, looking again so downcast that Brightside had an uncharacteristic urge to put an arm around his shoulders. "Worst holiday ever."

Beyond them, Fastitocalon straightened up, pressing a hand to his forehead. "Right," he said, turning back to the others. "This is a mess. I need to go back to Hell to pick up some equipment, and then we're going for a little chat with some other interested parties. I'm afraid I'll need your help," he added, looking at Crepusculus and Brightside. "This is going to be rather unpleasant but hopefully not for very *long*, but the weak point wants patching and I need all the strength I can borrow."

"Of course," said Brightside, thinking of himself in the café what felt like a century ago, making the decision to investigate the site of their last case: he hadn't *wanted* to, just as he didn't particularly want to do whatever Fastitocalon had in mind, but want and need were not the same.

"Do . . . you want me, too?" Irazek asked, not sounding at all sure of the answer.

"Well, obviously," Fastitocalon said. "You're the assigned Paris op; this is your *job*, Irazek. Talk amongst yourselves for a few minutes while I fetch the things I'll need."

*   *   *

Grisaille had felt this disconnected, cut loose from the ordinary world and flapping helplessly at the end of some long and twisting chain, once or twice before: *dispossessed*, all the things he had taken for granted ripped away and gone by the wayside.

It didn't get easier with practice. He had been astonished that the others wanted him to come with them to rescue Greta Helsing—and more astonished that she'd found her own way out despite the locks and bars and hazards of the underground; he could have slipped away then, possibly, while the others were focused entirely on Helsing and her welfare. He had, in fact, considered it briefly, and then thought: *Where would I go?*

So, trailing behind, he'd followed the little party through the brightening streets, hands shoved in his pockets, barely noticing the people they passed. The others were putting some effort into not being seen—Varney, carrying the woman, Ruthven beside him, St. Germain still on all fours— but Grisaille didn't bother, and got a few stares from the early-morning tourists taking photographs of the Église de la Madeleine. He knew what he looked like: a bedraggled Goth with bright red contacts, entirely out of place.

The werewolf lived in a thoroughly tony apartment on the Avenue George V, the kind of place he'd probably bought a hundred years ago; it smelled of expensive furnishings and faintly of dog. Grisaille was aware that the well-swept floors had a few drifts of silvery shed hair lurking in the corners. St.

Germain had turned back bipedal in order to let them into the house, and that was a little easier to deal with, a giant man rather than a giant wolf, but Grisaille was still a long way from composed when Ruthven drew him into another room and shut the door behind them.

Oh, thought Grisaille. *We're going to do more inquisition, aren't we.*

Aloud he said—knowing it was stupid even as he said it—"I don't understand how the hell she got out on her own."

Stupid, all right; Ruthven's big silver eyes went noticeably colder. They were huge, those eyes, almost luminous, each iris a bright silver bowl of ice. Grisaille couldn't help thinking of him in the Opera, back at the beginning—sleek dark head and ruby shirt studs, offensively perfect, doll-like with distance, seen from the fifth-floor balcony—and he had to look away.

"Not with any help from you, that's for sure," said Ruthven. "You *left* her down there, sunshine."

Grisaille wrapped his arms around himself, sat down on the edge of a chair. "*Yes*," he said. "What do you want me to say? Yes. I did. I left her there. Okay? We both clear on this point now? Do you want me to take out an ad in *Paris Match* saying to all the world what complete and utter scum I am in every single way, or would hiring a skywriter suffice?"

"Don't *wallow*," snapped Ruthven.

"What the fuck else am I supposed to do, pray tell?"

"Practically anything more constructive. Why *did* you work for that creature in the first place?"

"It—" Grisaille stopped, shoulders hunching. "It seemed like a good idea at the time."

"I can't believe you," Ruthven said, running his hands through his hair: it wasn't even slightly fair, Grisaille thought, that the subsequent disarray didn't look any less effective.

No, he thought. *You can't, and I can't explain it—*

"Look at me," he said before he could decide this, too, was the stupidest thing he could possibly think of to do, and when Ruthven did—those black-rimmed silver eyes focused directly on his—Grisaille let his own gaze blank out in a pulse of something like the opposite of thrall: an *opening*.

Let me show you, he thought, and then Ruthven was *there*, in his mind, cold and sharp around the edges, startled into curiosity. Grisaille reached for a sequence of images, like snapshots spread on a table, like cut-together film projected on a wall—

Ingolstadt, snow-cold and winter-bright, friendship, carousing, studying by lamplight while the windowpanes rattled with icy wind, sitting up talking all night long, Victor's easy laugh, the bright sparkling brown of his eyes—the gathering awareness that what his friend was talking about was not just wild theory but something worse, something edging into madness—

—the bitter sting of snow in his face and the knowledge, now, of what he had failed to prevent, of that unspeakable project and its conclusion—what he had not done, and could not now repair—fleeing Germany, fleeing Europe—the vampire's bite, the reshaping of the universe—and later, a series of poor decisions, leaders followed, leaders left, comrades gained—the unfa-

miliar thrill of faces turned to him for orders, and the sinking horror of losing them again, with no one to blame for it but his own incompetence—not again, never again, not that—

—Corvin, in Vienna, pressing schnapps on him, saying, "What do you want to do with your life?" Saying, "Surely there's more to existence than slumming. Join me; I could use someone like you—"

—I could use you, and how that had been the sweetest thing in all the world just then, someone to follow and not have to think about what it was he was doing—

—and Paris, and the things that Corvin did, hunting in Pigalle, the parties, the endless parties, carrying the bodies through the tunnels under the city when Corvin was done with them; a growing, gathering, miserable certainty that once again he'd made the wrong decision, with no other real option to speak of, and grimly hanging on until there was nothing left to hold, only the sick awareness of his own culpability, again, again—here, Ruthven, here, have it all, isn't it nice to consider, isn't it a lovely suite of memories to never be capable of fucking forgetting—

"Stop," said Ruthven, a long way away, shaky, and the connection cut off: the place where he had been inside Grisaille's mind hurt sharply like ice on a cracked tooth, dizzying.

When he could open his eyes again, Ruthven was still there, still quite close, still staring at him—but the expression was different. He looked ill, white around the mouth, and his eyes were too wide, but—absurdly—Grisaille thought there was a kind of recognition there that hadn't been before. Not quite sympathy, but recognition: *I see you. I see you very well.* All that Grisaille was, and had been. All of it. Dimly, distantly, he was aware of the familiar flush of shame.

"Don't *ever* do that to me again without warning," said Ruthven, sounding weary. "And—Christ, you've had a time of it, haven't you—when we're down there, we can all stand in line and take turns murdering him, to be democratic about it."

There was something in that voice, too, that Grisaille hadn't heard before, something that went with *being seen*, and he was almost sure he wanted to hear rather more of it; he had just about made up his mind to say so when St. Germain tapped on the door.

"There's coffee," said the werewolf, "and I think she's waking up; you'd better come out here so we can talk properly."

Ruthven got up, only just slightly unsteady; and after a moment Grisaille, rather more unsteady, went to join him.

CHAPTER 12

She had been somewhere very far away, dark and quiet, with no one else around. Somewhere safe and peaceful, and Greta planned to stay there for as long as humanly possible, savoring the sensation of being beyond the reach of responsibility. She floated in the blackness of deep and profound sleep—

And abruptly, with no warning, was no longer completely alone inside her head.

Greta?

After months alone, it felt uncomfortably *full* to have two people in there: the slot where the other had rested for several years had partly closed itself up, like bone filling in the empty socket of an extracted tooth. She hadn't expected to hear from this particular individual for some time yet.

Fass? Her mental voice was muzzy with sleep. *Fass, what are you doing back, you're supposed to be in Hell, aren't you?*

And you are supposed to be in England, so what on earth are you doing in Paris? In—he paused, as if trying to work out her location—*in the home of a three-hundred-and-sixty-something-year-old werewolf? Good grief, I go back to Hell for a few months and everybody gets into ridiculous amounts of trouble*—

It's a long story, said Greta, and abruptly she could *feel* him looking through her recent memory, flipping through the sequence of events in her mind: that wasn't a sensation you forgot easily, even if you could get used to it, the intrusion of one mind into another. *Could you maybe not do that quite so hard?*

He retreated a little. *Sorry. It's—I've apparently been in Hell long enough to forget my manners around humans, I do beg your pardon. And this is not so much a long as a bloody awful story.* In her head his voice was bitter-ice cold, colder than she had ever heard him. *I am going to*—*repair this mess with reality and* then *I want to go and turn all these vampires inside out, one by one, Greta, my dear*—

What's wrong with reality? she demanded.

Somebody has been playing silly buggers with it, that's what's wrong, summoning something without the proper care or precautions—

Lilith, said Greta, realizing it. *Lilith and her monsters. You'd probably better come over here, Fass.*

She could feel him going through the file cabinet of her memory again, a bit more gently now. *Yes,* he said. *I think I will, and I'll bring the others with me.*

What others?

Acquaintances of mine, he said unhelpfully, and withdrew—

most of the way. He was still there, a presence in the very back of her consciousness, but no longer an active participant in her thought process.

Greta opened her eyes. It was no longer even slightly possible to pretend she was asleep, and she knew she wouldn't be getting back to sleep anytime soon despite how bone-tired she still felt. She was lying curled up in a large and comfortable bed in a room that, though pleasant, was undoubtedly a spare bedroom: it lacked much by way of personality.

She got out of bed, hanging on to the bedpost through a wave of dizziness, and by the quality of the light through the windows, judged that it was still fairly early in the day. Greta looked down at herself; she was wearing her own nightgown, rescued with the rest of her stuff from the hotel—in need of a wash, but still enormously preferable to the remains of the ballgown, which was nowhere to be seen. She hoped the werewolf had burned it.

The whistle, however. She hurried into the bathroom to check, and was extremely glad to see that it was still there—clutched in the arms of her tiny wellmonster, which was lurking in the washbasin, looking as if it intended to stay there for the foreseeable future. She stroked its flat head with a fingertip, and squeaked a little when it let go of the whistle with one hand to grab her finger and subject it to a brief experimental gnaw.

Greta reclaimed her finger, after having it inspected and dismissed as possible foodstuff, and let the monster go back to guarding its prize. As she came back into the bedroom, a shadow she hadn't noticed detached itself from the curtains and rippled over to her: a familiar piece of torn red taffeta, with a crumpled face made of wrinkles. She grinned at it, despite feeling approximately four thousand years old.

"Hello," she said. "Nice to see you again," and offered her hand to the whistler—and was a little surprised when it didn't wrap hard little cloth fingers around hers but instead swooped in closer and pressed its wrinkled face against her neck. After a moment she lifted a hand to stroke it, feeling the invisible body underneath the cloth, wondering all over again what they'd look like if you could see them properly. This one stayed pressed against her for a few more moments before slipping away to take up position just behind and above her shoulder.

"I'd better introduce you," she said to it. "Maybe try not to menace my friends?"

The whistler rippled its taffeta as if to suggest that it couldn't promise anything, and Greta laughed. It felt strange, laughing, and she realized she hadn't done much of it for days.

Her clothes were basically one giant wrinkle after having spent so long in the suitcase, but they fit, and they were hers, and it felt absurdly comforting to pull on a pair of jeans and a shirt that she'd worn so many times before. She ran a brush through her hair, decided it was about as presentable as it was going to get, and went to see what the surface world was up to.

Following the sound of voices, she padded down a short hallway into a living room with huge windows looking over the white and grey mansard-roofed cliffs of Paris, and thought—briefly, disconnectedly—*I was having such a nice time, before all this.*

Varney had his back to her, sitting on a grey velvet sofa, but Greta had a clear view of the others in the room: St. Germain, rumpled and large, Ruthven, and—Grisaille.

Right there, large as life, amazing hair and all. Grisaille.

Oh, she thought, and then, *I wasn't imagining it, back at the Opera, that he got out, but what's he doing* here? *Did they capture him, or something?*

The conversation faltered as they looked up to see her standing in the doorway, and Varney got to his feet. "Greta," he said. "Did we wake you?"

"No," she said, "Fass did, because he's apparently back in my head again, which means he's on the surface for some reason, and—not to be rude, but could someone tell me what the hell *he's* doing here, please?" She nodded at Grisaille.

He met her eyes, red to blue, and she was a little surprised when his dropped first. It occurred to her that she hadn't ever seen this particular vampire looking quite so unhappy, and thought: *Did he leave, or was he thrown out?*

"He's been of some assistance," said Ruthven, with a curious kind of control in his voice, "and he won't harm you."

"He certainly won't," said Varney, heavy as lead. After a moment he sat down, and Greta came around the sofa to join him. It was simply pleasant to be *near* him, in a way she was not examining in any great detail: the constant anxiety of the past several days seemed to be deadened almost all the way to nothing with Varney next to her. She realized after a moment that the whistler was still hanging back in the shadows of the hallway.

"Are you all right?" Ruthven asked, leaning forward to look intently at her.

"No," she said after brief consideration, "I'm not, but I don't think there's anything permanently the matter. You're going to have company, by the way," she added, turning to St. Germain. "More of it, I mean. Fass is on his way over."

"Fass?" inquired the werewolf.

"Fastitocalon. He's mostly a demon. He said something about reality being messed up."

"It is," said Ruthven, "at least according to Irazek, who is also a demon, if not a very effective one. One of the unspeakable individuals who were responsible for your abduction had apparently been summoning something, Grisaille tells us, and that is apparently very bad for reality. Makes holes in it, sort of thing."

"Lilith," she said, and was a little surprised to see Grisaille wince. "I found the place where she does it," she continued after a moment. "Under the Opera. Her lair. There are— probably forty or fifty monsters down there right now."

"She's not doing it anymore," Grisaille said, sounding slightly unwell. "These were the grey things. They look like frogs. She'd also been breeding, or possibly just summoning, the hairy ones. I don't know how many of those there were; they kept escaping, and—what in God's name is *that*?"

He pointed. Greta twisted around to see Winston the whistle-monster hovering cautiously in the doorway, and was more than a little amused to note that the whites were visible all the way round Grisaille's eyes. "He won't harm you," she said, echoing Ruthven's assurance, and beckoned to the hovering creature. "He was extremely helpful in the process of escape. Unlike you. Are you the only one of Corvin's groupies to get out?"

"...Yes?"

"So you left everything behind and sauntered on up to join the forces of good, did you?"

He hunched his shoulders, very slightly. "Yes," he said again, and Greta watched him for a moment longer before nodding.

"I see," she said. "Well. Now what the hell do we do? Anyone care to suggest next steps?"

"We go down under the city," said Varney with awful delicacy, "and we root out the coven, and we get rid of them in a way which will not likely result in their reappearance in another city twenty years on. That would be my suggestion."

"Right," said Ruthven. "Could not have put it better myself. Alceste, have you got any handy wooden spoons I could sharpen the handles of?"

"Wait," said Grisaille. "Wait for midday. Another hour or so. It's—he's bound to be sleeping then, he'll be at his weakest, and he won't be expecting an attack. Wait."

Beside her, Greta could feel Varney tense slightly, and then make himself relax. "Very well," he said. "I suppose that's a valid point. The four of us can hang around a little longer before we leave."

"Five," said Greta. "If you think I'm going to sit around up here while the rest of you go off to battle, you are dead wrong, Varney; I've had enough of that, and I know my way around the lair."

"She does," Grisaille confirmed. "Bits of it anyway."

"*Greta*," said Varney, ignoring this, "under *no circumstances* are you to go back under the city. We only just got you *out* of there again—"

"No you didn't," she said. "*I* did. Remember? And if you want to murder Corvin, then imagine how *I* feel. I had to put up with him and his body glitter and his skull goblet and tiresome insinuations for several nights in a row. I get a say in this, okay?"

Varney blinked at her, his eyes flat and reflective, and then just sighed. She could tell the argument wasn't exactly over, just put on hold, and was glad when the doorbell rang.

"That's probably Fass," she said. St. Germain got to his feet, rubbing the back of his neck, and some of the tension in the air faded out a little when he went to let the newcomers in. Ruthven ran his fingers through his hair, disarranging it further than it had already been disarranged, and Greta saw him glance at Grisaille under the black curtain for just a moment before he pushed it back again. The look on his face was not one she thought she'd ever seen there before, or not quite in that configuration; there was a kind of sharp, almost *resentful* protectiveness she didn't recognize, unlike his usual interest and concern for the people—like herself—whom he tended to help. As if he minded *minding*.

That's interesting, she thought in the part of her mind that wasn't focused entirely on the situation under the city. *That's very interesting.*

At least he doesn't look bored.

And then everything else faded right out of her awareness, because St. Germain had returned to the living room with a little group of strangers—and with Fass.

It had been only a couple of months since she'd seen him, but it felt like forever; despite how sore and weary she was, the way every muscle seemed to be trying to out-ache every *other* muscle in her body, Greta practically levitated off the couch and flung herself at Fastitocalon. She had time to think, *Oh my God, he looks so much better, why didn't I insist he go to Hell before now*—and then her face was buried in his neat pinstriped shoulder and his arms were around her, holding her close. He smelled faintly of sandalwood; after the days spent in a fug of cheap perfume under the city, it was extraordinarily pleasant. Under her ear the beating of his heart was steady and slow, and she couldn't hear even the slightest rustle when he breathed.

You're better, she said, not bothering to use her voice.

I am. You, on the other hand—

Never mind me, what's going to happen with reality? And what are you doing up here anyway? You're supposed to be at the Spa.

That's a fascinating question, and I look forward to answering it in the near future, but for the moment we have work to do, said Fastitocalon, bone-dry.

She sighed and wriggled out of his embrace, opening her

eyes to find the rest of the group including the newcomers studying the ceiling, the mantelpiece, or in one case the line of upholstery tacks along the edge of a chair's arm rather than looking at Greta and her oldest family friend. There were three people she'd never seen before: one middle-aged guy who looked a bit like Jeremy Irons, one young hippie type, and one who had both bright orange hair and an expression of profound unhappiness on his otherwise unremarkable face. After a moment she realized he had tiny carrot-orange horns half-hidden in the hair.

"My apologies," said Fastitocalon, "I believe most of you know one another by now, but allow me to introduce Crepusculus Dammerung and Gervase Brightside, remedial psychopomps, and the demon Irazek. Gentlemen, Dr. Greta Helsing." He looked around the room. "Edmund, Sir Francis, a pleasure to see you again; you, I don't believe I've met before," he added, looking at Grisaille with an eyebrow raised. "My name is Fastitocalon; I represent Hell's Office of Monitoring and Evaluation; and thank you, Monsieur St. Germain, for your hospitality."

You represent M&E? Greta had to demand. *I thought that was—what's his face, the other guy, the archdemon—*

Asmodeus, said Fastitocalon. *Do hush, Greta, I will explain everything* later, *there's something rather more important currently at stake.*

Not only did he look and sound better, he had apparently developed a more decisive management style in the past couple of months. Greta wasn't entirely sure she liked it.

"Can I offer you some coffee?" St. Germain asked somewhat uncertainly.

Fastitocalon smiled, a brief flicker of expression. His face was narrow, lined, but deceptively ordinary: he could have passed for a middle-aged banker without a moment's hesitation, despite the infernal heritage. "Not for me, thanks," he said. "But don't let me stop you. Let's talk briefly about what's just happened and what we need to do about it."

"*I'd* like some coffee," said Grisaille. "If I have to go through this all over again. I'd like it even more if you put something heartening in it."

St. Germain sighed, and went into the kitchen. Fastitocalon eyed Grisaille—and then Ruthven, next to him—with one eyebrow raised.

"His name's Grisaille," said Greta. "He's probably all right. A defector. Used to work for Corvin, who's in charge of all the general awfulness under this part of the city, but he's all right, I think."

She watched the expression on Grisaille's face change briefly; he sounded rather less flippant and more intent when he said, "I'll help. I'll do whatever I can, I'll—help."

"Splendid," said Fastitocalon drily. "Tell me everything you know."

There was a kind of anesthetic in being managed by other people, in giving up the responsibility for being in charge of what happened next, that Greta found intensely soothing. It felt a little like being allowed to put down something very heavy after carrying it for days on end; nevertheless she didn't let herself do what she wanted to do, which was curl up in the corner of the couch and go back to sleep. Instead she listened to Grisaille providing his end of the story, which she could tell was somewhat edited to leave out the irrelevant gory bits regarding Corvin's activities. Both the strangers with complicated names and St. Germain had stared at one another when he mentioned Corvin's habit of nicking bones from the catacomb ossuaries to decorate his lair; presumably some tag-end of mystery had been tied up.

She wondered what exactly *had* happened in Ingolstadt. He'd told her a little about his studies, his tiresome classmates of a hundred and ninety-something years ago, but not precisely why he had stopped; what he'd seen or done or experienced that had made him throw over years of work and disappear into history, to return at some point as a vampire with questionable taste in leadership.

What he had to say covered mostly the parts of the story she already knew, and Fass and the two strangers filled in the other side of things. That the disturbance of the bones in the ossuary had been responsible for producing a manifestation sufficient to require Brightside and Dammerung's professional attention, and that Lilith's monster-summoning had had an unintended and highly dangerous effect on the planes of reality *allowing* such a manifestation to occur, had apparently been news to Grisaille as well. It did come as some relief to Greta that the strange timeslip experiences she'd had on the way out of the underworld were, in fact, not artifacts of her own neurology going haywire.

"You could think of 'em as eddy currents," said the younger of the two polysyllabic individuals. Greta noticed he was wearing a Led Zeppelin T-shirt. "Like, moving objects through planes sets up a brief metatemporal energy flow in the surrounding area."

"That's not exactly right," said Fastitocalon. Greta couldn't quite get over how *much* better he looked than he had the last time they'd met; he'd gained weight, his clothes flattering rather than emphasizing the thinness of the creature inside them, and he seemed to have finally managed to lose his chronic cough. She thought disconnectedly that she would really like an opportunity to chat with Hell's medical director—whatever they had done to him, it was a serious clinical success—and turned her attention back to what he was actually saying. "It's more like rolling out pastry too thin, so it wrinkles, and the places where the wrinkles touch can undergo a kind of temporal short circuit. The problem is the same: we, or rather I, need to throw a *hell* of a lot of energy into this bit of reality in order to first patch and then reinforce it. Orders of magnitude more than went into breaking it. And we have to do this before anything really nasty gets a chance to look in. Which brings me back to you," he said, turning to Irazek and the other two. "I am going to need you to come with me to the Opera—"

"To take advantage of the leylines?" Irazek interrupted, looking eager.

"To, as you say, take advantage of the leylines." Fastitocalon lifted a hand and swept it through the air as if washing an invisible window, and a map of the city made of blue light sprang into being in midair. Greta felt the static buzz of magic being done, and again thought, *He's so much stronger, he has the energy now to spare on doing pretty light shows. I so want to talk to Dr. Faust.*

Fastitocalon tapped the hovering map with a fingertip, and it expanded and began to turn slowly, streets and boulevards outlined in cyan light drifting through the air of St. Germain's living room. "As Irazek has pointed out, there are points in Paris where existing lines of mirabilic force intersect with one another—any town that's been around this long is going to have a few of them—and these loci represent coordinates where the effects of any given magical effort will be strongly amplified. The largest and most significant of these is the opera house."

They watched as the blue map lit up with yellow lines, crisscrossing the city; they were pulled into a kind of tangle surrounding the Opera, like iron filings drawn around a magnet. Fastitocalon made another little gesture and a point of throbbing red light appeared, waxing and waning, partially intersecting with the Opera building. "Is that the damaged part?" St. Germain asked.

"Spot on," said Fastitocalon. "My colleagues and I will take care of the metaphysical aspect of this situation, but the physical side is up to the rest of you. In order to focus my efforts, I'm going to need some of you to go down there into the actual location and put some very specific items in very specific places surrounding the damaged section, if the mirabilic geometry of this is going to be at all successful."

He reached into the inside pocket of his suit (Was that new? It *looked* new, even if it was cut just like his vintage 1950s pieces, double-breasted grey pinstripe) and brought out five thin rectangles of what looked like grey glass. They had an odd shimmer to them, a faint orange luster not unlike the one Fastitocalon's eyes sometimes showed, and when he set them down on St. Germain's coffee table, there were glints and flashes from inside the glass as if holograms were somehow sandwiched inside. "These won't do you any damage to touch unless any of you are carrying a recent blessing of any kind, which I sincerely doubt. I'll show you where they need to go."

"What *are* those?" Varney wanted to know.

"Interplanar communication devices," said Fastitocalon. "Our equivalent of the mobile phone. In this context, you can think of them as prisms, or possibly collimators in a linear accelerator to modulate and shape the beam."

"Wait," said Grisaille. "You can *collimate* magic using *hellphones*?"

"It's a very long story, and one day I am going to make him tell it to me properly," Ruthven told him. "I can explain what I do know about the science of magic later."

"Quite," said Fastitocalon. "Action first, lectures afterward, once the world's been stabilized. In order to manage it, you'll have to take care of the vampires first, assuming they're down there and will interfere with the operation—"

"That will *not* be a problem," said Varney silkily. "Believe me."

"There's one down there who's just a kid," Greta said. "Can't be more than nineteen, she's—very new, and she doesn't deserve this." *Body glitter*, she thought. *God help us, body glitter.*

"*Nineteen?*" Varney said, looking aghast. "They changed a *child?*"

Across the room, Ruthven hissed through his teeth. The pupils of his eyes were ever so slightly red. Greta looked from him to Varney and back. "Which one of them—" he began.

"Name of Yves," said Grisaille evenly. "I can point him out to you. A few months back. I told him at the time it was a bloody stupid thing to do, not that it helps very much. The girl's name is something intensely unmemorable—"

"Emily," said Greta. "Fass, tell me we can get her out of there."

He sighed. "Probably. That part is, I'm afraid, up to you and whatever methods you use to deal with the rest of them—I can't repair reality *and* help you fight vampires at the same time. At least this lot probably hasn't got poisoned knives and a possessed mercury-arc rectifier on their side."

"We'll do our best," said St. Germain. "I can't promise anything, Dr. Helsing, but we'll do our best."

"Yes," she said, "we will. I'm coming *with* you. We *did* this part already. There's five of those things Fass wants us to place; there's five of us. End of discussion."

"Greta—" Fastitocalon began, and she glared at him, fiercely angry all over again—for the things that had been done to her, for the things that had been done to Emily, for the whole miserable stupid mess of it, for Lilith's cassette tapes in the dark, for the monsters, for the ancient, decaying stuffed bunny, for *everything*. Some of it must have shown in her face, and rather more obviously he'd gotten a solid whack of it directly to the mindtouch, because he blinked hard and looked away.

"Show us where you want these phone things put," she said, picking one up. It was smooth glass, slightly warm to the touch, about the size of an iPhone 6. In other circumstances Greta would have loved the opportunity to play with it; right now she wanted very much to get this over with. "Is there an order in which we should place them, or does it not matter?"

"You always did ask good questions," said Fastitocalon, sighing, and canceled the blue-lit map of the city with a wave of his hand. In its place he called up a map of the *undercity*, the tunnels and mines and sewer pipes and utility conduits that made up the crowded space beneath the streets. Greta had wondered, down in Corvin's lair, what kind of shape all the mine tunnels and the catacombs would be, seen from out-side; now she thought again of those ant-nest sculptures cast in metal, dendritic networks of burrows intersecting with one another, intensely organic; there was no *tidiness* to it.

Fastitocalon spread his fingers, and the scale increased, zooming in on a section of tunnels. Beside Ruthven, Grisaille sucked in a sharp breath through his teeth. "That's it," he said. "That's the lair. There's the passageway that intersects with the sewer—"

"I went past that," said Greta, vividly remembering. "I was afraid I'd have to get *into* the sewer to escape."

"Oh no," he told her. "That's just where we'd dump the bodies if we didn't want to go all the way to the river."

"Convenient," said Greta, slightly brittle. "The way out through Erik's house—"

"Is the back way in," said Grisaille, and got up. "Can I?" he asked Fastitocalon, looking at the map.

"Be my guest," said the demon. Grisaille reached rather hesitantly into the glowing projection with a fingertip, as if expecting it to hurt, and then relaxed.

"Here," he said, tracing a pathway down from what Greta realized was the Opera itself—this map didn't show surface detail—through a large rectangular chamber that had to be the cistern underneath the building, through a series of smaller chambers that were undoubtedly the house set inside the foundation wall, and then along a narrow winding tunnel Greta recognized.

Where Grisaille's fingertip had passed, there was a faint line of light, tracing the route. "Here's the intercept with the storm relief sewer," he said, "and past that—*here* is where Corvin and his people live. Or don't live, if you want to get technical."

"That's the way we'll take, then," said St. Germain. "The main entrance is where?"

"Way over here," said Grisaille, reaching to the north. "In the cellar of a Pigalle bar. There are several others, but the main way in is through the cellar. It's convenient for their hunting grounds."

"Would it be better," said Brightside, who had been watching this in silence, "to wait until they're all *out* in said hunting grounds before you go down there and do this job?"

"Not if part of the purpose of the journey is to do some extermination," said Varney. "You can't reason with this sort; the only argument they understand is a snapped neck, I'm afraid."

"I tried reasoning with them once already," Ruthven said, pushing his hair back. "Didn't seem to take. All right, Fass, where do you want your magic things to go?"

CHAPTER 13

Greta had thought, not so long ago, that she'd had more than a lifetime's worth of crawling through dark holes underground during the whole Gladius Sancti affair, and here she was all over again, eyes wide in the relentless dark, walking toward a nest of vampires who had once already captured her and kept her in a cage.

I never claimed to be sensible, she thought.

At least she wasn't expected to join in the active fighting if it came to that: her role in this particular mission was to place Fastitocalon's five collimator plates, currently resting in her various pockets. They had decided to have her—the least-capable of physical violence—focused on that task, leaving it up to the others to make sure she *could* do that. If making sure involved gross bodily harm, then so be it. Greta could not bring herself to care about the ethics of the situation: she wanted it to be over.

They had come in the way Greta had escaped, and been

glad that the little boat was still waiting at the water stairs; the vampires could cross the underground lake simply by *flying* over it in bat form, but she and St. Germain were happy to take the surface route. It wasn't deep but it was cold enough that neither of them had particularly wanted to wade, or swim, the distance to Erik's house.

Something had been there since Greta had come through, however many hours ago. What had been simply a tableau of slow decay, wet and slimy, was now a chaotic mess of broken furniture, rotting pieces of the chaise longue and armchair hurled every which way. The gas lamp from which a particularly tiny monster had hung, slothlike, had been torn from the wall and bent viciously in half. There was no evidence of the monsters themselves, and Greta had no idea if that meant they had escaped the destruction in here or that they were all dead; at least there were no tiny grey bodies among the debris. She hoped like hell that they'd somehow gotten wind of Corvin before he showed up to trash the place.

"Got a temper, hasn't he," Ruthven had said softly as they picked their way through the wrecked living room and out into the tunnel proper. Grisaille said nothing at all.

Being down here again was awful, but it was the kind of awful she almost welcomed: This time at least she wasn't *alone*, and this time she didn't have to rely on a whistler to guide her through the dark—and oh but she wanted to *see* this happen. Wanted that insufferable smile to be knocked off Corvin's face once and for all. Wanted Paris to be safe from this particular group of monsters: she could think about the real world, about her responsibilities, on the other side of whatever lay ahead for all of them.

They had just passed the junction with the sewer when she was overtaken by a sudden, intense, complete rush of sensation: the tunnel they were walking through was no longer pitch-dark except for the others' eyeshine, but glimmering with the moving golden light of candle flames, and the silence and distant dripping of water were replaced with the clink of tools on stone and the undercurrent of human voices.

The miners, she thought. *The miners who dug these tunnels, way back when. It's the timeslip thing, it's happening again—*

And as fast as it had appeared, it was gone again, leaving them blinking in the sudden darkness.

"Did you see that, too?" said Greta, clutching Varney's arm tight in the darkness. "Tell me you saw that, too, that it isn't just me."

"Yes," said Grisaille. "It's been happening for a while, I think. I've seen the lights in the distance on and off, never knew what they were before. All thanks to Lilith and her Make-a-Monster games, poor silly bitch. Let's keep moving."

She didn't have much time to dwell on the thought of Lilith and her pitiful summoning circle before St. Germain and Grisaille stopped again, with Varney right behind them. "What is it?" Greta whispered.

"Vampire." St. Germain was a dim shape in the darkness, the only light being that cast by their various eyes, but she could still see him tense. "Up ahead, a little way. He must have set a sentry on the back door after all."

"Will wonders never cease," Grisaille put in, in an under-tone. "I suppose I'd better go and see to whoever it is. I might not yet be *persona non grata* completely."

"If he's set someone on watch," said Ruthven, "it's pretty likely that he *is* aware of your defection and wondering if and when you're likely to come back with a lot of friends intending to make him dead, or at least dead*er*. Could be a trap, is my point."

"Wait," said Greta, just as softly, "Grisaille, take me with you. You *haven't* deserted. You've simply gone out and recaptured the boss's errant toy."

She could feel it when he stared at her—feel the intensity of his gaze, even if she could barely make out his face in the darkness, just his eyeshine. Varney whispered "No!" at just about the same time as Ruthven and St. Germain, but Greta was looking directly into the two red pinpoints of light that were Grisaille's eyes, the lights she'd seen for the first time back in the Opera above them, a hundred years ago.

"That might actually work," he said thoughtfully. "For long enough for you to put those glass things where they need to go, anyway. Pity you've been and gone and got yourself some different togs than the ones you were last seen inhabiting, but beggars cannot be choosers. Shall we?"

He offered her his arm, as he had once before—and this time, with a brief passing squeeze to Varney's shoulder, Greta stepped forward and laid her fingers on Grisaille's forearm, aware of the absurdity of the gesture even as she appreciated it. She was on fire with adrenaline, every nerve lit up like a fiber-optic lamp, and thought: *Yes sir, I will walk and talk with you.*

*   *   *

Neither Brightside nor Crepusculus had relished the thought of returning to the Palais Garnier, not after the timeslip they'd experienced up in the dance studio tucked into the dome, but they didn't have a hell of a lot of choice in the matter. According to Fastitocalon, the mirabilic resonant frequency of the building, or something, dictated the point in space where they could take best advantage of its amplifying effects. Brightside was very, very tired of technical jargon, and the demon seemed to have a never-ending store of it to employ.

He looked up at the huge colonnaded facade, pausing for a moment before following the others inside. ACADEMIE NATIO-NALE DE MUSIQUE, it said, and Brightside thought, *It's not just music, it's* make-believe, *it's imaginary worlds stacked on imaginary worlds, God knows how many stories are stored in there, tucked away in the wings or under the stage; no wonder it's a complex weight on the fabric of reality.*

He shook his head, and as he passed through the main entrance, he could *feel* the building's atmosphere close around him, like the skin of a soap bubble. Fastitocalon and the others were waiting for him, and Brightside caught up without a word, following Fastitocalon into the huge echoing space of the atrium with its iconic sweeping staircase.

"Whoa," said Crepusculus softly. The decor—overdone, opulent, *gleeful* in a way—was pretty damn good, as a matter of fact, but it appeared to be lost on Fastitocalon. He led them up the central staircase to the portal flanked by a couple of disapproving stone women, through a brief red-plush claustrophobic corridor, and into the vast red-and-gold cavernous hollow of the auditorium, with no fanfare whatsoever. Things like admission tickets happened to other people.

The last time Brightside had seen this particular view, it had been in a nightmarish instant of temporal dislocation, and he had *witnessed* that chandelier begin to fall. He and Crepusculus looked at one another, looked up at the huge brilliant fountain of light far above them, and both sighed.

"When this is over," said Crepusculus, "let's go somewhere as far away from Paris as is possible while remaining on this planet?"

"You took the words right out of my mouth," said Brightside. "I hear New Zealand is nice this time of year."

"Does anywhere in New Zealand have an opera house?" Crepusculus wrinkled his nose.

"Probably, but I bet you none of them have got phantoms in. Let's get this over with, before he starts lecturing us about resonance and amplification again."

Crepusculus's expression intensified for a moment, and then he sighed and followed Brightside down the aisle. Neither of them looked up at the chandelier as they passed under it—all the way under it, and past, because apparently Fastitocalon intended to do this bit of magic from the middle of the orchestra pit.

He was already moving the folding chairs and music stands out of the way, assisted by Irazek, when the psychopomps climbed down to join them. "Why are we here exactly?" Crepusculus asked.

"It's the mirabilic isocenter of the building," Fastitocalon said, taking out a piece of chalk. He drew a circle on the floor, rapid and neat, with a couple of sigils around the outside. It seemed to glitter for a moment, brighter than white, and then was simply chalk once more. "Not, as you might imagine, directly under the center of the dome: the symmetry's not that simple. Take my hands," he added, holding them out, and they obeyed, stepping into the chalk circle on the floor: the demons facing one another, the psychopomps between them. The moment their hands closed around one another, Brightside could feel his hair trying to stand on end: Fastitocalon had been *completely* right about this place acting as an amplifier; even the slightest flicker of power that under ordinary circumstances would barely be noticed was significantly more impressive. With the circle closed, he could feel the mirabilic field lines around the four of them moving, a current beginning to build; he could *see* it with a little effort, a faint blue light surrounding them. The chalk line on the floor was brighter still.

Brightside knew that he himself almost certainly couldn't do what Fastitocalon planned on, even if he'd known how: using the combined mirabilic energy of all four of them, connected by the circle and amplified by the geometry of the building in which they stood, to—well, weld reality back together, was entirely not what he and Crepusculus were *for*. He couldn't help thinking about how frail and fragile Fastitocalon had seemed the last time they'd met him, and despite how briskly competent he currently appeared, *could* he do this, even with all their combined strength? He wasn't replaceable; Brightside knew he was the only one of them who had any idea *how* to manage the job, how to balance the forces involved. What would happen to them all if he suddenly ran out of strength in the middle of this operation?

We'll find out, won't we, he told himself, and a moment later Crepusculus's voice, faint but present—damn, they were linked, they could *hear* each other—said, *We will.*

We most certainly will, said Fastitocalon in his mind, dry, and then Irazek, small and rather frightened, *What are we waiting for?*

For the collimators to be placed, Fastitocalon said, and Brightside was a little surprised at the patience in his tone. *Greta has to put those where I told her to, or I won't be able to aim and focus accurately to do this right.*

How long is that going to take? said Crepusculus.

As you recently mentioned ... we'll find out.

It wasn't the first time Grisaille had re-infiltrated the headquarters of somebody he'd just betrayed—probably about the seventh or eighth, all told—but there was always still a little *frisson* of excitement to the situation. This time it was exacerbated by the presence of the human, whom he'd absolutely not expected to do anything nearly this reckless shortly after escaping from durance vile.

(How *had* she escaped anyway? Grisaille realized he'd never actually gotten around to asking; the last time he'd seen her underground was when he'd returned her to her cell after the

Lilith episode, and the next time they met had been at the entrance to the underground passage, where she'd made it to the surface by herself. Presumably she'd convinced somebody to unlock the cell door for her, but it puzzled Grisaille to try thinking of who other than himself might have done that deed. Couldn't be the new kid, she wouldn't dare do such a thing, so how *had* Helsing escaped?)

She was still flying high on adrenaline—that he could easily tell—and he hoped that when the high wore off, she wouldn't crash in a particularly inconvenient manner: they were relying on her to place Fastitocalon's collimators while the rest of them dealt with Corvin and his goons if this all went pear-shaped. He wasn't actually sure he'd be *able* to protect her, as a matter of fact. Not without proper weapons. All he had was a knife from St. Germain's kitchen, and why he was suddenly remembering Ruthven handing out the knives with a rueful expression and promising the werewolf a replacement set of Wüsthofs was entirely beyond Grisaille.

He looked down at her, and she could clearly feel the weight of his gaze because she looked right back at him, blue-green eyes wide in the near-darkness. He had been going to say something, and decided on the whole it was unnecessary—and then stopped, his hand closing around her wrist.

Beyond a bend in the tunnel there was the beginning of light visible—to vampire eyes anyway; he didn't know if she could see it yet—and he could smell the perfume from here, one of the Black Phoenix Alchemy Labs concoctions the Kindred favored, all sweetness and civet. He thought it was called

Dorian, or something equally unspeakable, and he knew exactly who was wearing it.

Leaning down, he put his lips to Greta's ear—God, humans were so warm, one forgot that—and whispered almost without sound, "Approximately fifteen yards ahead of us around that bend there is a vampire, presumably Corvin's sentry. His name is Aurélien, or at least he'd like people to think it is, and he will recognize both of us immediately. Stay quiet and let me do the talking."

Her breathing quickened, and he expected her to ask something like "What?" or possibly "Why?" but she simply nodded once, and Grisaille straightened up. He shook his hair back over his shoulders and concentrated on replicating the expression he'd normally worn down here: faintly amused, and more than faintly cynical, and above all unsurprised.

He let go of Greta's wrist and took her by the upper arms instead, propelling her before him like a prize, and together they walked around the corner and into what even for Grisaille was bright light after so long in the dark.

A tall figure in a floppy silk shirt with ruffles down the front stepped in front of them. "Halt!" it said. "Who goes th—*Grisaille?*"

"Me," said Grisaille. "Unbearably delightful to clap orbs on you, Aurélien. Look who's found the boss's wayward little pet and brought her home again; aren't I just the absolute most?"

"But we thought you were gone," said the vampire, who really ought to have been gently dissuaded from attempting flowing bottle-blonde Lestat waves of hair. Or possibly forcefully dissuaded. "That you *left*. Like, you *quit*. Corvin was furious."

"Don't I know it, ducks," said Grisaille. "An unfortunate misunderstanding, that's all. I expect he'll be terribly glad to see me back now that I've recaptured his prisoner. Is he asleep?"

"They all are, probably. Let me take you back to the cells so we can lock her up again?" He sounded as if he relished the prospect, and Grisaille's fingers itched to close around his neck; he made himself keep the mild expression and tone of voice nonetheless.

"That would be *super*," he said. "Come along, little human. Time you were safely back in your box, and don't open that pretty mouth of yours to bother trying to convince me not to put you there; I've had enough of talking."

Under his hands he could feel Greta's shoulders stiffen, just for a moment, and he had time to think, *Oh God, she's going to give the whole farce away*, before she relaxed again.

This might even actually work.

"It's working," St. Germain said in an undertone. "I can smell it—they're leaving together, all three of them, and there's no serious alarm or stress in the scent. Whatever he said to the sentry, it was enough."

"And now we follow," said Varney. "Closely. Let's *go*, all right?"

In the darkness he could see the werewolf nod, and then the three of them were moving again: completely soundless, wrapping themselves almost unconsciously in a layer of the don't-notice-me influence they all used to cover certain activities in public. A passing rat was startled when an unexpected shoe came down quite close to it: there hadn't been sound or sight or scent to warn of any other creature in the tunnel.

Varney's eyes narrowed as they entered the part of the passageway that was lit: electrical cables had been run along the corner between wall and ceiling, held in place by metal staples knocked straight into the pale stone. It was a professional job, and the lamp hanging from the ceiling was not tasteful but at least appeared to be installed correctly.

Someone with experience did that, he thought, and nothing Grisaille had told them earlier had given him any reason to believe that Corvin's group was well versed in electrical infrastructure. It had to have been a human, and he knew what would have happened to that human after they had done the job they'd come to perform.

He could smell vampire now, too, and a host of other things. As they moved deeper into the lair, and as chambers began to open up on either side of the passageway, a whole collection of scents assailed Varney's senses. Multiple kinds of perfume, some cheap and some less so, but all with the staleness of unmoving air, limited ventilation. Blood, and liquor, and the cloying sweetness of scented candles.

These people turned a child, Varney thought again. It was the cardinal sin for him. Killing was bad enough—but killing was at least clean, an act over and done with, and the person's soul would be taken care of in whatever fashion was appropriate. Turning someone was the worst thing Varney could imagine, condemning them to a twilight existence neither living nor dead, a creature of darkness that preyed on the living and gave nothing in return, a creature that was damned and could not die and reach that ending—

This is not the time or the place, he told himself, slightly amused to note how much the mental voice sounded like Greta Helsing's. It was right. He could reflect on the terrible things he himself had done, and the terrible thing he himself was, *later*. Now was for justice. Now was for retribution, and—if they were lucky—they might be able to rescue the youngest vampire, and at least attempt to help her adjust to the limitations of her new world, if not undo the damage already done.

And right up until someone far ahead in the tunnels shouted, "Corvin! Wake up! Everybody—Grisaille is back!" Varney thought things were going rather well.

There hadn't been enough warning for him to choke off the idiot's announcement before he could wake the whole lair. Grisaille shoved Greta away and grabbed Aurélien's head between his hands, breaking his neck with a single violent twist, but it was too late, the damage had been done.

"Fuck," he said, dropping the body, "that's torn it—get out of here, try to get those glass things in place," but doors were already opening, and people were there. Corvin's people. Sleep-blurred and blinking, but conscious and present, and when a moment later the other three members of the little impromptu infiltration force arrived, it was evident how badly they were outnumbered. Corvin himself emerged in a red silk dressing gown, his hair mussed, and stopped dead to stare at Grisaille and Greta.

"Hi!" said Grisaille brightly. "I'm here to ruin everything. Greta? *Run.*"

There was just enough time for him to see out of the corner of his eye St. Germain beginning a leap that started on two legs and landed on four, a dizzying *scrunch* of shape and form as he went from man to wolf, and then Corvin's uncomprehending expression settled into blank poisonous hatred, and he lunged for Grisaille's throat.

After that, things happened very rapidly. Grisaille was aware of the members of the coven all around him, and even as he ducked Corvin's grip and feinted to the left, coming back with a curled fist to hit his quondam leader so hard his hand went numb, even as the shouting rose and the meat-slab sounds of flesh against flesh rose with it, even as he dodged another vampire whose face seemed all made of white and snarling teeth and whom he'd watched waltzing extremely badly to techno only a day or so ago, he felt oddly distant. As if he were observing everything from a remove, dispassionate and without particular investment. That they had badly miscalculated the combined abilities of the now-fully-awake members of the coven was evident; that he did not, somehow, *care* so very much about this was equally unmistakable, if strange.

It wasn't something he had encountered before, and he wondered—catching a stunning redhead's wrist and snapping the bones of her forearm in three places—if the distance was simply a function of the awareness that he was, after so very long, perhaps finally going to die.

The fighting all around him rose and fell. He glimpsed Francis Varney, stone-faced, eyes ablaze, his shoulder wet-red and scarlet, biting the back of someone's neck, and had no idea if the blood was Varney's or somebody else's; saw a vampire go down under the killing jaws of the wolf in a spurt of blood and a choked-off cry. Saw, briefly, in a flicker, Greta Helsing on the other side of the heaving mass of combatants, pressing herself against the wall as she took one of the grey glass collimators from her pocket and set it into a rough niche on the wall. Saw Edmund Ruthven across the thrashing crowd thrusting a makeshift stake through the chest of Yves with sufficient force that the tip protruded from his back— and Grisaille, at that strange remove, was capable of noticing the odd serenity on those dramatic features. As he watched Ruthven pull the gore-covered stake free and turn with balletic grace to meet the oncoming advance of another vampire, Grisaille had the mental space to think, *That's beautiful*—

And something hit him in the back, a blow that stunned him for a moment, like the fall of a hammer, before the pain came and flooded his mind blank and terrible red.

There was an arm around him like an iron bar; he was pulled close, someone's face beside his, someone's mouth to his ear, and the agony in Grisaille's back flared red to white as the blade buried hilt-deep in him was twisted hard.

"So *this* is how you repay me," a voice snarled in his ear. Corvin. "I should have killed you months ago, you filthy traitor, but I'm fixing that unfortunate oversight"—another twist of the knife, and Grisaille moaned, helpless to stop it—"You go to hell," Corvin said, flecks of spittle cold against his ear and cheek, "and you tell the Devil that Corvin sent you."

Grisaille couldn't breathe, could hardly see: all the world was hazed behind that blank and sheeting agony. He had time to think *stabbed in the back, stabbed in the fucking* back, *of course, what did I expect, a glorious and heroic death in art-directed battle* before Corvin let go of him with a brutal shove, pulling the knife free; he stumbled, going to his knees and then collapsing completely. Someone trod on his outstretched hand; he scarcely noticed it through all that pain.

Had he really thought he was free of Corvin? Had he really thought there would be no repercussions from the years he'd spent, no price to pay? Had he thought he could simply— what had Greta said—saunter upward and join the forces of good?

What did I expect? he thought again, and wondered what dying would be like, and how long it was going to last before it was over. That he was going to die he already knew: not even a vampire's healing powers could do their job fast enough to repair a wound like this. He really *couldn't* breathe— something in his back bubbled, whistling with each attempt at inspiration, but he couldn't get any air; when he coughed, a mouthful of dark blood came up all at once, and oh God but that *hurt*, hurt like nothing he'd ever experienced. Grisaille moaned again: a soft rag of sound utterly drowned out by the din of battle.

Anytime now, he thought. *This can be over anytime now, come on*, and at first when the hands touched him, he didn't even notice through the pain; it wasn't until someone shook him, gripping his shoulders, making it hurt *more*, that he realized anybody was there. Was there, and was calling his name.

A distant voice, high and panicky. A *young* voice.

Grisaille made his eyes open, trying to see past the gathering haze, and could just about make out the face of Emily-called-Sofiria very close to his own. "Grisaille!" she said, and shook him again, and the bolt of pain that went through him tore a gasp with it, clearing his head a little. "Grisaille, come on, please, don't be dead, don't be dead, you can't be—"

He couldn't really get enough breath to speak, but he could whisper, and it took a lot of effort to make the words: "Sorry, I'm afraid...'s a done deal. Get out of here, kid. Get out."

"You *can't* die," she said again accusingly, and Grisaille was still trying to come up with some possible response to that when the sparkles obscuring his vision irised in all the way, and were followed by blackness; and he thought *oh good, finally* before the darkness closed over him completely, and took him down with it into the black.

Here is Greta Helsing, in a chamber underneath the city, flattening herself against the wall to stay out of the way of a moving, shifting mess of tangled vampires, all teeth and nails and mad burning scarlet eyes. Here is Greta Helsing setting a piece of grey glass behind a wall hanging of violet polyester with a shaking hand: two down, three to go, and she cannot get past the fighting to the places those last three need to be.

Here is Greta Helsing distantly aware of just how fast her own heart is beating, and just how easy it would be for it to stop, with just one bite—not even a bite, a *blow*, any one of these could crack her skull clean open with a flick of its wrist, snap her neck like a man might snap a piece of ice between his fingers.

Here is Greta Helsing vividly, viscerally aware of having felt weightless, high with adrenaline and the reassurance of companions, confident that this would be *easy*, and oh, but she could have kicked herself for it. Here is Greta Helsing wondering, *How in God's name are we going to get out of this—how am I supposed to get these glass things where they need to go before everyone gets killed—Fass will be so disappointed, the world's going to break because I didn't think things through, didn't plan for a pitched battle—*

—and being shocked out of the helpless fugue of terror by a hand closing around her wrist. It was a very strong hand, despite being small, and it was cold, and she was absolutely sure that whoever it belonged to was going to kill her dead—

And blinking through the haze at a face that *wasn't* frozen in a snarl, a face that was all huge shock-wide imploring eyes.

"You're a doctor," Emily said for the second time in their acquaintance, her voice high and quavering. "You have to come, please, right now, there's so much blood, he's—you have to come *now*—"

"Who?" Greta asked, but she was already letting Emily draw her forward—both of them flattened against the wall, trying to stay out of the way of the fighting—and it came as exactly no surprise to find that the crumpled form Emily had dragged out of the melee belonged to none other than Grisaille.

"Shit," Greta said, soft, and fell on her knees beside him as Emily did the same. "What happened?"

"I don't know, he's bleeding terribly and he was making this kind of—bubbling sound."

She leaned close. He was still making it, a faint unpleasant sucking liquid noise. Good. "Help me roll him onto his side."

She'd never dealt with a punctured lung in a sanguivore, but there was a first time for everything, and Greta had to hope that because he *was* still breathing, sort of, the weapon hadn't nicked his heart: if that was true, if she was fast and he was lucky, she might be able to stabilize him long enough for his accelerated healing to kick in.

Grisaille's shirt was slicked to his skin with blood: there was a puddle of it underneath him, and dark red bubbles swelled and popped at a point where the shirt fabric was torn. "Okay," she muttered, "right side, good, that's good, might have a chance—Emily, I need you to grab that curtain and pull it off the wall right now."

"Will that help?"

"*Do it*," she snapped, getting her fingers under the edges of the torn shirt and ripping it open to expose the wound. It hadn't gone all the way through, which was also good. Greta braced Grisaille with a hand on his chest and pushed her palm over the wound in his back, hard enough to jerk a moan out of him, hard enough to form a seal and keep the air inside his punctured lung; his ribs expanded almost at once in a deeper effort to breathe. She barely noticed Emily yanking down one of Corvin's decorative brocade hangings from farther down the hall, away from the main action, until the girl was right there with the cloth, thrusting it at her awkwardly.

"Fold it up into a square pad," she said, a little pleased that Emily hadn't simply devolved into hysterics at this point. When the kid was done, she grabbed the folded curtain— still keeping pressure on the wound—and as hard and fast as she could, she snatched her hand away and shoved the pad of cloth against his back.

"I need a belt," she said. "Something to tie this with. You got anything?"

Emily shook her head, her face shock-pale even for a vampire.

"Velvet scarf with fringe on it? Spiked bondage leash?" Greta continued. That got a tiny hiccup of laughter—*good*, she thought, *she's still on this side of hysterics, but only just*— and Emily shook her head.

"Then I need you to keep pressure on this. I'm going to roll him over onto his chest, and I need you to hold this against his back as hard as you can. It has to keep a seal. Hard as you can. Moving him in one—two—three."

Grisaille gave a terrible little moan as they rolled him over, and Greta pressed down on the pad of cloth over his wound, hard. "Here," she said to Emily. "Where my hand is. Push down *hard*. Going to move my hand now."

She was a little impressed at how fast and without question the kid obeyed, pressing down on Grisaille's back with her spread palm. He moaned again, a little torn-out shred of sound. "Harder," Greta said. "Put weight on it."

"But—that's going to hurt him," Emily said, looking at her with those shock-bright eyes again. Greta sighed.

"It sure as hell is," she said. "It also might keep him alive long enough for him to start healing. You keep that pressure on. I'm going to call for help."

"From who?" Emily demanded, the quaver back in her voice.

"The only person who might be able to answer," said Greta grimly and got to her feet. The knees of her jeans and the palms of both hands were dark with Grisaille's blood. The fighting was still going on, although there were fewer combatants: she saw Ruthven covered in blood, St. Germain with his fur black and matted with it—*Varney, where is Varney, no*—

She saw him for a moment in a gap between bodies. Hands red to the elbows, one arm hanging uselessly by his side, but *there*. Okay.

Fass, she said inside her head sharply. *Fastitocalon, I need you.*

Bit busy right now. When are you going to have those collimators placed?

I can't, that's what I'm trying to say, we're in the middle of bloody Agincourt down here, I can't get to the last three locations, we need some help and we need it right the hell now.

He paused, and she could feel him retreat, thinking fast, and then, *Stand by. And don't touch any of the stacked bones.*

What happens if I—

There was a sudden shock in the air, like a pressure wave, violent enough to send her staggering against the wall: her ears popped painfully.

That hadn't felt like *magic*, she thought. She'd been around Fastitocalon when he'd done actual magic enough times to recognize the static-electricity crackle, the smell of burned tin. That had been like *pressure*. Something coming into being all at once.

Fass, what the—

And then she heard the voices.

CHAPTER 14

Several hundred feet above them and perhaps a quarter-mile away, in the orchestra pit of the Palais Garnier, Brightside could hear a little of what Greta was broadcasting, the edges, echoes of her voice, through the link to Fastitocalon: he could very clearly hear Fastitocalon's response. *Stand by, and don't touch any of the stacked bones.*

What—Irazek began, through static.

Brightside, said Fastitocalon tightly, *are you and Dammerung one-way gates, or can you function in reverse?*

It took him a moment, dazzled with the sheer level of power that was building up all around him. *Can we bring ghosts back? I—we've never tried, I don't think.*

How about you try it now? said Fastitocalon. *The dispossessed. The bones they stole from the ossuary. Bring those people back to give our friends some reinforcements in the fight.*

Through the blue light, he looked at Crepusculus across the circle; could just about see him shrug: *I'm game if you are.*

350

It was more difficult than anything he could remember, the simple *effort* involved in projecting themselves through the planes while remaining physically part of the circle, but Brightside felt strangely exhilarated: they were *being used* for their purpose, even backward.

Finding the ghosts was easy by comparison. So was getting their attention. The resounding *YES* to Brightside's question—*will you let us bring you back through, give you physical strength, to revenge yourself on the ones who most recently disturbed your rest*—nearly deafened both of them.

And opening the way—he knew it was a risk, with this part of reality so attenuated and worn, but hopefully it was a risk that would pay off—opening the way for thirty ghosts at once to slip back into the prime material plane was like parting gossamer curtains. There was an instant of mental turbulence as the group went through, and then Brightside could think again, and let himself snap back into the circle in the Opera, shaking with effort.

That's done the trick, said Fastitocalon. *Thank you both. Not long now, I think.*

Greta thought for a moment that the timeslips were back, that she was inside a wrinkle of the past—but the sounds of battle continued underneath the guttural new voices, coming from behind her.

She turned very slowly, feeling her spine creak, and discovered herself staring at something she hadn't ever seen before outside of films or fever dreams: translucent, greenish figures with cold-burning eyes, points of pale light in deep sockets. There were...many of them. Many. And they were coming toward her.

There were more at the other end of the room, painting the lair with their corpse-light. And now Greta could make out something peculiar even by the standards of the current situation: all of the ghosts seemed to be missing something. A leg, an arm. Both. A head. A jaw.

It didn't seem to slow them down. The ones missing legs moved as if they still had them. The headless ones had eyes nonetheless, merciless little points of light hanging in nonexistent faces.

She watched, frozen, as the ghost army came on; watched, eyes apparently unable to close, as a translucent greenish arm hooked itself around a vampire throat and gave a sharp jerk. There was the bitter-ice crack of bone, and the vampire went limp.

Don't touch the stacked bones, Fastitocalon had said. Corvin's *decorative* bones, stolen from the ossuary.

These men and women had come, at last, to reclaim what was theirs. What had been taken from them.

Across the chamber, Ruthven was just as frozen in amazed shock as Greta herself: she could see it very clearly when he slipped out of that frozen state and back into *right, let's get this done* mode, and the battle joined again.

This time the advantage was in their favor. Considerably so. The remainder of the coven was driven back, away from the tunnel Greta needed to access. She felt for the last three pieces of grey glass tucked into her pockets, incredibly grateful they were still there. Now that the remaining Kindred were distracted, she could do the job they'd *really* come for.

It didn't take her long to find the other places Fastitocalon had indicated. They felt random; she knew they weren't, like the pieces of optical-illusion paintings that made no sense unless you looked at them from precisely the right angle to form the complete image.

She set the glass rectangles leaning against a wall here, flat atop a piece of furniture there, cradled in the fold of a wall hanging. Collimators, enclosing some kind of beam, shaping and aiming it at a particular part of the universe, and if she had been slightly less desperate and frightened, she would have found it fascinating to try to visualize.

I've done it, Fass, they're all in place—what happens now?

Thank you, my dear, he said. And *withdrew*, rather than answering.

Withdrew all the way, completely leaving her mind. The shock of it was like a door slammed against a gale-force wind, and Greta actually stumbled, hands going to her head. It *hurt* having that empty space there again; the last time he'd vanished like that without warning, five months ago, she had been convinced that he was dead.

This time she wasn't sure what to think—and was still blinking against that sudden empty shock when she came back to Emily and Grisaille, moving on instinct alone.

The kid was still holding pressure on his wound, hard enough to do it right: she could see the shapes of bone, glow-pale, under the skin of her knuckles as she pressed her hands down.

"What's—what's happening?" Emily asked in a strengthless little voice. "What are they? Those things?"

"People," Greta told her. "With a grudge. They're—here to help us. Thank you, by the way. You're doing very well."

"He's still breathing," Emily said as if offering something up. Greta picked up Grisaille's wrist, fingers resting over the pulse: there, slower now, steady but faint. His breath still came with the bubbling crackle of fluid movement; there was blood in there that would need to come up, but the seal was holding and his punctured lung could actually inflate.

"I think he's going to make it," said Greta. "If any of us are. Emily—something's going to happen soon and I'm not sure what it will be, which isn't helpful, but—if we do get through this, I want you to come with us back to the surface. With Varney and St. Germain and Ruthven and I. Be part of our world, instead of this one."

Emily stared at her, eyes huge, dried mascara snail-trails down her cheeks looking like war paint; she was about to say something, she'd drawn a breath, and then all the world went suddenly, brilliantly white.

This was magic, Greta knew, magic on a scale she'd never thought to imagine; the force of it was like a physical blow, like opening a furnace door and being knocked back by the heat, and the last thing Greta thought as the white swallowed her up entirely was, *We tried: that has to mean something at the end of it all, that we tried.*

Varney could remember an experience not unlike this once before, in another hole under the earth, the previous autumn. That one had ended with an even more improbable situation than *the walking dead.*

It had taken him very little time to observe, recognize, and assess the situation. After that peculiar and sharp kind of disturbance in the air, at least thirty dead people had decided to join the fray, and in doing so had tipped the balance sharply in their favor. He couldn't use his left arm, and the pain of his injuries was at the sort of level where it was making him feel distractingly ill, but suddenly that wasn't in itself a death knell.

The means by which the ghosts had appeared, or taken on enough physical form to be of use against the aggressors, did not bother Varney as he waded back into the fray; what worried him was that he couldn't see Greta anywhere. Had she managed to place the glass things and then sought safety somewhere else in the tunnels while the battle went on? Had one of the coven—

And even as the mental image flashed across his vision, Greta dead at the hands of one of these creatures, all the world blanked out in a soundless explosion of brilliant white light, brighter than anything he'd ever seen, brighter than the thing under London last autumn at the end of it all, nothing but white and white and white and then—

Varney felt himself *slide*. Instead of the terrible low-roofed chamber under the earth full of active carnage, he was in a different room, empty and dark; he was in a different room, flickering-pale with golden candle flames, the ceiling smudged carbon-black by God knew how many torches over the years; he wasn't in a chamber at all but sealed in solid stone, crushed by it, pressing against him with tons of weight in every direction, an explosion of pain; back to the chamber decorated only with a few hangings, then the chamber with bones, then the chamber full of drunken carousing vampires—

I'm lost in time, he thought to himself, his ribs creaking from the pressure of that stone even now: the stone not yet quarried that would become the chamber he stood in. *This place is not sure what time it is, and I'm lost in it.*

Through the haze, he could make out someone reaching for his hand. Ruthven, Edmund Ruthven, covered in blood that probably wasn't all his, white fingers with pointed nails, a solid grip in the middle of terrifying uncertainty. A moment later he felt Alceste St. Germain close a paw that turned into a hand around his own, warm with living heat, and—almost at once—a physical shock as Ruthven and St. Germain joined hands, the three of them closing a circle. They were together, a thing that existed, in the middle of wildly fluctuating temporal zones. They were real, against a universe that was suddenly and terribly unsure.

And the brightness flared again and ate all of them, swallowed Varney, Ruthven, St. Germain, everything still there in the chamber, and he could feel *all the times at once*, not sequentially: the blank pressure of solid stone before ever man tunneled through it, *and* the miners, through the ages, *and* the explorers, *and* the engineers, *and* the cataphiles, *and* Corvin's people. All times were one, overlaid on one another in a crushing dizzy flare of experience—

—and Varney could feel the world being stretched, feel the shock of power thrown into it, the dazzling destructive arc flash of history rolled thin and folded back together again, laminated like a plastic wrapping back into its proper order, pressed back into place, welded shut with an unthinkable burst of energy—

And reality *slammed* back again with vicious sharpness, bringing with it visceral awareness, pain, fatigue, fear. Varney was himself again, staggering back to lean against the wall of the chamber, gasping, aware that the remaining crowd of vampires was largely reduced to a collapsed confusion of terribly bent and bloodstained limbs; he had barely held on to consciousness himself, and presumably it had only been the combined strength of Ruthven and St. Germain that had held the three of them upright through the full force of the temporal flow.

He could just about make out Greta's pale hair across the room; she was lying facedown in a crumpled heap, and Varney had time to think, *If she is dead, then everything will have been pointless*, before he saw her shoulders move as she breathed. Nearby were the bodies of Grisaille and a very young vampire, both of whom seemed the worse for wear but still present.

A child, he thought, desperately weary. *They turned a child.*

St. Germain crossed the chamber and knelt down beside the three of them, still in two-legged form, and Varney had rarely felt so grateful to have somebody else taking charge of a situation. "Is it over?" he asked, aware of his own voice shaking.

Ruthven pushed back his hair. "No," he said. "Yet all's not done; yet keep the French the field, and this part I have to finish on my own."

"What—" Varney began, but the question died half-born as he watched Ruthven step over a tangled mess of limbs and reach down to haul someone bodily from the heap. And lift him off the floor, one hand around a blood-slick throat. Whoever it was had lost his shirt somewhere along the line. Blood-soaked black hair caked the pale face.

Corvin, Varney thought. *That must be Corvin.*

Half-conscious, the vampire scrabbled at Ruthven's wrist, choking, and then seemed to realize all of a sudden who was holding him. A change came over his face—still twisted, almost unrecognizable underneath blood and dirt—and Varney thought he actually looked happy. Or something close to satisfied.

"...it's *you*," Corvin rasped, clutching at the wrist of the hand that held him. "Finally. It's *you*—I've—waited for this for so long—"

Varney wondered if he *knew* exactly what kind of danger he was in. The platinum fang set with a ruby glittered behind Corvin's torn lips, bent at an angle. "Don't you remember me?" he asked Ruthven almost plaintively.

The air seemed to thicken, crystallizing around them, as if

something crucial was about to happen. No one else was currently bearing witness to this particular endgame; it was Varney alone who watched the awful little smile on Corvin's face tilt and slide off completely, to be replaced with a drowning kind of horror as Ruthven's own expression failed to change at all.

"Do I remember you?" Ruthven repeated, as if tasting the words. "Let me think about that—it's been a while—"

Corvin squirmed in his grip, choking, tried to say something, couldn't draw enough breath. "No," Ruthven told him after a deliberately drawn-out pause, his voice even. "I really can't say that I do; I have no idea who on God's earth you might be, and I'm afraid that I don't actually care."

Before Varney had time to register what was happening, he turned—still holding Corvin off the ground—and swung the dangling vampire like a sack of discarded clothing, hard, against the wall.

There was a small but horrible sound that Varney knew he would hear in his dreams much more clearly than he'd like, and Ruthven dropped what was left of Corvin in a heap. The shape of his skull had been radically altered, flattened on one side, and his eyes stared sightlessly at the ceiling.

St. Germain had risen to his feet while Ruthven was occupied, and the expression he wore made Varney wonder if Ruthven himself was going to be next in line; but the light in the werewolf's lamp-yellow eyes died out and he slumped a little, with a sigh. "Killing that one was my prerogative," he said. "I claimed the right."

"Terribly sorry," Ruthven said. "But it really *was* my job; I should have done it properly the first time I encountered that specimen, back in the nineties." He wiped his hands on his trousers. "Would have saved everyone a lot of time and effort and trauma. There's a few others left alive—"

"Not for long," said St. Germain. "I'm not having them come back, either. Doing this once is bad enough; I'm not planning on doing it again." He bent over the tangle of bodies on the floor, and Varney looked away.

"I can't fault the level of efficiency," said Ruthven. "Can you walk, do you think?"

The question was directed at Varney, who was leaning against the wall. The words were matter-of-fact, but the tone of voice belied how deadly sick he must be feeling. Varney blinked hard, pulling himself together. "Yes," he said, "I believe so."

"Splendid. Let's collect our people and get the hell out of here. I'd set fire to the place on the way out, but we've done enough damage to your city's infrastructure already, Alceste."

"I don't think we need an underground conflagration to finish off the day," said St. Germain, and sighed, straightening up with his hands on his hips, apparently finished handing out *coups de grâce*. Beyond him Greta was beginning to stir, and Varney let go of the wall and crossed the chamber to her, stepping over bodies.

With only one usable arm, it was both painful and awkward to lift Greta into his lap, but there was so much generalized pain sloshing around Varney's consciousness at the moment that it didn't seem to matter much—and the discomfort faded completely behind a spike of ice-clear gladness when she opened her eyes.

"Is it over?" she asked.

"Yes," Varney said. "I think so, anyway. You did it. You brought the things to the places where they had to go."

Greta sat up, squeezing her eyes shut for a moment, and leaned against Varney. "Yes, eventually, once the ghosts showed up and made that possible—where are they anyway? Did they split the scene along with all the terrifying visions?"

Varney looked around. There were no spectral manifestations present, or at least none he could detect. That they'd been motivated by some kind of profound emotion, he didn't doubt; that the deaths of all the vampires who had colonized these catacombs had released them seemed to logically follow. There was a strange, unfamiliar sense of *peace* in the air down here. Of spells wound up.

"Presumably," said St. Germain. "Is it safe to move him?" He nodded at the limp form of Grisaille, and Varney could feel the change in Greta as she slipped back into her professional mode—and regretted it, because a moment later she sat up properly and climbed out of his lap to examine her patient.

On Grisaille's other side, the young vampire moaned faintly, beginning to come around. Varney felt that stab of vicious protectiveness again—*they'd turned a child*—and he was briefly jealous of Ruthven for having been the one to end Corvin once and for all.

Not now, he thought. At least they could make sure the

girl had the necessary guidance and training she was going to need, even if they could not undo the harm that had been done to her; she would have support, and that was better than nothing.

"Yeah," Greta said after a brief interlude, sitting back on her heels beside Corvin's erstwhile lieutenant, wiping blood on the legs of her jeans. "We can move him. He's going to need a while to recover from this, but he's *going* to recover: he's begun to heal. I wasn't sure for a while there. But he needs a lot of work, and I don't have any of my stuff with me in this country—"

"We'll get you anything you need," said Ruthven rather quickly, and St. Germain nodded.

"In that case, let's get moving," she said. "All of us. Emily as well. And Varney—I think I have an idea for what you might consider doing with that country estate of yours, although possibly it's a conversation that can wait for now; and if I never ever have to go into any underground tunnels ever again in my entire life, it really *will* be too bloody soon."

At the instant when Fastitocalon had taken the entire force of their built-up energy and *bent* it, with his mind, his influence, taken it from a rapidly circling current to a focused beam, drawn off all that gathered and amplified energy and brought it to bear all at once, through the target outlined by his markers, on the wound in the prime material plane—at that moment Brightside had thought desperately, *It's not going to be enough, the four of us, even with this place acting as a giant metaphysical maser, the damage is too great, I didn't know how bad it was, I didn't want to know.*

He'd known that Fastitocalon could hear his thoughts, and hadn't cared in the blazing white-hot sense of energy pouring through him, of being a *conduit*, a part of something so very much larger than himself. It had been both a passive flowing-through and an active pushing, focusing all his mental force on Fastitocalon, feeling it drawn and taken and balanced and *tuned* through the five-point circle of the collimators to a brilliant and precise shape that could draw together and laminate the torn edges of reality. Brightside had felt the load on their circuit as he made that contact, power faltering for a fraction of a second and then surging as Fastitocalon adjusted his control—felt time change around him, felt himself outside of time completely, translated into a neighboring plane—and had felt his own self beginning to craze and crack around the edges under the ongoing drain. He had no idea how long it went on: minutes, decades, time had lost all meaning—

And then it snapped off, that load gone all at once, a ringing absence where the power had been, and Brightside's mind was his own again: their circle was still joined, he could feel the others through the fizz and static of aftershocks, and was exhaustedly glad to note that Crepusculus's mindtouch was still as strong as ever. But as they wound it down, drawing back their individual energies from the melded force Fastitocalon had guided, Brightside was astonished to discover that it wasn't just the four of them: that somewhere along the line, others had joined the circle, become a part of this, others who had not been among the dead they'd raised on Fastitocalon's command. He only realized it when they peeled off one by one, leaving the collective with a murmured word or two; and he was amazed to see who exactly had been aiding them.

Thank God that's *over*, said a weary American voice he immediately recognized: he'd heard it last singing, *The crystal ship is being filled, a thousand girls, a thousand thrills.* Then a woman's voice, French, just as weary and beautifully raw around the edges, and another young man's, speaking in French with a Polish accent, and half a dozen others—and a drawling, bone-dry voice Brightside would never be able to forget telling him, *I hate the cheap severity of abstract ethics.*

I thought you had better things to do than muck around with the shape of reality, Brightside said, sounding just as exhausted in his own mind.

Whenever other people agree with me, said Oscar Wilde, *I feel as if I must be wrong. Don't get any wild ideas, psychopomp: I enjoy it where I am.*

Wouldn't dream of it, Brightside said, and the voice of Wilde faded on a ghost of laughter. He was the last of them: Brightside was alone with his three colleagues, and a weight of exhaustion he had not felt since the killing fields of Vietnam and Cambodia.

Is that it? said Irazek shakily. *Are we done?*

Thank you, gentlemen. Fastitocalon, sounding just as weary as the rest of them but still surprisingly in control. *I think we have it. I appreciate your assistance, all of you.*

What happens now? Irazek wanted to know.

Now we go home, what's left of us. Irazek, I will escort you.

You don't need us anymore? That was Crepusculus.

Not at the moment. You've done very well and I'm extremely grateful for your help. That would not have worked, I think, without your ghost-transference skills.

All in a day's work, right, Brightside? Crepusculus asked.

Oh, entirely, he said—

And the group channel cut off completely, as Fastitocalon let go of their hands. The silence in his head rang strangely, after so long plugged into his neighbors.

Brightside sat down on a folding chair, rubbing his hands together to get the sensation in his fingers back, and thought on a much narrower band to Crepusculus: *Let's go. Somewhere a long way away, that hasn't had any monster incursions in recent history. I'm open to suggestion. New Zealand or somewhere in Micronesia or the very tip-top of Everest. You pick. And you do not get to snipe at me for drinking Pernod for breakfast, are we clear on this point, Dammerung?*

Some little distance away Fastitocalon had his arm around Irazek, and they popped out of existence with dual tiny thunderclaps—leaving Crepusculus and Brightside alone together in the orchestra pit. They looked at one another, up at the chandelier, back again.

Crepusculus sent him a flicker of imagery: a beach somewhere in the antipodes, green-blue surf and pale sand, a complicated drink with a little umbrella stuck in it. On the umbrella was a clock face, with the hours set at 8:45 a.m., and beside that a tiny sign on a separate stick: NO PHANTOMS ALLOWED.

Brightside found, to his considerable surprise, that he still remembered how to smile.

Returning to St. Germain's apartment this time had felt like coming home, in an odd way. Greta realized, as they limped about the process of getting themselves cleaned up and bandaged properly, that she thought about the werewolf's flat much the same way she felt about Ruthven's Embankment house, and for similar reasons: *safe haven.*

She'd said as much to him, eating delivery sushi in his kitchen, once the others were in bed. Grisaille was the worst of the casualties, of course, but Ruthven had at some point managed to crack a rib and had a couple of lacerations down his side, and Varney's arm was a mess. St. Germain's injuries were less severe, and he healed faster than an exhausted vampire could; he'd helped her with the others, and then suggested they eat something. Something, he hastily qualified, that didn't require him to cook.

"I really am sorry about standing you up," she said, a piece of tuna roll in her chopsticks. "In the beginning, I mean. That's been bothering me."

St. Germain's gaze went from the sushi to her face, and she had to smile at the *are you actually serious* expression. "You'd been *kidnapped*," he said. "By *vampires.* I can't think of a more cast-iron excuse for missing an appointment, except maybe having a meteorite land on you, and you're going to drop that tuna if you keep waving it about like that."

Greta rolled her eyes at him, but ate the sushi. It was something close to transcendent after having spent several days subsisting on nothing but mediocre coffee and chocolate pastries: she'd never really *understood* how sublime raw fish could taste. "I *do* feel bad about it," she said, "even if I couldn't actually help it. It would have been preferable to meet you properly in a civilized fashion before basically taking over your house, and you've been rather amazing through all this, so *thank you.*"

St. Germain went red. "Well, if I'd been doing my duty and actually keeping an eye on the city, this might never have had a chance to happen in the first place, so—anything I can possibly do to help, I want to do."

"Fair enough," said Greta. "Buying me dinner counts. And helping with the others. I don't actually know what happened with Fastitocalon and Irazek and those people with the odd names, but I'll find out as soon as I can."

"I hope they're all right," said St. Germain.

"So do I. But Fass is back in my head, at least, so *wherever* he is, he's probably going to be fine." She'd realized his presence was back soon after waking in the chamber, in Varney's lap, right after the final violent timeslip: very distant, very faint, but definitely *there.* It had been an enormous reassurance. "I don't know about Irazek or the other two."

"Irazek," said St. Germain, "is probably in Hell right now, which isn't necessarily a bad thing, and the others can take care of themselves." He yawned enormously. "I'm sorry. I think I may be reaching the end of my usefulness for now."

"It's all right," said Greta. "Go sleep. I'm going to spend the night in Grisaille's room; I want to be there in case he needs anything in a hurry."

She had flipped over the sleep-deprivation edge point where it was now *difficult* to fall asleep, and she knew it would catch up with her but didn't care: right now she could still make use of it.

Sitting up beside Grisaille while the world turned toward morning, she had reached for Fastitocalon, and after a long while he had replied, sounding weary and rough but in acceptable spirits. Greta had demanded that he tell her the whole story. Had, in fact, demanded that he show up in *person* and tell her all about it, but it hadn't been until halfway through the next day that he arrived—still visibly exhausted, but apparently in one piece, wearing a different but equally beautiful grey three-piece suit. They *were* new, the suits. Cut by the Devil's favorite tailor, on Plutus Boulevard, in the fancy part of Dis.

Over glasses of St. Germain's sherry, Fastitocalon explained an outline of recent events Below that had resulted in his promotion. "Asmodeus had been skating on increasingly thin metaphorical ice for—oh, ages now," he said. "Several decades at least. See, for example, the fact that nobody had ever bothered to assign a second operative to the Paris station to help that rather ineffective ginger chap do the job, which in some part undoubtedly contributed to the current issues. There's also some concern that the poor performance of M&E might have camouflaged signs that something larger is going on that's buggering up reality, but we don't have a lot of hard evidence for that—the angels aren't being forthcoming about their own situation, which isn't new, but it's yet another thing to worry about. I've been tasked with working out what we know and don't know, which will take a while. The mess last autumn with the M&E department not catching any hint of that hostile entity's presence or activity was just too much for Sam to ignore."

She'd met Samael only once, briefly, but she would never be able to forget the sensation of the Devil's butterfly-blue eyes looking all the way through her like an arc-lamp searchlight, reading what was written on the inside of her skull. He was terrifying, but he did seem to have Fastitocalon's best interests at heart.

"What did he do?" she asked.

"Gave him a leave of absence," Fastitocalon said, looking rueful. "Called it a black sabbatical, not a suspension, to let Asmodeus save face—at first Sam was still willing to allow that—but the deputy head of M&E who took over was *completely* Asmodeus's creature and absolutely nothing changed practice-wise at all. Same lack of oversight, same approach to quality control and performance management, same laissez-faire attitude toward paperwork." He rolled his eyes. "Classic Asmodeus. That lasted a month or two before Sam discovered that Asmodeus was still running the department by proxy from his nice dacha on the banks of the Cocytus."

Greta had to smile a little. "Do I want to know what happened then?"

"Upon the discovery of which," said Fastitocalon, straight-faced, "the deputy head was fired and Asmodeus himself got turned into what I understand to be a large banana slug."

"A *banana slug*?"

"A large one. About so big," he said, holding his hands eight inches apart. "Bright yellow. In which form he will be forced to stay for a term of no less than one hundred years, although I do gather he will be allowed to retain the right to wear a crown or crowns of his choosing, presumably scaled down to fit."

Greta started to say something and then shook her head. "No, I don't want clarification on how slugs wear crowns, I think."

"Probably best not to inquire," he agreed, still solemn and straight-faced. "I don't imagine he'll be making many public appearances, crowned or otherwise. It could have been worse; Sam could have turned him into something completely without charm, such as a giant cockroach."

"When you put it like that, I suppose the banana slug is merciful," she said. "But what about you? That's what I'm curious about. The rest cure seems to have worked. You're in remarkable shape, even after whatever it was you had to do to fix that rip in the world. What exactly did they have you *doing* down there?"

"Lying around and being intensely bored," said Fastitocalon. "And…all right, fine, some tiresome experimental treatments with the mirabilic resonance scanner, which isn't supposed to *treat* so much as *diagnose*, and which I've grown to cordially detest. Although it has apparently done some good."

"Mirabilic resonance scanner," Greta repeated, wide-eyed, and took him by the shoulders, shaking him gently. "I *have to get to talk to your doctor*, that's—I can sort of imagine how it might actually work, Fass, that's—do you *know* how cool that is?"

He smiled at her, the corners of his eyes crinkling. "I might have some idea," he said. "Exposure to very strong and highly polarized mirabilic fields in rapid sequence having some effect in resetting a damaged pneumic signature. You could write a paper about it, if anyone up here would believe you. Incidentally I did mention to Sam that you'd been agitating to have a chat with Dr. Faust, and he says he'll see if something can be arranged."

Greta was totally unable to squash a huge, excited grin. "You're *wonderful*," she told him. "How'd *you* get to be interim Not-Asmodeus, though?"

"Well, I'd been sitting around twiddling my thumbs in between sessions in the high-energy mirabilics lab, and after the fiasco with Asmodeus's successor, Sam came to see me and said effectively *congrats on your promotion, I need someone who knows what the hell they're doing, go and put some proper clothes on and meet me in tower six in twenty minutes.*"

"I can picture that so clearly," said Greta, smiling. "Oh, Fass. I'm glad for you. My father would be *very* glad for you, and it sounds like the place sorely needs a sane person to keep it running—and deal with angels, and do longitudinal studies on the state of reality—but you'd *better* not let it wear you out or I will come down there myself to shout at you. I just wish Dad could have been around to see this, you know?"

"I know," he said, and curled his arms around her, and when she rested her cheek against his chest, the easy effortless sound of his breathing was a lovely thing to hear.

The rest of that day, and most of the next two, passed without Grisaille's conscious awareness. He had no idea how much time had gone by when he woke out of slow, complicated dreams to find himself lying in a bed that was not his own, looking at a white ceiling that was not chiseled out of limestone, in a room full of cool green light: sunlight through blinds.

The last thing he could clearly remember was the chaos underground, a determined little face thrust close to his own, someone saying, *You can't die*: either he had, and this was a particularly specific version of Hell, or he hadn't, and—

He turned his head on the pillows: it hurt, everything hurt, moving at all woke a stab of quite remarkable pain in his back and chest, but his curiosity outweighed the physical discomfort. It was not exactly a surprise to find that Greta Helsing was sitting by the bed.

It probably should be, he thought to himself. *Maybe I've run out of the capacity for surprise.*

She put down her book, smiling a little. "Back with us?"

she said. "You're going to be all right, even if it was a bit touch-and-go at first. *Don't* try to sit up," and he abandoned the attempt, blinking at her. "Not until after you've had something for the pain. You've lost a great deal of your own blood, and we gave you lots of someone else's but it's still going to take you a while to get over a knife through the lung."

"Corvin," said Grisaille, his voice rusty. "Stabbed me in the back. In the actual back."

Greta rolled her eyes. "Christ. Of course he did. I should have worked that out myself, it's so completely *Corvin*. He didn't do a very good job of it, at least; anyone with even rudimentary anatomical knowledge could have done you much more damage. Didn't even chip a rib."

"What...happened?"

"Fastitocalon happened. And before that, so did a lot of ghosts. Here." She offered him a glass of something dark red with a bendy straw in it. "Managing pain for sanguivores is a complicated business; you metabolize everything fast and hard and you don't respond to opioids except in highly recreational doses, but I've been working on some experimental compounds and this ought to help at least a bit."

Grisaille took the glass, a little appalled at how unsteady his hands felt, and was both irritated by and grateful for the convenience of the straw. The glass's contents were mostly fortified wine, with a hit of something bitter underneath it and a faint anise-like numbness on the tongue; it wasn't unpleasant. He found he was desperately thirsty about two sips in, and finished half the glass before looking back up at Greta.

Now that he was a little more awake, he could pay attention to detail. She looked somewhat battered, a bruise across one cheek and a couple of steri-strips holding together a cut on her forehead, and the stains under each eye spoke of a sleep debt that wasn't even close to being paid—but she also looked calm, back in her element, doing her job. She was wearing fresh clothes, which made a difference; fresh, and to Grisaille's admittedly discerning eye, quietly expensive.

"Where are we?" he asked.

"St. Germain's flat. He has very kindly allowed us to stay here as long as we need, which is probably going to be at least another couple of days before you can travel."

"Travel where?"

"England," she said. "Unless you have a burning desire to stick around here for old times' sake. Ruthven says you can stay with him while you heal, which I do recommend you take him up on: he's got a magnificent house on the Embankment and a serious-business espresso machine."

Grisaille blinked at her. He felt rather as if he'd missed a page in the script—namely the bit where these weird and apparently friendly and affectionate people without question took him in, when all he'd ever done for them was imprison one and act as occasional guide and general source of irritation for several others.

"You don't have to," Greta said, apparently mistaking his silence for something other than surprise. "I mean, it's entirely up to you, whatever you end up doing, but I do suggest you give the vampire-coven-lieutenant gig a rest for a couple of decades. It's not a good look on you. Doesn't do you any favors."

He laughed without meaning to, and she had to steady his hand around the glass while he got his breathing back under control: that had *hurt*, hurt like being struck all over again with something pointy. Greta was looking somewhat contrite.

"Anyway," she said. "You don't have to decide now. Finish that, and get some more sleep. You're safe here, I can promise that."

"What about—the others," he said, breathless.

"Varney's arm is a mess, he'll be in a sling for another week or so, and Ruthven has managed somehow to evade damage to his pretty face but he's banged up as well. St. Germain's in better shape. And Emily's all right, even if she's having trouble adjusting to the diurnal cycle."

"She's here?"

"Oh yes. We got you both out, at the end of it all. She's under Ruthven and Varney's protection, which is practically the best possible situation for a kid in her position; they'll make sure she gets whatever help she needs, and they can tell her how to be a vampire in a more sustainable and less self-destructive sort of way."

He nodded, subsiding. Thought about Corvin at the beginning of all this, standing at the Opera balcony looking down at Ruthven and Greta moving through the crowd. Thought about himself, sidling up to his leader, looking down as well. Thought about how much he'd wanted, even then, before all of this, to have someone else in charge.

I can see why you want to pull his head off, he had said. *It's a nice head.*

Grisaille was glad, in a forceful if formless sort of way, that Corvin hadn't succeeded in that particular task.

Greta took the glass back, and reached down to rest a hand gently against his forehead. "Good," she said, "you're making excellent progress, I'm very pleased. Does it hurt any less?"

He realized that it did. The pain was still there, but it had been blunted, overlaid with some kind of insulating factor, or perhaps he simply didn't care about it quite so much. "Yes," he said, and was rewarded with a bright and genuine smile.

"I had hoped for that. Get some rest, Grisaille. Today—"

"Is the first day of the rest of my unlife?" he drawled, raising an eyebrow. She nodded, mock-solemn.

"You are not a number," she informed him, "you are a free man."

"You know, I cannot *believe* you missed the opportunity to tell me I was in the Village when I woke up," said Grisaille, but he was smiling helplessly. It had been a small but pleasant surprise to find that *his* prisoner had a sense of humor, back in the tunnels under the city.

"To be honest," said Greta, rueful, "neither can I."

CHAPTER 15

Greta came into the kitchen with Grisaille's empty glass. From the doorway she could look out into St. Germain's drawing room, full of the slant-light of early evening. The dark figure of Varney stood by the windows, out of direct sunlight, looking out at the cliffs and canyons of Paris, the distant green of the Tuileries and the Trocadéro, the arching spike of the Eiffel Tower on the far bank, away to the southwest.

He was standing very still, but a flicker of movement caught her eye: she looked up to find her whistler hovering in a corner pretending to be a bit of curtain drapery, and had to smile. The creature had been waiting here when the whole group of them returned, limping and battered, from the tunnels under the city, and even through the exhaustion and general horror, she had been touched at how glad it had apparently been to see her. Being clung to by an invisible being wearing shredded red taffeta was among the more peculiar of her recent experiences, but by no means unpleasant.

Since then she had coaxed Winston into trading in the ripped piece of ballgown skirt for a much nicer and more tasteful high-thread-count bedsheet in pale pearl-grey, and he looked quite respectable—if unavoidably eldritch: the classic ghost. Greta took a step into the room and the hovering monster swooped down to greet her, pressing a horrible little wrinkled cotton face into her own; she stroked him gently, and was reminded again of what she'd meant to discuss with Varney.

Who was turning from the windows, drawn out of his reverie by the whistler—and who smiled at Greta, a kind of weary shy smile that did odd things to her insides. "Hello," he said. "How is your patient?"

"Mending," said Greta, coming forward into the room, with the monster still nestled against her neck. "We did the whole where-am-I, what-happened bit, and he's responding to my experimental concoctions most satisfactorily. What about you? How's the arm?"

"Also mending," he said. "Slower than I would like, but steadily."

"Good. Don't try to do too much with it yet—we can't go anywhere until Grisaille can travel anyway; it's going to be a few more days. I've given up worrying about the clinic for now: Dez and Anna and a couple other kindly souls have been wonderful and I will thank them fulsomely when I get home, but right now I'm going to worry about things I *can* have some effect on."

"Quite right," said Varney, and his smile warmed as he

looked at her and the monster. "That creature ought not to have quite as much charm as it, in fact, has."

"I know, it's entirely illogical," Greta said, and joined him by the windows. In the indirect light, the lines on his face were graven very deep, and she found herself wanting to touch them. "I did want to talk to you about something," she said a little hurriedly, and was a bit surprised at what looked like hope in that face, just a flicker, here and then gone. "About the monsters," Greta clarified, and watched Varney's expression change back to mild and melancholy interest.

"What about them?" he said.

"So there are a *lot* of them. St. Germain and a couple of the other Paris supernaturals have been going through the underground to try to find the rest—there are feral tricherpetons loose in the city, and more baby wellmonsters than you could shake a historically significant femur at. They apparently *did* get enough warning to hide before Corvin destroyed the old house by the lake—and they need somewhere to go." The wellmonster that had come out of the underground with her had colonized St. Germain's bathroom sink and refused to be dislodged until they found it a large stoneware bowl in which it could lurk instead, which it had accepted with reasonable grace, still clutching the silver whistle.

"Go on," said Varney, sounding as if he had some idea where this was headed.

"And—well, there's no way I can take them, my flat's tiny and I'm never there and it's completely inappropriate habitat-wise, but…" She sighed and ran a hand through her hair. "You've got quite a lot of land down in Wiltshire, haven't you?"

Varney's eyes narrowed, and for a moment she thought, *Oh God, this was a mistake,* before a remarkably sunny and totally unpremeditated smile broke over his features: an expression quite unlike him, and so bright it dazzled Greta.

"That I do," he said. "There's a great deal of room in the stable block for monster kennels. And an ornamental lake which may or may not contain skeletons. And water gardens that are frankly a mess of overgrown grottos and stagnant ponds, *and* I think there's an abandoned well in the stableyard."

"That's ideal," she said, smiling back helplessly. "Are the cellars damp?"

"Extremely," he told her. "Heavy on the cobwebs, as well. And there's *nitre.*"

"I could not imagine anything better," said Greta, "except this is going to be expensive, and they're going to need to be taken care of, and that will require hiring people to do the taking-care-of, and it's—it's a lot to ask of you."

"My dear," said Varney, "do you realize how long it has been, how abominably long, since I had a purpose other than to prey on the living and get myself chased by angry pitchfork-wielding mobs? An actual purpose, with—responsibilities, and useful tasks? A *constructive* use of time? Do you realize quite what you're offering me?"

"Not really?" she said, looking up at him. His eyes were dark silver, reflective, metallic. She could see herself in them, two tiny upturned Greta-faces, as he regarded her. "But…I offer it gladly," she added, feeling the glittering edges of his thrall, held in check but always present, feeling as if she were stepping up to the edge of some unknowable precipice, feeling the empty space of clear air in front of her, waiting for that last and final step. "Gladly," she repeated, softer now.

"And *gladly* I accept," said Sir Francis Varney, and took her face between his two cold hands—gently nudging the whistle-monster out of his way—and bent to kiss her lips.

Greta was still pink and feeling as if she were floating an inch or so above the floor an hour later, when she went to knock on Emily's door. St. Germain had done a bit of rearranging in order to accommodate them all, and Greta, Ruthven, and Varney were sleeping on various couches around the flat; it had been evident to all of them that the youngest vampire needed the privacy of a room to herself. She was trying to adjust to a crepuscular lifestyle, if not a diurnal one just yet, but it was proving difficult—and coupled with the stress from her recent experiences, Greta didn't blame Emily for wanting to spend most of her time asleep.

Still. She knocked again gently. "Emily?"

There was a sound of movement from within, and a minute or so later the door opened to reveal Emily in a pair of vastly oversized borrowed sweatpants and a similarly huge T-shirt advertising Rammstein, her dyed-red hair in a messy braid over one shoulder. It was about as far as one could get from frilly underwired lace sleepwear and hairsprayed ringlets. She looked heartbreakingly young and also entirely human: the only visible signifier of her nature was the color of her eyes, the same white-silver as Ruthven's, with the black rim to the iris.

"Mnnh," she said, and rubbed at those eyes. "What time is it?"

"About six; the light's lost most of its intensity. Do you feel up to having something to eat?"

"Not really," said Emily, "but I guess I have to, right?"

"I'm afraid so. You'll get the shakes and cold sweats if you don't feed at least a little every twenty-four hours or so, and that's not even slightly fun. Did you get some sleep?"

"Kind of. I—can I talk to you about something?"

"Of course," said Greta. "Anything you like."

"Okay. Let me get dressed. I'll be, like, two seconds."

She nodded, and the door shut again. Greta hadn't spoken very much with Emily since their return from the caves under the city—mostly she'd been too busy with Grisaille and the walking wounded—but she knew the young vampire would be full of questions, and hoped she'd actually be able to answer some of them, now that she'd had a chance to talk to Fastitocalon.

She hadn't been leaning against the wall for very long when Emily emerged in a pair of jeans and a dark purple shirt, both newly purchased from quite expensive boutiques on the Champs-Élysées, as was Greta's own clothing. Ruthven had accepted what was apparently a standing invitation to join a couple of Parisian lady vampires for an evening on the town that had involved *shopping*, clearly pleased at having an excuse; he'd come back with bright color in his face, a spring in his step, and an enormous number of shopping bags. As always, he'd been eerily good at judging not only size but personal taste and making decisions accordingly. Emily looked pale, beautiful, but ordinary. The whole Grand Duchess of the Body-Glittered Dead bit was nowhere to be seen.

"Very nice," Greta said approvingly. "Come and have some dinner and ask me whatever you like, although I can't guarantee I'll have an answer."

"It's *weird*," said Emily, but fell into step with Greta anyway. "The—having dinner in a kitchen, like—out of cups, like people, not—from a victim outside in an alleyway or during a party."

"It's certainly a change," she said. "But on the whole, this version of things works just as well. Sit down, I'll manage."

Emily subsided into one of St. Germain's kitchen chairs and watched her as she rummaged around in the fridge and came up with a swollen plastic packet of something dark and red. "Okay," said the girl, "first question, if that's real blood, how did you guys get that stuff? Did you, like, rob a hospital or something?"

"'Or something,'" Greta said, cutting the edge of the pouch open with kitchen scissors and pouring the contents into a large mug, adding a dash of wine and some spice. "St. Germain is a pretty big deal in this town, as well as being a pretty big wolf, and he knows people everywhere: there's a couple of supers that work in various healthcare facilities around Paris and were willing to do him a favor. What you had last night was fresh, though: Ruthven went out to dinner and took a flask along."

"This is so *weird*," Emily complained again, and there was real distress under the whine. "Before—in Corvin's group—I had to learn to bite people, there wasn't any other choice, and they did that thing with their eyes a lot, I don't remember parts of it, but there wasn't, like, blood in the fridge."

"Pretty much every single thing they did to you was atrocious," Greta said, folding her arms. "I'm so sorry that you went through that, and that it is going to be unavoidably difficult to unlearn all that rubbish and learn more sustainable and sensible techniques—but Ruthven and Varney want to help, very much."

The microwave went *ding* after the manner of its kind. Greta had half hysterically expected French microwaves to make a different type of sound, the first time she'd used it, and then cursed herself for an idiot. She set the mug in front of Emily, and the rich coppery smell of warmed blood filled the kitchen almost at once. You never really did get used to that smell, although it got easier to ignore.

She watched the rapid sequence of reactions pass across Emily's face: first instinctive, residual disgust, and then a ravenous almost mindless need that eclipsed the revulsion completely.

Half the mug was gone before she looked up at Greta and licked her lips. "You put something in this," she said, sounding a little surprised. "It's nicer this time."

"I did," she said. "I thought you could probably use it. Better now?"

"Yeah," said Emily, and sighed, relaxing. There was color

in her cheeks, faint but present; she looked much more like a living person than a dead one. "Thank you. It's really nice of you. All this." She waved a vague hand at the kitchen.

"You are extremely welcome," said Greta, and made herself a cup of tea. Shortly the others would be congregating for the evening, but she thought they had half an hour to talk in relative peace. "What did you want to ask me?"

"Oh," said Emily. "Right. The—in the lair. When the— those were ghosts, right? When they appeared, and then everything went white. What *was* that?"

Greta sighed. "The short answer is 'I'm not exactly sure,' but the long one involves a friend of mine who happens to be sort of a demon. You—do you know about the reality rip, the damage Lilith was doing as she summoned all of those monsters?"

Emily's eyes had gone huge again. "Reality rip," she repeated.

"...I'll start from the beginning."

In fact, it took about twenty minutes, all told, before Greta finished, and she had to admit Emily was taking it rather well; then again, the kid had had to readjust her worldview quite starkly to incorporate a number of improbable truths in the past couple of months.

"So it's fixed," she said when Greta had stopped. "The hole. It's—there's not gonna be that weird Time Lord shit happening anymore with the flickers of the past and stuff?"

"Yes. It's fixed. According to Fass anyway."

"I still don't really get the Hell thing," said Emily. "It's—it sounds like a big giant bureaucracy, not a bunch of eternal tortures."

"Some would say the two overlap," Greta told her, wearily amused. "But the eternal tortures are provided for the clients, not the staff. There's apparently all sorts of dreadful things being done to sinners as per spec, but the place is run very efficiently by—as you say—a big giant bureaucracy. What's fascinating to *me* is that Fastitocalon's got a proper job down there again, and—rather an important one actually. I'm rather proud of him, even if it does mean he's mostly going to be spending his time Below, rather than in London. I'm definitely going to miss him—he was all the family I had for a while—but I'm happy he has a real job again and that he's finally been allowed to come home. For a long time he couldn't, he was sort of living in exile up here, and it must have been incredibly lonely."

Emily looked down into the empty mug, and Greta could see the muscles of her jaw tense for a moment. "Family," she repeated. "Yeah. I—don't get to have one now, do I. I'm dead. I can't go home to my mum and dad and say *Hello, I'm a vampire now, cheers*, exactly."

"No, you can't," said Greta. "And that's unfair, and I'm sorry for it, Emily. The people who did this to you took that away, but—in time, if you want, you can *find* yourself the beginnings of a new family."

"How?" Emily said bitterly. "How am I supposed to do that—look, I can't even do *normal* stuff. That was the one thing they didn't lie to me about. I don't have a home or a family, I can't go back to school, I can't *do anything* like real people do now."

"Yes you can," said a voice behind her, and both Greta and Emily looked up to see Ruthven leaning in the kitchen doorway, arms folded.

There was something a little strange about his appearance, and after a moment Greta realized what it was: he'd done his hair differently, without the high-shine firm-hold product he normally used, and it fell in a soft black wing across his forehead. "You can in fact do *almost* anything you want to do," he continued, "as long as you are willing to put in the effort and devote the necessary patience to the task. Your condition doesn't make things impossible, just difficult."

He was wearing a new shirt, too, Greta noticed. Dark red with a hint of iridescence.

"You sound like one of those stupid self-help books, all *follow your dream, work hard, and you'll get to become whatever you want to be.* It's not *like* that, I'm *stuck*, I can't—be anything in the real world other than a fucking *vampire*," Emily said, her voice rising with the threat of tears.

Greta reached out to touch her hand, and then drew back. The girl needed to say this.

Emily looked up at Ruthven through messy red bangs and sat up straighter, almost spitting the words at him. "I'm *dead* and I'm a *monster* and I'm always gonna be, and I can't *do anything about it.*"

"What do you want to do?" Ruthven asked.

His voice was calm and mildly interested, but it cut through the air of the kitchen as if he'd snapped at her. "What had you been planning on doing, before this happened?"

"...I don't know," said Emily, and her shoulders slumped. "I was—gonna get my degree in English, and then—find a job, like—teaching or something, I don't know. I don't have special talents at anything, I'm good at writing papers, I like reading and studying stuff and that's just—that doesn't *matter* now. Nothing does. I'm not smart enough to find a way to deal with this, okay?"

Greta and Ruthven shared a look over her head. "I think you can do more than you realize," Greta said gently. "You kept your head in the battle, while we worked on Grisaille— you did very well in a terrifying situation, and you have managed to survive and adjust to an incredibly traumatic change without subsuming your personality into something else."

"That's different," said Emily. "In the fight, he was—I thought he was gonna die and you said *hold the pressure on his wound* so that's what I did, it wasn't *difficult*—what actually was that about, anyway? Why'd you need me to push so hard that it hurt him?"

Greta looked back at Ruthven, and this time she was smiling slightly: after a moment, so did he. "A lot of people wouldn't have been able to do that, Emily," she said. "And— here, give me that notepad, I'll draw you a diagram of the rib cage and the lungs; it's easier to explain sucking chest wounds with pictures."

"Can I learn how to do stuff like that?" Emily asked, her silver eyes suddenly wide, as if this had not previously occurred to her. "Like—can I learn how to fix people, and not just bite them?"

"Of course you can," said Greta, smiling. "You can learn how to do a hell of a lot of things, including medicine. There's no reason you can't study to be a doctor."

Emily looked from her to Ruthven, who nodded. "There really isn't," he said. "I mean, yes, there's absolutely going to be *challenges*, tiresome things to deal with along the way based on your new physiology, but they can be overcome. And forget all about money; if you want to go back to school, all you have to do is get accepted. You need never have to worry about a penny of tuition or fees. I can promise you that right now."

"Really?" Emily said in a small voice, and looked back at Greta.

"Really," she told her, warm and certain, and Emily burst into tears—huge, helpless, racking sobs, the kind that come out after they've been repressed for much too long.

Ruthven cursed under his breath and came forward into the kitchen as Greta put her arms around the girl and held her close, stroking the messy braid of her hair. Emily clung to her almost tight enough to hurt—she didn't know that yet, didn't know how strong she was—and Greta held her, rocking both of them slightly, as Ruthven rested a careful hand on Emily's back.

"It's not true, what they told you," he said, his voice gentle. This close, Greta noticed he was wearing garnet studs in each earlobe, a glitter and wink of deep wine-red; she'd never realized he had pierced ears until now. "You can't go back to the home and the family you had before, but that doesn't mean you'll never have one again. What's true is that you are only starting out now, and you can *make* your own family, with the people you find along the way, and the home you will come to is one you will build yourself."

"I don't know *how*," Emily sobbed into Greta's shoulder.

"But we do," Greta said gently. "We do. We're all learning, all the time. And we'll help—all of us. Ruthven and Varney and me, and our friends, and the friends you'll make on your own. We'll help. You don't have to do this alone."

"We'll help," said Ruthven, echoing her. "I'm glad we came here, in the end, because we've found you, Emily. That's worth it all."

Greta could feel Varney's presence in the doorway before she looked up to see him standing there, and the expression on his face made her feel as if all her insides had turned to hot liquid gold, threatening to spill over. She hugged the girl tighter. "I'm glad, too," she said.

"And I," Varney said. "For what it's worth."

Greta met his eyes—silvery, reflective even at this distance—and some of what she felt must have shown on her face, because he blinked at her and began to smile—that odd, uncharacteristic, brilliant smile, like the sun rising over a fieldful of mist, turning it from blank impenetrable barrier to opalescence. *It's worth everything*, she mouthed, and color flared and faded in Varney's thin face.

Everything? he said without a sound. She could read his lips as clearly as if he'd spoken for the whole room to hear, and she was pretty sure he could read hers.

Everything, she mouthed back. *Varney—I want to go home,*

too. So much. She stroked Emily's hair. *I want to go home, too, if you will take me there.*

I can, he said. *I will.*

She saw that St. Germain had joined him in the doorway: that all of them were there, except Grisaille and Fastitocalon; and for the first time since her own father's death, Greta was truly aware that she herself was *not* alone; that Ruthven was right, and family was what you made it; that despite everything, in the end, there *was* no home lost that might be found, if sought.

EPILOGUE

Spring came that year to London late but gloriously, all at once: the gardens at Hampton Court, the daffodils at St. James's, and the tulips in Regent's Park, the brilliant wealth of azaleas at the Isabella Plantation and rhododendrons at Kenwood House, the wisteria draping the Hampstead Heath pergola, all seemed to come into fulminant bloom within a week or two. The maples lining the Embankment had lost their reddish seed clusters and were hazed with the delicate green of new leaves, jade-clear and unfolding, deepening into a richer color as they expanded day by day.

It was extremely beautiful and it meant that there was a hell of a lot of pollen in the air all at once, and Edmund Ruthven found himself a slave to the demon antihistamine. He made his way downstairs quite late these mornings, still wrapped in an embroidered silk dressing gown, half-asleep, in search of blood and coffee—and for the third day in a row had to pause and sneeze in the echoing marble-floored entryway before entering the kitchen.

Grisaille was reading the *Times*, bare feet propped on the table, and eyed him with an eyebrow raised as he came in. Ruthven sighed.

"It isn't fair," he said, consonants slightly blurred by congestion, "that not only should you escape this particular inflammatory hell, you consistently look better in my dressing gowns than I do. I object."

"Of course I do," said Grisaille, and sat up, putting the paper down. It was true: he had purloined one of Ruthven's favorites, blue and green peacocks with little jewels sewn into the embroidered feathers, and it set him off much better with his dark skin and red eyes than it had ever done for Ruthven. "I'm thoroughly decorative; we know this to be true. Also, I'm allowed to lounge around in silks of more-than-oriental-splendor; I'm a convalescent."

"You *have* convalesced," said Ruthven, and pushed his hair back. He had done some experimentation and discovered a range of hair products that gave him some hold while avoiding the sleeked-down wet look, but it was difficult getting used to having his hair flopping over one eye. "Past tense. I saw you nip up the stairs yesterday like a damn gazelle; you're fully recovered."

"I had a *knife* through my *lung* three and a half weeks ago," said Grisaille, looking hurt, and coughed for effect. "You wouldn't throw me out on the streets in my condition?"

Ruthven sighed. "Oh, hush. Of course I wouldn't, you know that."

"I know that," Grisaille agreed, and got to his feet with a single limber movement, going to put the kettle on. "You, however, look like hell. Here, read the thing about the people trying to tear down Trellick Tower and put up another unspeakable glass prong in its place; I'll make you something for your allergies."

Ruthven stayed standing a moment longer, and then flopped into a chair, pulling the newspaper toward him. "I hate Trellick," he said, and sniffed. "But I hate the glass prongs more."

"I know," said Grisaille fondly, and Ruthven looked up to watch him. There was less silver in his hair these days, Ruthven was sure: the dreadlocks fell in a wealth of rich darkness over his shoulders, here and there glittering with tiny jeweled rings, as he got things down from cabinets and mixed and poured. It was much more pleasant to observe Grisaille work than to read about architectural atrocities, and he didn't even try to look as if he hadn't been watching when the other vampire turned from the counter to set a steaming mug in front of him.

"What's this?" he inquired.

"Just drink it," said Grisaille, and Ruthven took a sip: the richness of blood plasma and the sharp smokiness of lapsang souchong tea blended remarkably well with honey, lemon juice, and brandy. He blinked, and felt himself smiling helplessly as the stuff began to ease the miserable congestion in his sinuses.

"Thank you," he said, cupping his hands around the mug, for once without a witty rejoinder; and when Grisaille put a slim dark hand on his shoulder, Ruthven covered it with his own. "You'll *have* to stay," he said after a few moments, with a bit more self-possession. "Who knows how long this wretched tree orgy is going to last?"

"Who indeed," said Grisaille. "You'd better keep me around for medicinal purposes. It's a good thing for you that you met me, Mistress Bona."

"My thoughts exactly," said Ruthven; and the spring breeze passing by the Embankment house carried with it the faint but undeniable sound of laughter.

At Dark Heart, the spring rains had drenched the parkland, filling up half the ancient and neglected water-garden ponds with stagnant green murk, and Varney's newly hired team of builders trooped back and forth from their vans to the main house and to the stable block in a sequence of muddy Wellington boots.

He was slightly *aware* of playing the part of the country squire much more effectively than he'd ever managed in previous iterations, and of enjoying it for the first time, as he pulled on his own muddy boots in the back pantry of the house and set out for the stables with a pail of expensive dog food kibble in one hand and a plastic bag half-full of cobwebs in the other.

This was not a scene Varney had ever envisioned in his concepts of the future. Neither was the fact that as he came down the terrace steps, shoulders hunched under his waterproof against the misting rain, the crew hard at work replacing the broken terrace flagstones greeted him with grins and a cheerful "Mornin', sir."

He nodded to them—there was noticeable progress made, apparently hiring people who *wanted* to work for you made a bit of a difference results-wise—and thanked them for coming out in the rain; and could feel the eyes on him as he walked through the weed-choked parterre toward the stables. He was used to being stared at. He was not used to being stared at *approvingly*.

The stables were bright and warm and dry, and full of bustling activity. He handed over the pail of kibble to one of the young women who were managing the logistics of feeding their thirty charges, and tucked the cobweb bag into his pocket as he walked down to the last stall on the end. The bag was for later, when he went to see the wellmonsters in their new homes. Now was for—

Well, for this. Varney leaned on the half-open door of the stall and looked down at something wonderful.

Greta Helsing sat crosslegged in the straw with Emily beside her. She was cradling a reddish-brown curly-coated tricherpeton's head in her lap, making notes on a clipboard.

Greta looked tired but glowingly happy, her hair pulled back into a loose knot, but what was really the center of attention were the four newborn trich pups nestled into the curve of their mother's body as she lay exhausted with her head pillowed on Greta's knee. They wriggled and made soft little noises as they nursed, and Varney could not help being aware of a certain unwarranted flicker of pride.

Four pups, and—a fifth, because Emily was bending over something very small cradled in the cup of her hands: a tiny scrap of mortality, half the size of its brothers and sisters, and quite unlike them in color: all the others were the warm auburn of their mother, but this little creature was a peculiar, almost iridescent pale champagne-gold with what looked to Varney like blue overtones in its coat.

"Good heavens," he said, and both Emily and Greta looked up, startled. "I'm sorry. I didn't mean to disturb you, but— what a remarkable color."

Greta grinned. "Isn't it? I wish we had any idea which of our other gents—if it's any of them—this lady had relations with, because the genetics on this are fascinating. Can you come in or are you on your way elsewhere?"

"I am, but it can wait," said Varney, and let himself into the stall. Very carefully he settled down in the straw, heedless of its cleanliness or lack thereof, and peered at the tiny tricherpeton in Emily's hands. Hesitantly she held it out a little for his inspection.

"Will it be all right?" he asked. "It's so small."

"Probably," said Greta at the same time as Emily said "*Yes*," and she had to smile. "Probably yes. It's a runt, so we'll see if it can manage to get enough out of Mum unassisted to survive, and if it's not, we'll do the hand-feeding every two hours. But we're determined." She looked from Varney to Emily and smiled, and he had to smile, too: the young vampire looked so intent on her handful.

"May I see?" he asked, and held out his own hands, and after a moment, hesitant, Emily set the little pup into them. It looked even tinier in the broader expanse of Varney's palms; in fact, it fit quite well into one of his hands, and he stroked it very carefully with a fingertip. The tiny quivering delicacy of its life was very vivid to him. Very vivid.

That I should be trusted so much, he thought, looking down at it. *That I should be allowed to hold this creature.*

He very gently settled it back into Emily's hands, and could see her relax. There was a confidence in her that he hadn't seen in France, and hadn't even seen here outside the stables or the water gardens: she was *better* here. As if the things that had happened to her mattered less. He didn't know what specific aspect of Dark Heart had wrought that change, and didn't care, as long as it worked—but he was slightly, slightly proud that there *was* this version of Dark Heart to be there at all.

"You're doing beautifully," he told her. "Thank you."

"I want to," Emily said, looking up at him suddenly. "I want to. To do this. More than anything else. Can I—is this something I can learn to do properly?"

"Yes," said Greta, stroking the mother's soft ears. "Yes, you can. The world very much needs more monster vets. It's not going to be easy, but there are some people you can train with; you've got the instinct, and the monsters like you; and I'll help as much as I can."

Varney wasn't prepared for the sudden, astonishing brilliance of the girl's smile: it seemed to light up the warm dimness of the stall like a candle flame. Almost without thinking about it, he held his hand out and Greta laced her fingers with his, and Varney thought for the space of a few slow heartbeats that he actually sort of understood what all the wretched poets had been on about with their fulminations on joy, on happiness, on—*satisfaction*.

Outside, the rain intensified, pattering against the stable block's slate roof; beyond the stables it drifted in grey curtains, like a sigh, across the hills that marked the western boundaries of Dark Heart's park; and beyond that, up the low rise of the chalk downlands like a vast green whale-back, past the hedgerows and fieldlets of the valleys at the foot of the chalk, past the wrinkled rings of greensward cut into hill-forts six hundred years before the birth of Christ, all the way to the distant gold streak of the Chesil Bank and the flat blank sea, and all the worlds beyond; and with it, on the breeze borne with the drifting veils of rain, came a feeling of peace extraordinary in its sweetness: a feeling like coming home.

The story continues in...

GRAVE IMPORTANCE

A Dr. Greta Helsing Novel

Keep reading for a sneak peek!

ACKNOWLEDGMENTS

First and foremost, my eternal thanks to my wife, the author Arkady Martine, who kept me as sane as possible throughout with judicious applications of single-malt and sympathy; I love you, dear. Also: Stephen Barbara, best of agents; Emily Byron, Lindsey Hall, and Sarah Guan, editors par excellence; M. R. James, Victor Hugo, and Gaston Leroux, whose influence will be readily apparent; and my parents, Owen and Penny Bamford, who made it possible for me to visit Paris twenty years ago. As you can see, it made something of an impression.

extras

orbit

meet the author

Photo credit: Emilia Blaser

Vivian Shaw was born in Kenya and spent her early childhood in England before relocating to the United States at the age of seven. She has a BA in art history and an MFA in creative writing, and has worked in academic publishing and development while researching everything from the history of spaceflight to supernatural physiology. In her spare time, she writes fanfiction under the name of Coldhope.

if you enjoyed
DREADFUL COMPANY

look out for

GRAVE IMPORTANCE
A Dr. Greta Helsing Novel

by

Vivian Shaw

*Oasis Natrun: a private, exclusive, highly secret luxury
health spa for mummies, high in the hills above Marseille,
equipped with the very latest in therapeutic innovations
both magical and medical. To Dr. Greta Helsing,
London's de facto mummy specialist, it sounds like paradise.
But when Greta is invited to spend four months there
as the interim clinical director, it isn't long before she finds
herself faced with a medical mystery that will take all her
diagnostic skill to solve.*

extras

A peculiar complaint is spreading among her mummy patients, one she's never seen before. With help from her friends and colleagues—including Dr. Faust (yes, that Dr. Faust), remedial psychopomps, a sleepy scribe-god, witches, demons, a British Museum curator, and the inimitable vampyre Sir Francis Varney—Greta must put a stop to this mysterious illness before anybody else crumbles to irreparable dust...

...and before the fabric of reality itself can undergo any more structural damage.

CHAPTER 1

"I've just had to rescue a *third* groundskeeper from drowning in the ornamental lake," said Sir Francis Varney over the phone, sounding put-upon. "I am beginning to suspect the wretched ornamental lake of harboring something unpleasant and tentacular that drags people into it—or possibly with this rain everyone has become sufficiently wet and cold to develop suicidal tendencies. Also part of the roof's fallen in. Again."

It was pouring. Greta Helsing watched out of her office window as debris bobbed and swirled in the gutters of Harley Street—hardly gutters so much as small rivers, after the second week of practically ceaseless rain. Autumn this year had apparently given up on the mist-and-mellow-fruitfulness bit as a bad job and gone straight for the Biblical aesthetic instead.

"Which part of the roof?" she asked. Varney's ancestral pile, Ratford Abbey, went by the much cooler epithet of Dark Heart House, and had only just been renovated at considerable expense.

"The part over the green drawing room, which is not exactly benefiting from the experience. I rescued all the bits of jade and malachite that could be moved. At least the wellmonsters seem to like this weather; they're having a lovely time splashing around in the gardens."

"Well, that's something," said Greta. Dark Heart and its park had been pressed into service as a shelter for dispossessed supernatural creatures earlier in the year, and one of the species housed there was somewhat amphibious. "Is—"

Over the phone she could hear someone else's voice, and Varney's inventive cursing. "Sorry," he said, after a moment, "Greta, I've got to go; the stable-block is apparently flooding— I'll call you later, all right?"

She could picture it, and bit her lip. "Yes, of course. Go sort things out; don't worry about me."

"I can't help it," said Varney, "I think it's a permanent condition. Talk soon."

Click.

She took the phone away from her ear, and it was probably only her imagination that the rain seemed even louder as it spattered against her window. Only her imagination, now that Varney's voice wasn't there with her. When she set the receiver back in its cradle that sound, too, felt much too sharp.

I could go home, she thought. There weren't any appointments in her calendar, and it was extremely unlikely that anyone would bother slogging their way through this mess to come to see her, this late in the afternoon—

But if they did, she finished, not without bitterness, *they'd really need me, and anyway being out in this weather appeals even less than sitting here and listening to the clock tick.*

She watched through the moving blur of rain on the window as a plastic lemonade bottle negotiated a series of rapids across the street, wondering vaguely if it was going to escape the maw of the storm drain in its path or simply vanish into the darkness of the undercity. Into the coigns and brick-arched vaults of Bazalgette's Victorian sewers, where anything might be waiting for it.

extras

I hope the ghouls are all right, Greta thought, not for the first time. They lived in the deep tunnels under the city in the places rarely, if ever, visited by humans; she knew they were more than bright enough to have evacuated the lowest-lying tunnels as soon as the weather really turned vicious, but it was still a present worry in the back of her mind. Presumably they could, if necessary, seek shelter in the cellar of Edmund Ruthven's house, as they'd done once before under rather different circumstances. Assuming the cellar wasn't already full of water.

She hadn't heard from Ruthven in several days, and allowed herself a brief flicker of resentment at the fact that he was hundreds of miles away in Geneva, probably having an absolutely lovely time with his unsuitable boyfriend—and thus not around to let *her* stay in his Embankment mansion until the weather stopped being quite so vile.

Greta was, in fact, still so wrapped up in the thought of Ruthven's warm bright kitchen and the luxurious spare beds, plural, he had available for guests—nobody did hospitality like a vampire—that it took her three rings to notice the phone's renewed demand for her attention.

"Dr. Helsing," she said when she picked up, aware that she didn't sound quite as brisk and in-charge as usual, not caring enough to really make the effort.

"Greta," said the voice on the other end, warm with relief. "Thank *God* you're in town. Are you terribly busy?"

She sat up. It had been at least a year since she'd talked to Ed Kamal at a supernatural medicine conference in Germany; his job kept him too busy for much by way of socialization. "Ed? No, I'm not in the middle of anything. What's the matter?"

"I absolutely hate to spring this on you with no notice whatsoever, and I completely understand if you can't do it," he said, sounding both apologetic and hurried.

"Do *what?*"

"I—something's come up and I have to go back to Cairo, more or less immediately, and there's no one I can really leave in charge of the spa, nobody with the experience to oversee the patients we've got, nobody who really understands the therapeutic regimens and the principles we're using—you're so good with mummies, and it'd only be for a few months, four at most—"

Greta stared at the phone, and then at the rain spattering against the windowpane. "Wait," she said. "Let me make sure I've got this right. You want *me* to spend four months in *Marseille* overseeing *Oasis Natrun.*"

"I know it's a hell of a lot to ask," Dr. Kamal said, sounding wretched. "I mean—my nursing staff's fantastic, I'd never want to imply they're not competent to keep the place going, but I need a medical director who knows this stuff inside and out and—we have some very important patients just now and I can't leave without being sure they're going to have an expert managing their care whom I trust without question—"

Oasis Natrun. The private and exclusive mummy spa and health resort. Where Greta had sent her own mummy patients who could afford a course of treatment whenever she possibly could. Where cutting-edge therapeutic, restorative, and cosmetic techniques were being pioneered all the time.

Which was located in *the south of France.* Where it almost certainly was not currently pouring with rain.

"Ed," she said, cutting him off in the middle of another compound-complex self-referential loop of apology, "I think the phrase I am looking for here is *oh god yes please.*"

The mummy Amennakht was over three thousand years old and on his third set of replacement fingers, but this didn't severely impact his typing speed. On a good day he was capable of about sixty-five words per minute.

It was useful to be able to work from home—he hated the word *telecommute*, he wasn't *commuting* at all, that was the point—when you couldn't exactly go out in public without people noticing certain peculiarities in your personal appearance. Nobody cared what you looked like when you existed solely as a source of emails and completed assignments.

(Sometimes, when he was feeling particularly philosophical, Amennakht reflected that in certain senses the function really did shape the entity: he *was* a Thing That Emailed, and a Thing That Sent In Code, and he could *feel* the metaphysical parameters of that in a way that people who weren't largely made up of magic would never be able to manage.)

The other benefit of working from home was that you could fuck around on the Internet as much as you liked, as long as you were getting the job done, and no nosy manager could peer over your shoulder to read your RP posts or critique your Twitter banner-image design. Amennakht had a couple of Slack channels open almost all the time while he coded; he was an expert at flicking back and forth between windows without taking his hands off the ergonomic split keyboard. Right now he was half-paying-attention to an ongoing conversation about the likelihood that anyone would ever design a functional fusion reactor while he slogged away in SQL. *Not in my lifetime, however long that is*, he thought, and smiled a little: his face creaked faintly. He at least *had* most of a face; he considered himself pretty good-looking, as Class A revenants went, even if he did need rewrapping rather badly.

He was halfway through a line when abruptly, *viciously*, a wave of terrible dragging weakness flooded through him. It felt like being pushed downward by a sudden g-force—the strength he was using to simply sit upright at the desk was not *there*, and he both felt and heard himself creak as he slumped forward—he felt like he was *falling*—

And just as suddenly as it had come, the feeling was gone. Well. Mostly gone.

Amennakht sat up again, slowly, with another creak. He still felt faintly weak and dizzy, but the awful *weight* was gone as if it had never been there at all.

He looked around. Nothing at all had changed: same cluttered apartment overlooking Boston's Mattapan neighborhood, same stacks of magazines, same canopic jars sitting in a neat row on the mantelpiece. Nor did he himself look any different.

He saved his work—that was automatic, a completely ingrained habit—and then after a moment closed out of the fusion-reactor discussion channel and opened a rather different one, with a more complicated name. There weren't many people in it at this time of night: mostly *his* people were either in various parts of western Europe or in Egypt, and the time difference was kind of hilarious.

Weird question, he typed, after a minute of staring at the screen, *has anyone else had a kind of…dizzy spell out of nowhere recently?*

Nothing. He went on staring, the dim pinpoint reflections of his eyes looking back at him. And then, from his friend Mentuhotep—what he was doing up at four in the morning London time was a mystery in itself—*You too?*

if you enjoyed
DREADFUL COMPANY
look out for

PRUDENCE
The Custard Protocol: Book One

by

Gail Carriger

When Prudence Alessandra Maccon Akeldama ("Rue" to her friends) is bequeathed an unexpected dirigible, she does what any sensible female under similar circumstances would do—she christens it the Spotted Custard *and floats off to India.*

Soon, she stumbles upon a plot involving local dissidents, a kidnapped brigadier's wife, and some awfully familiar Scottish werewolves. Faced with a dire crisis (and an embarrassing lack of bloomers), Rue must rely on her good breeding—and her metanatural abilities—to get to the bottom of it all...

CHAPTER ONE

The Sacred Snuff Box

Lady Prudence Alessandra Maccon Akeldama was enjoying her evening exceedingly. The evening, unfortunately, did not feel the same about Lady Prudence. She inspired, at even the best balls, a sensation of immanent dread. It was one of the reasons she was always at the top of all invitation lists. Dread had such an agreeable effect on society's upper crust.

"Private balls are so much more diverting than public ones," Rue, unaware of the dread, chirruped in delight to her dearest friend, the Honourable Miss Primrose Tunstell.

Rue was busy drifting around the room with Primrose trailing obligingly after her, the smell of expensive rose perfume following them both.

"You are too easily amused, Rue. Do try for a tone of disinterested refinement." Prim had spent her whole life trailing behind Rue and was unfussed by this role. She had started when they were both in nappies and had never bothered to alter a pattern of some twenty-odd years. Admittedly, these days they both smelled a good deal better.

Prim made elegant eyes at a young officer near the punch. She was wearing an exquisite dress of iridescent ivory taffeta with rust-coloured velvet flowers about the bodice to which the officer gave due appreciation.

Rue only grinned at Primrose's rebuke – a very unrefined grin.

They made a damnably appealing pair, as one smitten admirer put it, in his cups or he would have known better than to put it to Rue herself. "Both of you smallish, roundish, and sweetly wholesome, like perfectly exquisite dinner rolls."

"Thank you for my part," was Rue's acerbic reply to the poor sot, "but if I must be a baked good, at least make me a hot cross bun."

Rue possessed precisely the kind of personality to make her own amusement out of intimacy, especially when a gathering proved limited in scope. This was another reason she was so often invited to private balls. The widely held theory was that Lady Akeldama would become the party were the party to be lifeless, invaded by undead, or otherwise sub-par.

This particular ball did not need her help. Their hosts had installed a marvellous floating chandelier that looked like hundreds of tiny well-lit dirigibles wafting about the room. The attendees were charmed, mostly by the expense. In addition, the punch flowed freely out of a multi-dispensing ambulatory fountain, a string quartet tinkled robustly in one corner, and the conversation frothed with wit. Rue floated through it all on a puffy cloud of ulterior motives.

Rue might have attended, even without motives. The Fenchurches were *always* worth a look-in – being very wealthy, very inbred, and very conscientious of both, thus the most appalling sorts of people. Rue was never one to prefer one entertainment when she could have several. If she might amuse herself and infiltrate in pursuit of snuff boxes at the same time, all the better.

"Where did he say it was kept?" Prim leaned in, her focus on their task now that the young officer had gone off to dance with some other lady.

"Oh, Prim, must you always forget the details halfway through the first waltz?" Rue rebuked her friend without rancour, more out of habit than aggravation.

"So says the lady who hasn't waltzed with Mr Rabiffano." Prim turned to face the floor and twinkled at her former dance partner. The impeccably dressed gentleman in question raised his glass of champagne at her from across the room. "Aside from which, Mr Rabiffano is so very proud and melancholy. It is an appealing combination with that pretty face and vast millinery expertise. He always smiles as though it pains him to do so. It's quite...intoxicating."

"Oh, really, Prim, I know he looks no more than twenty but he's a werewolf and twice your age."

"Like fine brandy, most of the best men are," was Prim's cheeky answer.

"He's also one of my uncles."

"*All* the most eligible men in London seem to be related to you in some way or other."

"We must get you out of London then, mustn't we? Now, can we get on? I suspect the snuff box is in the card room."

Prim's expression indicated that she failed to see how anything could be more important than the general availability of men in London, but she replied gamely, "And how are we, young ladies of respectable standing, to make our way into the *gentlemen's* card room?"

Rue grinned. "You watch and be prepared to cover my retreat."

However, before Rue could get off on to the snuff box, a mild voice said, "What are you about, little niece?" The recently discussed Mr Rabiffano had made his way through the crowd and come up behind them at a speed only achieved by supernatural creatures.

Rue would hate to choose among her Paw's pack but if pressed, Paw's Beta, Uncle Rabiffano, was her favourite. He was more older brother than uncle, his connection to his humanity still strong, and his sense of humour often tickled by Rue's stubbornness.

"Wait and see," replied Rue pertly.

Prim said, as if she couldn't help herself, "You aren't in attendance solely to watch Rue, are you, Mr Rabiffano? Could it be that you are here because of me as well?"

Sandalio de Rabiffano, second in command of the London Pack and proprietor of the most fashionable hat shop in *all* of England, smiled softly at Prim's blatant flirting. "It would be a privilege, of course, Miss Tunstell, but I believe that gentleman there...?" He nodded in the direction of an Egyptian fellow who lurked uncomfortably in a corner.

"Poor Gahiji. Two decades fraternising with the British, and he still can't manage." Prim tutted at the vampire's evident misery. "I don't know why Queen Mums sends him. Poor dear – he does so hate society."

Rue began tapping her foot. Prim wouldn't notice but Uncle Rabiffano would most certainly hear.

Rabiffano turned towards her, grateful for the interruption. "Very well, if you persist in meddling, go meddle."

"As if I needed pack sanction."

"Convinced of that, are you?" Rabiffano tilted his head eloquently.

Sometimes it was awfully challenging to be the daughter of an Alpha werewolf.

Deciding she'd better act before Uncle Rabiffano changed his mind on her father's behalf, Rue glided away, a purposeful waft of pale pink and black lace. She hadn't Prim's elegance, but she could make a good impression if she tried. Her hair was piled high atop her head and was crowned by a wreath of pink roses – Uncle Rabiffano's work from earlier that evening. He always made her feel pretty and...tall. Well, taller.

She paused at the refreshment table, collecting four glasses of bubbly and concocting a plan.

At the card room door, Rue reached for a measure of her dear mother's personality, sweeping it about herself like a satin capelet. Personalities, like supernatural shapes, came easily to Rue. It was a skill Dama had cultivated. "Were you anyone else's daughter," he once said, "I should encourage you to tread the boards, *Puggle dearest*. As it stands, we'll have to make shift in less public venues."

Thus when Rue nodded at the footman to open the card room door it was with the austere expression of a bossy matron three times her age.

"But, miss, you can't!" The man trembled in his knee britches.

"The door, my good man," insisted Rue, her voice a little deeper and more commanding.

The footman was not one to resist so firm an order, even if it came from an unattached young lady. He opened the door.

Rue was met by a cloud of cigar smoke and the raucous laughter of men without women. The door closed behind her. She looked about the interior, narrowing in on the many snuff boxes scattered around the room. The chamber, decorated without fuss in brown leather, sage, and gold, seemed to house a great many snuff boxes.

"Lady Prudence, what are you doing in here?"

Rue was not, as many of her age and station might have been, overset by the presence of a great number of men. She had been raised by a great number of men – some of them the type to confine themselves to card rooms at private balls, some of them the type to be in the thick of the dancing, plying eyelashes and gossip in measures to match the ladies. The men of the card room were, in Rue's experience, much easier to handle. She dropped her mother's personality – no help from that here – and reached for someone different. She went for Aunt Ivy mixed with Aunt Evelyn. Slightly silly, but perceptive, flirtatious, unthreatening. Her posture shifted, tail-bone relaxing back and down into the hips, giving her walk more sway, shoulders back, jutting the cleavage forward, eyelids slightly lowered. She gave the collective gentlemen before her an engaging good-humoured grin.

"Oh dear, I do beg your pardon. You mean this isn't the ladies' embroidery circle?"

"As you see, quite not."

"Oh, how foolish of me." Rue compared each visible snuff box against the sketch she'd been shown, and dismissed each in turn. She wiggled further into the room as though drawn by pure love of masculinity, eyelashes fluttering.

Then Lord Fenchurch, unsure of how to cope with a young lady lodged in sacred man-space, desperately removed a snuff box from his waistcoat pocket and took a pinch.

There was her target. She swanned over to the lord in question, champagne sloshing. She tripped slightly and giggled at her own clumsiness, careful not to spill a drop, ending with all four glasses in front of Lord Fenchurch.

"For our gracious host – I do apologise for disturbing your game."

Lord Fenchurch set the snuff box down and picked up one of the glasses of champagne with a smile. "How thoughtful, Lady Prudence."

Rue leaned in towards him conspiratorially. "Now, don't tell my father I was in here, will you? He might take it amiss. Never know who he'd blame."

Lord Fenchurch looked alarmed.

Rue lurched forward as if under the influence of too much bubbly herself, and snaked the snuff box off the table and into a hidden pocket of her fluffy pink ball gown. All her ball gowns had hidden pockets no matter how fluffy – or how pink, for that matter.

As Rue made her way out of the room, she heard Lord Fenchurch say, worried, to his card partner, "Which father do you think she means?"

The other gentleman, an elderly sort who knew his way around London politics, answered with, "Bad either way, old man."

With which the door behind her closed and Rue was back in the cheer of the ballroom and its frolicking occupants – snuff box successfully poached. She dropped the silly persona as if shedding shape, although with considerably less pain and cost to her apparel. Across the room she met Prim's gaze and signalled autocratically.

Primrose bobbed a curtsey to Uncle Rabiffano and made her way over. "Rue dear, your wreath has slipped to a decidedly jaunty angle. Trouble must be afoot."

Rue stood patiently while her friend made the necessary adjustments. "I like trouble. What were you and Uncle Rabiffano getting chummy about?" Rue was casual with Prim on the subject; she really didn't want to encourage her friend. It wasn't that Rue didn't adore Uncle Rabiffano – she loved all her werewolf uncles, each in his own special way. But she'd never seen Uncle Rabiffano walk out with a lady. Prim, Rue felt, wasn't yet ready for that kind of rejection.

"We were discussing my venerated Queen Mums, if you can believe it."

Rue couldn't believe it. "Goodness, Uncle Rabiffano usually doesn't have much time for Aunt Ivy. Although he never turns down an invitation to visit her with a select offering of his latest hat designs. He thinks she's terribly frivolous. As if a man who spends that much time in front of the looking glass of an evening fussing with his hair should have anything to say on the subject of frivolity."

"Be fair, Rue my dear. Mr Rabiffano has very fine hair and my mother *is* frivolous. I take it you got the item?"

"Of course."

The two ladies drifted behind a cluster of potted palms near the conservatory door. Rue reached into her pocket and pulled out the lozenge-shaped snuff box. It was about the size to hold a pair of spectacles, lacquered in black with an inlay of mother-of-pearl flowers on the lid.

"A tad fuddy-duddy, wouldn't you think, for your Dama's taste?" Prim said. She would think in terms of fashion.

Rue ran her thumb over the inlay. "I'm not entirely convinced he wants the box."

"No?"

"I believe it's the contents that interest him."

"He can't possibly enjoy snuff."

"He'll tell us why he wants it when we get back."

Prim was sceptical. "That vampire never reveals anything if he can possibly help it."

"Ah, but I won't give the box to him until he does."

"You're lucky he loves you."

Rue smiled. "Yes, yes I am." She caught sight of Lord Fenchurch emerging from the card room. He did not look pleased with life, unexpected in a gentlemen whose ball was so well attended.

Lord Fenchurch was not a large man but he looked intimidating, like a ferocious tea-cup poodle. Small dogs, Rue knew from personal experience, could do a great deal of damage when not mollified. Pacification unfortunately was not her strong point. She had learnt many things from her irregular set of parental models, but calming troubled seas with diplomacy was not one of them.

"What do we do now, O wise compatriot?" asked Prim.

Rue considered her options. "Run."

Primrose looked her up and down doubtfully. Rue's pink dress was stylishly tight in the bodice and had a hem replete with such complexities of jet beadwork as to make it impossible to take a full stride without harm.

Rue disregarded her own fashionable restrictions and Prim's delicate gesture indicating that her own gown was even tighter, the bodice more elaborate and the skirt more fitted.

"No, no, not *that* kind of running. Do you think you could get Uncle Rabiffano to come over? I feel it unwise to leave the safety of the potted plants."

Prim narrowed her eyes. "That is a horrid idea. You'll ruin your dress. It's new. And it's a Worth."

"I thought you liked Mr Rabiffano? And *all* my dresses are Worth. Dama would hardly condone anything less." Rue deliberately misinterpreted her friend's objection, at the same time handing Prim the snuff box, her gloves, and her reticule. "Oh, and fetch my wrap, please? It's over on that chair."

Prim tisked in annoyance but drifted off with alacrity, making first for Rue's discarded shawl and then for the boyishly handsome werewolf. Moments later she returned with both in tow.

Without asking for permission – most of the time she would be flatly denied and it was better to acquire permission after the fact she had learned – Rue touched the side of her uncle's face with her bare hand.

Naked flesh to naked flesh had interesting consequences with Rue and werewolves. She wouldn't say she relished the results, but she had grown accustomed to them.

It was painful, her bones breaking and re-forming into new shapes. Her wavy brown hair flowed and crept over her body, turning to fur. Smell dominated her senses rather than sight. But unlike most werewolves, Rue kept her wits about her the entire time, never going moon mad or lusting for human flesh.

Simply put, Rue stole the werewolf's abilities but not his failings, leaving her victim mortal until sunrise, distance, or a preternatural separated them. In this case, her victim was her unfortunate Uncle Rabiffano.

Everyone called it stealing, but Rue's wolf form was her own: smallish and brindled black, chestnut, and gold. No matter who she stole from, her eyes remained the same tawny yellow inherited from her father. Sadly, the consequences to one's wardrobe were always the same. Her dress ripped as she dropped to all fours, beads scattering. The rose coronet remained in place, looped over one ear, as did her bloomers, although her tail tore open the back seam.

Uncle Rabiffano was mildly disgruntled to find himself mortal. "Really, young lady, I thought you'd grown out of surprise shape theft. This is most inconvenient." He checked the fall of his cravat and smoothed down the front of his peacock-blue waistcoat, as though mortality might somehow rumple clothing.

Rue cocked her head at him, hating the disappointment in his voice. Uncle Rabiffano smelled of wet felt and Bond Street's best pomade. It was the same kind of hair wax that Dama used. She would have apologised but all she could do was bow her head in supplication and give a little whine. His boots smelled of blacking.

"You look ridiculous in bloomers." Prim came to Uncle Rabiffano's assistance.

The gentleman gave Rue a critical examination. "I am rather loathe to admit it, niece, and if you tell any one of your parents I will deny it utterly, but if you are going to go around changing shape willy-nilly, you really must reject female underpinnings, and not only the stays. They simply aren't conducive to shape-shifting."

Prim gasped. "Really, Mr Rabiffano! We are at a ball, a private one notwithstanding. Please do not say such shocking things out loud."

Uncle Rabiffano bowed, colouring slightly. "Forgive me, Miss Tunstell, the stress of finding oneself suddenly human. Too much time with the pack recently, such brash men. I rather forgot myself and the company. I hope you understand."

Prim allowed him the gaffe with a small nod, but some measure of her romantic interest was now tainted. *That will teach her to think of Uncle Rabiffano as anything but a savage beast*, thought Rue with some relief. *I should have told her of his expertise in feminine underthings years ago.* Uncle Rabiffano's interest in female fashions, under or over, was purely academic, but Prim didn't need to know that.

He's probably right. I should give up underpinnings. Only that puts me horribly close to becoming a common strumpet.

Speaking of fashion. Rue shook her back paws out of the dancing slippers and nudged them at Prim with her nose. *Leather softened with mutton suet, resin, castor oil, and lanolin*, her nose told her.

Prim scooped them up, adding them to the bundle she'd formed out of Rue's wrap. "Any jewellery?"

Rue snorted at her. She'd stopped wearing jewellery several years back – it complicated matters. People accommodated wolves on the streets of London but they got strangely upset upon encountering a wolf dripping in diamonds. Dama found this deeply distressing on Rue's behalf. "But, Puggle, darling, you are wealthy, you simply must wear *something* that sparkles!" A compromise had been reached with the occasional tiara or wreath of silk flowers. Rue contemplated shaking the roses off her head, but Uncle Rabiffano might take offence and she'd already insulted him once this evening.

She barked at Prim.

Prim made a polite curtsey. "Good evening, Mr Rabiffano. A most enjoyable dance, but Rue and I simply must be off."

"I'm telling your parents about this," threatened Uncle Rabiffano without rancour.

Rue growled at him.

He waggled a finger at her. "Oh now, little one, don't think you can threaten me. We both know you aren't supposed to change without asking, and in public, *and* without a cloak. They are all going to be angry with you."

Rue sneezed.

Uncle Rabiffano stuck his nose in the air in pretend affront and drifted away. As she watched her beloved uncle twirl gaily about with a giggling young lady in a buttercup-yellow dress – he looked so carefree and cheerful – she did wonder, and not for the first time, why Uncle Rabiffano didn't *want* to be a werewolf. The idea was pure fancy, of course. Most of the rules of polite society existed to keep vampires and werewolves from changing anyone without an extended period of introduction, intimacy, training, and preparation. And her Paw would never metamorphose anyone against his will. And yet . . .

Prim climbed onto Rue's back. Prim's scent was mostly rose oil with a hint of soap-nuts and poppy seeds about the hair.

Given that Rue had the same mass in wolf form as she did in human, Primrose riding her was an awkward undertaking. Prim had to drape the train of her ball gown over Rue's tail to keep it from trailing on the floor. She also had to hook up her feet to keep them from dangling, which she did by leaning forward so that she was sprawled atop Rue with her head on the silk roses.

She accomplished this with more grace than might be expected given that Prim *always* wore complete underpinnings.

She had been doing it her whole life. Rue could be either a vampire or a werewolf, as long as there was a supernatural nearby to steal from, but when given the option, werewolf was more fun. They'd started very young and never given up on the rides.

Prim wrapped her hands about Rue's neck and whispered, "Ready."

Rue burst forth from the potted palms, conscious of what an absurd picture they made – Prim draped over her, ivory gown spiked up over Rue's tail, flying like a banner. Rue's hind legs were still clothed in her fuchsia silk bloomers, and the wreath draped jauntily over one pointed ear.

She charged through the throng, revelling in her supernatural strength. As people scattered before her she smelled each and every perfume, profiterole, and privy visit. *Yes, peons, flee before me!* she commanded mentally in an overly melodramatic dictatorial voice.

"Ruddy werewolves," she heard one elderly gentleman grumble. "Why is London so lousy with them these days?"

"All the best parties have one," she heard another respond.

"The Maccons have a lot to answer for," complained a matron of advanced years.

Perhaps under the opinion that Prim was being kidnapped, a footman sprang valiantly forward. Mrs Fenchurch liked her footmen brawny and this one grabbed for Rue's tail, but when she stopped, turned, and growled at him, baring all her large and sharp teeth, he thought better of it and backed away. Rue put on a burst of speed and they were out the front door and onto the busy street below.

London whisked by as Rue ran. She moved by scent, arrowing towards the familiar taverns and dustbins, street wares and bakers' stalls of her home neighbourhood. The fishy underbelly of the ever-present Thames – in potency or retreat – formed a map for her nose. She enjoyed the nimbleness with which she could dodge in and around hansoms and hackneys, steam tricycles and quadricycles, and the occasional articulated coach.

Of course it didn't last – several streets away from the party, her tether to Uncle Rabiffano reached its limit and snapped.